CITY OF THE DEAD

A Grimm Story

CHRIS J. CRANFORD

Forged Iron Press

BOOKS BY CHRIS J. CRANFORD

THE FERGUS GRIMM SAGA
Ghost Town
Recon Team Four
City of the Dead
An Ethereal End
Crown of Bones
Storm of Souls
City of Second Chances

The Crosse Series
The Deadening Wake

The Reality Thief
The Black Horizon

Finn Gallagher
The Chronicles of the Wolf

Acknowledgments:

A special thanks go to my mother Patricia, my sister January, and my ride-or-die brother Chris. All family, all part of my inner circle, who together were the first three to dive into this particular rabbit hole. The story may or may not have been your cup of tea, but this mad hatter certainly appreciated you coming to the party.

All your thoughts and feedback were invaluable, and you've helped make this story better, not just by reading it, but by being a part of my life. I hope you found something reading the story, that reminded you of something we did together.

Whether we drank hot chocolate off the stovetop after sledding in the snow, ate cereal with ice-cream flavored coffee creamer, or finished a few cold beers long after the party was over, there are moments with you three that will stay with me forever.

Thanks again to each of you.

CHAPTER ONE

It was a new day. Never mind that we had left Grafton only that morning. That most of us were exhausted from the battle, the night before. It was new, because we were all alive. Together. *Free*.

We were at a gas station. It was early in the drive, but we needed a break. Walk around a minute, grab something quick to eat.

The sky above was an empty, pale blue. It was marred only by faint, dark smudges of smoke that rose above the hills north of us. The sun drifted its way westward, a yellow orb radiating little warmth. We were still in the mountains, and the air carried a chill only late autumn could bring. Not many hours of daylight were left, and when night fell it would bring the icy cold promise of the coming winter.

I stood, gas nozzle in hand, staring at the empty skies above me, the cold hills we descended out of. I took a deep breath, inhaling the strong smell of manure from the gently sloped land around the station. Farm animals, in the fields around us.

The mountainside behind us took on the shape of a slumbering giant tucked under a blanket of browning grass, dotted with black specks of cows. Here and there I could see the giant's features, the slumbering head, tilted to one side. The crook of an elbow. The round shape of a knee ...

I tried to ignore the dark columnlike clouds above the giant in the north. The trails of smoke lifting high over Grafton. The homes there must still be burning, and tall ashlike fingers stretched into the skies, one last grasp of a town no longer alive.

No longer anything.

Just a few hours ago I had killed Raphael. Nick and Johnny and I had buried Father Ben. Sarah and Jen had hugged and cried. Nick and I had talked, apologized, and forgiven each other.

Then we had driven out of town.

I put the handle into the tank and squeezed it, felt the hard pump of gas kick through the hose, followed by the rippling feel of gasoline pulse into the tank. The smell of gasoline drifted from out of the tank, which oddly enough, I liked.

Nick and Johnny were in the store, seeing what food they could scrounge up with what little cash we had. Sarah had gone with them, quiet and withdrawn but staying by Nick as much as she could. Something she had never done when we were kids. Which was just one of the changes in her.

They had used science and dark magic back in Grafton to turn Sarah's blood into a drug. Any vampire who bit her would be able to control other vampires, in much the same way as a curse could control me.

The same process that had changed her blood had also turned her into some kind of supernatural time bomb. Sarah's clock was ticking. I didn't know how much time we – *she* – had left. And I had destroyed the place that could have reset her clock to zero.

No one had mentioned that problem yet, but in the rearview mirror I had seen her in the backseat, jaw set tight, wincing at every loud noise. We needed to find a fix. A cure. The sooner, the better.

I had broken what might have fixed her, back in Grafton. I didn't know what I had done, back at the factory. I was just trying to rescue Jen. But in the middle of a fight, as I was pulling ghosts, an explosion had burst out of me. A wave of force that had cracked the concrete floors of the factory, destroying the sigils and the equipment the doctor had used to create Sarah and the drug controlling the vampires.

Before that moment, I was just a guy who could see ghosts, and who could tap into the ethereal plane through each spirit, using the energy to make myself faster, stronger. I had never exploded anything before. Well, not without a lot of C-4.

Things had changed for me in Grafton. Armor had grown out of my skin. I had healed Jen. I had met my mother. I had killed Raphael, one of the most vicious monsters I had ever faced.

Danny had been a large part of that victory over Raphael. Even though his ghost was long gone, I still felt his spirit like the echo of a song that stayed in your head. His ghost had appeared and shown how to forgive myself, and I had used what Danny had given me to kill Raphael and rescue my friends.

I had missed the sleight of hand, though. The real reason I was in Grafton. By the time I had realized that everything happening had been to distract me, it was too late. Like a three-cup game, I had been so focused on following the ball I hadn't seen the trick.

I looked to the south and felt the pull of the Key. Azazel still had it, was drifting away from us even now. It would be hard to catch him, and although I didn't regret my choices, in Grafton, it was hard for me to just let Azazel go. The demon liked his games, and though I felt like I was more of a match for him now than I had been, I was tired of playing.

But all of that was before.

Now was for after.

"Hey." Jen leaned out of the passenger's side of the car and smiled at me. One of her hands drew circles on the outside of the car door, and her long blond hair wisped a bit in the slight breeze.

I could get used to that smile, but I wouldn't.

"Hey." I grinned back at her. Amazed at being with her, again.

"What'cha thinking?" she asked.

I motioned north. "It's hard to believe we can still see the smoke."

Jen twisted a little in the window to look, one hand covering her eyes. The smoke had hung behind us while we were driving, always present in the rearview mirror, tiny columns of darkness that twisted and turned and thinned out over the distance like slender, smoky fingers of a beckoning hand.

A shadow hanging behind us, the smoldering flames over our past, not quite ready to dissolve away.

"It's hard to believe that was the town we grew up in," Jen said.

"So much happened there," I said. "And now it's all gone."

The town was dead. And along with it, people who had taken care of me. Whom I had cared about. Miss Tammie. Parker, Danny. Even Father Ben, Greg.

All the deaths didn't seem worth what I had figured out about myself. I had learned I couldn't protect those I cared about by running. I learned that I needed to be there, for them. I just couldn't protect them all.

It didn't seem fair. And I had killed the person responsible. But I hadn't killed Azazel. And now I had lost the Key. I looked south again, feeling its pull.

Jen got out of the car. Shut the door and leaned against me a moment. Her body was warm against mine. Her scent of honeysuckle and fresh rain overpowered everything. I took a breath and, as always, felt a little better.

She nuzzled her face into the hollow of my throat and ran her hand up and down my arm. My skin tingled in response, like I had stuck my finger into a light socket. It was electric.

"I can't figure out whether it's you doing that," I said. "Or it's you *doing that*."

She waggled her eyebrows against my cheek. I laughed. Jen was a storm witch, something I didn't know until yesterday. It was hard to believe the woman I had come to Grafton to rescue was the same woman who had been throwing lightning bolts like she was striking out a side.

But it wasn't hard to believe she was the same girl I had fallen in love with. Back when we were kids, eating cereal on the couch, watching Saturday morning reruns. Back when she could smile at me, and I felt a little taller.

"Have we figured out where we're going?" Jen asked.

I shook my head. We were headed south for now, it being the fastest way out of Grafton. But also because of the pull of the Key. It still called to me, even though Azazel had it.

The demon had warned me off from following him. I had buried the Key while in Grafton, and Nick had found it and given it to Azazel in exchange for Sarah, after thinking I had been killed. Not that I faulted Nick. I hadn't been the best Keeper, just the latest one, and I would make the same trade if had meant saving Jen.

He had left one last message to me. I could protect my friends, or I could come after the Key, but I couldn't do both. But I had learned a valuable lesson in Grafton. Protecting my friends wasn't all on me. Life sucked sometimes, and I needed to take responsibility not only for the lives of my friends, but for their deaths as well. Not everyone always made it, and I would always try, but I would no longer run from my failures.

Azazel wanted me twisting in the wind, worried about my friends, and worried what would happen if the demon released his brothers and sisters. The person I had been a few days ago would have been terrified. The new me had learned a lesson, to lean on my friends' strengths, to include them in a burden shared. It wouldn't just be me coming after Azazel. It would be me and Jen and Nick and Sarah and Johnny.

"You got serious quick," Jen said.

I didn't answer. She knew I wasn't one for a lot of words. Especially when the words mattered. It felt good to be with her, to be with my friends, to be with people who counted on me and believed in me and in turn wanted me to believe in them.

But it also felt strange. The dynamic was something I needed to get used to. I had been alone for a long time, and I hadn't been a great friend before then. I was trying to learn how to be one now.

I looked over to the gas station. Jen's sister was in the station with Nick and Johnny. The magic she carried would kill her, if we didn't get her help. As much as I wanted to beat Azazel at his game, my friends would come first. I had learned that lesson now.

Jen sensed what I was feeling. Kissed me lightly on the cheekbone and whispered in my ear, "Be right back."

She was never going to press. Jen was just always going to be there. I was having trouble getting used to that kind of acceptance, of having someone always in my corner. Maybe a little irrationally, I feared losing it.

She strode toward the gas station, legs and curves and athletic grace. The door to the store opened. Jen walked in as Nick and Johnny walked out. The two guys were arguing which candy bar was better, and the argument got louder as they came near. There was a serious discussion about whether a peanut butter cup could be allowed into a candy bar debate.

"What do you think, Grimm?" Johnny asked.

The nozzle for the gas pump kicked off, and I pulled it out of the tank and hung the handle on the pump. I stared at them both. "Peanut butter cups have to be allowed."

"Told you." Nick grinned.

"Then you can't have a debate," Johnny said. "Nothing beats a peanut butter cup."

"Exactly," I agreed.

"No one lets airplanes get into a fastest car discussion," Johnny said.

Nick made a motion that meant, *see what I'm dealing with?*

"That's because planes aren't cars," I said.

"Then peanut butter cups aren't candy bars," Johnny argued. "Right?"

"I think I'd say that once you fly somewhere in a plane, you realize it's the peanut butter cup of how to travel." I patted the roof of my car a few times to let her know no hard feelings. "No matter how fast the car."

"But they're not a candy *bar*," Johnny said. "Emphasis on the square shape."

I raised my eyebrows. "It's candy, though. So for the purpose of this discussion, I'm firmly in the peanut-butter-cup camp."

Johnny rolled his eyes.

"Guess what?" Nick handed me a Coke and some kind of clawlike pastry, the kind with white icing and thick cinnamon filling. "Those witches we saved? They were here yesterday."

I remembered Tabitha at the factory. She had been an earth witch of some power. She had left with her daughter and the rest of the witches after I had freed them.

"Nick thinks we should find them," Johnny added.

"It's not a bad idea," Nick said. He looked over at the front of the gas station. In the window we could all see Jen talking to Sarah. "They might know something that could help."

I looked over at Jen and Sarah, at Sarah's pinched, withdrawn face. At Jen's worry. At Nick, earnestly looking at me.

Just a few days ago Nick had punched me. And up until this morning, he hadn't trusted me. And I understood why. Up until a few days ago, I had let all of my friends down. Maybe Nick, most of all. And even though it was Nick's fault that the demon had the Key, I understood his reasons there as well. I told him I would have done the same, and I would have.

Nick and I had forgiven each other. Though he seemed tentative around me. Nervous maybe, stuck somewhere between the hard man he was now, a man who walked shadows, and the younger kid brother he had used to be.

Or maybe he was just worried about Sarah. The girl he had grown up with a crush on. Whom he had stayed in Grafton for, even though she – at the time – had wanted nothing more than his friendship.

Raphael, the vampire I had killed, had created a mind-controlling drug, one vampires were massively addicted to. Though he needed some kind of control for the drug, and had made that with Sarah. She had gone through some kind of ritual that had turned her blood into the power by which Raphael could control any of the vampires that drank his drug.

Sarah was paler now than earlier today. Her eyes were constantly pinched. Jen had told me Sarah had thrown up that morning at the hotel, and she was having trouble eating since.

We would have to find her help soon. The witches were as good a bet as anyone.

"Sure, man," I said. "Let's look for them."

Nick whooped loud enough that both Jen and Sarah looked at him from inside the station.

Johnny winked at me. I took a bite of pastry, tasting the sweet icing and the cinnamon, and waited for the girls to come back out. When they did, they had a variety of sugary snacks and a couple of bottles of fancy water, the colored kind with electrolytes. Jen was talking Sarah into drinking some.

Sarah's skin was even paler than a few hours ago. Little black lines, like thin veins, appeared and disappeared under the surface of her skin. She had bought a baseball cap in the store, and had it pulled snug over her head. The rim laid a shadow across her eyes.

I watched Sarah force down a swig of the water and grimace at the taste. "You okay?"

She nodded. We had been close once. She had been like a little sister. I remembered a girl who loved teasing Jen and me whenever we were snuggled together on the couch. Now, out of all my friends, Sarah and I had grown the most apart. Or at least there seemed to be a larger gulf between us than before.

It hurt me, back when I had first come to Grafton. I had seen Sarah, and she had told me to save her sister and go. Like Sarah believed she herself wasn't worth saving.

It hurt deeper at the time, because I had come into town with just that intention. My full plan was to rescue Jen and run. It still hurt now, even though I believed I had changed. At least, I wanted to change.

"Nick mentioned the group of witches we rescued from the factory," I told her. "We're going to find them and see if they can help."

"Okay," Sarah said, simply. She eased past me to get into the car. Nick climbed in after her, and Johnny slapped me on the shoulder before getting in.

I took another bite of the pastry and walked around to the other side of the Camaro and got in. I hoped somehow we could help Sarah. Or what happened to her, that would be all on me.

Johnny started up the candy bar debate again, this time trying to get Jen on his side, talking about square shapes versus round ones. Listening, as I fired up the car, I thought it sounded as if he fought an uphill battle. It was four to one against. But he still argued on.

I grinned. There was a sense of the old us, the old times, of the Wolverines, with Johnny. With just the argument about a candy bar. Or a peanut butter cup. It was a feeling I'd missed, and it was nice to be reminded that it was the five of us versus the world.

I drove the Camaro out onto the road. The car accelerated quickly and bounced over a rough spot where the on-ramp met the interstate. Sarah winced, hard, and grabbed for Nick's hand.

Farther back behind Sarah, in the rearview mirror, were the faint smudges of smoke over Grafton. Trailing over the mountains. A past we all were trying to leave behind.

I focused forward. South. Where the Key still pulled at me. Toward Azazel, and whatever game he wanted to play.

My foot pushed harder on the gas. The Camaro surged forward. Jen gave me a questioning look, which I shrugged off.

Sarah. The Key. Maybe it was the life I had lived up until now, but I had a feeling those two were going to collide. It was a premonition I could not shake, no matter that it made no sense.

CHAPTER TWO

An hour later we left the interstate and pulled into some town in Tennessee. A local place with an army base nearby. It had the typical look of a military town: suburbs containing row after row of the same model house, each suburb tucked right off the main roads leading out from the base. Mailboxes all lined up at each house. American flags flying from every porch. Every home association looked like a nicer, newer version of the old base housing I was used to.

I had been in the military for a bit. I shook off the déjà vu as we drove past the homes. I looked at the gauge for the gas tank. Even though I had filled the tank earlier, the needle had stayed at half-full. I tapped the glass.

Jen looked at me. "Something wrong?"

I shook my head. Then I tapped the gauge again. It was just something I would have to pay attention to. The car had taken a beating in the past few days.

"How are we going to find them?" Nick asked.

"Shouldn't be hard," I said. "A big van full of women. They'll draw a crowd."

"They'll want to be inconspicuous," Johnny said.

"They'll want to be," I said. "But it's a military town. It'll be tough."

It would limit where they could go. Soldiers had a way of finding women, especially near the main strip. So they would have to hide away from that, in some of the smaller areas of town, which we could find and search.

Tabitha had told me the witches were headed to Lewiston. But I also knew the witches would want to make sure they were safe from what had happened in Grafton. From any possible blowback. So even in this town the women would be hiding, and they would have something prepared for anyone who came looking for them.

But I didn't want to bring that up now. We just needed to get looking. Jen gave me a small smile, and I winked back at her.

The Camaro cruised along the main road into town. It felt much the same as other bases I had been on. To our right ran the long wall of the base, thick red bricks stacked for miles, broken occasionally by gates. To our left there were rent-by-the-hour motels, liquor stores, and mobile-phone stores next to one another. As well as barbershops, strip clubs, fast-food places, and bars.

Sarah remained silent in the back. I looked at her in the rearview mirror. She had never been a loud person, but had been extremely quiet since Nick and I killed Raphael. Sarah noticed my glance at her, and frowned back at me.

"I could eat something," Jen mentioned.

We passed a diner then, something long and tubular and metallic painted. I kept driving on, though. Ms. Tammie was too recent for all of us.

A fast-food place was next. Something with dirty windows, overfull trash cans in the parking lot, and a sign that said Drive-thru Only After 10 PM.

The restaurant was right next to a motel, which was as seedy a place as any I had seen. The paint on the outer walls peeled, some kind of tan stucco mixture molded in spots. Dust lay heavy on the curtains inside the yellow windows. Trash fluttered over the walkway in front of the doors.

But there was a nice enough coffee place across the street, something new with a round green sign. Plenty of people going in and out. All in all, we had the essentials nearby for people on the run, and this was as good a spot as any.

I had called it the trifecta, back when I was running from Azazel. A place to sleep. A place to eat. And a place with caffeine.

"Three for three," I said to no one in particular, and pulled into the motel parking lot. The Camaro shut off like it was ready for a break.

Johnny, Nick, and Sarah went over to get a head start on food. Jen hung around while I grabbed a couple of rooms from the motel attendant. Both of the rooms were outside and right in front of where I had parked my car. The attendant hadn't cared much about who I was, just how much cash I was handing over. I paid for a couple of nights in advance.

I handed Jen one of our room keys. She was smiling and looking back at me. "You know, at some point we're going to have to get new clothes," she said.

"I'm not sure we can afford it." I still had my wallet open, and a few twenties stared back at me. Money was going to become an issue. I had taken the odd job here and there while I was on the run, and had resorted to less scrupulous ways of acquiring funds, but a party of five was going to need money quickly.

"We'll look for a thrift shop somewhere," Jen said.

I took a deep breath, folded up my wallet, and slid it back into my pocket.

"I'm glad we're looking for them," Jen said.

"Will they be able to help?"

"Maybe better than anyone," she said. "They were there with the experiments going on. And … witches have different talents. I work with weather. Tabitha could manipulate earth. We need someone in the more physical realm. A healing witch."

"What's Sarah?" I asked.

"She's not that," Jen answered. Somehow her hand had found mine while we were talking, and I gave it a squeeze.

"We'll find them, then," I told her. Conscious of the pull of the Key even when I said the words. Azazel was out there, and I didn't know how long we had until he freed his demon family, but Sarah would come first. For a moment both of us stared across the lot at our friends in the fast-food place. Until my stomach rumbled.

The corner of Jen's lip curved a bit. "Treat you to lunch?"

"Always."

We walked over to the restaurant. Nick, Johnny, and Sarah were already almost done eating. I tossed them a key to their room and followed Jen up to the line. She got us a couple of big burgers, hot fries, sodas, and a large milk shake. I opened my eyes at the milk shake.

"I need my calories." She grinned.

We sat down at a table for two next to the group and ate silently. It struck me that this was the first time I was eating a meal with Jen since we were teenagers together. The first time we all had sat down together in a long time, and it felt good.

Jen ate fast. The burger disappeared. And the milk shake was down a quarter. And some of my fries ended up missing.

"Hey," I said.

"Hey?" She paused, mid-milk-shake, and threw a questioning eyebrow my way.

"No sharesies on the fries."

Johnny snickered from the next table. "Aren't they cute?"

Nick pretended to gag and rolled his eyes. Even Sarah smiled. At the same time I watched Jen sneak a couple more of my fries. Which got Johnny laughing even harder and the rest of us giggling, like kids back in school.

I pulled the fries closer to me and guarded them carefully while I ate. Even so, they disappeared faster than they should have.

CHAPTER THREE

It was a short walk back to the motel from the restaurant. Sarah had trouble making it.

We all wandered over, feeling good after the meal. Being together. Dusk had fallen while we ate. When we left, I had my arm around Jen, like all of us were walking home from school.

Halfway across Sarah cried out. Nick grabbed her before she fell and held her up. Sarah pressed both of her hands tight to her temple. She pressed so hard her ball cap fell off.

Nick looked at me. His eyes open, worried. Jen placed her hands over Sarah's and held her face up. As I watched, little black symbols, like tattoos of hieroglyphs, surfaced and disappeared all over her skin. They flickered and changed, almost like they were counting down. It reminded me of the first tattoo I had seen on her, in Raphael's car up on the hill in Grafton, but back then it was just a few lines and symbols wrapping gracefully around the side of her neck.

"Fuck," I said. We needed more time. Whatever was going to happen to Sarah couldn't happen now.

Jen told Sarah to take a deep breath. She repeated the words, over and over, trying to get her sister to focus on something other than the pain. Sarah looked like someone about to give birth.

"Can't you do something?" Johnny asked me.

"Like what?"

"You healed Jen."

"I'm not really sure how I did that," I said. "That might have been a onetime thing."

"Can it hurt to try?" Johnny said.

Everyone looked at me expectantly.

I swallowed, hard. If something happened and Sarah died, I would be the person who killed her. I didn't know if I could handle that. Back at the factory I had destroyed the circle that could have reset her curse. And at the same time, I had killed the doctor who could have performed the ritual.

I had done it unknowingly. I had done it to save Jen. But that didn't mean it still wouldn't be my fault, if the curse killed Sarah now. She was a friend, she was Jen's sister, and whether I tried or didn't try right now, to help, I was afraid I had already done enough damage. I was scared that anything I did now would make it worse. Maybe, most of all, I was afraid of being the person who failed, yet again.

Jen laid her hand on my arm. Five points of warm contact, plus her palm, on my skin. Not directing or pleading or squeezing. Just there.

I took a breath. "Let's do it."

Nick picked Sarah up. She wriggled in his grasp. We carried her to one of the motel rooms. He laid her on one of the beds. Briefly he stretched his hands out to Sarah, and then he pulled them both back to the bedside, as if scared to touch her.

Jen kneeled on the other side of the bed and held on to her sister. Sarah writhed and pressed her hands to her temples, biting back a scream.

I flicked on my ethereal sight.

The hieroglyphics fading in and out on her skin were more prominent now, surfacing across Sarah in thick, dark red outlines. Forever changing. Ticking down, maybe. Currents of purple ran through her veins. Deep inside her chest flickered a tiny white light.

"I have no idea what I'm looking at," I said out loud. And I didn't. I was winging this. And it didn't feel good.

I reached for the nearest ghost, knowing there was one in the motel parking lot. I always looked for them, when staying somewhere. They made good watchdogs, and old habits die hard. This ghost was the spirit of an older woman, fat with many layers of different clothes, a ghostly image of a shopping cart full of junk in front of her. One of her hands held the cart tightly and would not let go.

"Here it goes." Ethereal energy poured into me. Jen held her sister down against the bed. I took the energy and touched the side of Sarah's neck, where I had seen the first tattoo. Figuring I would try to feel what it was.

When my hand made contact, all the purple and red blotches inside Sarah immediately gathered inside her chest. The lines stopped fading in and out on her skin, and the hieroglyphs stopped shifting. I took a breath.

Then the purple and red exploded outward.

Like a punch.

A crack – like a tree exploding in a fire – echoed through the room. A smell of sulfur flooded the place. I flew back through the air and crashed into the dresser, falling to the floor. A cheap flat-screen television wobbled on the top of the dresser, and then fell on top of me.

I let go of the ghost and shook my head. A tingling ran across my skin, and large goose bumps rippled up and down my flesh. It was like the spell on Sarah had attacked me.

Two hands moved the television off me. Johnny. He looked worried. "You okay, man?"

"I think so," I said. I still had my ethereal sight up, and two tiny white punctures stood out on Johnny's dark skin. It was easy to forget he was a thrall. I shook my head again; that word wasn't right for Johnny. He reached down and helped me up, patted me on the back.

The purple currents in Sarah's veins swam slower now. The hieroglyphic tattoos flickered at a slower rate, and there were fewer sparkles of red. Had I exhausted the spell? Maybe worn it out?

I blinked back to normal. It had been only a few moments, but Sarah was asleep. She looked peaceful, and took normal, deep breaths. It was hard to tell in the motel room, but she looked less pale, and like she carried less pain.

But not healed either—that wasn't what I had done. I had just provided an outlet for the energy of the curse to go.

"She better?" I asked.

"I think so," Jen said. Her face was scrunched in worry.

"We need to find those witches," Nick said.

"Yeah," I said. "Probably no time like the present."

"I'm going to stay with Sarah," Jen said. She ran one hand up and down her sister's arm.

"That's okay," I said. "We only have the one car. One set of eyes is as good as many."

"I'll come with you," Johnny said.

"I'll go on my own," Nick said. "It's dark out. I'll cover more ground by myself."

I didn't know if I had bought more time for Sarah or not, but I didn't believe what I had just done would work too many times. Whatever the spell was that bound her, it had sensed me and reacted. No telling what it would be ready for the next time I tried it. "Let's do it, then."

The three of us walked out to the parking lot. Dusk had grown into night. Nick took a couple of steps into the darkness and melted into the shadows, disappearing from view.

"Freaky," I said.

"No more than you bouncing off a dresser," Johnny said.

"Maybe." We both got into the Camaro. I fired it up. It coughed once or twice before it caught. I patted the dash once or twice, a little worried about my car.

"You got any idea where to go?"

"Start on the strip," I said. The main road that paralleled the base. "We'll go from there, and keep an eye out for the factory van."

"That's not a great plan," Johnny said.

"I'm listening, if you have something better." I pressed the gas and cruised the strip. Johnny stayed quiet for a bit. We each kept our eyes on our side of the road. Bars and bars and more bars passed us, all with garish signs listing drink specials, ladies' nights, and local bands. All part of the military experience. I frowned.

After five miles the road peeled away from the base and headed into the main part of the small town. There were a few small city blocks, a town hall, and a church. We stopped then and hit up a gas station to grab a town map. Johnny gave me a funny look.

"What?"

"Man, let's get a couple of phones," he said. "They got better maps than that thing."

"You have any money on you?" I asked him.

Johnny shook his head. "I had a sugar mama."

He was talking about Gabrielle, daughter of one of the vampire clans in Europe. Who was back home now after what had happened in Grafton, explaining things to her father.

"Then we're doing the paper map thing tonight," I said, showing him what I had left in my wallet.

He whistled at the couple of bills I had left.

"Yeah," I agreed.

We took a couple of roads out of town, circling around some areas between the town and the base that headed into the country, but Johnny and I were throwing darts blind. I left the roof light on in the Camaro, and he kept tracking the map with his finger.

At some point around midnight we stopped to put more gas in the car and grab some cheap food to eat. Neither of us expected to find anything. But neither of us had a better idea. We were hoping to get lucky.

The whole time driving around I felt the pull of the Key. Steadily tracking south. I wasn't sure where Azazel was headed with it, and why he hadn't freed his brothers and sisters yet.

"What about asking your ghosts?" Johnny asked. He was onto his second pastry.

"They're not my ghosts," I told him. "And it doesn't really work that way. Most of them don't pay great attention to what's around them. It's more like what they remember."

For the most part, that was true. Ghosts did take more of an interest about the world when I was around, though. And recently, when I had killed the doctor responsible for Sarah, his ghost had been aware enough of what was happening to try to attack me. A few other ghosts had done similar things, lately. Which told me something had changed, either in the world I lived in or with me.

"They'd be a big help."

"Sure, it'd be nice if one popped up with a foam finger pointing out where the witches had gone," I said. "But it's just not what they do."

"That's a shame."

We kept driving for a bit after that. Johnny took over driving after he caught me napping at a red light. It had been a long day and the fight with Sarah's curse had drained me more than energy drinks could keep up.

We were cruising through yet another of the same military neighborhoods. Johnny had both hands on the wheel, and used his blinker to make a right turn at the end of the road. I wondered if there was another reason he wanted a phone.

"You and Gabrielle good?"

"Sure," he said. A little too quick. "It's good for me not to be around right now. Her family would use me as leverage."

"What's that mean?" I asked, curious.

"You gotta know her father isn't happy about her being with some guy from a town in mid-America," Johnny explained. "He might use what happened in Grafton to, you know …" He looked over at me and made a little throat-cutting motion.

"Really?" I asked.

"Really," Johnny said. "Her family rules Europe, man. The whole clan is out there. Victor Dumont wants more for his daughter. Well, he wants more for himself, but I think he rationalizes it as for Gabrielle."

I got the sense there was a long history there, a lot of discussions between him and Gabrielle. "Or maybe he doesn't," Johnny finally said. "The guy's an ass."

"Huh," I said. Wondering if Johnny had met Victor. Or just knew him from Gabrielle. Wondering how Romeo and Juliet their relationship was. "You tell her everything?"

Gabrielle had been sent to Grafton to figure out how to replicate the drug Raphael was making, but her family – all vampires, really – were interested in how Dominic had created a real vampire from a human child. Thanks to me, the drug, the recipe, and the factory had been destroyed.

And Raphael, his creation was mostly due to Azazel. He had been a weird mix of human and demon and vampire. It wasn't an experiment that could be replicated. But Victor wouldn't know that, and Gabrielle might suffer the consequences of her perceived failure.

We headed out along a country road, single-lane in both directions. The headlight caught dark blacktop and faded double yellow lines separating the lanes. Johnny checked the rearview. Adjusted the mirror again, like he couldn't get it just right. "We covered enough. I'll catch her up later. We've been apart before."

"Okay," I said. I wondered if they were having issues, and what that might cause for Johnny. He was tied to her blood in a way that would make it hard for him to be separate from her, for long.

"Don't worry, man," Johnny said. "With how Sarah is, Gabrielle didn't want to be tempted."

I nodded. I hadn't thought about that. The calling of Sarah's blood, the temptation of the drug coursing through her body, begging to be bitten, to take *control*, might be too much for Gabrielle, one the vampire might not be able to resist.

Johnny had picked traveling with us over anything else he could have done, though. Of all of us, he had the largest reason not to come. But here he was, driving a tired me around, with both of us looking for the witches who might help Sarah.

A farmhouse rolled by. The lights were out, and no barn around. No van and no place to hide one. "We get some time tomorrow, I'll get some money. We'll get a couple of phones."

Johnny hit the blinker again. Another turn. "That would be appreciated, man."

"Tabitha told me they were headed to Lewiston," I said. "They must know someone here. Maybe we hunt them down that way."

"It'll take more time, if we have to look for them that way," Johnny said.

Time we probably wouldn't have.

Dammit.

Somewhere close to sunrise we headed back.

CHAPTER FOUR

The faint wisps of the sun broke through the clouds in little orange streams, illuminating the bellies of the clouds in orange and reds. Johnny pulled the Camaro into the motel and nudged me. Nick was standing in front of the door to Sarah's room, a big grin across his face..

"You ever see that guy smile?" Johnny asked me.

"He found them," I said.

Nick waved us to stay in the car, and climbed behind me to get into the backseat. He was giddy. He had found where the witches had hidden themselves, and a few of them had already come back to the motel to get Sarah and Jen.

Tabitha, the older lady I had rescued from the factory, thought they could do something to help. With all of the witches together, there was a variety of experience and expertise to pull from. Nick had waited for us to show back up. He told us Sarah had woken up feeling better. He patted me on the shoulder, once.

"Man," I said, thinking of all the ground Nick had had to cover. How impossible a task that seemed. He must have walked shadows all night, and I asked him about it.

"It wasn't hard," Nick said. Though he was happy, dark shadows circled his eyes. "We need to get some phones, though. I had to wait hours for you guys to show up."

"Tell me about it," I said. I had never needed them before. When it had just been me on the road. They would be convenient now, though. I just had to get some money. "You got any cash?"

Nick shook his head. "I'm dead broke."

We followed Nick's directions, only stopping to get a ton of ninety-nine-cent breakfast items. Bags of sandwiches and burritos were handed inside the car. The smell of sausage and eggs and pancakes filled the Camaro.

Nick directed us out of town from there. We headed away from the base and over a hill. Off in the distance a small lake shimmered in the morning sun. Hay fields rolled by to our north, big rolls of hay wrapped up in man-sized pinwheels. A long run of tall power poles cut through the fields. Nick pointed to the top of one.

"I saw the van from the top of that one," he said.

I winced thinking about it. Those things were high up and running enough juice to fry anyone who accidently crossed a couple of the wires. To shadow-jump across those things all night must have taken immense guts. But one thing I had learned about Nick, he carried no fear.

We rolled down a last hill and around a couple more turns, before pulling onto a dirt road that wound around to the lake. A large white farm-house sat there, a few big oak trees in front.

"I don't see the van," I said.

"We moved it last night," Nick said. "The women worried when I told them that was how I had found them."

Nick had accomplished a lot while Johnny and I were driving around.

A couple of women waited out on the front lawn. A middle-aged woman and someone much younger. Johnny parked the car off to the side and we all got out. Nick waved a quick hi and headed right for the house, carrying the bags of food. Tabitha introduced us to her daughter, Zoe. She was a thin-faced replica of her mother, with the same severe lips and tightly pulled back hair, just more black in it. The last time I had seen them they were fleeing the factory and Zoe had been one of the women on the cots. Her blood had been used to help make the vampire drug.

I asked Tabitha about Sarah.

"She's okay," the earth witch said. "We might be able to slow down what's happening, but she's going to need more than what we can do."

"Do you have any idea what they did to her?" I asked. The factory floor and all the medical equipment had been inscribed with demonic symbols and various pentagrams. The doctor had been combining science and dark magic not only to make the drug, but to turn Sarah into whatever controlled the vampires infected with the drug.

"I was there for a few weeks. Browner liked to talk to me. Research, he called it," Tabitha said. She shook her head. "He was a geneticist, and somewhere he had encountered someone supernatural. He was convinced there was something in a person's DNA that explained everything."

"Everything?" I asked.

"Like why witches are born with different powers. Why mother after mother works with earth, and suddenly a daughter is born that can work with fire. Why vampires can't tolerate sunrise," Tabitha said. "Browner was convinced science would explain it all."

Would science explain away how I could see ghosts? The ethereal plane? Why plates of armor grew out of my skin, then just as suddenly disappeared? Maybe it could. Maybe it couldn't. It was hard to believe everything I could do was because of some bits of genetic code, but what was the alternative? Was there a reason for my powers? Or was I just some random throw of DNA dice?

"You were up too late to be thinking that hard," Johnny said, and playfully punched my shoulder.

There were a lot of scientists in the world. And a lot of supernatural. But not a lot of crossover. The supernatural world existed around us. People could see it if they just looked at it. Problem was, it was human nature to explain away things they didn't understand, to shy away from things they feared.

Which helped evil to swell in larger numbers than ever. *Recruitment numbers were low*, Greg had told me, just a day before he had been killed. The Catholic Church had been minimized with years of legislation, such as reducing nativity scenes, eliminating prayer in school, and even a campaign against saying Merry Christmas.

Chances were, not a lot of doctors or scientists today believed in the supernatural. Even though monsters were around in greater numbers than ever. I didn't think we'd be able to find a scientist ready to explain the things we could do, or walk into an emergency care and find Sarah help. And although I was able to get her curse to expend its energy, I was unsure that continuing to do that wouldn't end up killing Sarah, or me.

"Thanks for the help," I said to Tabitha. "It's better than what we could do."

"It's the least we can do," Tabitha said. "We still owe you."

I had only been at the factory for Jen. Saving the rest of the women there had just happened along the way. "I just happened to be there."

"Do you remember anything?" Zoe asked me. Her voice wavered a little. It was a lot lighter than her mother's. Almost airy.

"What do you mean?"

"When you were fighting the cops."

All the bullets that had hit me and bounced off. The armor plates that had grown out of my skin. The explosion that broke everything. All the ghosts I had burned through. Zoe had been one of the women on the cots, providing their blood to make the addictive drug for the vampires. She hadn't been near the fight, though.

"Yeah." I remembered. I didn't understand some of what had happened, but I would not forget it.

"My daughter is a spirit witch," Tabitha explained.

"I couldn't see anything," Zoe said. Her voice didn't waver so much as drift in and out in intensity. Like she had to push herself to speak, and when she didn't, her voice tailed off. "But I sensed the spirits. A lot of them, all at once. And then they were gone."

Zoe looked at me, a question in her eyes. "You used them up, somehow, didn't you?"

Other than my mother, I had never met another person who could see a ghost like me. Or knew much about their realm. "I did. I don't understand how I can do it, or why."

"I have never heard of anything like that before," Zoe said.

I shook my head. I had searched across the earth for any hint of someone who could do what I do, and hadn't found it, and hadn't always gotten an understanding response. Walking in and telling a priest I could see ghosts usually led to a phone call to the local authorities, or at the very least a phone number to a help line.

It didn't make sense to me that the priests I had tried speaking to didn't understand me better. In the movies and the books, every priest could do exorcisms and every church held off demons. But most of them, when I asked, seemed unaware that vampires and demons and monsters really exist. That ghosts are real.

I regretted not spending more time with Father Benjamin. He had been the first priest I had met who had moved in the same supernatural circles I had. He had been part of the Templars, in some function. He had known things, but he was dead now too.

Zoe was the first person I had met with a supernatural ability overlapping mine. It would be interesting for the both of us to connect to the same ghost. I wondered if she could tell me what they were thinking as I used their energy. As I lived their memories.

The last image of Browner's ghost came back to me. The doctor had been furious. It spoke to me of a self-awareness in the ethereal realm I had been unaware of before.

"It's how I do what I do," I said. "You can't see them?"

Zoe shook her head. "I can just speak to them. Sense them when they are around. Some of them talk to me, some of them never answer. I can always sense them around, though. They leave a spiritual footprint where they walk. But I have never seen them just disappear. There was nothing of them left in this world. Like they had been erased."

Was that what I did? Burn through ghosts with energy from the ethereal plane until I erased them from this world? Should I feel guilty, if I erased what was left of Browner from the earth?

I hadn't felt guilty in the past. I didn't like living their memories. Every time I did, it was like they left that part of them inside me, that I was the rapist, the murderer, the person who fed poison to his neighbor's dog. And that was the main reason I didn't pull from ghosts all the time. Not because of any sense of guilt.

I wasn't even sure why ghosts existed. Most of the ones I encountered seemed to belong in hell. And I knew a certain demon there who would be happy to take them. So why did some ghosts hang around, and some make the trip? Was there a membership-only privilege involved? I shook my head. I didn't know anything about what I was doing, and I couldn't understand my powers. Why I had them. What they could do.

My mother had said there were originally seven of us. She and my father were what was left of those seven, and myself. I needed to go back to the beginning, and see if I could learn more. The creation of the geas. But Sarah would come first. Then I had to get the Key back from Azazel. And then maybe I'd figure out more about myself.

Tabitha led us into the house. Inside was a bustle of activity. Sarah stood in the center of the living room, surrounded by a multitude of witches, all of them asking her questions and poking and prodding. Every now and then Sarah would pull her shirt aside to let them get a better glimpse at one of the tattoos. I hadn't noticed before, but she wore a necklace. A thin silver chain, with a small clasp hanging from it.

When we walked in, I could see the skin of her back ripple, as if something wriggled underneath one of the large sigils on her back. Sarah turned and saw us right then. She caught Nick's eyes and frowned, pulling her shirt down to cover herself. The wince in her eyes was back.

Jen leaned against the wall, watching her sister carefully. She offered a small smile when Sarah flashed an exasperated glance her way. Johnny and I walked over. Jen gave me a quick hug, her chin tucked into the nape of my neck, squeezing hard one time with both arms before letting go.

We had been together just a few days now, and I couldn't imagine a life without her. My breath caught once or twice as I let it out. "Everything okay?"

She tilted her head back and forth. Yes and no. Her hand snaked into mine. "I'm glad you're back."

We watched the show. Some of the witches stood around Sarah in a trancelike state, others whispered words that sounded spell-like, others poked and prodded Sarah and then wrote in little black books. Other witches stood aside, talking to each other in low voices. There was an air of expectation and worry in the room. Sarah undertook it all with a pinched face.

I flipped on my ethereal sight. Sarah glowed there, a mottled purplish red. The same bright white light hidden in her chest. Unlike back at the motel, though, the flickering words had surfaced permanently here. Held in place by a spell, maybe. The script lay all over her skin. Like someone had taken a quill and used Sarah as a canvas.

The witches had done something to bring out every word of the script, every symbol, every etching. Long lines of an unreadable language ran all over her skin, each of the lines part of a pattern, and the pattern was easy to see now.

A pentagram.

Azazel. "Damn," I said. Jen looked at me, worried. I kept my voice low. "It's a pentagram, but not like any I have seen before. Each line of script forms the outer triangles, and each of the triangles has a symbol at its apex."

In the middle of the pentagram, where maybe the energies were the most focused, was the wriggling I had seen. Like something was held there. Maybe what powered the curse.

Tabitha had spoken to another witch there, a tall lady with blond hair bound back like a Valkyrie's. Tabitha looked small next to her. The tall witch shook her head once or twice.

Tabitha walked over to us. "We've been able to stabilize the spell, but we're not sure how long we can keep it that way."

"What's that mean?" Jen asked.

"It's going to start counting down again," Tabitha said. "We can slow it maybe, but the longer the count goes on, whatever it does it's going to do more and more."

"You don't know what it does?"

"We can tell some of it by the behavior of the curse," Tabitha explained. "But why it's there and how it functions, we don't know. Some of the spell is demonic. The other part is written in High Vampiric."

Johnny spoke up. "Um, I might be able to read and write a little High Vampiric."

We stared at Johnny. He had never been a great student in school. "Really?" I asked.

"Gabrielle was teaching me," he explained. "Something I was supposed to learn, if I was going to be a part of the family."

I frowned at his use of the past tense.

Tabitha was excited. "We need your help, then. If you can decipher some of the script for us, we might be able to help Sarah more."

"So you can't cure it?" Jen asked. "You can't break the curse?"

Tabitha shook her head. "Whatever we do, it's only going to give her time. And help you know what's going on. But we can't expel the demon part of the spell. At some point, your sister is going to need a real exorcism."

"Where do we get one of those?" I asked.

"Not just any priest," Tabitha said. "This is a powerful curse. Intricate. It's going to take someone in the church with real power."

Father Benjamin would have been able to help us, then. And if he couldn't, he would have at least known a direction we could go, a place to look, a person to find. But the last I had seen of the priest had been his ghost, red cross on his tabard, holding the point of a sword into the ground. "The Templars," I said.

"Father Benjamin," Jen said.

"We need to find the Templars," I agreed.

Tabitha looked at me curiously. "Do you know the demon who put this on her?"

"Yeah," I said. "I'm pretty sure."

"It's as intricate a curse as I've seen," Tabitha said. "There's going to be traps there. Whoever is going to break this is going to have their work cut out for them. Knowing the name of the demon might help, though."

Knowing Azazel like I did, knowing his name would only hurt the person trying to unravel it. It would lead them into poking into every corner, looking for a trap so hard they never saw the real one. But what did I know about curses?

A loud sizzle crackled inside the house. There was a bright flash of light, so bright I winced. The tall Valkyrie witch next to Sarah was picked up and thrown across the room. Sarah cried out and collapsed to the floor. Jen and Nick were the first people there, helping Sarah to sit up. Other witches ran over to help Valkyrie.

Tabitha looked at me. "We can buy you time, I think. But that's all we can do. Whatever your next step is, you need to figure it out. Quickly."

CHAPTER FIVE

An hour later the witches had taken Sarah up to one of the bedrooms, where she complained too many people were around. Most of us left her alone. I gathered a couple of the breakfast sandwiches, damp and cool in their plastic wrappers, and walked outside with Jen.

The sun shone over the farmhouse, the sky a brilliant blue with tiny puffs of white clouds floating by. Life seemed much happier. I took a deep breath of the clean air, the smell of fresh-cut hay on the breeze, felt the rays of sun on my skin. Somewhere a big fish plopped in and out of the lake.

Jen and I sat under one of the large oak trees, our backs against the bark. We finished the sandwiches and shared a bottle of water. Her hand lay on the grass between us and idly traced patterns through the grass. The green blades sprang back after her fingers passed. A few other trees stood between us and the lake, tall and windy, limbs draped with shades of orange and yellow. When the breeze stirred up, the limbs shook like they were on fire.

It felt so peaceful here, out on the lawn, in this moment. But inside the farmhouse a group of witches were doing everything they could to keep Sarah alive a few days longer. Even as the demonic curse counted down the moments Sarah had left.

Outside was just the sunny air and the cool breeze. The splashing of fish and chittering of squirrels. Like the house and everything inside it didn't exist.

"We have time," I said out loud. I felt better after saying the words. Jen looked at me and smiled, but her mind was elsewhere.

The Templars would know how to help. I was sure of it. I just had to find them. I needed to find a church. But recruitment numbers were low. It would be hard for me to believe every church in every town had one. But if I was lucky, I would find a place to begin. The oldest Catholic church in town would be the best place to start.

I ran the idea by Jen.

"Let's do it," she said. I think she, like me, wanted to do something other than waiting.

We got up and headed over to the Camaro. After Sarah had asked us all to leave, Nick had grabbed a box of tools from somewhere and was now leaning over the hood of the car. I think he, like me, was looking to fill his time with something. Tabitha stood to his left, lips pursed, glancing down the passenger side of the car.

"My father loved classic cars," she said. She looked past the car for a moment, at the road behind it. "He had a fifty-seven Ford Thunderbird. Cherry red. We used to drive it in the country, top down. I loved it."

I actually didn't know much about cars. I knew the major models, like everyone did. Mustang, Camaro, Charger. Other than that, all I could do was change the tires and swap out the oil.

And, I guess, drive them.

Tabitha shook her head for a moment, and looked back at the passenger side of the car. The bullet holes punched down the side of it. The broken window. The dents from running over vampires.

"You should stop driving into gunfights," she said.

"I just drive," I said. "The fights are never my idea." I felt bad for the Camaro. The side of it was dotted with places where the cops had fired at Nick and me, back in Grafton. There were bumps and dings from where the vampires had run into it, when I led them up to the water tower. The dented roof and broken window, from the fight with Azazel at the motel, before I had even known Jen and my friends were in trouble.

I ran the Templar idea past Nick. He and Tabitha liked it.

"The oldest church in town is close to the base," Tabitha said. "I think it's on Charleston Avenue."

"No time like the present, then," I said.

Nick held up a hand. "If you're okay with it, I'm going to work on the car a bit. Get some window replacements, tune it up. There's a junkyard close by here."

"You can take one of our cars." Tabitha pulled a key fob out of her jacket. "I'd like to look at your car myself."

I arched an eyebrow at her.

"Earth witch," she explained, and smiled. "I helped my father, back in the day. I might be able to work some magic."

A somewhat kidlike giddiness washed over me. There was hope for my Camaro. I thanked Tabitha and handed my keys to Nick. Then took a moment to grab the town atlas out of the glove box. Before I shut the door I patted the dash of the car a couple of times.

"You have the house number," Tabitha told Jen. "Call anytime for an update."

Jen and I headed over to a four-door silver sedan., with tinted windows. The car beeped when I clicked the fob, and started up with a soft purr. I immediately didn't like it. The engine whined every time I pushed on the pedal.

I turned off the driveway onto the road and headed south, back into town. Jen had the atlas out and occasionally pointed out where to turn next. The Key tugged at me from over the horizon, the pull of the stone faint, as if it had moved farther away. Behind us was Sarah, getting more and more distant. Of a sudden, I felt stretched between them.

"You okay?" Jen asked.

"I don't like this car," I said. Maybe it was the sedan, maybe it was me. Would I know if the Key had been opened? Would the sense of it just disappear? I turned a little hard around one curve, used to the easy glide of the Camaro and not the sharp response of the sedan. Jen raised both eyebrows at me.

Finding a cure for Sarah would come first. I had made a promise to myself concerning my friends. But old habits die hard. I hated to think of what would happen, what I had let happen, if Azazel was able to open the Key. I hated to think of what would happen if we couldn't find a cure for Sarah.

And this car was slow when I wanted it to be fast. I pressed down on the gas, and the car jerked to respond. I let off the pedal, taking a deep breath. This car just didn't have it. That was all I was feeling now. Just the car.

"You're exhausted." Jen put her hand on my arm, her fingers light and yet warm on my skin.

"That too," I agreed.

"Whatever we find, at the church let's get back to the motel and get you some sleep," Jen said.

"We should go back to the farmhouse," I said.

"Sarah's in the best place she could be," Jen said. "We need to make sure you are too."

I took another deep breath and let it out. It was still tough for me, talking to others. Letting them in. Then I nodded.

"Hey," Jen said. "Just tell me."

"Just a feeling." I waved my hand between pointing to the south and the north. "The Key is pulling at me still. And then there's Sarah. What we need to do for her. That's all."

"You sure it's not something more?" Her eyes were a deep blue in the shadows of the car.

There was something more. She knew it. She just wanted me to say it.

"We have to move," I said. "We're not safe."

"Tell me," she said, simply.

"Staying in one place for too long makes me nervous, Jen," I said. "I've been on the run a long time, and I've never stayed in a place longer than a day. When I do, bad stuff happens."

"What kind of bad stuff?"

I pointed behind us with my thumb. "Grafton kind of bad things."

Her eyes narrowed. "Surely Grafton is the exception."

I thought about it. My army days, all the people who had died right before I found the Key. Grafton. A donut shop in Philadelphia. The list went on. I shook my head. "It's not."

"That's crazy," Jen said. Her fingers tightened on my arm. "I believe what you're telling me, Gus, but we're not in a town of vampires here. And no demon is chasing you for the Key anymore."

Maybe Jen was right, but I couldn't shake the feeling that we needed to move. Azazel had talked about a new game, back in the jail cell in Grafton, when he finally revealed himself to me. He had left Jen alive at King's Lodge, and he had left a glass of whiskey by her bedside.

Azazel wanted me to chase him. And part of me was ready for that. I couldn't leave the Key in his hands. But I also knew my friends would be a part of the chase, and I would do anything to protect them. Part of protecting them was to stay on the move.

I was going to have to walk a fine line. I knew it. But knowing something and doing it were two different things, especially with my history. "I know everything you're telling me, Jen. I just can't shake the feeling something bad is going to happen."

Both of us were silent for a long moment.

"We both know we're going to get Sarah a cure first," I said. "Whatever it takes. Maybe I just have to fight this feeling I have, but it's hard. Staying in one place too long, it's just something I don't do."

"I understand, I think," Jen said. She squeezed my arm one more time. "And I'm here no matter what. Just consider, maybe you worry too much."

"Maybe," I said. My worry had kept me alive. Running had kept me alive. I trusted my instincts. I wanted the others to trust them too. "Maybe."

We pulled up to the church. It lay on the corner of Charleston and Fourth. It wasn't anything fancy, an old granite structure with a plate on the outside telling us it had been founded in 1932 by someone long dead now. The doors were thick oak, and stained-glass windows ringed the sides, and as we pulled up, a bell sounded the hour.

The street around the church was mostly empty. It was a weekday, so maybe that was normal. The sedan clicked off silently. Jen and I got out and walked up the steps to the church. To the right of the church doors there was a square black sign with white letters listing the times of the services for the day.

Jen and I walked inside. Neither one of us blessed ourselves at the font. The church was quiet inside, with only a couple of parishioners spread out among the pews. A few candles burned in the votive under a statue of the Lady Mary, at the front of the church.

Stained-glass windows ringed the inside walls. One of them was of an angel with a sword and shield. The shield had a blazing yellow cross on it, and the angel and shield were outlined in gold. There was a history there, in the stained glass of the church, in churches across the world. A force of good, standing against evil. A graphic novel of supernatural characters played out over colored glass.

Jen was staring at the same thing. "Did you know Father Benjamin well?" I asked her.

"We talked a lot over the last year," Jen said.

"Did you know about the Templars?" I asked. "That he was a part of them?"

The first I had seen him, when I had come back to Grafton, he had traced symbols in the diner. Wards that glowed in my ethereal vision. He had told me he wasn't like Greg, and I didn't know what that meant, but the last sight of his ghost had revealed the priest as a holy warrior: the golden glow, the sword plunged into the pavement in the motel parking lot, Father Benjamin on one knee.

Her eyes flicked up to the stained-glass window I had been looking at. "There's so much we don't know."

"And most of it can kill us," I said.

"I wish I had talked to him more," Jen said. "My guess is, the church knew something about Dominic and Raphael and had Father Benjamin sent there to keep an eye on things. But when we talked, we danced around things. I think we trusted each other, but the church and witches, there's some history to get over there."

"I think that's Saint Michael." I motioned to the window. "The Archangel."

"The lead soldier against Lucifer," Jen said.

"Yep," I said. "If you believe in that kind of stuff."

Jen tilted her head. "You don't?"

I shook my head. "I've never seen Lucifer. I've never seen God."

"You've been chased by a demon," Jen pointed out.

"Sure," I said. "What does that even mean, though? Demons exist, evil exists. Monsters are just monsters. That doesn't mean there's some ultimate power behind demons and vampires. There's enough evil in most of us, I'm not sure we need to blame someone else for it."

"But ... ghosts," she said. "You see them. What do you think they are?"

"I don't know," I said. "I've burned through a lot of them, Jen, and there's nothing there leading me to believe something good is waiting for us in the afterlife."

She paused for a long moment. "What about Danny?"

I think she knew that would hurt. Danny had been an exception. I had never encountered a spirit like his. Or what I had been a part of, with what he had given me. So I looked away from Saint Michael, from Jen. "There's an exception to everything."

"You really believe that?" she asked.

A young man with the collar of a priest walked up. His eyes had dark circles underneath them, and he paused a good distance from both of us. "Can I help you?"

"We're hoping so," I said. "We came here looking to find out more about the Templars?"

His eyes opened wide. "You have to leave."

"Father," Jen said, "we're in need of help."

"I apologize, miss," the priest said, looking around at the people in the church. "But I have nothing to say. I won't help you. The best thing you could do now is just leave, and not come back."

Jen and I paused, perplexed. I stepped close to the priest, who took a step back. "Look, Father, we're both looking for a little information. And you're in a business that is supposed to help others. So I apologize in advance, but we're not leaving."

The priest surprised me. He gathered himself and stepped close to me and looked me directly in the eye. "Whatever help you need from the Templars, you can get on your own. I'm done with them here."

Some of the people in the church looked over at us. A teenager sat by the confession booth, tucked into a pew there, almost hidden in the corner. When I noticed him, he got up and left.

"Father," Jen said.

"You leave now," the priest said. He watched the young man leave, and shook his head. "Or I'll call the police and ask them to remove you."

We stood like that for a moment. The priest was shorter than me, and up close I could see he hadn't shaved in a few days. His eyes were bloodshot. But his jaw stayed shut. He wasn't going to tell us anything. And we couldn't afford the notice of the police.

"We're going," I said. And both of us walked out.

The teenager was waiting outside. A boy, actually. Maybe ten or eleven years old, pale with a shock of red hair, freckles decorating his face. He stood with his chest stuck out, and when he spoke, his voice was high-pitched. "Were you asking about Templars?"

"We were," I said. "What do you know about them?"

"So you knew my dad, then?"

I had a hard time picturing Greg as this man's father. They looked completely different. Still, I described the man to the kid. "Tall man, Middle Eastern? Hawklike nose, spoke with an accent?"

The kid sank in a little. "You mean Greg."

"You knew him?" I asked. "Was he your father?"

"He's dead too?" The kid sighed. "He and my dad, I think they were partners. My dad was killed a week ago."

Jen placed her hand on the kid's shoulder. "I'm sorry."

"It's okay," the kid said. His jaw clenched. "I understand. I know what he did was important."

Greg had told me he had lost his partner recently. And the priest had told me he had taken the news hard.

"Greg was just here a few days ago," the kid said. "I didn't know what my dad did until then. But he explained parts of it to me."

"Can you help us?" Jen asked. "We need someone who can do an exorcism."

"Like in the movies?" The kid's eyes opened wide. "Wow."

"Not wow," I said. "But needed."

"I don't know much," the kid said. "Just what Greg told me. He came down and told me all about my father and the good he's done. He gave me some money. And then he got into a fight with Uncle Donald."

"Marcus, we've talked about this." The priest stood there in the door-way, one hand holding the door open. "Please come inside the church."

"Why don't you help these people?" Marcus asked. One of his small fists had balled up. "Are you scared? My father would have."

"My brother was a foolish man," the priest said. "And look where it got him. He died doing foolish things."

"These people need an exorcism." Marcus had stepped past me, toward his uncle. "Isn't that something you're supposed to do? Something the church should do?"

The priest's eyes opened in fear. He stepped quickly down to Marcus and pulled the kid up the stairs. "You think these things are just games."

Marcus twisted in the priest's grip. "All that evil needs to win is for good to do nothing."

"What do you know?" The priest's teeth showed themselves in a snarl. "All that evil needs to win is for good people to keep dying."

He pushed the boy into the church and shut the door behind him. Then he turned back to us. "I want you to leave this boy alone."

The whole thing had happened so fast, in front of us. Jen's eyes were pinched in concern. I didn't know Marcus's father, but whatever had killed him had left its mark on Greg. It would have been a bad death to leave that kind of sadness behind.

Still, Sarah needed a miracle. And the only shot we had of one started here.

"Then help us," I told the priest.

"I can't help you," he said. "I knew what my brother was into. What Greg was doing. If they couldn't take care of it, it's far beyond me."

"I don't understand," I said. "Whatever your brother died doing, it's got nothing to do with us. Her sister needs an exorcism or she's going to die. Won't you help us with that?"

"I can't help with what you need," the priest said. "It's beyond me."

"Then tell us who," Jen said, stepping forward. "She's my *sister*. Surely you understand how that feels. If you could have helped your brother, wouldn't you have?"

"I'll thank you not to talk about him," the priest said. "And who would I be helping? Two churchgoers? Two believers? From the looks of you, you've got blood all over your hands. I'd be willing to bet your sister does as well. Let me ask you, what happened to your priest in Grafton?"

Father Benjamin had died. Saving Jen. But he had died. I didn't say anything, but the priest saw it in my face.

"I thought so," he spat. "It's people like you who get people like my brother killed. He was a fool."

The door opened again. Marcus pushed himself out through the priest's hands, swinging tiny fists against the man. "You don't say that about my father!"

They fought for a moment, until the priest got his arms around Marcus and held him. The boy ran out of energy and stopped suddenly, crying into the priest's robe. They stayed that way a long time, until the priest looked over Marcus's head and met my eyes. *See?* his eyes seemed to say, looking at the top of the boy's red hair, and back to us.

Jen grabbed my arm and pulled me back to her. "We'll figure it out," she whispered.

I understood.

The priest swallowed then, and patted Marcus on the head once and then twice. Marcus's sobs died off, and he gripped the priest tightly.

"Knowing what my brother was into," he said, "if you need an exorcism, then there's only one person on this continent who could help you. Bishop Jean-Louis of New Orleans."

"New Orleans?" I shook my head. That was a long way away from here.

"He's the archdiocese there," the priest said. "I have no idea if he'll help you. But he would be able to, I think."

"Thank you, father," Jen said.

The priest blushed a bit. "You all should probably leave. I did call the police. I'm sure they are on their way."

I sighed. It was a hell of a day when a priest calling the cops on you was par for the course.

CHAPTER SIX

We got back in the car. It had a cherry air freshener that smelled funny, to me. I let out a deep breath and leaned back against the headrest. "New Orleans is pretty far."

"Yeah," Jen said. "We'll figure it out."

"I know." I rubbed my eyes with the palms of my hands. "It's just one more thing."

"Let's go back to the motel," Jen said. "You need some sleep."

I started the car, feeling the transmission engage the tires and lightly tug the car forward. We headed down the street until we joined the strip in front of the base, and stopped only once, when we saw a thrift store. Ten minutes later and with a full bag of jeans and T-shirts, we headed back to the motel.

The lumpy mattress felt like heavenly, floaty marshmallows. I stretched and felt the cool, thick pillows underneath my arms. Jen got on the phone and called the number Tabitha had given her, speaking to someone for a few low minutes. When she hung up she told me that Sarah was okay and still sleeping. Johnny was helping them with some translations, but they hadn't figured out anything yet. And Nick was still at the junkyard.

"So we have nothing to do now but rest." Jen grinned and lay next to me. She threw her arm over my chest and nestled her chin into my shoulder.

I exhaled a long, relaxing breath, and smiled back at her. We stayed like that for a while, and though it was dark in the room, the midday sun still outlined the thick drapes covering the window and lit up the corners of the room. It seemed a little bare. There was only the lone bag of clothes we had, which made me think of the cash I didn't have.

"When night comes I'm going to make a quick money run," I said.

"I'll come with you," Jen said.

"It's okay," I said. What I did to get money wasn't lawful, by any means, although morally I didn't have much trouble with it. Sometimes I was a scavenger, and preyed on those less fortunate. The recently dead usually had something around I could use for money. It was how I had survived, and though I was okay with it, it wasn't a part of me I wanted Jen to see. Not yet, at least. "I won't be long."

"You sure?"

"I'm sure." I turned my head just a little and placed a tiny kiss on her forehead. Her skin was warm and soft under my lips.

Tomorrow would be the second day in this town. Azazel had caught me, just a few days ago, because I had hung around a different motel for two days. So deep down a part of me wanted to keep running, and take Jen and Nick and Johnny and Sarah with me, but I fought that feeling down. We would be safe. I would protect them all. I made it a promise.

We drifted into sleep. I slept for a large part of the afternoon, getting up an hour or so before midnight. Jen moved sluggishly next to me. She must be as exhausted as the rest of us. Only the day before she had been in bed, a sword having cut through her stomach. I kissed her carefully, before I left.

"Be careful," she murmured, her lips falling away from mine. I smoothed her hair, softly. I wasn't worried too much. Careful was my middle name.

It was good and dark out when I headed out. The parking lot was lit by a mix of yellow motel lights and bright white streetlights. I got into the sedan, and the cherry smell still bothered me. It was too strong. Too fake.

I turned it on. It was a four cylinder, and I couldn't feel the engine rumbling under the hood like I could my Camaro. The car couldn't convince me it was running, even after I let my foot off the brake and allowed the transmission to back the car up a bit.

At least the car wasn't too noticeable. Especially since I was about to do something not quite legal. It was just another four-door sedan among thousands.

I drove around, searching through the area with my ethereal senses. I sensed ghosts all around me in this town, like dots on a radar. An old man had passed earlier that day to the north of me. A recent ghost on the base nearby, maybe a training accident. Another ghost on the road as I drove by, where someone had stepped into traffic. Fields of dots lay west of me, laid out in rows and lines that usually signified a large graveyard.

The old man was my first bet, and I headed that way He was in a run-down house on the corner of an old street, where all the homes had the tan vinyl siding that had been used a lot in the eighties. The neighborhood was old enough that there weren't any sidewalks. Privacy fences were few and far between. Some of the lawns were well manicured, but many had weeds in the yard and scatterings of brown, brittle leaves.

I parked on the next street over and snuck through a few backyards to get to the house with the ghost. There wasn't a lot of activity. The neighborhood was old and so were the people who lived there. The back door was easy to jimmy and I snuck into the home.

The ghost was in the living room. The body was old and laid-back in an old yellow easy chair, with the footrest kicked up and facing an old tube television. A half-eaten peanut butter and jelly sandwich lay on the floor next to him, the plate a few feet away. His ghost sat overtop the body and looked at me briefly as I came in before turning back to the blank television. One of its ghostly hands clicked a nonexistent remote.

I walked through the house quickly. The man's wallet was on the kitchen counter and had almost nothing in it, just a few small bills, which I took. There was a nice watch beside the wallet, and a few pieces of jewelry upstairs, but nothing that would sell for anything at a pawnshop. I usually would take everything and get what I could, but I didn't want to have to explain hawking a dead man's watch to Jen. I didn't think she'd judge me, but I wasn't proud of this part of my life me, even if the dead didn't need to tell time.

I ended up striking out here. Which was typical. I normally had to poke around a few old ghosts before finding enough things to sell. Sometimes I would find enough cash to last me a few days. Occasionally, and rarely, I would find an ATM password written in a wallet. One time, I had found the keys and title to a sixty-eight Camaro, stuck in a garage.

I snuck back out, making sure to wipe down the areas I had touched, and to close the door so that everything looked like it had when I arrived. I didn't think anyone would think the old man had been murdered by a peanut butter and jelly sandwich. I got back in the car and scanned my radar for a better score.

There was a ghost that had passed away the past weekend, an older lady this time. She was across the other side of town. Even though she had died maybe a week ago, I headed that way. Sometimes people left homes alone for a bit, when their loved ones passed away.

On the way, though, two ghosts popped up immediately on the radar. One, then the next. Both of them young, and when I sensed the ghosts, they came with an overwhelmingly dark feel of violence. Both had been shot.

This would be more promising. And more dangerous. That kind of violence usually only happened in gangs, and that meant cash on hand. If I was lucky I could get there quick and find a real score.

I pressed the pedal down on the car, and the engine whined. I drove into a run-down part of town, one of those areas where bars ran lengthwise across not just the shop windows, but homes. Broken bottles and brown bags littered the sidewalks. All of the lawns were fields of knee-high weeds. A slight discomfort settled over me as I headed deeper into the neighborhood, like someone was in the seat behind me, dragging a chilled knife's edge along the back of my neck.

I knew nothing was there, but I couldn't help it. I kept checking my rearview.

A few blocks later and I was at a corner house on a run-down block. The house at one point had had a nice yellow stucco exterior. Lights were on in the front of the house, and there were some empty forties stacked up on the porch. The lawn was decorated with broken leaves, torn plastic bags usually from a gas station, and white foam cups. A screen door waved back and forth, beckoning. Somewhere in that place were two ghosts who had shot each other.

I turned the corner and parked in the shadows of the street. For a moment I sat there, then I took a deep breath and reached out to the first ghost. A young man, talking to a man named Luther.

"Luther, you a damn fool," the young man laughed, tilting a forty back on the couch and swallowing a few big gulps. I felt a little jacked up as his ghost, like I had drunk a thousand cups of coffee. "Jo ain't gonna go for that."

"I don't care what Jo wants," the other man said, sitting in a chair next to the couch. This man had his hand on a pistol, and his bottle lay unopened on the table between them. A few twists of plastic baggies, filled with white powder, lay sprinkled around the bottle, and a round circle of hundred-dollar bills was held together with a rubber band. Luther kept looking at the door. "He's done gone off the edge."

"You ain't takin his stuff, though," I, or the young man's ghost, said.

"I got a right to the shit I earned," Luther said.

"Dawg, Jo runs this crew," I said as the ghost again, and laughed. "You ain't got shit for rights here."

Luther tumbled over the chair then. A loud cracking sound popped through the house. Then another. As the ghost, I watched Luther look from behind his chair and fire back down the hallway to the house. I dropped my forty, the beer spilling all over the couch, and scrambled around for my gun.

More shots from the back of the house. Luther collapsed to the floor, and a big man walked in from the hallway, dark-skinned, hand pressed to his stomach.

The young man's ghost thought Jo's eyes never looked right. They always were much wider than a normal person's. Like he saw more. The big man put a few more rounds into Luther's body and looked at me. Or the ghost. Well, me as the ghost.

"Jo, I ain't listened to him," I said, and put up my hands. "I swear."

The man looked at me, and looked at his stomach. Blood bubbled over his fingers. "Yeah," he said. "You did."

He looked at me and pulled the trigger.

I jerked back in the car and sat there for a moment, breathing heavily. Violent deaths were tough to live, but sometimes it was the best way to check and see if the coast was clear. Or what I might run up against. I had been desperate enough, at times, to go in and finish the job.

As I sat there a third ghost popped up in the house. Jo. He had died of his stomach wound. So tonight the coast was clear. I had gotten here in time, and no one else was in the house. And the police probably weren't headed this way. It wasn't that kind of neighborhood. The image of the roll of hundreds on the coffee table came to me mind; I likely had a few minutes to go in there and see what else was there.

Quickly, I got out of the car. The night was quiet. In the distance I heard the occasional eighteen-wheeler rumble down the nearby highway. No lights turned on in any other houses. No one shouted a challenge, asked what I was doing, or what was going on. No one cared about three guys killing each other here.

I pushed myself to get into the house. I wasn't looking forward to seeing the ghosts. Something about Jo had seemed off. I avoided violent deaths and violent ghosts when I could. Still, I had done things like this before, and it wasn't like I had a day job.

It was slightly chilly out, and the T-shirt I wore now did little to hide me from the cold. I missed my army jacket. I had had that jacket a long time, but it had undergone a lot of altering in Grafton, mainly from getting shot at, and at the end I had thrown the coat away.

It occurred to me that I wasn't carrying a gun. Everything I had was in the Camaro. Maybe an oversight, but at least there were ghosts around to pull from, if I needed to.

I strode up to the house. I walked like I belonged there. I'd learned over the years that was the best way to go about something like this. If you walked like you belonged, then the people watching assumed you had business there. And if you had business in a place like this, most people who saw you would rather look away than ask about the guy walking into a trap house.

The screen door still lay partly open, with part of the screen ripped out and folded over on itself. The front door was shut, but the jamb to the door was broken where the dead bolt would be. I shoved on the door. It opened, and immediately the metallic, acrid scent of gunpowder flooded over me. I set my jaw, ready to grab a ghost if I needed to.

The house felt empty. There was a silence in the place, like the quiet that descends right after a thunderstorm. I couldn't shake the feeling of the cold knife on the back of my neck, though, and uneasily stepped into the house.

"Hello?" I called out, and then rolled my eyes. I already knew who was in here. No one. But for some reason, I was still afraid of going in.

I walked into the living room, with the three bodies and matching ghosts. The ghost of the young man I had been still sat on the couch and occasionally lifted a ghostly bottle of beer to his lips. Luther's body lay sprawled next to the recliner, and his ghost sat back in the chair, staring alternately at the coffee table and then down the hallway.

Jo had made it to the kitchen, and had a wad of old towels pressed up against his belly. All the towels were dark with blood, and his ghost stood above the body and looked down with a wide frown at the corpse. He was as large in real life as he had been when I was living the ghost of the third man, easily a head taller than me, and muscled like a bodybuilder on steroids. There was a lot of blood over the floor.

Luther had a nine-millimeter by an outstretched hand. The thick roll of cash lay on the coffee table, and I quickly grabbed that and stuck it in my pocket. A quick search of the recliner and couch found me a few more rolls of cash, and there was a bag of it in the closet in the hallway. The young man and Luther had some rolls in their pockets.

I ended up finding a few places with more cash and heroin, like the attic in the hallway, and the bedroom closets, and the toilet tanks. There were some plastic grocery bags all around the house. I stuffed all the cash I found in a couple of those. I had hit the jackpot.

This is what I did for my spare change. It was quick and dirty and, if not wrong, not quite morally right either. It had gotten me by in the past, especially while I was running from Azazel, and had helped me survive. Sometimes all I found was a nice necklace to pawn. Or someone with a wallet full of bills. But that was far from the norm. Most of my spare cash came from something like this. A bad part of town, a shoot-out, a stabbing. Rapid uncontrollable violence.

The ghost of the guy in the recliner stared at me, frowning a little, as if trying to put it all together. Sudden death does that sometimes to ghosts. They live on afterward, trying to figure out what had happened, and what was keeping them from getting up and going over to so-and-so's house.

I had to double-bag the cash, it got that heavy. I tied the knot and looked at the ghost of the guy in the recliner one last time. He had wanted to leave the gang, leave Jo. He had wanted to do something different, and maybe better. At least that was my hope. In the midst of all the violence and the drugs and the gang wars, I wanted to believe there were people who wanted more to life.

I think I needed to believe it. I went to tie off the last bag when a loud boom echoed through the room.

A hot piercing pain shot through my back and burst out of my stomach. Blood sprayed from my front onto the body in the recliner. A second sharp pain followed the first and repeated the spray of blood. Gunshots. Two of them.

I fell between the couch and the recliner. I had been shot. And it was bad. Splintered white bones poked out of the holes. My heart pounded at the sudden loss of blood, and a large red puddle spread across the carpet around me.

I grabbed ghost. An immediate reaction, like dodging something thrown at you. A reflex as soon as I felt the pain, as soon as I saw the blood. I had lost a lot already, even in just these few seconds. I needed to heal quickly. Then figure out who was shooting me and handle that.

The first ghost I tapped was the guy next to me. On the couch. His memories filtered through me …

Riding around in my boy's Monte Carlo, holding my nine loosely out the window. Yellin' at the bitches and tossing some drink back. Popping shots off down the street. Heart racing, I reached down for some more of the purple sizzurp …

Electric tingles spread across my stomach, little pins and needles of nerves firing, and the gaping holes in my front started to close. At the same time, I picked up Luther's nine-millimeter. And I prayed it was loaded.

Someone cursed behind me. My heart loped hard in my chest. It didn't have enough blood left to pump. The first ghost disappeared under my pull, so I switched to Luther. In my midsection organs regrew themselves, bones knit back together, and skin stretched across the holes in my stomach.

But none of that was happening fast enough. I rolled over and heard more shots. Felt another bullet slam into my stomach from the front, another hit my shoulder. I used Luther's ghost to strengthen the skin I had left and heal what I could.

Luther stashed some more cash in his room behind the vent. It was a dumb place to hide it, but there was so much cash from their last score he thought it wouldn't matter. He needed the money to cut out. He didn't like what Jo did to his women anyway, and it only had gotten worse. Luther had to get out. He hoped he could take Tank with him, but Tank was more concerned about the girls and the drugs than whatever Jo was doing.

More ethereal energy poured out of the plane and through Luther's ghost. I used it to strengthen whatever skin I had left, whatever muscles would fire, and to keep my heart trying to beat. A small thin man was at the door in a white tank top, a semiautomatic pistol pointed at me from one hand. The barrel of the gun moved slowly, tracking my roll. Another bullet had left the gun and headed tortoiselike through the air. I pointed Luther's nine-millimeter and pulled the trigger quickly.

The thin man spiraled around and tumbled out the door, leaving it wide-open. The last bullet tore through my side. A spindly, wiry ghost appeared above him, finger still pulling a gun that wasn't there.

My stomach cramped. I rolled over to my side and threw up blood and screamed at the pain erupting from my belly. I tugged on the thin guy's ghost, and the spirit disappeared almost as soon as I started pulling.

Some ghosts never lasted that long. I didn't have enough. I needed the last ghost. It stood in the kitchen, a mountain of a dark spirit. The ghost no longer looked down at his own body; he stared directly at me. Like the specter could see everything that happened. His eyes were wide-open and maybe I imaged it, but they seemed to burn red in their sockets.

I swallowed once, then pulled. Beggars can't be choosers. The giant ghost fought me from the first touch. I yanked hard at the energy he tried to withhold from me, like an ethereal tug-of-war. Jo's mouth opened in a soundless roar and the tug-of-war stopped, the energy balanced between us. I set my jaw and screamed and pulled as hard as I ever had –

I had my pants around my ankles, and I was rock hard. Pushing in and out of the tiny cheeks in front of me, just drilling her. I was close to coming and I pushed hard and harder, and told that bitch to scream for me. She didn't, though. I told her again and she looked back with wet, scared eyes and THAT BITCH WAS CRYING. So I reached around and grabbed her throat hard. I clasped down until she bucked over and over.

I kept pumping until she screamed. I felt her throat work hard against my hand. Then I came, and she bucked one last time and fell limp. I pulled my hand away from her throat and saw the blood on my hand and coming out of her mouth and told that bitch that's what she gets.

I threw up all over myself. My stomach cramped more and I threw up again, this time blood and bile mixed. I rolled over to my knees and pushed a hand hard against my stomach and held back a scream at that memory. I retched over and over, dry heaves where nothing came out. I prepared myself and pulled more.

More and more of Jo's memories flew through me. I lived each one of the girls he'd murdered after that one. Each one he had raped. The women got younger and younger, all kinds of shapes and sizes and race. Each one he had snuffed out, in sicker and sicker fashion.

My hand shook against my stomach. I would always remember the first girl's death, from Jo's memories. I had lived her death, and at the same time Jo's anger and excitement; both feelings warred within me. I still felt his hand gripping the poor girl's throat, felt her muscles work as she tried to breathe, felt Jo's hand close tighter and tighter until his fingers broke through the skin.

I had lived all of that. I was sick beyond belief. And angry beyond measure.

Jo's ghost stared down at me. Still murderous in its gaze, though the specter had faded somewhat. As I met his eyes, Jo's ghost smirked at me. Then he licked his lips and grabbed his crotch.

I balled my shaking hand into a fist and *pulled*. The memories kept flying through my mind and I tried to push them all away, but each of them left their own sordid trail. Girl after girl died by Jo's hands, and I lived them all. I screamed so hard muscles in my abdomen tore around the wound. But in the end the ghost finally disappeared.

I let out a trembling breath and healed myself with the energy that was left. It was just enough that the wounds closed up on my skin, but a warmth still spread inside my body, from where I had been shot. Blood still pooled inside; I still was mortally wounded.

That guy, that ghost, so many women he had raped and snuffed. I had them all, but I would never shake the first of Jo's memory. The excitement of the twisted man and the power he had felt. The fear and pain and the tears of the poor girl.

Sirens blared in the distance. Someone had finally called the police, or the police had finally decided to head this way. I wobbled as I stood up and waited a moment as a wave of dizziness overcame me. My blood pressure was low, partly because I had leaked a lot of blood, and partly because I was still open in my insides. I was almost at the door when I remembered the cash. Thankfully I had double-bagged all the rolls; blood was everywhere.

I staggered to the car. My hand shook as I tried to open the door. I finally got in and realized I was still bleeding. Nothing to do for it now. Somehow I was able to start the car and drive away. Along the way I passed the ghost of the guy who had stepped into traffic, and was able to pull enough from him to stop the bleeding and stitch together my insides.

I shook and shook. I was sure anyone watching the car weave along the road thought I was drunk. I was fortunate, though, and didn't get pulled over, and actually made it back to the motel.

The fast-food place was closed. The motel lights were off, but the streetlights still lit the parking lot up with a stark whiteness that outlined corners of buildings and cars with dark shadows. I turned off the car, got the money, and went to the door to our room.

Jen opened it as I got there. She took one look at my face and blood-covered clothes and pulled me into the room, shutting the door behind me. I held the plastic bag of money tightly to my belly, the plastic crinkling in my grip.

"Gus." She gently tugged the bag from me and set it aside. She pulled me in and wrapped her arms around me, and I let myself lean into her. Her voice was low and close to my ear. "You okay?"

I shook my head. She held me close, her arms warm around my back. Every breath I took was shaky. My hands opened and closed, and opened and closed, over and over. Part of them could still feel the throat of that young girl as she died.

I had lived rapes before, pulling power from ghosts. I had lived memories of rapists and murderers and thugs. Ghosts of some of the police in Grafton, the doctor in the factory, what he had done with Sarah. But this act, and this ghost, had been too evil. Too psychopathic. A sick enjoyment colored every sense I had, a feeling that wasn't mine, but a sickness left inside me from what I had experienced.

I worried that living the memories would change me. How could they not? I experienced evil in many ways, I *lived* the evil for a time, as I used ethereal energy. A rotten apple spreads its rottenness just through touching another, and I had touched evil many, many times.

Bile burned the back of my throat, and I swallowed to keep it down. I stood in Jen's arms and shook. She rubbed her hands up and down and murmured words into my ear, her voice calm, comforting. I buried my face into her neck and cried. She kept telling me it was okay, everything was okay, over and over and over.

I couldn't stop crying. Jen just held me. Kept telling me she was there. One hand stroked the back of my head and trailed down my neck, over and over, the touch softer and softer. For a long time I stayed in the cocoon of her arms, wanting all the memories I had just lived to go away. I didn't think they ever would, but after a while they did recede, like a tide, slowly pulling back from shore. At some point, when I could, I let out a big, shuddering breath.

After a while, in a tiny, personal whisper, Jen asked me to tell her about it. Just a little encouragement. A little bit later, I did.

I started with bits and pieces. What I usually did to get money to live by. How that usually happened. Then I told her about tonight. What had happened in that house, the furious face of Jo's ghost as it had fought me, and his memories of what he had done, what he had left with me.

"Gus." Her voice low and throaty in my ear. Her arms tightened around me. "I'm so sorry."

"I'll be okay," I said, my voice a little too loud. Fragile. I said it again, and again, like a mantra. Like if I said it enough, I would be. The whole time I did, Jen's hand lingered in my hair, finally cupping the back of my head, and holding it against her shoulder. I whispered the words against her shoulder, and she held me and let me get it all out.

The tipping point passed. My hands stopped shaking. My cheek pressed against Jen's shoulder, my chest rose and fell, slowly and regularly, against hers. Her heart beat softly in return, and my heartbeat slowed down to match.

Some of the memories, the worst parts of them, dimmed a little.

Jen pulled me into the bathroom, and stripped me of my bloody shirt and jeans. Those went into the trash. She started up the shower, testing the water before pushing me under the hot spray. A moment later she joined me, grabbing the tiny block of motel soap and lathering her hands up with it, then rubbing me up and down.

The hot jets of water hit us both, ran down both of our bodies. Jen's hands were silky smooth against my skin. She worked and scrubbed the blood away from me, letting the water take all the dirt and grime and gore down the drain.

I leaned my forehead against the shower wall and let her work. Jen started shampooing my hair, her fingers digging into my scalp. There was a rhythmic push-pull to her hands, and my head nodded back and forth under the hot spray. I shuddered and let out a long, deeply held breath.

She rinsed my hair, then did the same with the conditioner, working her fingers into my hair, little shivers of pleasure running down from my scalp and through my body. She turned me around to face her, and tiny bubbles of soap slid down us both, mixing with the rushing water.

She smiled, laying her wrists on my shoulders, using her fingers to dig into either side of the base of my neck. Everything felt so good that I moaned, and Jen smiled at the sound. Water ran along her arms like clear streams, flowed along her skin, down her breasts. Her blue eyes were open and guileless and weren't really asking me a question, so much as telling me there was an answer.

All I heard was the pounding of my heart and the pattering of water in the tub.

Then I whispered her name.

She pressed against me, putting her mouth against mine. Her lips were soft and warm and gentle. There were little kisses between us, accompanied by little moans. Skin soft and wet and silky smooth flattened against me. For a long moment it was just us, our bodies, and a long, passionate kiss.

Then her mouth opened, her tongue flicked out over her upper lip, and she rubbed her body against me, our bodies sliding in the soap. Our kiss got harder, more animalistic. The moan became a cry, Jen's breath came out in a quick gasp, and the innocent moment between us erupted into a sensual, physical need.

I moved Jen, putting her back to the shower wall. Our bodies slid against each other, slick and warm and wet. Her hands slipped down and tried to grip me. My hand slid down the small of her back and cupped one cheek. She lifted that leg a little and I slid carefully in. She let out a small moan, her hip moving in my hand, back and forth.

The kiss between us kept going. Jen rocked in little, slow motions. Our lips stayed together, each of us leaving only briefly to take little bites of each other, nibbling an ear, the nape of her neck. I let out a breath and braced my hand against the shower wall, Jen's hair lying thick and heavy over my arm, dripping water.

Then Jen moaned in frustration, and wrapped her other leg around my hip, arching her back and working me deeper inside her. I echoed her moan and thrust forward, and Jen matched the motion with her hips. We moved, slowly at first, until we found a rhythm. With all the little kisses and short breaths and sighs and moans of each other's name.

The rhythm slowly beat louder. Harder. Jen lifted her face to me, and we kissed hard enough that her teeth grated against mine. She leaned back against the wall and pulled my face into her chest, her hair plastered around her face, stuck to the side of the shower.

Droplets rained everywhere, trailing down her face, little wet trickles outlining every line and curve. A soap bubble rested on the top of one breast, shiny and iridescent in the bathroom light. She turned my face up so that my eyes found hers. We locked our gazes as Jen moved her hips slow and hard. Rocking.

I groaned. She rocked harder, and bit her lower lip. We moved a little faster and then a little faster, until she gasped at every thrust and I buried my face into her neck, holding a moan back.

Then she pushed hard with her hips and cried out loud, pulling my face up to hers and kissing me as hard as she could. Our moans mixed together. She shuddered, I shuddered, and both of us sighed softly into each other's mouths.

For a long moment I stood there, not trusting that I could move, and yet not trusting my legs to hold us both in place. Jen shifted a bit, trembling. I closed my eyes and braced myself against the wall, letting the water wash over her, over me, over us.

I breathed in and out, and felt her chest rise and fall to match mine, and I shook just a little on my next breath, feeling better than I had felt in a long, long time. Both of us breathing hard, mouths still pressed against each other, our lips curved in a smile.

We stayed like that for a moment.

Then Jen bit my shoulder.

I jerked back a bit, looking down at several more marks on my shoulder and chest. Something I hadn't felt, when it had happened. I arched an eyebrow at Jen.

She stared at me with an impish grin, blue eyes twinkling. Her skin glistened wetly, and looking like that, I imagined her as one of the sirens who could lure a sailor to his death. With just that grin.

I smiled in returned and kissed her, a long kiss that spoke more of being complete, of being whole, than any kind of need. The hotel water ran from hot to warm. Cold would be next. We worked ourselves until we both were standing again, and Jen turned us around so that she was under the spray.

We both finished washing off, taking turns lathering each other up and standing under the spray until it finally did become cold. Laughing, making little jokes. Being together. Forgetting about the rest of the world. Sometime later we fell asleep in a lumpy hotel bed, and I hadn't felt more comfortable or safe or happy in my life.

CHAPTER SEVEN

I woke early the next morning. Spent some time staring at Jen. She slept like she had when we were teenagers, like we had fallen asleep on her mother's couch, having stayed up talking and watching television until the late show had finished.

There was an innocence to Jen all the time, but it came out most when she slept. A peacefulness and contentment and even, deep breaths. All I wanted to do was wrap my arms around her and hold her tight against me. Feel her chest rise and fall against mine, hear her breath against my ear, and wish her peaceful dreams.

She opened her eyes and caught me watching her. "Hey."

"Hey." I smiled.

"What're you doing?"

"Watching you."

"Ugh." She pulled the blanket over her head, so her next words came out muffled. "You should get us some coffee instead."

"Is that the deal?" My grin widened. It seemed I couldn't stop it this morning.

Coffee did sound good. Maybe something to eat with it too. I got up and got dressed in some of the clothes we'd gotten yesterday. Some kind of metal band logo on my T-shirt: a monster strumming a guitar in front of some pyrotechnic lights.

"You want breakfast or anything?"

All I got back was another *ugh*. I laughed and shut the door and took a couple of steps away from the door. The sky outside was bright blue, the air was cool, but the sun shone low over the horizon and promised to warm the day up.

I stepped onto the parking lot, heading over to the coffee place across the street. Far in the distance behind the shop lay the tall brick walls of the army base. Immediately a cool, wet breeze blew across my face with a slight hint of rain in the air. A slow rumble of thunder cracked loudly overhead.

Fat, heavy drops pattered around me.

I looked back at our motel room, raising my voice. "Really?"

The window muted some of the laugh from inside our room, but not all of it.

A big cloud appeared in front of the sun and threw a shadow between me and the coffee shop. A heavy rain began to fall. I raced across the street, avoiding a car stopped in one lane, its blinkers on and windshield wipers flipping back on forth. A few more rumbles of thunder rolled around the skies, and I dove into the shop. Dripping wet.

Inside, people muttered and looked out. The skies had opened up. A guy by the door looked at his phone with a furrowed brow. He thumbed the screen until a weather app revealed a bright yellow sun. He glanced at me as I stepped past him.

The shop smelled like freshly ground coffee and warm milk. A number of people already stood in line. Other customers sat in black-wire chairs around tiny round tables. Plates of half-eaten pastries and cookies lay here and there.

I waited in line. The baristas took orders and called out names. People grabbed their cups and walked out into the rain. The line slowly chugged forward. The lady in front of me smiled and wished me a good morning. I smiled and replied that it was. We neared the counter, with large thick squares of coffee cake under the glass, the top layer of crumbs, thick and gooey. My stomach rumbled.

I ordered a couple of flavored lattes this morning. Life felt different today. Maybe it was time to stop drinking the easier-to-get black coffee. I also added a slab of coffee cake to the order. The barista put a large piece on a tiny white plate and handed it over to me. I smiled at the weight of it.

I turned around to look over the shop and took a bite of the cake, enjoying the cinnamon-sugary sweetness on my tongue, licking my thumb and forefinger after the bite.

The crowd of people waiting for their drinks parted before me. A man sat at a table right in the middle of the coffee shop, wearing a white pin-striped suit with a black shirt. Overdressed, in this part of town. A wide cup holding an overfoamed latte off to the side of the table. The man's legs casually crossed each other, his body lay back relaxed in the chair, and he held a newspaper loosely open in front of him.

The sweetness of the coffee cake disappeared. I swallowed and clenched my jaw. Azazel.

The demon looked at me and motioned to the chair at his table.

I tapped the closest ghost I could find.

Azazel looked at the people around us and raised an eyebrow at me. I rolled my eyes; Azazel had never been one to worry about collateral damage. And he did love to talk.

I took a deep breath. The wind picked up outside with a low, whistling roar. A smattering of rain slapped the side of the shop and washed across the glass.

We both waited.

The ghost was the old homeless lady by the motel, the one with the shopping cart. There was some initial resistance as I pulled from her, an awareness from the ghost of what I was doing that hadn't happened before Grafton. She turned a gap-toothed smile toward me, from the parking lot across the street. A strange scent of ginger cookies flooded my senses. I strengthened my grip on the ghost, and the resistance wavered and disappeared.

The corner of Azazel's lip turned up in a small curve. His eyes opened as if he could feel the tension rise between us, as if he breathed it in and relished it. He made a show of folding the newspaper together neatly and placing it on the table. Squaring the paper to the corner.

Behind me, across the street, Jen was snuggled in her blanket and waiting for coffee. Farther away, Sarah was fighting for her life, with Nick and Johnny and the witches. And if Azazel was here, they were all in danger.

I took in more energy, feeling myself get a caffeinelike jolt. Voices around me were louder, sharper. The air felt cleaner. My lungs pumped more oxygen into my blood. All of my muscles got ready to twitch in a moment's notice.

Azazel pushed the chair out from across from him with a foot, then looked at me with both hands palm-up.

I swallowed the remaining bits of coffee cake still in my mouth. The cake was dry now, and I worked to get it down. I kept my link up with the ghost and walked over, taking the chair across from the demon. I set my plate on the table between us.

Around us conversations continued, customers unaware of what sat in their midst. Of what I sat across from. Most of them talked about the sudden storm. There were clinks of coffee cups hitting saucers, scrapes of forks hitting plates as they cut into pastries, mutterings and murmurs, and over it all was the silence between the demon and me.

"How'd you find me?" I finally asked.

"I've been finding you for years, Grimm." Azazel took a sip from the large latte cup, looking at me over a zigzagged tree pattern in the foam.

"Then why'd you find me?" I asked. I searched for the Key, hoping it was on the demon, but found the pull of it still south of me. Not here. "I would think now that you got what you wanted, you'd be freeing your friends."

"Grimm, you've been the most fun I've had in a thousand years," Az said. "What makes you think I'm going to leave you alone?"

"You can't have it both ways," I said. "You can't chase me because I have the Key, and then chase me because I don't have it."

Azazel snorted. "I'm the reason people say *damned if you do, damned if you don't.*"

I frowned at the demon. Here he was with me, playing word games, when he could be opening the Key. I wasn't sure how he was going to open it, but I was sure that he wanted to, so the fact that he was here meant something.

I had to keep my mind open. I couldn't focus on just the Key. Azazel always played a game within the game. I needed to figure that part out.

"I just missed you, Grimm," he said. "The quality of the people who can appreciate what I do in hell has diminished over the years. There's a lot of murderers, rapists, killers. That stuff is easy to do. It always has a quick payoff. What I do is more layered." The demon leaned forward a little. "For instance, how's Sarah?"

"If you're going to go after my friends," I said, "we might as well have it out here and now."

"Sure, Grimm, sure," Azazel said. "How's having it out with me worked for you, over the years? You got your gun around, the one with the silver bullets?"

I didn't. And without something to banish the demon with, even temporarily, any fight between us would go on for a long time. Until he got tired, or I ran out of ghosts. I focused on what Azazel hadn't answered. What he had tried to steer me away from.

"So, why isn't the Key open?" I asked. "You have what you've wanted for thousands of years. You finally *have it*. Why isn't it open already?"

The demon took a breath and looked up at the ceiling, tilting his head back and forth like he was thinking on how he wanted to answer the question. He did really enjoy playing human.

"Maybe you don't think your brothers would appreciate being locked up for all these years," I said.

Azazel kept staring at the ceiling. "You have no idea what you are talking about."

"Or maybe I'm onto something," I said. "Maybe you're worried you won't be top dog anymore in hell."

"If that was it, Grimm, then I wouldn't have been chasing it for so long." Azazel looked back down. "Maybe this was a mistake. Maybe I remember our chase a little more fondly than I should. Maybe I just haven't properly incentivized you."

"Maybe you should remember what you said, the last time I was in a cell," I said. "About you fearing me."

"Yes." Azazel took a deep breath and let it out, like he was savoring each molecule of oxygen in the air. "Exactly. Now we're to it. A real game has to have real stakes."

Why would the demon fear me? I couldn't kill him. I had tried over the years. Everything I had done, had tried, and he had always been back on my heels a day or two later.

But I remember when he was pretending to be Cole, and watching me in the middle of the fight back at the factory. Remember him having run after the explosion. It was the first time Azazel had ever run from me. I remembered the shimmering black gauntlets that had somehow grown out of my arms back then. I could be something he was afraid of. I had to figure that out somehow.

Azazel twitched his nose.

His ultimate game had to be the Key. I was sure of it. Azazel had taunted me back in Grafton. He had let me know he had it, and that if I chased him to get it back, he would take it out on Jen. On my friends.

But then I had asked him about the Key. He had returned with a question about Sarah. Were those two things connected? How could they be? Was I missing something, or was Azazel just trying to confuse me?

The rabbit hole could run deep, when you were trying to figure the demon out.

"I think you thought that I would just be gone," Azazel said. "I think you thought you could come and get the Key whenever you wanted."

"You don't know if I was ever coming," I said.

The demon rolled his eyes. "I know you, Grimm, better than you know yourself. You're coming. You're struggling right now with helping your friend. And you've promised yourself your friends will come first. But will they?"

"Make no mistake, I'll open the Key. When I want to open it," he continued. "Everything I do has a purpose. Maybe you've forgotten that. Maybe you think you have all the time in the world to come after me and get the Key. Maybe you're okay with me opening it, and unleashing seven different types of hell across the earth."

The demon looked at me, and whereas before he had been relaxed, every fiber of his body was taut with anger now. "Maybe you believe you can protect your friends *and* retrieve the Key." Azazel grinned. "I'm here to tell you, that's not going to happen. It's going to be one or the other. You can bet on that."

A flush heated my face. I had promised my friends that they would come first. That I would protect them. Just yesterday I had told Jen we would do whatever it took to help Sarah, and yet I still tracked where the Key was going. I had promised to protect my friends, and at the same time felt like we couldn't stay in this town long. A town with a military base and a coven of witches, where they might be safest. And where Sarah would get the best help she could, for now.

"You can't force me to chase you," I told Azazel.

"That, Grimm, is where you are wrong." Azazel grinned. "You and your lady have a nice shower last night?"

Energy poured into me. I had pulled from the ghost without realizing it. Quickly I pushed the memory of the spirit aside, the *quick flash of needle pricking the inside of my elbow, then a sharp pain racing to my heart …*

I bent forward, getting closer to the demon. None of the customers paid any attention to us, but still my voice was as low as it could get. "I'm just going to tell you this once, Az. Leave my friends the fuck alone."

His voice was light but carried a thread of iron. "I'm going to tell you this in return. Stay here, chase me, it doesn't matter. *I'm* going to make sure it doesn't matter. Whatever you do, I'm going to make sure you travel the bloodiest road. I am going to make you choose, Grimm. Friends or the Key. I will make you walk a trail of corpses until you make that choice."

"We might as well start now, then," I said.

"Random slaughter is pretty blasé." Azazel shrugged. "But it's never something I'm opposed to."

A fight between us here would kill everyone around me. And it would end up over at the motel. And then Jen would be in the middle of it.

So I shoved the anger down. I was making my choice. I would not drag my friends into this, no matter what Azazel wanted.

"Just so we're clear," I told him "if you make me come find you, Az, I will. And I will tear everything down around you. If anything happens to those I care about, I will make sure you understand the error you made, right before I make sure you can never do it again."

Azazel leaned back of a sudden. Chuckling. All of the intensity before just … gone. The demon pointed at me with his forefinger and thumb and clicked his thumb forward like he was shooting a gun. He smiled. "Now, that, Grimm, is a game worth playing."

The barista called out my name. It didn't break the tension between me and the demon. I got up slowly. Still holding on to the ghost, nearby. "This isn't a game, Az."

He shook his head. "It never was."

The barista called my name again. I waved a hand toward the counter and got up, keeping an eye on Azazel. The demon picked the paper back up and opened it with a snap of his wrists. A large advertisement caught my eye, something about a new international phone company building a large network infrastructure across the world, with a new faster technology. Newer cables, newer towers. Already in some of the bigger cities in Europe, and coming to a metropolis near you.

Right beside the advertisement, though, was a picture of Grafton. It was a black-and-white image of Main Street from years ago, with the water tower hanging over the far end of town. The headline read *Wildfire catches town unprepared*.

I took my coffees and headed outside. Both cups were warm in my hands. The rain had stopped, though it was still overcast and patches of dampness spotted the street. I crossed over to the motel. The air felt wet, like another storm hid inside the sky, one that could happen anytime, anywhere.

Jen had fallen back asleep. The blanket was pulled up over her face, and her hair spread out across the pillow. I placed her coffee on the nightstand and sat myself in the chair next to the window. Like in all motels, the chair reminded me of something I would find in a grandparent's house. The seat was hard and covered with a thin, feltlike cushion.

I left the drapes closed, though the sunlight got past the edges, leaving the room an interesting mix of light and dark. I shifted in the chair to find a comfortable spot; the cushion was hard and the back of the chair was too straight. I took little sips of my coffee. It was creamy with a hint of vanilla and a nice note of roasted caramel coffee beans. Definitely better than what I usually got.

I had felt it in my gut yesterday, talking to Jen about staying on the move, and that premonition had been right. Azazel was going to be a problem. I had hoped he would be content with having the Key and freeing his brethren.

Grafton was just a couple of days ago. I had hoped to have the time to figure out a cure for Sarah. But one thing running had taught me: the running comes first. Time to think about things and make plans, in the little moments where I could take a breath.

I didn't think that moment was now. But we had a coven of witches now willing to help, and able to help, at least some. Those people who could help us didn't just exist anywhere. We had been lucky to find these. So running – *right now* – was out of the question.

I would have to learn how to protect my friends better, then. I watched the blanket rise and fall over Jen's sleeping form and took another sip of my coffee. I didn't know how I would handle it, if any of them were hurt because of me. Danny had helped me to accept his death, back in Grafton. But a tiny piece of me could not forgive myself, would never forgive myself, and that part screamed loudly now that it was time to go. To *run.*

I forced that part down and pinged the ghostly radar that was always in the back of my mind. A number of spirits hung around this town. I would have plenty of power available, although what was happening with the ghosts lately worried me. Fighting me while I tried to tap their energy. The psychotic, hideous memories I had to live while doing so.

I would have to push through that. Azazel seemed intent on breaking me. It was more important to him than opening the Key. Why would he delay that? He had been chasing the Key for thousands of years, me for just the last six. Life was never easy, or fair. I knew that better than most. Azazel just didn't want the Key, he didn't want to free his fellow demons, he wanted to do it in a way that entertained him.

Unfortunately, I had been a great entertainer for the demon for the past few years. My friends were going to be in danger all the time. That was something I had accepted as we left Grafton. With us all together again. But there is a wide gulf between knowing and understanding, and I just now stood at the precipice of that comprehension.

How long could I walk that tightrope, between entertaining Azazel and protecting my friends? That same tightrope had gotten Danny killed, when I was a teenager. When I had been trying to protect my friends from Raphael.

I slowly became aware of Jen watching me from the bed.

"Want to tell me about it?" she asked, quietly, as our eyes met.

I did. I started with Azazel in the coffee shop, but I drifted far into the past from there. I talked a little bit about my time in the army, and finding the Key overseas. How I had first met Azazel; after that, the running, and the chase.

Her face softened during some of the tale, like when I had told her about finding the Key. The end of that battle, after thinking we had lived, after talking to them, buried in the rubble. After joking with Lilly about movies. And then finding them all dead. Some of their bodies unrecognizable.

I hadn't realized they were dead until I had dug out from where I was buried. Until I had seen them. What was worse, they hadn't known they were dead either. We all had felt the exhilaration of surviving something incredible, and happy to live another way.

Each of their ghosts, of my friends, after that moment of realization, they had looked at me, confused. Some had cursed. Some had just gone silent. My team leader, he had asked me for understanding.

Which I couldn't give him. I couldn't give any of the understanding. I could not give them any peace. I couldn't tell their loved ones why they had died, or how. I couldn't explain any of it. Maybe, most of all, I hadn't understood myself why I had been the only one to survive.

The Key had been there, among the dead and the fallen. I had staggered down the rubble that had been the monastery, and I had found one of the men who had stood with us, a guy in a Pakol cap named Azir, his legs crushed. About to be murdered, by another man.

I had shot that man. He had also been responsible for the death of my team. After that, Azir had given me the Key, and had tried to make me understand what it was. He had told me it was a prison for demons, and had me promise to keep it safe.

I had humored Azir, a dying man. At the time I was still in shock, or I might have walked away. But he had told me to give the death of my friends some meaning, and that had agreed with something inside me.

I remembered how heavy the Key had felt when Azir had pushed it into my hands. I remembered the panic in his eyes, all the way until they emptied of everything. He had held on, until I had accepted, and then he had let it all go.

Then Azazel had shown up.

I only knew a little about the Key, but I shared that too. I had gotten some of it in Azir's memories. Solomon had created it a long time ago, imprisoning some of the worst demons of hell. Part of the ongoing fight between good and evil, during his time. He had made it in response to a many-years battle, one the good side had lost, and took heavy losses.

I kept talking. I told Jen about running, after that. Fleeing, day after day. About all the times I had stopped somewhere, for a day or an hour too long. About the times, the very seldom times I had tried to help someone. How Azazel would always show, how the demon would ruin any kind of help I gave, or just kill those around me.

I remembered trying to help someone in Vegas. There was an advertisement for a concert there, one I wanted to see. I had mentioned it a few times. Part of me had thought I was crazy, being around that many people.

So I listened to it from the parking lot. In a car by myself. So when the shooting started, I heard it clear, over the crowd screaming. And when the papers talked about it the next day, they talked about the guy who just wanted his girlfriend back.

But I knew who really had been behind the massacre.

I told Jen about everything, from when I had left Grafton ten years ago, until a couple of days ago. All the way up to that motel the night she called me, where Azazel and I had fought it out. Even about Azazel's speech to me there, before the fight.

As I talked, I felt that there had been a long period in my life of doing the same thing, over and over and over. There had been a rhythm to it. It had been consistent, even if it had been horrifying. And it had begun to feel safe, in the way that a person can get used to anything, even failure, if he encounters it over and over and over.

Until it was beat into them. Lately, though, things were accelerating. It felt like I was in the front seat of an out-of-control roller coaster. The wheels *clack-clack-clacked* faster and faster, the carts tilted up off the rails, and images kept flashing by, in my mind, of Sarah, Nick, Johnny. Jen. People I cared for.

People I was afraid to care for. Afraid I would hurt them, just by being around them. A part of me would always feel powerless, against Azazel. I had helped fewer people than had died on my watch.

Danny, Miss Tammie, Parker all rocketed past me. Greg and Father Benjamin. My Ranger team. People I had failed. People who never had a chance in life, because they had met me.

Then there was Jacob, Rand, Marks. My mother, Dominic, Dr. Browner, even Raphael. All of those faces flashed by again and again as the cart raced along, some dark fate waiting for me at the end of the tracks. People who had killed me. People I had killed. Others, fates still unknown.

In the quiet of the moment, when I had finished speaking, I could still hear the screams behind me. Reaching out, drawing me back into my past.

Jen had grabbed her coffee sometime in the middle of me talking, and sipped it slowly, watching me, both hands curled around the cup. Her legs were crossed Indian-style and the blanket was pulled up over them. She wore just a T-shirt, but it was one she had bought for me at the thrift store, another dark shirt with a bunch of people playing guitar on the stage, all wearing painted white masks.

I had stopped talking. Everything from that point forward led to now. What was left of my coffee was cold, and the cup shook slightly in my hands.

"Gus," Jen said, her voice soft and warm. She spoke as if talking to a frightened animal, cornered. "It's okay."

I swallowed, and tried to put myself together again. It took a few more breaths. A few more sips of cold coffee. A few more glances at Jen, who waited patiently for me to speak. "I figured it was something I was owed," I finally told her.

"No." She set her coffee aside, got up, and came and hugged me. I was still sitting, so she gathered my head in her arms and pulled it into her chest. I took a deep breath and let it all out.

"I don't know what to do," I said into her stomach. "I don't know what Azazel is going to come up with. He wants to do this. I don't want to be the guy that let that Key get opened. But even more, I don't want to be the guy that gets his friends killed."

She held me against her, placing the flat of her hand against the back of my head and running it slowly down to my neck, over and over. "Have you ever thought this demon may have been playing you since the very beginning?"

"No," I murmured. "It would fit his style."

"You've told me how much this guy likes to scheme," Jen said. "Everything he does is with a purpose. It strikes me that he could have set this up from the start. Made you the Key Bearer."

"I had never thought that," I said. "But why me? That part doesn't make sense."

"So we figure out what makes you special," Jen said. She winked down at me. "Other than being with me."

I smiled then, a real smile. "I wish I knew."

"Something about your ghosts," Jen said. "Why you can do what you can do."

"Yeah," I said. My mom had given me as much as she could about this. That there had been seven of us, in the beginning. We had been under the geas for thousands of years. She had left me sketches on the concrete floor of a jail cell of a feather, a staff, and a shield.

Solomon had created the Key in response to something the demons had done. He had imprisoned seven of the worst of them, to bring balance back to the world. Seven.

I snorted. "Ridiculous."

"What?" Jen tilted her head at me.

"Nothing," I said. I stopped thinking of what my mother had hinted at. I could see ghosts and use the power they were bound to. Maybe the doctor had been right back in the factory, and it was all some twist in the chain of my DNA. That was easier to believe. "It's absurd."

"Share it with me, then, Gus."

I laughed and stood up. The two of us hugged for a moment, and I loved the way her body relaxed into mine. "Jen, if I did, you'd think it was crazy."

There was a long pause. She would keep asking me. But she would do it later, and not press it right now. "Okay."

I kissed her, and she kissed me back. The kiss deepened. Sometime later we were on the bed, under the blanket, learning more about each other with long, careful touches, light whispers, and sudden gasps. A little less of the mad urgency of the night before, a little more celebration of being together. When we finished, I lay there and promised myself if I did anything else in this life, I would keep Jen safe.

No matter what Azazel thought he could make me do.

CHAPTER EIGHT

Sometime later we both got ready to head back over to the coven's house. I broke out the rest of the money and separated all the cash rolls, putting one in my pocket. I liked having them in rolls of a thousand. A nice round number. The rest of the money I stuck into the duffel bag of clothes we had brought back from the thrift store and carried it with me.

We got in the sedan. Jen's face whitened when she saw all the dried blood in the car. Her hand grabbed mine.

The horrific memories of the past night had receded some for me. But seeing it in the car brought it all back. It was a lot of blood. I had lived through worse, but barely.

We stopped by a car wash and cleaned as much of it as we could. We went through a number of the cleaning wipes. After we finished, we picked more food at the same place I had picked up the breakfast sandwiches the day before.

Nick was detailing the Camaro as we drove up. It looked almost brand-new. No bullet holes. Windows replaced. Grimm-sized dent in the roof gone. I whistled as I got out, and felt a little better about the day.

Nick grabbed a bag of the breakfast burritos and dug into them.

"How'd you do all that?" I asked.

"I didn't do it all." He munched around a big bite of food. "Tabitha did a lot of the bodywork."

I ran a hand over a side panel, feeling the clean line of the car. The metal felt brand-new, polished. Smooth and cool to the touch. I wondered what her father's Thunderbird car looked like.

"If I had a few earth witches and a body shop I could make a lot of money," Nick said.

Did witches have regular jobs? I had, for whatever reason, always imagined them as librarians, Gypsies, or running a shop selling knick-knacks and charms and New Age books. I grinned a little on the inside. Jen would make a hell of a weather reporter.

"How's Sarah?" she asked Nick.

"Better." He frowned a little. Whether she was better or not, angry or not, Nick had probably been on the receiving end of all of it. He had always been her relief valve. "She's slept a lot."

"I'm going to see if she wants breakfast," Jen said.

"You guys go ahead," Nick said, grabbing another sandwich. "I've got a few more things to do."

"Thanks, man," I said, clapping him on the shoulder. "I like this car."

The Camaro had saved my life, more than once. Nick's lips twisted in a half smile. His eyes moistened over, just a little. He took a deep breath and looked back at the house, then turned back to me and bobbed his head, maybe in thanks.

I clapped his shoulder again. I understood. Then I followed Jen to the house.

Inside had calmed down from yesterday. A few witches sat at a long oblong wooden table in the dining room, talking to each other and writing in their books. Jen dropped the bags of food on the table, and all of them dug in.

Johnny was on a couch in the family room, side by side with Tabitha and the tall witch that reminded me of a Valkyrie. Each of them held large square pieces of paper, and each of the papers were covered in sigils and words. I recognized some of it from Sarah's tattoos.

Tabitha looked up.

"Thanks for the car," I said.

She smiled. Her gray hair was still tied back in a bun, and her face was too thin to be called beautiful, but the smile lit up her face. An image popped up of her with her father, riding in his car. Just a girl and her dad and the open road.

"We're trying to identify some of the tattoos," Johnny said. "I got most of the Vampiric, but these symbols are demonic. It's a weird mix."

"Have you figured out what it does?"

"A little," Johnny said. He looked at the witches.

"This is something that should not exist," Tabitha said. "Somehow they took dark magic and blended it with demonic curses. We can figure out bits and pieces of it. The Vampiric part is basically a calling. The way it's written, how the spell reads, is much how I imagine a heroin junkie feels about their next fix."

"Which means?"

"Sarah is the drug. The spell puts out a calling to come get the drug," Tabitha said. "She'll manufacture it in her body, and as she does the calling will get stronger. Reach further. Vampires that encounter her will want to drink from her to get the drug."

The big Valkyrie nodded. Close up, the tall witch was thinner than I had guessed, like her body had undergone significant weight loss. Paler. It had only been a couple of days since Grafton. She spoke, her voice deep and methodical. "And what's worse, getting bitten actually releases some of the energy of the spell."

That must have been how she survived in Grafton. With Raphael milking her, when he needed the cursed blood to control other vampires. Images flashed in my mind. Sarah standing up behind Raphael, holding her neck. Tiny wells of blood underneath her fingertips. Raphael holding a glass of crimson liquid and smiling at me. Right before we went to meet his father, and Raphael called an army of vampires to help him.

"So there are a couple of options," Tabitha said. "She'll have to be bitten regularly, or the spell will get more powerful. Call louder. Bring more vampires to her. The spell can be mitigated in that way, for a little while."

I frowned. "What's door number two?"

"We're trying to slow the buildup down. Bring the calling down to a lower level," the Valkyrie said. "But all we're doing is getting you time. It's still going to build. It's a siren song for vampires. It's calling them even now, at a low, low level. No matter how much we slow it now, the curse is going to ratchet higher and higher, until every vampire around hears it, or until the spell gets toxic and kills her."

"We've almost stopped it for now," Tabitha said. "And we can maybe put some things in place to hold it for a bit. But it's storing that pent-up energy, and at some point what we've done will break. When that day happens, Sarah will die."

Jen heard that and went rock-still. I rubbed her back lightly. Her neck muscles were tight under my fingers.

"The exorcism is the key," the Valkyrie added. "You have to get one done in the time we are able to give you. The best we can understand, the spell is powered by the demonic sigil. An exorcism should remove the energy source and drive the Vampiric part of this to go dormant."

"We found out something at the church," I said. "The priest there said only the archdiocese of New Orleans would be able to help us. Bishop Jean-Louis."

Johnny whistled. "That's a long way from here."

It'd be a few days of a drive, even if we drove it straight. A couple of states over and down. If we could take the interstates, it could be done. And hopefully with plenty of time for Sarah.

I flipped through the sketches of the spell. Lots of curvy scripts in a language I didn't recognize, with written explanations underneath. An older symbol by itself on one page. It looked familiar, and I realized where I had seen it before. The Key.

My expression must have changed. "You recognize it?" Johnny asked.

"I've seen this one." I pointed to the symbol I recognized. Something that looked like an child's sketch of a truck, with a small front hood and three U-shaped wheels underneath The fourth wheel was an upside-down cross. "It's one of the symbols on the Key," I said.

Tabitha looked at me curiously. The witches didn't know about the Key. I explained. "It's the name of one of the demons imprisoned in a stone."

"So your buddy's involved," Johnny said. "The demon."

"I'm beginning to think he's always a part of something," I said. The Key still pulled from the southwest, not feeling any farther, but not feeling any closer. And I'd found out, the location of the Key didn't necessarily tell me where Azazel was.

"That sigil seems to hold something," Tabitha said. "Or maybe it was built to hold something."

It was the symbol on her back, the one underneath which I had seen the wriggling. "I thought maybe it was what her curse was powered from," I said. It seemed, at least to me, that the energy was most concentrated there.

"Do we know which demon the sigil is for?" Tabitha asked.

I glanced at the sigil again. The symbol looked very much like it had been drawn by a child. If I blurred my vision it looked like a three-eyed winged scorpion, with the segments of the body and a small curve of the tail. Upside-down crosses blackened its wing. That was just a best guess.

Who knew what the symbols meant? I had carried the Key for years, and had been on the run the entire time. I rarely had the chance to research symbols in a library.

I shook my head. "I couldn't tell you."

Jen spoke up suddenly. "How much time do we have?"

Tabitha and the Valkyrie looked at each other. The older witch responded, "A day or two at most, right now. But tonight we hope to give you a week."

"What's tonight?" I asked.

"It's a full moon," Tabitha explained. "We'll be able to use the full power of the coven then. What we cast will be stronger. We can bind the curse then. Slow it down more."

"We think," the Valkyrie added.

Jen's face had paled a little. Our hands met and I squeezed hers lightly. "Go spend some time with her," I told her. "I'll take the car and get a few things for the trip."

She squeezed my hand back.

I ducked my head a bit to the witches. "We'll leave right after the casting, then. We appreciate everything."

The Valkyrie's face remained pinched with worry. Her words were still paced, spoken in a slow measure. "We wish we could do more."

CHAPTER NINE

J en went up to visit with her sister. I spent a little time with them. Sarah was quiet, though, lying in bed, her face withdrawn. She looked out the window the entire time I was there, occasionally closing her eyes for long minutes at a time.

I stood in the corner of the room, afraid somehow of intruding on the silence between the sisters. Jen sat in a chair next to Sarah's bed. At times her hand would reach out for her sister's, and then she would pull it back. Once Jen glanced up at me, her blue eyes sad, lost in thoughts or memories.

There was a lot of tension hidden in the room. We all knew we had to do something. That Sarah's life was on the line. And we all knew we had no real understanding of how to save her. Just guesses, and maybe a few days to figure it out.

After a bit I ended up leaving to get supplies for the trip. Johnny and Nick went with me when I left. We had given them some of the thrift shop clothes, and both of them took quick showers and changed. The three of us looked like a walking poster of metal band fans from the eighties.

The Camaro fired up with a roar outside and shook gently with the cycling of the engine. I took a deep breath of new car smell. The carpet was vacuumed, the dashboard wiped down, even the seat belts looked new. That Thunderbird must have been incredible.

I spun off down the road. We saw a buffet place, one of those restaurants with endless plates stacked up at the end of the salad bar, and the three of us stopped by to wolf down some food. We all needed the calories.

Nick and Johnny got into an ice-cream-eating contest. Both were on bowl number five, but Johnny argued that he had eaten more because he topped his bowls with fudge, caramel, and sprinkles. Nick was an ice-cream-only guy but had maybe piled his bowl higher with the soft-serve.

The contest took our minds off what waited back at the farmhouse, just for a bit. It was something Johnny was good at. He would joke and wheedle and poke fun until all of us had our minds off whatever was bothering us. I had missed him.

"I'm right, aren't I?" Johnny said. Fudge smeared a little of his cheek, and a pink sprinkle had stuck to one of his teeth.

I raised my eyebrows at Nick. "It's rare, but I agree with Sprinkle King."

Nick rolled his eyes, but he still grinned and got another bowl.

I went for another plate of lasagna. I loved stretchy cheese and ground beef and rich tomato sauce by the plateful. Pasta seemed to hold back the hunger, especially if it was the last meal I ate for a while. Johnny and Nick came back with more ice cream, and the waitress refilled our sodas.

"I'm taking it we have some money now," Johnny said.

"We do." I tugged a few rolls out from my front pocket, sliding one each to Nick and Johnny.

Nick's eyebrows rose when he picked it up. "Where'd you get it?"

"From people who no longer need it," I said.

They both gazed at me with the obvious question.

"It's not stolen," I added. And then, after a moment, "At least, it's not money I stole."

I think they both sensed I didn't want to talk about last night. Experiencing the memories of Jo's ghost wasn't something I wanted to do again. Not even in the telling of it. But I did want to talk about what had happened this morning. So I went over getting some coffee and what had happened with Azazel in the coffee shop.

"So he's coming after us," Nick said.

"And he's probably going to hound us the whole trip to New Orleans," Johnny added.

I nodded. "It's going to get rough. I just wanted you all to know. Just in case you wanted to take off."

"Us?" Nick frowned.

"Spit it out, man." Johnny grinned. "Just say it."

It was tough. I had promised I wouldn't leave my friends again. That I would find a way to protect them. But they could always choose to leave of their own free will. I rushed through what I wanted to say. "Being around me gets people killed. And Azazel is going to force that issue. It might be best for Sarah, for all of you, if you all headed to New Orleans without me. I can keep Azazel busy for a day or two, I think. Maybe so busy you all could get there and get her help."

They both stayed quiet for a moment. "I don't think so," Nick said. "I think we should be in this together."

Johnny grinned at me, like I had said something ridiculous and ulti-mately unbelievable. "Man, we're a family."

"So, what can we do?" Nick asked.

"I don't know," I said. I was relieved they wanted to stay. "I felt like it was something you should know. I wanted you guys to be aware. Stay on your toes. Azazel is going to try something. I just don't know what it'll be."

"I'm sure Azazel coming after us is going to be bad," Nick said slowly. "But tonight we start running to New Orleans. We get Sarah help there. And then we'll show that demon what it's like to mess with us."

That might have been the most I'd heard out of Nick at one time, except for maybe back in Grafton, when he had stood outside my Camaro and thanked me for hanging around, for trying to help rescue Sarah. Johnny switched his stare to Nick, as if he was just as surprised.

Nick winked at Johnny and kept eating his ice cream.

"You win," Johnny said, rubbing his stomach. A little round mound pushed out from underneath his shirt. "My tummy is starting to hurt."

"I hear sprinkles will do that." Nick smiled, and dropped his spoon into an empty bowl.

We left the restaurant a lot fuller, and somewhat sluggish. I drove through a coffee place and got us a few coffees. Nick still fell asleep in the backseat.

We stopped by one of the big retail stores after that. One of those places with clothes and electronics packed into a supermarket. I yanked a cart out from the long line at the front of the store and the three of us walked through the aisles, getting what I called necessities. Things we might need on the road.

Johnny looked at the cart after a few aisles. "Energy drinks and protein bars?"

"It's gotten me by so far."

"What gets you by and what gets me by are very different things." He left and came back with a few boxes of toaster pastries, s'mores flavored.

"Go back and get some frosted blueberry," I told Johnny. I had my favorite, just like everyone else.

Nick just added water. He didn't seem to be picky about what he ate, as long as he did eat. He could pack food away, for being skinny.

We wheeled around the store. I picked up a new jacket, something with pockets that could hold a gun. I added a few rolls of paper towels, trash bags, and a box of wipes. Flashlights, batteries, and a battery-powered lamp. There was a ninety-nine-cent travel aisle, and there I found a bunch of things like toothpaste, toothbrushes, and mouthwash. At electronics I picked out a few of the cheap monthly plan phones, and Johnny had me put them back.

"We need the smart phones," he said, and grabbed a few of the more expensive large, square, flat phones. He grabbed cases and Bluetooth headphones, gift cards for digital stores and monthly plans, chargers, everything we could possibly need for them.

I let him pick everything out. I had never needed a phone before, and I tended to buy the cheap stuff because things just didn't last long around me. For this, I'd defer to his experience. "You set them all up, then."

"Deal."

We went to automotive and sporting goods next. Nick perked up there, selecting a toolbox and a set of tools: ratchets, wrenches, screwdrivers. We got a couple of tents, things that would fold up well, and a few sleeping bags. I tossed in a couple of small red plastic gas cans. Tonight we were going to start a long drive, and I was prepping for anything and everything. The life I had lived until now had prepared me quite well for this type of thing.

Johnny came back with a few baseballs, a bat, and a little baseball that was meant to hang from the rearview mirror. He tucked them all into the cart, which was full. The three of us, Nick, Johnny and I, had played all of the sports back in Grafton. Football and basketball and baseball. But the one sport all of us had played, the girls, us, and Danny, had been baseball.

"I saw the bat," Johnny said. "And thought we could maybe bring Danny with us."

It was an odd moment there. Johnny had always been the jokester. Danny had meant a lot to us. And his ghost would be a mystery to me. It had been so pure, so happy. There was a peaceful contentedness I had never felt from another ghost, but it had seemed so *Danny* at the time.

"I think you're right," I said. Both of us kind of looked away from each other. I blinked a few times at the sudden wetness in the corner of my eyes. "We could always use him around."

I also stocked up on ammo, buying the limit of what we could buy, grabbing some buckshot and shells for the shotgun, and nine-millimeter, .38, and .357 rounds for the pistols. The guy selling me the ammo looked at me and my cart curiously but made the sale. I figured this close to the army base, a lot of ammunition getting sold wasn't a big thing. And it just looked like we were going on a hunting trip.

I had Nick and Johnny go back and buy what ammo they could as well. Nick came back with a few hunting knives, silver ones with bone handles, and a bunch of smaller blades.

I looked a question his way.

"When you work out of the shadows," he explained, "you like the quiet things."

My eyes opened a bit. My old friends had some new faces. I was impressed and maybe a little scared of this one from Nick.

We spent some time packing all of the items into the trunk of the Camaro correctly. Finding the right space for everything, and giving us the access to the items we might need in a hurry. Nick hung the baseball from the rearview, and the ball spun there for a moment.

Somehow the toaster pastries kept showing up in front of the bag of ammo. I discreetly tucked the shotgun between the driver's seat and the door. Put the .357 in the glove box. And a few of the nine-millimeters in the backseat.

"You know," Johnny said, "if you had asked me a few days ago, I wouldn't have said I'd be stashing guns and ammo around a car in broad daylight in the middle of a hypermarket, getting ready to outrun a demon to New Orleans."

"Hell of a life, right?" I reorganized the trunk a little, moving the pastries to the back again.

"It's not what school prepares you for, that's for certain," Johnny said.

I was worried about the next part, but it had to be done. I drove the Camaro back over to the old church. It was just as quiet today as it was outside. I popped the trunk, got the gas cans out, and went inside.

To me it appeared as if the same few people sat inside the church today as the day before. An old woman with a black veil in front of her face. A younger man up toward the front, on his knees. But no Marcus hiding by the confessional. The stained-glass window still remained, still looking down on me. The one of Saint Michael that brought about thoughts of Father Benjamin.

The priest was there, up around the front altar, instructing a couple of young altar boys in white. He saw me come in and rushed up to me, his chest stuck out in his robe. His voice was high-pitched and rushed. "I helped you yesterday. And I asked you never to come back."

I held up the gas cans. "I was hoping I could get some holy water from you."

"This is how you repay me for helping you," he said.

I shook my head. "I wish I didn't have to come back, but I promise it's the last time."

"This is what happens in your world." He shook his head. "You all take a little, and a little more, and a little more. You always take more, and I don't want any part of it."

"I know you don't, Father." I said. "But what's happening, it's here anyway. Your brother was killed. I understand, I've had friends die too. I didn't ask for the life I'm living. I'm just trying to do my best."

"What you all don't see"—the priest's voice cracked—"is that your best isn't good enough."

"I don't believe that," I told him. "And you don't really believe it either. I'm going to keep swinging, or go down trying. And you believe that too. It's why you're trying so hard to keep Marcus safe."

He deflated a little in front of me. A chink of metal on metal came from up front. One of the altar boys carefully caught a goblet he had been setting on a plate.

"I promise you, Father, we are leaving town tonight," I said. "But we could really use your help."

The priest had noticed the altar boys as well. He turned back to me. "What do you need?"

"Just holy water," I said. "If you could bless some water for us, that's all."

He took a deep breath, then grabbed the cans from me. "I'll be back."

I stayed there. The priest walked up to a door on the left of the church, taking a moment to admonish one of the altar boys.

It was quiet in the church. I walked up to the last pew and sat in it. The wooden surface was hard and unforgiving. I picked one of the Bibles from where it rested, in a slot on the back of the pew in front of me, and thumbed through it.

Seven demons. Seven of us, my mother had said. I went through the Old Testament, flipping through pages. The paper was really thin under my fingers, and the words were jumbled together in tiny rows, tiny and black on the page. I didn't know what I was looking for, so I wasn't surprised when I didn't find it.

The front doors of the church opened and closed. The priest hurried toward me, a plastic can hanging from each arm. The old lady with the black veil and the young man both watched him walk down the aisle. The priest handed the cans to me when I got up.

"Thank you, Father," I said. "Trust me when I say I hope never to come back."

He paused. "It's tough for me. It goes against what I believe, not helping those in need. But I was the first person to find my brother, and I …" The priest swallowed. "I will not have that happen to Marcus."

I had recently encountered something I never wanted to experience again, with the memories of the spirits I was encountering. But I wasn't going to be lucky enough to avoid having to live ghosts, in my future. I held up the Bible. "May I keep this?"

The priest nodded. He went to say something, then stopped. "Certainly."

I put the Bible under the crook of an arm and grabbed the gas cans from him. The priest was excited to see me go. I didn't blame him. It's not like vampires and demons were everything on this earth. There were other evils, other things to take care of. He had a kid, parishioners, to consider.

Maybe when he had found his brother, this other supernatural world, with monsters and wights, had become all too real for him. He stood there, watching me.

"It's not a bad thing to want to hide sometimes, Father," I told him. I had spent a long time doing just that. "But you're going to have to make a decision. You can either run and hide or stand and fight. And people who run from things, well, it's my experience those things never stop chasing you."

The priest didn't answer, he just stood there. Waiting for me to leave.

"Thanks again," I said. And then left.

Nick was sleeping in the back of the Camaro when I came out. Johnny was cutting through packages and putting the phones together. Getting them working.

I opened the trunk and tucked the cans in the back. Then I got in the car and fired it up, feeling the pedals rumble a little against the bottom of my feet.

"Why gas cans?" Johnny asked.

"I used to get just gallons of water," I said. "But it was easy to mix those up. Remind me to tell you about the time I drank the holy water and used the regular water to bless my bullets."

Johnny laughed. "It must have been a hell of a night."

"It's something you only do once," I told him seriously.

I drove onto the street and headed back to the motel. Johnny looked tired, and Nick was still sleeping. It wouldn't be a bad idea for the three of us to get some real sleep, in preparation for tonight.

"What if you needed gas?"

"If my car ran out of gas, and I needed to get some quickly?" I shrugged. It was why I usually topped the car off, whenever I had a chance. I didn't like a low tank. "I probably wouldn't be here now."

"Good point," he said.

We pulled into the motel parking lot. I went to the front and made sure we were good for another night. I wasn't surprised to see our rooms still vacant. Or that the maid service hadn't made it there.

Johnny and Nick went to their rooms. I poured a little of the holy water into one of the bathroom clear plastic cups so Nick could work on his knives. Then I let them both get a good nap in. They had probably not been able to sleep well at the coven's house.

I packed up the car again, making sure I hadn't left out anything from the hotel. My old clothes were there, covered in crusted blood, and I cleaned all of that up. It felt weird, being in the same place for a consecutive day. For years I had moved on each day, from one place to the next, never cleaning up after myself. In the past I would have left this room alone.

I hit redial on the room phone. One of the witches picked up. I asked for Jen and got her a minute or two later.

"Hey," she said.

I shivered a bit when she said hello over the phone. Like her voice had resonated up my spine. "Hey."

I told her everything we had done. What we had tried to prepare for. And then I told her we were going to get an afternoon nap in. We'd be ready to go tonight. And then I asked her about Sarah and the preparations for the ritual.

"Sarah is … Sarah," Jen said. She sighed. "She's pushing through the pain, but she's not telling me anything."

I waited.

"Sometimes she just closes up," Jen said. "It got worse when she started seeing Raphael. She just shuts up and won't say anything."

"I've got some experience with that," I said. "Being closed up."

"But she's not alone," Jen said. "I keep telling her that. And I keep telling her we're not going to let her die."

I agreed with Jen, but I maybe understood something more about her sister. "She's not worried about herself. I mean, there's the pain, and I'm sure she's afraid. But it's more likely she's thinking about all the decisions she's made to get to this point, and what she could have done differently. I'm sure the choices Sarah's made haunt her. She probably feels they are the reason her friends, and her sister, are in danger."

There was a long pause from the other end. "You're a smart man, Gus."

"Like I said," I said, "I have some experience there."

"I miss you," Jen said.

"Me too," I answered. "When's the ritual start?"

"Don't laugh," she said. "Midnight."

"The famous Witching Hour," I joked. "Need me to bring a big black cauldron by?"

Jen laughed. "No, you goofball. They have one here, full of frog toes, bat wool, and eyes of newt."

I laughed back. We talked about little things for a bit, and it felt to me like we were back in Grafton, with me in the kitchen at Parker's house, talking to Jen at her mother's. Two teenagers tied together by a phone line. At some point it had to end, though, with Jen needing to get back to her sister.

"I'll plan on getting us there around eleven," I said.

"It's a date," Jen answered. Both of us held the phones to our ears for a bit, waiting for the phone to hang up. Then we both laughed some more, and hung up together.

I got up and pulled the drapes tighter around the window. I was still a bit wired from the night before and thought I'd have trouble sleeping. I lay on the bed and set the cheap motel alarm. The square digital numbers of the clock stared at me, glowing red bars morphing from one minute to the next. The mattress was too soft. There was still an indentation from where Jen had been that morning, and I missed the person who filled it.

I had been trained to get sleep where I could. It was tough, but sleep finally came.

CHAPTER TEN

I woke to the blaring beeping coming from the alarm. Amazing how much sound could come out of a tiny plastic box. I turned it off and stretched in the bed. I took a quick shower and got dressed in the same clothes I had worn this morning. They had a thrift store smell to them, a little like dust, and a little like mothballs.

The yellow sunlight behind the drapes had been replaced by the bright white outline of streetlights. It was closing in on eleven o'clock, but it would only take twenty minutes to get to the coven. I was sure they didn't want us hanging around while they got prepared. My experience with rituals told me they were a serious thing and any deviation could mean a backfire for the casting, the spell not working, or even death.

I went to the Camaro and got some of the pastries from the trunk. The air was cold tonight, but muggy. It was a weird feeling. It was like I stood in a numbing fog of dry ice, spreading over the lip of a boiling pot where something cold and malignant bubbled.

Nick opened the door to their room. It looked like he had gotten up a while ago. He had put a couple of sheaths horizontal on his belt, at his back, and a knife handle stuck out from each one. Another sheath hung from his right hip, and he wore a jean jacket that hid who knows how many more.

"I went over at dark," he said, meaning he had shadow-walked there and back. "So far, so good."

He was back to short sentences. I prodded Johnny. "Come on, slowpoke."

Johnny got up reluctantly, but moved faster after that. I tossed them both a foil package of pastries. We all ate in silence. Nick never talked much, and Johnny was too sleepy to crack a joke.

Some coffee would be good. While they were finishing up getting ready, I stepped outside to see if the coffee place was still open.

Blue and red lights flashed over me from two police cars, lighting the walls behind me. Both cars were in the middle of the parking lot, one slightly in front of the other. The initials LPD on the side of the cars, Lewiston Police Department. A *blooping* sound came from the first car, and quickly cut off.

A policeman got out of the car, one hand on the top of the door, one hand on his holster. He was young, black hair cropped tight, but his eyes were focused. He had a partner on the passenger seat holding a shotgun. Both of them were dressed in dark black body armor, and had their badges hanging from the armor.

"Fergus Grimm?" the cop asked, although it sounded more like a statement than a question.

"Officers," I said. I held my hands up and open. There were some small noises behind me, and the motel door quietly closed to almost shut. *At least Johnny and Nick would be safe.*

"We'd like to ask you to come with us," the cop said. There was latching and unlatching of doors, and the pair of cops in the second car got out. Both stayed behind their doors, bracing semiautomatic pistols on the window frame. "And any of your associates."

"May I ask what this is about?" I said. "I was just about to get some coffee."

"You know what this is about," the cop said. He looked at his partner holding the shotgun. "Someone set fire to a town up north of here."

The second cop swung out of his side of the car then. He was grizzled, with a gray flattop, and a scar along one cheek. He looked enough like the younger cop that they might have been family.

The older cop ratcheted the shotgun slide and pointed it at me.

"Wholesale murder, son," the older cop said. "An Officer Cole put out an APB this morning."

Azazel. I stopped myself from clenching my fists.

"We've got your description and everything," the young man said, flicking his eyes to the older cop and back.

"You can get in the car now," the older cop said. "Or you can wait and get loaded up in a body bag."

The younger cop rose his eyebrow. His hand was still on his holster. "Let's make this peaceful, okay? Come on in, get yourself a lawyer, and figure it out."

The old lady's ghost still stood in the parking lot, one hand still gripping a ghostly grocery cart. The cart was covered in a blanket, with little melonlike bumps here and there.

I swallowed and pulled from her. A hint of ginger cookies drifted over my tongue, from her memories. And the ghostly humming of a song. "I'm not going to do that, Officer," I said.

The young man placed a hand on his gun. "No?"

"No, sir," I said. "We can sit here and talk for a bit, though. Maybe figure out something."

"Grimm, I'm going to tell you that you're in no position to bargain," the young officer said. "That bulletin read like a gang war."

"I'm not armed," I said. "Shooting me standing here and holding my arms up is going to look awfully funny on the news."

"This is a military town," the older cop said. "We're a little more liberal in how we interpret things."

Johnny whispered to me from the side of the door, "Nick says the witches are okay. He wants to know if you want him to take care of the police."

Bright streetlights lit both cars, but there were still shadows there. I had no doubt Nick could kill them, quietly and quickly. But I didn't want innocent blood on anyone's hands, and I had a ghost nearby. I could get us out of this.

I shook my head. "No killing," I said.

"Who are you talking to in there?" the cop asked.

I shook my head and started walking again. The first cop spoke into the two-way radio on his shoulder. At the same time, the shotgun fired.

The slug whistled as it brushed past me. Plaster erupted from the motel wall behind me, and tiny white bits sprayed out across the parking lot.

I stopped, and pulled a little more ghost into me. I didn't want to get shot up two nights in a row. The older cop pumped the shotgun again.

"Harrison, cut that shit out," the first cop ordered. "People could be in there."

"Not innocent people," Harrison said.

"I said cut that shit out."

I had stopped not quite halfway to the police car. Pulled more of the old lady's ghost and got ready for the fight I saw coming. Fucking Azazel and his games.

"You saw that bulletin," Harrison said. "I'm not letting that guy walk away from this."

The younger cop took a breath. "Look, Grimm, let's not get to a point that we all can't walk away from. More cops are on the way. Just come to the station with us. We'll get you some donuts. We'll wait for Lieutenant Cole to drive down and we'll get you a lawyer. You can work it all out from there."

"Do you even know Officer Cole?"

"Why do I need to know him?"

"Just wondering how that all works," I said. "Harrison's about to blow a hole through me on the basis of some bulletin. What if this Cole is lying?"

"It's why I'd like everything to be done peaceably," the young cop said. "If he's lying, we'll figure it out when he comes down. I won't even handcuff you. Just come in and let us sort it all out. Because in a couple of minutes, it's all going to be too late."

The young cop's voice stayed even when he spoke to me. He wasn't scared, just trying to do the right thing. But I couldn't go back to a cell, not if Azazel was still playacting as Cole. He just made getting to New Orleans that much harder. Every cop in the country would be looking for us now.

And they would look for us even harder if I started a gunfight here. I wasn't worried about the ritual; the witches could handle that without us. But they couldn't wait a day or a week while I waited in a cell. Sarah didn't have that kind of time.

In my heightened senses I heard more sirens, farther away. The pitch of the sirens changed as they came closer. And somewhere overhead, the chopping blades of a helicopter. They were coming in force.

I didn't want to kill anyone here. But at some point this pot was going to blow. Harrison was all kinds of ready to shoot me. So I had to move now.

The lead cop saw me make the decision. I gathered up ghost. He shouted and started to pull his weapon. Harrison's shotgun fired. I hardened my skin and felt a stab of pain as the slug bounced off me. I staggered forward and pulled a lot more. A couple of pops as bullets hit my chest. I caught my balance and dove at an angle into the front of the first cop car.

I pulled more ghost and leaped through the air, pushing the power into my jump. I hit the grill of the car with a crunch, and the front end of the police car slid a few feet across the pavement. It hit Harrison and slung the cop out of the way. I rolled to the ground and got to my knee, finding the shotgun in front of me. I appropriated the gun and blew out the front tires of the car.

So far, so good. No cops hurt, or better yet, no one was dead. Now I just had to disable the second car and tie up the cops, and the three of us could get away. Easy as pie.

The feeling of a hard metal finger punched into my back, repeatedly. Three or four times. Gunshots. I had enough ethereal energy burning through me that my skin deflected the shots, but the force threw me on the hood of the car. I turned to see the young cop loading a .357.

I took a deep breath and pulled everything the ghost had. Deep memories flooded through me. *Hot chocolate and gingersnaps. The creak of a rocking chair. I watched my hands knit a pattern into the scarf as I rocked. A pile of scarves next to me in a basket by the chair.*

The cop snapped his revolver shut. I was a blur, running over the ground. Before he got the gun up I had broken his thumb and forefinger and tossed the gun aside. Then I tossed the cop.

He rolled over the ground a few times, holding his hand to his chest. I felt bad about having to break his fingers, but a cop that can't shoot can't shoot me.

I watched him roll to a stop. Then a car hit me.

I shot through the air and smacked into the wall of the motel. I fell to the ground in front of the wall. Somehow I stayed conscious and watched

Harrison back up the car. The hood shook when he shifted it back into drive.

My head felt fuzzy. I tried get up, but one of my legs wasn't working the way I needed it to. The rear wheels of the car screeched and spun against the pavement. In less than a second I was going to be between a vehicle and a brick wall, so I winced and pulled all the ghost I could hold.

Images of another life flew through me.

The rocking chair. The smell of gingersnaps. Two wrinkled, mottled hands kitting a scarf. A hundred scarfs in a basket next to the chair. The sounds of kids playing. The long knitting needles were blackened at their tips, and I was an old woman, or she was me. She laughed and cackled to herself, rocking back and forth faster and faster.

I was an old lady. Living her memories. Knitting and listening to kids play. Baking cookies. What could be bad about that?

A timer dinged. The old lady set aside the needlework. Stopped rocking. Pulled herself out of the chair. She opened the oven and pulled out the tray, and the warm smell of ginger and sugar flooded the house.

"Children?" she called out. "Children, you want your cookies?"

She cackled again. Of course they wanted their cookies. They were probably starving, dear things. The old woman placed each cookie carefully on a tray and carried the tray to a door, opening it and setting her hip against it to keep the door open.

"Children?"

No response. They were always playing. She chuckled to herself. They would need their energy. Slowly she made her way down the stairs, one stair at a time, balancing the tray on a hip while holding the bannister with her hand. Stopping to wave occasionally at a fly. "Did you all leave the window open again?"

The buzzing got worse as she got to the bottom of the stairs. She set the tray on a tiny stand to the left of the stairs, and flipped on a switch. A ceiling fan started up and the flies buzzed to the walls of the room.

"There you are." The old lady stood, hands on her hips. Tiny bodies lay across the floor, some bloated, some decomposing, some fresh. Hand-knitted scarves wrung the necks of all of them. Smiling, the lady grabbed a cookie and bent over a kid lying by her feet. She smoothed his hair back on his rotting scalp and pushed the cookie between swollen lips. When the

kid didn't eat, she clucked her tongue and made a chewing motion with his jaw.

"All my kids have to eat," she said. Bits of the ginger snap had fallen out, and she pushed those back over the kid's swollen lips, rubbing the lip a little, and made the chewing motion again. Unconsciously, she licked her lips.

"Eat some more, children." She moved over to the next kid. "There's cookies enough for everyone."

For the second time in twenty-four hours, I had to fight to keep from throwing up. Old people had the worst ghosts. Pain shot through my leg as a bone knitted itself back together and a kneecap realigned. My vision blurred, then cleared just in time to watch the police car streak toward me.

Back in Grafton, when I was trying to save Jen at the factory, armor had grown out of me. It had been strong enough that it could deflect bullets. I remembered watching the vambraces almost sprout from my arms.

I could certainly use that armor now.

It didn't appear though. And I didn't know how to bring it out. Maybe I just needed more energy than what I could currently pull. I braced myself for the hit and hoped I had enough ghost to keep from becoming a human pancake.

Nick suddenly appeared in the passenger seat. He yanked the wheel hard to the left. Then he disappeared again.

The car swerved drastically to my left and crunched through the motel wall. The air bag deployed with a loud popping sound, and Harrison stayed underneath it. He was out.

Nick appeared next to me, materializing from the shadows. He smiled a little smile. "Did you just get hit by a car?"

"I believe so," I said. Slowly. Trying not to think of the grandma and all the dead kids in her basement. Of the feel of her fingers pushing cookie crumbs past rotting lips. "But just the once. Thanks."

Nick helped me up. Gingerly I probed myself, finding myself to still be in one piece. The two cops in the second cop car now lay on the ground there. A third police car sat unmoving down the street, its lights flashing, but no alarm blaring.

Nick had worked fast.

Johnny poked his head out from the room. "We good out here?"

"Yeah." I was in pain, but everything seemed to be working. I staggered over to the lead cop. He was sitting on the ground, holding his wrist. His face taut with pain.

"I didn't want to do this," I said.

"You should have come in," he said.

"You need to let this go," I said. "It's not what you think."

He spat again. "I tried to do the right thing."

"Yeah," I said. "Me too."

The whirring chopping of a helicopter drew closer. The cop looked up in the air for it. I took the walkie-talkie off his shoulder and yanked the cord out of the handset. Then Nick, Johnny, and I hurried into the Camaro. I fired it up and we spun down the street in the opposite direction of where we needed to go, after which I doubled back through some back streets and directed us toward the coven.

CHAPTER ELEVEN

I t was dark out, so dark the headlights of the Camaro didn't seem to penetrate deep enough into the gloom. I feathered the brakes a couple of different times when a sudden turn surprised me. As fast as I drove, the ritual had still begun by the time we arrived. I slowed a ways from the house and coasted to a stop at the very head of the driveway. The three of us got out and quietly strode toward the house.

The air had been chilly before. It was freezing now. I tugged my jacket around me and felt cold air pockets against my skin where bullets had punched through it and perforated my shirt. I couldn't seem to keep a jacket long these days.

The house itself was dark with no lights on. The entire coven was outside, arranged in overlapping patterns around Sarah. Not a pentagram, and not quite a circle, but a mix of the two. The overall picture reminded me of a starfish, swollen and floating across the deep ocean bottom, its arms curled upon itself here and there.

In the center of the pattern the witches had laid a folding cot on the ground. Sarah lay on it, a few feet above the grass. Each witch held something, a candle, a lighter, glasses of different liquids, a hand fan. Tabitha held a large rock. Others held symbols of the moon on a chain, tiny slivered metal half arcs. Jen held a long, thin rod.

We all stopped and watched. Sarah's eyes were shut tight. The tattoos covered her skin spreading out from under her clothes and sprawling across her cheeks, running under her hair.

A soft chanting carried through the air. There was a breeze that rustled some of the leaves of the big oaks in the front yard. The three of us stood well outside the circle and remained quiet. I put a hand on Nick's shoulder, though he didn't acknowledge it.

As the chanting continued, a tiny wisp of white light streamed off Sarah, disappearing into the night. The stream grew thicker, reached higher into the sky. A white glow surfaced over Sarah's skin, muting the tattoos, just a little.

The moon, high above, carried the same soft glow. Then it grew so bright the lunar surface began to blur. A second stream, larger, thicker, drifted down from the moon and descended through the heavens toward Sarah.

The chanting grew stronger. It carried a basslike undertone that resonated in my bones. The words were not something I understood, but images and impressions of things flashed through my mind, of fire and lightning, of mountains and oceans, of snow and rain. Even the feel of a corpselike grave. All hints of the real world mixed with a magical one.

The opalescent glow above Sarah spiraled around itself and stretched higher and higher, thinning into the distance. The thick column from the moon pushed downward, punching through the atmosphere like a million-watt spotlight. Somewhere high above Lewiston, the two met.

A thunderclap cracked across the sky and echoed along the hills. The soft white glow tugged the lunar beam back, quickly, and wrapped itself around Sarah. She twisted some on the cot, her brows lowered against pain, her hands balled into fists.

The ground trembled. The beam from the moon thundered down around us and illuminated the circle of witches in a bright lunar light. Nick and Johnny and I stood in the dark, outside the sharp edge of illumination, bracing ourselves against each other. Each of the witches in the circle had her magic superimposed over herself. Tabitha looked as if she was made of stone. The Valkyrie was encased in ice. Forks of lightning ran across the rod and streaked over Jen.

The chanting stopped. The lunar beam disappeared, leaving a superimposed black-and-white image of the witches in my eyes. A few of them fell where they stood. And a chill wind blew across the coven, stirring the robes of those still standing.

Jen raced to the circle. I held Nick back, unsure if the ritual was done.

Sarah still had her eyes closed, as if she slept. Her hands had relaxed, though. And the tattoos I could usually see seemed to have slipped back underneath her skin.

Jen finally looked up from Sarah at me, her eyes wet, but smiling. I let out a breath I hadn't known I was holding. The ritual had worked. I let go of Nick, and he walked in to kneel beside Sarah, across from Jen. He reached one hand out to Sarah, laying it on her arm for a moment, and then quickly pulled it back.

I felt for the guy.

Some of the witches who had fallen were getting back up. Others were being helped. Tabitha made her way across the pattern and stopped by me.

"It's done," she said. "You should have three days."

Three days to get to New Orleans and convince the bishop there to perform an exorcism on Sarah. With every cop between here and there looking for us. And a demon.

"Going to be tight," Johnny said.

Tabitha's eyes were angry. She almost looked inward, as if she felt like she had failed. "You need to know, all we could do was reduce Sarah's pain. Keep her from feeling the curse. It's still going to call to vampires. It's still going to build and kill her."

Zoe came up beside Tabitha. The daughter was a thinner image of her mother, and looked exhausted from the ritual, with hollow cheeks and bags under her eyes. The daughter still held her talisman in one hand, a tiny opaque globe, about the size of a billiards ball.

"I understand," I said.

"It's poor repayment," Tabitha said. "I can never thank you enough, for helping us back there."

I looked away for a minute. Rescuing the women there, that had been an accident. If I hadn't seen them, I would have just grabbed Jen and left. I didn't know that I was worthy of their thanks. Or their repayment.

Sarah was, though. And three days of time was more than I had expected. It was nice to have people help, for a change. Help – freely offered – wasn't something I was used to. I shook both of their hands, an acknowledgment of a debt paid.

"Come back, if you can," Zoe added. "Maybe we both can sit with the same spirit and compare notes."

I shivered. I didn't want to talk to someone like Jo, or the old lady's spirit from this night. The memories seemed to be getting worse. Could a spirit feel sorry for something it had done in life? Would that same spirit lie to Zoe, or acknowledge what it had done?

Up until now, most of the ghosts had seem like automatons, doing the same thing they had done in life right before their death. But more and more seemed self-aware now. And they fought me pulling them. Especially the ghosts of the recently deceased. I'd heard stories of séances, where a poltergeist had torn through the room. Could that be another ghost like Jo?

There were too many questions for me. I wished I had more time. Zoe was maybe the first person I had met that might be able to help me discover more about what I could do. About what happened to the ghosts I used. There was a reason behind it, according to my mother. And a Bible, in the glove box of the Camaro, that might tell me more.

"Time always seems short, to me," I said. "Maybe someday."

The witches understood. Jen came up and put a hand on my arm. She leaned on me, just a little, her palm warm even over my jacket. "I was worried about you."

She looked tired too. I remembered the forks of lightning running up and down her body from the ritual, the electricity tracing her cheekbones, running through her hair. "We made it okay."

"The cops are going to make it harder to get to New Orleans," she said.

I didn't tell her that I thought the cops were just Azazel's opening move. The coffee shop seemed like a lifetime ago, but it was only this morning. The demon wouldn't wait long before making another. "Yeah. We probably need to go. The clock is ticking."

Jen patted my arm and went back to her sister. She already had what she and Sarah needed packed up in the house. I went inside and grabbed a small black bag while Nick carried Sarah to the Camaro. Somewhere he had wrapped her in a thick blanket.

Tabitha and the Valkyrie spent some final words with Jen, by the passenger side of the car. Offering a little advice, passing whatever bits of knowledge they thought might help, though most of what I heard was just hopeful thoughts and wishes for us to be safe. I did learn the Valkyrie's name was Gertrude, and that seemed to be the right kind of name for a witch, if not for a Valkyrie.

I opened the trunk and stuffed the black bag in there. After a moment I yanked out another shirt and changed it out with the one I was wearing. Then popped open an energy drink. It was citrusy with a lot of carbonation. I picked out a second can, something coconut flavored, and got into the car. After the fight at the motel, it was going to be a long night.

Nick and Sarah were already in the backseat. Sarah was behind me, asleep, leaning on Nick. Her face looked younger than it had recently. Nick sat in the middle, and he had his head back against the seat.

Johnny let Jen get into the backseat. She patted me on the shoulder, then buckled her seat belt, laid her head against the inside of the car, and closed her eyes.

I fired up the Camaro, feeling my seat shake in a rhythm to the comforting rock of the eight-cylinder engine. Johnny got in and shut his door and buckled up. In his hand was one of the smart phones.

"Figured we'd want to take the back roads out of here," he said. He hooked the phone to the dash and plugged a charger into the cigarette lighter. The phone had a map on it, with my car represented as a tiny blue vehicle. The top of the screen had the next turn I was about to take on it, and the time it would take to get to Birmingham.

"The time's not accurate," he said. "I'll have to reconfigure it every so often. We're going to hit construction, accidents, whatever. But I thought Birmingham was a nice first stop."

"I gotcha," I said. I pressed the gas pedal down. The Camaro surged forward. I followed the phone's direction and took turn after turn, heading slowly and inexorably into the countryside. There, the map opened up a bit, the car rolled along effortlessly, and we counted down the miles. For a long time it was just the headlights on the road, the thrumming of the engine, and the night.

CHAPTER TWELVE

Our first problem happened in Tennessee. Construction around Nashville had slowed us down by hours. Each direction was two lanes, but there was roadwork along the shoulder, and traffic cones and concrete barriers took the interstate to one lane for ten or so miles. Even though there were no workers present, this late at night.

Adding to that, all of the side roads seemed to funnel all the traffic to the interstate, pulling everyone west to Nashville. There were two wide lanes in both directions, but the lanes headed toward Nashville got thicker and thicker with cars. We joined the stream of vehicles heading west. I was counting on the sheer numbers of cars to hide us from anyone that might be looking for a classic car out of Lewiston.

We drove through the rest of the evening, all the way until early-morning twilight. I almost drove to the pull of the Key, far to the south, always turning in that direction before checking the map. Occasionally a text message bubble would pop up on the phone, and Johnny would take it down and type in a few things. He told me it was Gabrielle, and we talked about that in low whispers. She was fine. Her family was disappointed. Maybe a little more.

"She wants to know how you're doing," Johnny said.

"Other than being hit by a car?" I asked. "Fine."

"She means with the geas," Johnny said. He kept his voice low. "Like, are you feeling anything from Dominic?"

I had put that from my mind. But it was a concern. My mother was under the real geas; what controlled me was just a part of it. I knew from experience that the farther I was away from Dominic, the harder it was for him to get control over me. So the farther I headed out of Grafton, the less I had worried about the geas reaching out. Especially with Dominic fighting the drug in his system.

I shook my head. "Not yet."

"Man, she is curious," Johnny said, and stopped asking me questions after a bit. He texted awhile more. We took a brief stop to gas up and get a bathroom break in, then got back in the car. Sarah slept the whole time through.

We were sixty miles outside Nashville when the interstate morphed into a parking lot of taillights, pairs of red eyes blinking here and there as dozens of cars slowly rolled forward a few feet and then stopped. A van advertising a new cellular network sat on my left for a long time, and it tickled something in the back of my brain. Then I remembered the advertisement in the paper the other morning, and let it go. For a while we waited underneath a digital sign flashing the number of road fatalities this year. The construction would only up that number, if this was what heading into work was like every day.

Some cars sped along the shoulder of the road. I wasn't sure how far they thought they could get. Gravel kicked up and rapped off the Camaro. Part of me wanted to follow them, but the risk of being stopped was too great. We still had days to get to New Orleans, and getting into a police chase wasn't the way to speed that up.

Sarah still slept, though Jen or Nick woke up from time to time, looking at the red lights of traffic around us, before falling back asleep. Johnny turned on the radio and found a traffic station, and a monotone voice went down a list of traffic jams around Nashville, construction hot spots, and accidents. The voice reported an accident existed in our construction zone: a car had been forced into one of the barriers. Soon, the phone app reported the same accident.

It took a few hours for us to move to a place where we could take an exit. The problem was everyone tried to do the same thing. The side streets became a flood of slow-moving cars and SUVs and even eighteen-wheelers. The huge parking lot on the interstate became many smaller parking lots on the side roads, the entire lots of cars moving from stoplight to stoplight en masse, at every flick from red to green.

"There's no beltway or anything," Johnny said. He had pulled the phone off the dash and was doing something to the screen with his forefinger and thumb. "They have something called Briley Parkway that circles around the city some, but no interstate bypass loop."

That seemed silly, with this amount of traffic. I hit the brakes for maybe the thousandth time. In my rearview mirror the sky had lightened from dark, deep space blue to a gray. The gray was tinged with burning reds and oranges in the east, as if the sun hid behind thick-fingered layers of clouds. The morning was humid enough that the windshield kept fogging up the inside. I got into a defogging rhythm: I'd turn the heater on to clear up the glass, then the inside of the car would get uncomfortably warm, so I'd turn the heater off and wait for the fog to reclaim what had been cleared.

We made our way to Briley Parkway and blended into traffic there. It wasn't fast, but it was moving. We headed around south to southwest, stopping in places where all the traffic stopped, darting forward when there was room. For some reason, every exit and entrance ramp caused a logjam of traffic, like people couldn't figure out how to blend together.

Sarah finally really woke up, and she was hungry. I caught a real smile on her face, a smile like a younger, thinner Jen, and the expression seemed to wash her pain away.

"Can we stop and get something to eat?" Jen asked.

We had used one of the plastic grocery bags for our trash. It was full of energy drinks, toaster pastry wrappers, and an empty jumbo bag of trail mix. Johnny and I had eaten as much from boredom as from hunger. I wasn't too hungry, but we could all use a break, and a real meal with some coffee would be nice. "Sure."

The sun had climbed out of its slumber and had burned away the morning clouds. Every exit and entrance ramp was packed. We took one with a lot of restaurant signs on it. From there we navigated to a buffet-style place with pans of eggs and bacon and pancakes next to a row of lettuce and tomatoes and other chopped vegetables. We walked in to the smell of sausage and fried potatoes and my stomach rumbled even though I had snacked all night.

We were seated in a booth, where we ordered juice and coffees and then went to the bar to load up. I piled a lot of pancakes on my plate, and a lot of syrup. Jen sat next to me and picked a few bites off my plate, even though she had pancakes too. Maybe my syrup was better.

Sarah came back with a huge salad. She saw my questioning look. "I'm a vegetarian."

"Really?" Johnny asked. He had paused with a huge forkful of sausage and eggs halfway to his mouth.

"Yes," Sarah said. Every now and then, when she spoke, I saw her as I had back in the movie theater, with tiny punctures on her neck, still leaking a little blood. She let out a shy smile. "Silly, right?"

I got it and snorted holding back a laugh. Jen elbowed my ribs. Nick rolled his eyes at me across the table, but he still grinned. Sarah's smile grew more confident, and she dug into her salad.

Sarah did end up eating a lot. Maybe vegetables had a lower caloric intake than pancakes, but there was still a question of room in the stomach. The sheer amount didn't seem possible, in a person that thin.

It struck me that this was our first meal, all together. Our first meal sitting together, each of us somewhat relaxed. I couldn't remember the last time we had all sat down, but Miss Tammie was probably the one feeding us. And I smiled for a moment, wondering what Miss Tammie would have made of a vegetarian, in that diner. I worked to push away the sadness that came over me, thinking of the diner, and just focus on the good. On the now.

Johnny and Nick each got a bowl of ice cream and immediately looked at each other as they ate. I think there was a subconscious truce between them. Jen was happy her sister felt well. I felt her happiness in little ways. Jen's light touches on my arm, a hand on my leg, stealing more bites of my pancakes. I liked all of it. At some point the two of us lay back in our seat, my arm around her, Jen fitting next to me like we had been made for each other.

We'd have to get back on the road soon. We had passed a lot of cops through Nashville, and each time a blue-and-red bulb popped up on the phone app I worried more. I didn't know if the APB described the car or not, or if the police had gotten my license plate in Lewiston. I had been on the run, been prey, for a long time. And I trusted the instincts I had developed while I was on the run, and those instincts flared up with fear every time we passed a cop car tucked underneath a bridge, radar gun pointed down the road.

But maybe Jen was right, back in Lewiston. Maybe I worried too much. Maybe I had been prey so long I couldn't see things the way they were. I was learning how to be something different. It was hard to navigate how I felt about this. Because we *were* prey. But also, we were hunters. And as Nick said, once Sarah was okay, we'd show Azazel what it was like to mess with us.

Jen had stopped stealing from my plate. She had noticed I had gotten contemplative and had turned a quizzical eye my way. I winked at her. It would be okay. I'd figure it out.

We paid the tab and got back in the car. Jen and Johnny switched seats. Nick offered to take over the wheel, but I was used to driving long pieces of road at a time and still felt good. I stretched a long moment in the parking lot. The sky had deepened to an oceanic blue, and a gathering of clouds rolled along from the west like waves, crest after crest lined one behind the other. The sun stood high in the east, a pale yellow eye, facing the cloudy horizon. I shook myself a final time, taking a deep breath of the cool autumn air, grabbed an energy drink from the trunk, and fired up the Camaro.

Like us, the car rumbled in contentment. It had eaten a lot of road, and was ready to eat more. We got on I-65 South to Alabama and slowly worked our way out, passing large cloverleaf ramps exiting onto eight-lane highways, with hundreds of stores and gas stations and apartment buildings and shopping malls at each stop. Like small cities.

"So many people here," Nick commented. "I wonder what they all do."

I didn't know. Millions of people lived here, apparently. I didn't know how that many could exist in one place, or what they all did. Did people in large cities support each other, with their jobs, and what they did? Or did they all just get up and go to work and go home, every day?

Hundreds of years ago cities rose up around ports, where goods could be harvested or built and sold. People were attracted to them to either sell or purchase what they needed. They developed communities, those communities built products, and sold them to others.

I couldn't apply the same thought process to Nashville. What could possibly exist in the city that provided a livelihood to everyone who lived there? Who purchased or sold what? How was enough food produced to feed everyone? What industries were here that could support all these people, the hotels and the restaurants and the millions of cars on the road?

I didn't know, and couldn't imagine. Sign after sign rolled by along the interstate, each one advertising something different: the next country artist coming to town, the local news show, or a lawyer I might need if I had encountered asbestos in my life and suffered from a bunch of different symptoms. Didn't seem like any of that would put a lot of food on people's plates.

I kept driving. The exits grew farther apart. The small cities around each exit thinned out to just suburbs. Newer neighborhoods for people who would have to fight a large commute to get into Nashville. Then the exits disappeared altogether, though occasionally I would just see a ramp leading to a short road with one gas station off to the side. Tall, peaked hills rose up ahead of us in the distance, each hill feathered with green pine trees. The tail end of the Appalachian Mountain Range, sinking back into the earth.

The mile markers counted down the distance to Alabama's border. We passed a sheriff's station at an exit, and my spine tingled on high alert for a few miles after. I made sure to drive the speed limit, until too many cars passed us, and then I sped up and kept inside a pack of cars.

Jen turned on the radio, something with a lot of pop hits. I caught her singing to one, softly, and I raised my eyes at her. She had never been a teenage pop queen. She just smiled.

Sarah sat in the middle, her head on Nick's shoulder. Every now and then they would talk, softly. He caught me looking at them in the rearview mirror, and both of us looked away.

We crossed the border with no issues. All of us gave a little cheer at the Welcome to Alabama sign. A rest stop was a few miles away, and in a few more hours we would be closer to Huntsville.

Johnny had been thumbing through his phone. He stopped and held the phone up to the front seat. "Recognize this?"

Jen grabbed it and showed me the face. It was the same demon sigil that was in the middle of Sarah's curse. "Yeah."

"The internet is a wonderful thing," Johnny said. "Demon, thy name is Buné."

Sarah and Nick had stopped their side conversation. Jen turned the radio off.

"That's the demon powering the curse?" Sarah asked.

"Yeah," Johnny said. "He's like one of the seventy-two demons in Solomon's Lesser Key. He's called a great Duke of Hell, with thirty legions of the dead under his control, and … hold on." Johnny held up a finger. "It says here he can change the places of the dead."

"And that's the same tattoo on me?" Sarah turned her head around in both directions and moved around in the backseat, as if she could see the symbol on her back.

"Changing the place of the dead," Nick said. He talked so seldom that when he did, it felt important. His gaze looked at me. "Why would that demon power this type of curse?"

He had linked it before I had. Changing the place of the dead sounded suspiciously close to what I called living their memories. Was it the same? "What's that mean?"

"*Occultipedia* doesn't say," Johnny said, still skimming the phone. He still looked tired, but not tired enough to miss a joke. "And it's not like I'm an expert in demonology. I didn't even stay in a Holiday Inn last night."

"Maybe that part doesn't have to tie in," I said. "Maybe it's like Tabitha said, and it's just an energy source."

"Knowing any names is important," Jen said. "So is knowing the reason behind the name."

"And back in that club, you could see what the drug did. It created an addiction, and there was a carnality to it. The club always turned into a mass orgy," Johnny said. He held his phone out. "Here's the perfect demon for that kind of thing. Asmodeus, the Demon King of Lust."

"When you put it that way," Nick said. "It feels like using Buné is kind of like putting unleaded fuel into a diesel engine."

We all were quiet for a moment. I knew nothing about old demons, the major players back in the times of the Old Testament. I had only learned what I had needed to keep me alive, running from Azazel. I had never had the time to dig deeper, and I had the feeling that lack of knowledge could come back to really bite us now.

"A count would be easier to manipulate than a king," Sarah ventured.

"If it's just about powering the spell, maybe it's just a question of what demon would be easier to control?"

I grunted. Jen looked thoughtful.

"Yeah." Johnny's face was still on his phone. "Maybe."

"What I do is more layered." Azazel's words rang back to me. "For instance, how's Sarah?"

Azazel had a reason. He had as much as told me. But we would figure it out or we wouldn't. Thinking about it right now would only worry us all, and all that mattered right now was getting Sarah to New Orleans.

"It's the internet." I shrugged. "Can't believe everything you read."

Jen reached a hand back to her sister. Sarah's fingers locked up with Jen's, and all of their knuckles were white. A great pit of worry grew suddenly in my chest.

The Key pulled at me then. Hard. The tug of it was like was a fishing line between us, with someone slowly turning the reel. I had gotten so used to it that I only noticed it when I consciously looked for it.

However, the Key had never pulled at me like this. It was as if I were on a hook, deep in the ocean. The Key was the person in the boat on top of the water, jerking on the fishing rod, yanking me towards it.

The Key's pull grabbed me. A stabbing pain shot through my chest. It was so strong I fell forward against the steering wheel. I immediately tried to push myself back, and straighten in my seat, but my foot jabbed against the brake and we all lurched forward in the car.

A horn blared from behind us. There was nothing I could do. Agony burned through my body. The best I had was letting off the gas and the brake pedals, bracing my feet instead against the floorboard of the Camaro. The car began to weave in traffic.

Jen grabbed the steering wheel. At the same time a gong sounded in my brain, like a heavy cavernous bell had been rung in my skull. The echoes reverberated in my brain, and I found myself pressing my temple with both hands, trying to hold my skull together.

The Key ripped open. It felt like a zipper had burst open. Or maybe the lips of a womb grew apart, the labia stretching and tearing as an evil pushed itself out of it. A scream only I heard ripped through the sky.

And just as suddenly as it had been opened, the Key shut.

The car swerved across the interstate. More horns blared behind us. I pumped my foot on the brake a few times, more a reflex than a conscious action.

The Camaro skidded wildly. Jen had the wheel and directed us off the shoulder. There was a long screech of burning rubber, the car skidded, and dirt kicked up in the rearview mirror. We slowed down quick and ended up in the tall grass to the side of the road, bouncing up and down a few times at the end, and then the car stalled out.

Nick and Sarah and Johnny were all holding each other. Jen gripped the steering wheel, each finger wrapped tightly around it. All of them looked at me.

I shook my head, and pressed one hand against my temple. "The Key."

"Shit," Nick said.

"It's been opened," I said. I shook my head to try to clear it from the ringing of that bell.

"This is Azazel forcing the issue, right?" Jen said.

I nodded. A demon had been released. Either to come after us, or to make us come after Azazel.

"Can you drive?" Jen said.

My hands shook. I needed a moment to get myself back together. Whatever tie I had to the Key stabbed me like a hot, sharp pinprick in my chest. Like a needle stitching the flesh together over a deep cut, with the thread tugging through my skin. *This is on your watch,* it seemed to say.

"I might need a minute," I answered, trying to smile. "Or two."

A truck had pulled off to the side, a dark red Ford 150 with big chrome wheels. A guy was getting out of the side, one hand holding a cell phone to his ear. I hoped he was still talking to whoever he had been talking to, and not 911.

"We still need to go," Jen said.

We switched seats. Jen started up the Camaro. It took a couple of times to chug to life, as if protesting. Slowly she worked it back to the edge of the road and then blended back on the interstate, punching the gas. The guy by the truck watched us as we passed. I waved a hand at him slowly, as if saying, *That was close, right?*

I watched him in the sideview mirror. The man got back in his truck. The phone still close to his ear. Then the Camaro crested a small hill, and I lost him from sight.

CHAPTER THIRTEEN

A few miles later a rest stop appeared, the first one we had seen in Alabama. We saw the sign for the welcome center, and then right after the sign there was a large stand of trees, with the nose of a space rocket poking out high over the woods.

It looked like the rockets they launched back during the moon race, tall and white with a black circle right under the nose of the rocket, and United States spelled out in black letters down each fin. The rocket was easily taller than a city apartment building, and all kinds of wires led down from the nose of the craft to anchor it to the earth.

Jen looked at me, and what she saw worried her. "Let's get you some water."

She drove off into the lot. There were a number of other cars there, and she pulled a bit farther away from them, to the edge of one of the lots. A lot of people were there, walking back and forth between the parking lot and the welcome center, and the welcome center and the rocket. This would be a bad place for Azazel to catch us.

Jen got out and then helped me out. My legs still shook some, and I stood for a minute and leaned against the side panel of the car. Jen popped the trunk and got a bottle of water out, and I stood there and drank it.

The Key had been opened. I don't think I shook from the pain of the opening, or the fear of whatever it had let out. I think I was shaking because a part of me knew Azazel wanted me to make a choice, and he had just brought his biggest gun to that fight.

I searched for ghosts. It was hard during the day, like a thick film covered the ethereal plane and masked everything underneath it. But I got lucky. There was a large lot behind the rest area for big-rig trucks, and in the woods there I sensed a small dot on my radar. A spirit lurking deep beneath the surface. I knew the spirit was female, and she was hidden in the woods, way past the tractor trailers. I didn't want to think of what could lead a woman to that spot. Or if her body was still there.

Everyone else got out of the car. They stood around me for a bit, concerned but not knowing what to say. Nick maybe seemed the most worried, and maybe he felt like he should be, since he had given the Key to Azazel. But I had told him then that I would have done the same thing. Nick just looked like he had trouble believing it now.

I took a deep breath and let it out. We needed to move. "Let's make this quick."

Jen cocked her head. "Are you sure?"

"Yeah," I said, then slid a little against the car before catching myself. "If the Key is open, we need to hurry more than ever."

A demon to the south, and cops looking for us everywhere. A rock and a hard place. A hammer and an anvil. All of that flashed through my mind.

"It's bathroom time," Johnny said. He forced a grin. Sarah started to follow him, and Nick did too after looking at me a long moment. I waved him off.

"Gus, you okay?" Jen asked again.

"I'll be good," I said. She placed her hand on my chest. I pushed it away. My tone was short. "I'm fine, Jen."

She looked at me, arching an eyebrow at me and standing there. Waiting.

I took a breath or two and realized I was being an ass. I was great in a fight, and I was great running. Sometimes I wasn't so great in the times between the two.

Jen had been the only real relationship I had had in my life, before I had left Grafton. I had never had one in the time since. Being chased by a demon kind of did that to a person. So I didn't know how to do it properly.

But then, Jen and I had never been a relationship. We had a connection deeper than that. From the moment we had seen each other, it had always been her and me. And I didn't need anything to figure that part out, or some fancy language to explain it.

"I'm sorry," I said.

She rolled her eyes at me, then smiled. Her eyes twinkled at me. "Was that so hard?"

"No." I shook my head. "And yes. I haven't done this in a long time, Jen."

"Done what?"

"Worry about others," I said. "Something like this happens to me and I get right into battle mode. Fight or flight. I shut down and push through and over or away from things."

"You have help with all of that now," Jen said. She placed her hand on my chest, and this time I let it happen. Her palm felt warm through my T-shirt. "So just get used to it."

I was afraid to, I realized. Danny had forgiven me for his death, had shown me that forgiveness was possible. And I had accepted it. But I still maybe hadn't forgiven myself.

I kept working through this same issue. Protecting my friends. Each of them had accepted the danger and wanted to be a part of this. And each of them had their own strengths, strengths we all would need if we wanted to win this war against Azazel.

But each of them could die, as well. I wondered if I could accept it. Part of me was in front of Jen, feeling her hand against my chest, as if holding me up. Another part of me looked south and shook my head no. I still felt the difference, between my brain accepting the danger my friends were in, and my heart understanding that any of them could die, at any moment.

Somewhere, Azazel was loving this.

And that image tipped the balance for me right then. That thought allowed me to push past my fear, in the moment. I wasn't someone who let others win. So I focused on that image, of Azazel being pleased at the dilemma he had put me in, and took a deep breath. In my heart, I was someone who reacted to bullies with a great vengeance. I would measure my reaction to Azazel's action, every time.

If my friends died, it would be long after I had given everything I had, and was a cold, dead corpse myself.

I guess Danny's lesson could only help me so far.

I finished off the water, the thin plastic bottle crinkling in my hand as I crushed it. Jen and I headed to the welcome center. Inside there were a number of people, racks of pamphlets of things to do in Alabama, and an old guy wearing a security officer's uniform.

I went into the bathroom and used the urinal. Then stood at the sink for a long moment. I waited until a confident man stared back at himself.

We'd be okay, I told myself. Azazel had the Key for the sole reason of opening the prison. It was just a matter of when the demon wanted to. Whatever purpose he thought it would serve. I just had to be ready for whatever happened next. And figuring things out on the run was something I was good at.

I washed my hands and splashed my face with the lukewarm tap water. I ran some more of the water through my hair, feeling the black strands curl as they got wet. There were no paper towels to dry my hands, and the hot air dryers never turned on, no matter how many different ways and angles I held my hands under them. So I shook my head, a little like a wet dog, and dried my hands on my jeans. My jaw had clenched some, so I tried a cocky grin on until it stuck.

Then I headed back out. Nick had wandered back to the car and had popped the hood, looking at the engine. He had pulled a flashlight from the trunk and ran his hand through his hair, like he was just looking over things.

In one of the buildings there was a line of vending machines behind the thick metal bars. Johnny stood in front of them with a few dollars in his hand. He pointed toward the rocket. Sarah and Jen stood over there, by a large sign.

I walked over there as well. They both were reading the information plaque there. The rocket was one of those Alabama had built in Huntsville. One of the Saturn models that had tested out the lunar modules, before the Saturn V rocket had taken the astronauts to the moon.

Jen and Sarah wanted to walk a little more. Jen had patted my back as they took off. I think she wanted some time with her sister. A few other people stood around the rocket and took pictures, talking among themselves.

The rocket reached high up in the sky, towering over me. I wondered about the power of the thrust required, to force oneself out of an orbit and onto a new trajectory. The cones underneath the rocket, where the propellant would burn its way out, were thick and dark gray, each of them taller and wider than a person. Millions of pounds of force and fire bursting from each, all to take a person to a place he had never been before.

Johnny stepped up to me. He had a pack of animal crackers in one hand, and munched on them absently. I couldn't remember the last time I had eaten one, so I took one out of the bag and tried it. A lion. The cookie crunched in my mouth and a sugary-shortbread sweetness melted in my mouth. I went ahead and got a second one. A lion again.

"Ever wonder why we never went back?" Johnny asked.

"I hadn't really ever given any thought to why we had gone up in the first place," I said.

"It was something Gabrielle is fascinated with," Johnny said. It surprised me, a little, but their relationship was like that.

"Really," Johnny said at my look. "We talk about things like that. We humans used to be these great explorers. Pushing the boundaries of where we could go. And then after the moon, nothing.

"Gabrielle, she wonders still," he continued. "Some of the vampires as well. A few of the younger generation feels like space is built for them, and if there are others like them in the universe. Is there a place for them, where they could exist and see a sunrise?

"I don't know that I want to be a vampire." Johnny kicked the foot of the sign. "But they have one thing going for them. Immortality makes space travel a little more feasible."

"Huh," I said. When I had looked up at the stars as a kid, it had only been because I had imagined Jen doing the same thing from her house. I always felt connected to her, in that way. For Johnny, the stars were something different. Did he look to get away? To find something different? Or a greater understanding? "I never knew that about you."

He finished up his crackers and crinkled the bag up in his hand. "We all have dreams, I guess. Some more real than others."

A man stepped up next to us. A slight whiff of wet hair radiated from him, like the smell of wet dog, mixed with maybe cheap cigars. When he spoke, his voice was hoarse but quiet, and intonated in a strange rhythm, like he was unused to speaking aloud. "This is a thing man built, to escape the earth?"

"I guess," Johnny said, then looked at me, making a little circling motion with his finger by his ear, and rolling his eyes.

"Huh," the man grunted. He stared up at the rocket, as if lost in wonder. As if lost in figuring out the reason. "What do they think they can accomplish?"

"Exploration," Johnny said. "Discovery. Finding new things in new places. Looking for something better."

We all stood still for a moment, until the man snorted.

"What do they think to find out there?" the man asked. I wasn't sure if he was asking me or just talking about loud. Musing. "Do they think to escape us?"

Something in his tone made me take a harder look. The man was big, taller than me, and dressed oddly. He wore black jeans and a dark red shirt, like a thick flannel. A black trench coat, almost like a cape, feathered out around him.

And the handle of a black sword jutted out from behind him.

Oh shit, I thought. *The demon.*

The demon looked at me and grinned. He was bronzed-skinned, black hair tight to his head, except for a sharp fade on the sides. He was huge. Something about him reminded me of a barbarian. His eyebrows were elegantly thin, one arched at me in a very precise motion.

The sun darkened, as if a thick cloud had passed in front of it. A group of people stood not far behind him, taking pictures.

"Fergus Grimm." The demon nodded. He unsheathed his sword in a fluid motion.

I pulled from the ghost of the girl.

The demon swung at Johnny.

The fight began.

CHAPTER FOURTEEN

As had been the case with the most recent spirits, the ghost of the girl fought me, briefly. I was ready for it, though, and pushed past the resistance, tapping into the ethereal plane as fast as thought itself.

As fast as I was, the demon was faster.

It was a near thing.

I strengthened my skin and turned in the same moment, grabbing Johnny in a big bear hug. Johnny had just turned to look at the demon, a quizzical expression on his face.

I had hardened my skin in time. The blade barely cut into me. The demon's sword hit my back as if it were a bat, like he was an outfielder swinging for a home run. Johnny and I flew across the exhibit and bounced off the rocket, landing on the concrete pad underneath the cones. A large gonglike sound echoed from the old spacecraft. I turned and let Johnny go, and he rolled up behind a fin.

I went to get up then, but the demon was already on me. He swung the sword down and I moved fast enough that the black steel struck sparks from the concrete. Then I spun around his legs and pulled myself up the demon, clambering up him like I was climbing a tree.

I had to stay inside the reach of the sword, and I was fast enough to do it. He punched me with his free hand, I head butted him a few times, and then I wrapped both hands around his sword arm. The demon roared and shook his arm like he was trying to shake off a dog that had bitten him. I hung on tight and kicked him repeatedly in the stomach and chest. I yanked at his grip on the sword. It was less a sword fight and more a back-alley brawl.

He took a couple of steps forward and swung me against one of the cones of the rocket. It rang like a church bell, but I held on. He looked at me after the first swing, puzzled, and then swung again. Each time bones snapped in my back, numbing hot pain would shoot through my spine, and I would pull ghost to fix the breaks and to keep my skin as hard as possible.

Where in the world were the vambraces when I really needed them? The armor over my skin? The burst of energy that had occurred back in the factory?

I worked the demon's grip on his sword. It was all I could think of doing while he was pounding me against the rocket. The cones shifted underneath me each time I hit them, and around us there was a snapping of tension wires, sharp *cracks* and *twangs* in the air.

The demon beat me a few more times against the cone. I pulled enough ghost to stay conscious and finally broke a few of the demon's fingers, in tiny pops. His sword clattered to the ground. I hung from his arm and kicked him another time in his belly.

The demon set his jaw and swung me headfirst into the cone. I heard a bell ring out, like a long gong sound. Then I realized the bell was inside my head.

He swung again.

The gone rang even louder. My skull stayed together but everything inside seemed to jumble around. I fell to the ground. A boot connected with my ribs and I tumbled across the concrete before my body hit something hard and I jerked to a stop.

Warm blood ran down the side of my face from my scalp. Cobwebs in my brain held every thought captive. I couldn't link sentences together. I had to do something, but puzzling out what that something was supposed to be was beyond what my mind could put together.

The fight had taken just seconds. There were a few shouts around me. Something squealed and then there was a bang and a crunching sound, like one car had hit another. My vision blurred. Every image around me was doubled up, no matter how many times I blinked.

I finally remembered the ghost. I sucked energy from the spirit, enough that a memory began …

This guy kept making her blow him on the road. She wished she hadn't taken his offer, back at the last truck stop. But she had argued with Gretch and was tired of that fight. There were enough truckers for all of them to make a little money there. No need to get mad about it.

So she had jumped when the guy said he was headed south. And she got a little nervous, after the last time. He hadn't come and had gotten angry. And he kept looking at her funny…

I shook my head to clear it. Both from the cobwebs and the memory. It was harder now than ever, with my brain constantly ringing that bell. Or that bell ringing inside my head. But even as I tried to avoid the memory, there was a feeling of my hands, the tiny hands of the girl, pushing back against the big hairy belly of the trucker. I could still feel the memory of the trucker's hands, grabbing the back of my hair and tugging my face hard against him.

The ghost girl gagged. I did as well. Then I set my jaw and focused. Got out of that memory. Tiny snaps and pops came from my body as broken bones knit back together.

My vision cleared. I lay against a water fountain, on the sidewalk in front of the rest area. I had hit it hard enough the brick foundation had cracked, and water spilled out down the sides. Far away, Nick was still in front of the Camaro. He was only, just now, looking up from under the hood of the car, his eyes wide-open and staring at something behind me.

A large groan cut through the air, the groan of something moving for the first time in decades. The groan of an old man, tired, finally getting up out of his recliner. The groan of large pieces of metal, once anchored to the earth, now free.

The rocket tipped over. Slow at first, then accelerating as it fell. It crashed through the trees and the thick trunks shattered with large booms, the wood exploding under the weight of the spacecraft. The tops of the remaining trees waved back and forth after the passage, the ground trembled under the rocket's weight, and as it settled a slow rumbling sound rolled over us all.

Eight cones faced me now, empty black orbs that had once thundered with flames. People had started to run from the exhibit now, from around the back of the rocket, from the welcome center. The demon looked back from the rocket and turned up the corner of one lip when he found me. He looked for his sword, found it a few feet away, and picked it up.

Bodies lay around the rocket. I didn't see Jen or Sarah, but I did find Johnny. He had dived from where he had been hiding and was lying across the pad, just a dozen or so feet from the demon. Johnny looked at the demon and tried to get up.

The demon found Johnny as well. He threw both arms into the air, holding the sword high with one, and screamed into the sky. The scream sounded like a thousand voices in his throat.

I was too far from Johnny to do any good, but I got up and started to run. Taking as much energy from the ghost as I could. Running as fast as I could. There was nothing I could throw at the demon, nothing I could stop him with.

I still ran. Though it was useless. I couldn't save Johnny, not in time. No matter how much ghost I pulled.

All that got me was living a memory of a girl getting murdered in the woods.

I screamed and ran fast as the wind. I flew across the pavement. Johnny tried to get up. The demon launched himself into the air and fell toward Johnny, sword held with both hands high over his head.

It looked like slow motion to me. Like a movie. And I still wasn't going to make it in time.

Then a burst of air flashed across my face. Cool and wet. It brought the scent of rain and a slow rumbling sound of thunder. Lightning forked across the concrete pad and connected with the demon. There was a sizzle and a sharp pop and the demon was thrown back over my head, landing close to the welcome center.

Jen walked around from where the rocket had collapsed. Lightning traced around a balled fist and ran along her arms. Both of her eyebrows were lowered. She had her game face on. Sarah hung behind her sister.

The demon picked itself back up and screamed. Jen let loose another bolt of lightning and threw the demon through the front of the welcome center. The large glass windows shattered.

I slid to a stop and headed back that way, after I pointed a finger at Jen and grinned.

I liked having a heavy hitter around.

The demon picked himself back up inside. People lay across the floor, limbs and arms tangled up, not moving. A ghost stood above one, fading in the daylight, the spirit still looking at a pamphlet his real body must have been staring at just a moment before. A few people were racing out of the bathrooms and heading toward the front doors of the center.

I jumped through the broken windows and launched myself at the demon. We traded punches for a bit. He seemed a little slow—I guess lightning strikes will do that to someone—but gathered himself together quick. It was a stalemate for a bit. Every punch I landed seemed like I was punching concrete. Finally, I ducked a wild swing, grabbed that arm, and threw him into the wall.

The wall broke underneath the demon. Part of the ceiling collapsed. Sparks spat down from the lights, and a cloud of dust rolled into the room.

I located the demon's sword. It throbbed when I picked it up, and felt chill to the touch. I threw it back out the window, and stopped to watch it circle high into the air and over the highway. However we were going to finish this fight, it was going to be without that thing.

I was in the middle of a ghost burn, and everyone else still moved much slower than I did. Johnny was getting up. Nick was at the back of the Camaro, my shotgun in one hand, the trunk open. Jen headed this way, and lightning played over her face in slow motion.

I turned back. The demon was climbing back out of a large hole in the wall. A few ceiling tiles fell behind him, and white dust coated his bronze skin and hair.

"I can see why Azazel is interested in you," he said. His voice came out the same as earlier. Hoarse, yet soft.

"Yeah, well, the next time you see him, tell him he needs to up the depth of his bench," I said.

The demon tilted his head. "I see no need to tell Azazel how to craft his seats," he said.

I grinned. If this guy had been locked inside the Key for thousands of years, he wouldn't know anything about a sports metaphor. "Your name wouldn't be Buné, would it?" I asked.

The demon laughed then. It sounded much like his scream, thousands of hoarse voices chuckling among themselves. "That fool?"

I frowned. It seemed like the demons in the Key weren't on speaking terms. Maybe they were less of a family and more like casual acquaintances. Or maybe being locked up together for thousands of years made enemies of everyone.

"You face Kimaris, Grimm, not some soft-spoken gatherer of souls." The demon's chest swelled out under his shirt. The last of the lights popped out above him. "I was made to ride the earth, and bring battle wherever I go. I create the Nephilim, and bring rule to the world."

Dark black tendrils snaked out from him there, quick even in my heightened senses. They snapped out and touched the people still in the welcome center, the bodies on the floor. The tendrils even flew outside and flicked upon people in the cars.

Five tendrils, then twenty, then hundreds. Each person the tendrils touched became a likeness to the demon. Their skin bronzed over, became rough, and cracked in places. Whatever their size, they swelled some, as if packing on more muscle. And their eyes all paled into white orbs.

The screams got louder outside and became cries for help. A loud horn of a big rig blared from the interstate and tires squealed. Lightning boomed heavier around the building, sharp claps of thunder that vibrated along the earth in strike after strike.

I swung at the first Nephilim, a clone of Kimaris, if a little smaller. Another grabbed me from behind. Then a third. They each had the strength of the demon and all of them pounded on me until I had to pull at the new ghost just to stay standing. I kicked and punched and head-butted everything around me, but each of the warriors was just as strong as the demon. I was going to run out of ghosts before I could get free of these things.

Somehow we ended up near the bathrooms. One of the Nephilim threw me against the wall. I lay against it and took a deep breath. Whatever was happening outside, I needed Jen to finish it up and bring some lightning in here. Quick.

That didn't happen. But a hand reached out from the shadow of the door and placed a large hunting knife in mine. One of the silver ones that had been dipped in holy water.

Nick.

He stepped out of the bathroom, holding the shotgun. The Benelli boomed, the holy-water-dipped buckshot burst through a couple of the demon Nephilim, and they disappeared in puffs of ash. I cut a third Nephil with the knife and the same thing happened to it.

I made a little pinching motion at Nick, with my finger and thumb. He winked back. I quickly worked my way across the room, slicing at any clone that got too close. Ash clouds filled the welcome center.

The demon had cocked his head, like he was listening to a voice. He glanced outside at the forks of lightning, and then at me, and then at Nick, still in the shadows behind me.

Kimaris didn't look confused, so much as thoughtful. He turned his gaze to me. "What does Azazel want from some witches, a vampire's lackey, a shadow walker, and you, Grimm?"

"Why don't you ask him that, next time you see him?" I said.

I rushed forward. Kimaris slid to the side. Nick appeared in the hole of the wall directly behind the demon. The shotgun boomed and a blazing red hole appeared in the belly of the demon. A mix of buckshot and cold black blood spattered across me, the buckshot sticking to my shirt here and there.

Kimaris, though, disappeared in a flash of light and a settling of black ash on the ground.

I pumped my fist. Nick ratcheted the shotgun slide, but as soon as the demon disappeared the rest of the Nephilim did as well. The forms fell to the ground, human again, but lifeless, in a way that made me think of a marionette after its strings has been cut.

"Did we kill him?" Nick asked.

I shook my head. I didn't know how to kill a demon. Whenever I had been lucky enough to get Azazel with a blessed bullet, he would disappear for a day or so. I always thought he needed to heal from the wound, and that shooting him gave me some time to get ahead. But I didn't trust that feeling now, didn't trust anything that had anything to do with Azazel. Everything he had shown me could be a lie. "It might give us some time, though."

The lightning had died down outside. My car was maybe a hundred yards away. The trunk was closed now, a few of our things on the ground behind the Camaro, as if they had been tossed out. Nick had made some room, then climbed in and shut the trunk behind him, using the shadows there to get to a place he knew inside the center.

I was impressed at how quickly he had thought of it. "Glad you could make it."

Nick and I both looked at the bodies of the people around us. Innocents, all. And dead now, for no other reason than stopping to take a break on a drive and see an attraction. There was an older lady in a flowered dress and a big huge purse. The security center guard. A young man, maybe a teenager, with a pattern shaved into the side of his head and wearing blue sunglasses.

I shook my head. There was nothing we could do for any of these people. We headed outside. More bodies lay there, by cars, by the vending machines, by the little picnic tables off to the side. All dropped like the life had been cut from them. Whatever Kimaris had done to take them over, the process killed them. And he was only one of the seven demons in the Key.

Black marks streaked the ground and became furrows of smoking earth and charred stone. Jen and Sarah and Johnny all made their way toward us from the concrete pad of the rocket. All of their eyes opened wide at the destruction and the death. Jen held a tiny red shoe in one hand, its tongue hanging out and laces dangling below.

Jen hugged me, holding on for a long time. The shoe pressed hard into my back. She was probably thinking of what I had said earlier, about always staying on the move. That staying in one spot too long got people hurt. And maybe now she understood a little more about the life I had lived. I ran to always be one step ahead of something like this.

Of course, she was right as well. Running only prolonged the death and destruction. Avoiding something never resolved it. I couldn't both run and take care of Azazel at the same time. At some point, everything was going to come to a head.

Jen held on tight, like she might fall if she let go. I wondered how much strength it took to work that much lightning. And she had just taken part in the coven's ritual. It was easy enough for me to recharge, as long as another ghost was around. I wondered how Jen did.

I leaned my head into her hair, taking in the scent of honeysuckle, and said softly, "Hey."

"Hey," she answered into my chest, and hugged me harder.

She was beat. I was tired too, and pulled out the keys to the Camaro and handed them to Nick. "You guys got the watch for a bit."

He nodded and took them. Nick had always been quiet, and efficient. He never minded staying in the background, at least he hadn't when we were kids. He hid behind his glasses, and never stood out.

I would never have guessed that kid to be the killer in front of me today. The silence around him wasn't someone hiding in the background; it was a deadly silence, the quiet of a killer. The stillness of a predator, a calmness Nick had learned to move around with, or in.

I was glad to have him around.

Sirens sounded in the distance. The interstate was a huge pileup next to the center. Multiple eighteen-wheelers had crashed into one another and piled up right beside the exit ramp. Cars and trucks had run into the trucks from behind, maybe fifteen or twenty cars all locked up together.

One of the rigs was a tanker, and an amber liquid jetted out of a tear in its side. A large puddle worked its way across the highway. Bodies lay all around the accident, but I couldn't tell if they had been thrown from the crash or had been turned into Nephilim. It was eerie, though, how silent the crash site was. As if no one lived.

We all froze for a moment, looking out over all the death and destruction. We had all been together in Grafton, and had killed a lot of people there, but mostly everyone there had either been a vampire or someone working for them. It had been easy, going into that last battle, knowing that it was either their side or ours

Here, more innocents lay around than combatants. I'm sure it shocked all of my friends, the realization of how many could be hurt in a fight. Of us all, only I had seen something like this, back overseas in the army.

My friends would want to process this, to walk around and find any survivors and help put the dead to rest. Jen would want to find the kid missing that shoe, dead or alive, and either bury him or help him. I knew those things, because I had lived them. It was how we as humans got through life.

But we didn't have that kind of time. And we definitely couldn't be caught here. The clock was ticking, and we were fugitives.

"We've got to go," I said aloud.

Jen looked up, her eyes wet. We all took a breath and started to move to the car. Each of us gathered ourselves in little ways, breathing, looking up into the sky, looking at all the bodies lying on the ground.

I wanted to remember what happened here, adding it all to the price I wanted Azazel to pay. I wanted my friends to understand too what it meant to be in a world with him hunting us. Because I knew he would never let us go.

Nick and I packed up the trunk. I changed shirts, throwing away the one I wore. I took a minute while my shirt was off to rinse myself with a bottle of water, and then I pulled out some bars and got into the backseat. Jen sat next to me, and Sarah to the other side, behind the driver's seat. A tight fit.

Nick got in behind the wheel and adjusted the seat a bit. Johnny got in last and put the phone up on the dashboard, the map up and ready.

The car rumbled loudly when Nick fired it up. Like the Camaro was upset it had missed the fight, and was trying to make it up. Nick backed up and navigated us through the lot, driving around a wreck and a few bodies on the road.

The last car in the lot was a minivan. It was old and dark blue, with some of the paint peeling, and had a faded bumper sticker that had the word *BELIEVE* inside an oval, crossed at one end, like a child's drawing of a fish. A tiny face was pressed up against the window in the middle seat. Too young to know whether the face was a boy's or a girl's, but the cheeks were wet against the glass and the eyes were wide-open and scared.

CHAPTER FIFTEEN

W e took the risk and drove the interstate for a bit. The car engine thrummed along. The sun was out and heated up the car, so we cracked the windows and listened to the wind whip by.

After a short bit we heard sirens and slowed down. Cops raced the other way on the other side of the interstate, heading back toward the accident. At least a dozen of them, all their lights flashing, with a fire truck and a couple of ambulances giving chase. Not one of the police cars turned around and chased the last vehicle heading south.

I wondered if any of them would remember us when they got to the rest stop. Who knew what kind of video footage they might get at the welcome center? Or possible eyewitness accounts. What could they get, and would they remember us on the road, and link everything to the APB in Grafton?

We kept driving, though, taking the interstate as long as we dared. The car rumbled along, and as always the rumble was soothing. Jen instantly dropped asleep, her head lying on my chest, and one of my arms supporting her.

Sarah looked over at us and gave a tiny smile. I remembered her hiding behind Jen, back at the center.

"If Jen can work storms," I asked, "what can you do?"

She shook her head. "Nothing now." She picked at her shirt. "Until these tattoos are gone."

I hadn't known whatever curse and spell had been put on her, had robbed her of her powers. It must be doubly frightening for Sarah, having that curse, being under its power, and being powerless to stop it or protect herself.

There was always the geas. Something that bound me. Made me powerless. I felt like I understood her, a little better than I had.

"We'll get you fixed," I promised.

Sarah kept the smile and kind of half shrugged a shoulder. Then she turned back to the window, the wind fluttering out strands of her hair.

Johnny took some time to map out a way around Huntsville using older roads out in the country. He shook his head. "It's going to be slow going."

"Slow is better than stopped," I said.

Nick just kept driving. Interstate or country roads, it all seemed the same to him. When the time came he exited to the right and smoothly transitioned to the highway.

"Watch for cops," I reminded him.

He looked at me in the rearview mirror, one eyebrow raised. The tiny baseball swung back and forth under his gaze.

Sometimes I did sound like a parent. I rolled my eyes at myself. "I know, I know."

Jen woke up. She patted my chest and grabbed a small purse, tucked beside the passenger's seat.

"You have a purse?" I asked. I had never seen her with one, and for some reason watching her dig through a handbag made our relationship feel more real, more adult.

She frowned a quizzical look at me. I guess I was two-for-two on dumb comments. She dug through makeup cases, lipstick, and a slim, elegant wallet until she found the other phone Johnny had bought.

Jen pulled it out and turned it on, started searching the internet. The first thing she found were reports on the welcome center. Hundreds of people were found dead all along the road. There were pictures of people in environmental suits holding equipment around the area. Dozens of body bags were lined up on one side of the stop.

The sheriff at the site postulated a gas leak combined with some kind of explosion. Possibly a terrorist attack. The bodies would be taken in and autopsied, and they would get to the bottom of it. He had been asked about survivors, and had mentioned the few that had been found were in too traumatic a state to provide any help.

The new site Jen was on had a link to video. Jen clicked on it and we both watched some cell phone footage. The video started with the rocket tipping to the side. It jerked around as the rocket fell, and then the sidewalk rocked by as the person with the phone started running.

Jen hit a button, and we heard sound. The person was yelling at someone else to get to the car. The voice was high-pitched and shaking. There was a sharp crack of thunder, and then another. The person turned back and held the phone back out. A young woman screamed at him to unlock the car.

The hand holding the camera was shaking, and so was the video. It caught a blur that was me jumping through the front window of the welcome center, and then shadows moving inside the building that was me and the demon swinging it out. The front door opened and a group of people flooded out of the center.

The first part of that fight had only taken moments. I had been moving fast. There was another crash inside the center when I threw the demon into the wall. And then a flash of light when I had thrown the sword out the window.

Right after that dark black tendrils flicked out of the front window, like a thousand-armed octopus sat inside the center, reaching out to whatever prey swam too close. The tendrils whipped around the open air, and the people running outside the center froze as soon as dark appendages touched them. I couldn't quite see if the people turned bronze on the video, or swelled a little in size, like I had noticed during the fight. The camera wasn't that great, and there was too much motion.

The video only lasted a moment longer. The tendrils stretched out past the sides of the person holding the camera. The young lady stopped screaming. We heard the eighteen-wheeler's horn and then the long screech of tires locking up on the interstate.

Then a dark, thin strand flicked directly past the camera. The camera immediately dropped to the parking lot and bounced a few times before lying facedown on the blacktop. All we could see was the blacktop of the parking lot and part of a white line of a parking space, but the audio still captured all the screams and the explosions of lighting.

Jen stopped the video.

What I kept going back to was that Kimaris had shown up next to me. The demon had made sure I saw him. Only after that did Kimaris try to kill Johnny. Part of me was sure that was all Azazel. Maybe a condition for letting his brother out of the Key.

We all went quiet for a while. The car rumbled along and Nick deftly navigated the curves, taking the inside of each one and coming out accelerating, as if he could make up minutes every mile. The sun beat down on us and heated up the back of my neck, and my arm by the window, but the wind got to be too much for Sarah and Jen. Their hair kept whipping around, and one of the things we didn't have was hats. So we rolled up the windows and turned on the air-conditioning, and I waited for the cold air to make its way to the backseat.

The Camaro drank up the gas as we rode, and the needle dipped down below a quarter-tank, so we finally stopped at an old gas station. It sat at a crossroads in the middle of nowhere. Trees stood at three of the corners, then the gas station, and the roads stretched long in all directions.

It was the best chance for us to get out and walk around. Take a break. Nick pumped the gas. I went in to pay, and Jen followed me. There was an old man sitting on a stool at the counter, in a white T-shirt and grease-stained coveralls. He was chewing bubble gum and listening to the radio, from which a young male voice read out news headlines in an energetic fashion. As if by will alone, he could bring in more listeners.

I bought a couple of cold energy drinks. Jen grabbed a number of paw-shaped pastries with cinnamon and sugar and lots of icing. She eyed my drinks, and I gave her pastries the same look.

"They're not all for me," she explained.

I got another energy drink. "And now these all aren't just for me."

She rolled her eyes. We packed up some candy bars and avoided a spinning wheel of hot dogs under an old heat lamp. There was no telling if the hot dogs were hours old or weeks. The old man rang everything up and packed it all in a bag for us, and added the fuel.

"Shame about those people," he said after he was done.

We had been headed out. A fear or discovery ran through me. Jen stopped at the door, and I paused next to her. I tried to make my voice sound curious. "Which people?"

"All those people at the rest stop," he replied. "I figure it's the government." The way he said it, the word sounded like *gubberment.*

"You mean the gas leak?"

"It weren't no gas leak," the man said. "It's the gubberment, mark my words. They never liked that we 'bamans helped put people on the moon."

"Huh," I said.

"All foreigners now," he said. *Forinerrs.* "You unnerstand. You drive American-made."

I nodded to the man, as if I did agree with his wisdom. Jen pulled me out of the store. We left the old guy still perched on his stool, jaw working his gum, watching the radio as if he could imagine everything the monotone voice described in vibrant colors of Alabamans and everything else.

"Takes all kinds," I said with a grin.

"I think we're just lucky he doesn't have a television," she said.

Nick finished pumping and signed to me he was going to use the restroom. Jen and I stood there and looked down the road. Thick woods stood at each corner, the leaves mostly green, even this late in the year. It seemed like they stayed green longer, in the South.

Telephone poles ran down one road, away from us, thick lines looping from pole to pole. The lines ran down the station and headed past us into the distance. Every now and then one of the poles would tilt out at an angle, like a jagged tooth.

The gas station had a garage next to it, the roll-up door open. A breeze shifted by us and brought a slight hint of gasoline and used oil. The woods made all kinds of sounds around us, made larger by the quiet of the empty roads. Rustling leaves in the wind, creaking branches, the chittering of squirrels, and the tweeting of birds.

It was warmer down here than in Tennessee, and more humid. The air felt heavier to breathe, harder to pull in. I took a deep breath and felt my chest swell against my shirt.

"So, that's what it's like?" Jen asked. "Every time? Every fight?"

She meant the rest stop. The bad jokes in the store, my attempts for a quick laugh, faded away in the sibilant sounds of the forest. "Yeah," I said.

"That's what you were worried about? Something like that happening?"

"It's what he does," I said. We both knew I meant Azazel.

"So, how do you live with it?" Jen asked. I knew the tiny shoe was still in her mind. The baby it had belonged to. All the other people there.

I waited a long moment to answer her. "I don't know that I do. I just push it all down, Jen, and keep running. Before, a part of me had convinced myself it was part of the cost of keeping the Key from Azazel. That it was better if one or two people get hurt, than him getting the Key. Then people hurt became people getting killed, and two people became three, and then ..."

I shook my head. "And then the days became years."

What had happened at the stop had happened in other places over the years. Innocents died wherever I had been. It had started small with Danny, had moved to my regiment when I was overseas, the forward operating base, and then spiraled from there.

The best I thing I did, back then, was stay on the move. And keep away from as many people as possible. Through the years as Azazel chased me, I even had become a little numb to the deaths around me. Deaths to other people because I lived. I was ashamed of myself, thinking of some of the times where I kept moving, when people might have needed help.

I was trying to be a different person now. More of the person I had been, before Danny. The guy who stood up for others.

It was tougher to find that person now. I'd had an innocence once. I had believed in right and wrong. But over the past ten years I had lived a lot of memories, and each time they were murderers, rapists, thieves. Pedophiles.

It was tough to believe in the good part of me now. The guy who stood up for people, when I carried those memories around. It was tough to do the right thing, when every time I used my power I lived the atrocities of some spirit. It was tough to believe that I could do good, that I could *be* good, when faceless person after faceless person was killed by a demon just because I had happened to stop in their town that night.

Somewhere in the past I had combined the horrors of the ghosts' memories with each person who had died around me, and had pushed them all into some deep, dark place inside me that I hoped would never open again.

That door was opening now.

And it was letting others in as well.

"I understand what you were saying, back in Lewiston," Jen said. Her eyes were open and soft, and carried a bit of a wet shimmer. "I keep seeing that shoe, back in the welcome center."

"Yeah," I said. I looked away then, and worked hard to shut the door of horrors inside me. I didn't want the individual memories popping up. The poor girl back at the truck stop. Miss Tammie, back in Grafton, and Parker.

There was a cashier at a donut shop in Philadelphia, who had just cracked a joke to me about the sprinkle patterns on the donuts she had just sold me. It was such a corny joke I couldn't help but laugh, at the time. I didn't remember the joke now, but I remembered the cashier's eyes opening wide as Azazel walked in and started shooting.

All these people had died because of me, because Azazel had been chasing me with the Key. All their lives had meant nothing to the demon. I think I had hoped to maybe find a reason, but Azazel had the Key now. So that cashier's life had been wasted. My running had meant nothing. And now even more people were dying because of it.

"You know where it is now, don't you?"

"Yeah," I said. It had gone silent, right after it had been opened, but the pull was back now. The fishing line gently tugged me to the southwest. I looked that way.

"It's not your fault that he has it." Jen's gaze had followed mine, and her eyebrows came down just a bit.

I would keep being surprised at how much Jen understood, reading me. And how fast. There were a million ways I blamed myself. I could have hidden the Key somewhere else in Grafton. Or dug it up and given it to Jen, before the last battle. Or told my friends all about it in the beginning. Only I hadn't thought about the Key at all in Grafton, because the trap was about my friends, and I couldn't see past them to understand the endgame then.

Something tickled my mind then. I reached for the thought, and lost it.

Jen tugged on my arm. "Hey," she said. "Did you hear me? It is not your fault."

"It is and it isn't, Jen," I said. "I can push this down with the rest of the stuff and keep moving. Or I can take responsibility for it and try to fix it."

"By keep moving, you mean get Sarah help," Jen stated.

Jen's eyes were a little angry, and a little afraid. I wondered if she worried I might leave them to go after Azazel, even after my promise to her. My track record wasn't great, in the past, but I hoped she believed better of me, even if she knew the reason why I was worried.

I let out a deep breath. "Yeah."

Saving Sarah would cost a lot more people their lives. I couldn't determine if her life was worth more than some other. I could only determine what that one life meant to me.

For years I had carried a weight of billions of lives, running with the Key. And what had all that running really accomplished? Who had I really helped? No one. And I had left a trail of dead bodies along the way, each time Azazel had caught up to me. The welcome center was only the latest collection of innocent corpses.

I was starting to believe that the best person I could be started with the small things. Being a good friend. Protecting and caring for those around me. Not what I had done before, in trying to protect *everyone*. That thought struck me, and felt right to me. I had to do right by those in my care, build that foundation, and grow from there.

"Whatever Azazel throws at us, Sarah will always come first," I said. "Trust me."

"I do, Gus," she said. "But I worry about you."

Nick had said much the same thing about Azazel. As soon as Sarah was healed, we were going to get the bastard. I was less alone now in what I faced than before the welcome center. I had help shutting that door. But I would not forget any deaths, I would keep tallying up the cost and lay that bill at Azazel's feet, the day it came due.

And I would grin when I collected it.

"You know what?" I asked. "I'll make a deal."

"What?"

I smiled at Jen. "You keep throwing lightning around, and I'll worry about things a lot less."

She laughed, and it was a real laugh between us. Jen leaned into me in the way she always did, where her curves fit me just right, and warmth spread out from her body into mine. She patted my chest with her free hand. "I can't do that all the time. Especially if you're going to get on me about eating cinnamon pastries. I need my calories."

"We'll make a deal, then," I said. "I get one bite of the pastries, and I won't make fun of you eating them."

Jen looked up at me, her eyebrows narrowed just a bit. "A small bite."

"Deal," I said. I was a fan of cinnamon and sugar too.

CHAPTER SIXTEEN

The Camaro rolled along the country road, sinking into the dips and lifting slightly into the air over the top of each hill. Nick kept the pedal down, and we saw very few other cars. The sun descended ahead of us, and the windshield became a bright flash each time the road took us west. Nick put the sun visor down. The map on the phone stopped working, the signal was just too spotty, so Johnny pulled the phone off the dash and clicked it off.

We all remained quiet. The welcome center was not that long ago. I understood, I had been in battles before. The aftermath always came, and when it did there were thoughts, regrets, and wonders. People always walked away wondering how they'd survived. Or if they had done this instead, would more people have lived? Or how they hadn't seen it coming.

Trees flashed by the windows and became pastures of black and brown cows, munching grass in small groups. Pastures became farmland, rows and rows of tall green cornstalks, slightly brown at the tops, the leaves dried up and barren. We passed a large green tractor on the road, pulling a cart holding ears of corn. A young woman with a big floppy hat sat on the machine, rumbling along, and she waved as we went by.

Every now and then fields of cotton would appear, acres of short bushes next to each other, sticks poking out and holding tiny puffed balls of white. Barns dotted the fields, looming red-sided buildings with large, slanting peaks. Matching silos stood tall, as if on watch, beside them.

Then the process reversed. The barns thinned out and became farmland. The acres of corn became pastures of cows, and then was broken up by small gatherings of trees. Then, on the horizon, an empty overgrown pasture with a broken-down barn. The sun edged down in front of us, and a dirt road broke off the highway and led up to the barn.

Jen had been quiet this whole time, but she looked at the barn. "Let's stop here for a bit."

Nick slowed down and the Camaro bumped up and down as we turned onto the road and headed up to the barn. The doors of the building were open, and a little daylight broke in through open holes in the roof. He pulled the car all the way in, and then we all got out.

Even out of use, the barn smelled like a barn. I took a deep breath of moldy hay, wet earth, and cow patties. Some of the stalls still had walls, a rusty pitchfork lying in one of them, but otherwise the barn was empty.

I switched on the battery-powered lamp and set it by the car. Then we all grabbed a few snacks to eat. Protein bars, pastries, energy drinks, and water. Sarah picked out what she could from the trail mix. I'd have to look for something she could eat at the next stop.

I sat on the ground, my back firmly against the Camaro. Jen sat next to me, and Nick and Sarah sat across from us, back against part of a stall. Nick had gotten a baseball from the trunk and tossed it up and down, the ball thumping in the palm of his hand. Johnny sat cross-legged off to the side. We had gotten a few bars of service, and every now and then he'd pull up the phone, checking for messages.

The night before seemed far away. The ritual. The police at the motel. They felt like they had all happened weeks ago, instead of hours.

Jen and I ate some pastries. She ate hers and then snuck bites out of my frosted strawberry tart. She sipped on her water and left me my energy drink. She was deep in thought. I remembered the look from many times, back when we were young. We'd be on her mother's couch, watching television, and she would be next to me, but her mind would be far away.

"So, what's up?" I finally asked, nudging her with my elbow.

"Figuring out how to say this right," she said. "But I can't."

"So just say it," I said.

She looked at her sister. Then she looked over at me and waited a long moment. "How long to New Orleans?"

"Can't really say," Johnny said. "By interstate, eight or ten hours from here. But the way we're going? Maybe double that, to be safe?"

"Plenty of time, then, right?" Jen said.

"Sure," Johnny said. "Depends on what you want to do."

"It's what we need to do," she said. "We need to make a plan."

"Is that what you've been thinking about?" I asked. "Isn't the plan getting to New Orleans? Find the bishop, get an exorcism done?"

"That's your kind of plan." Jen raised her eyebrows at me. "I'm talking about a real plan."

"Ouch." I put both hands on my chest and pretended to be hurt. "Is this you figuring out how to say this right?"

"This is just me beginning." Jen smiled, and wiggled up so she was sitting straight against the car. She held up three fingers and looked over all of us, counting each point off when she spoke next. "The way to get a proper plan is to outline what we know, what we think, and then what we can guess. Once we have all that information, we talk about what we can do about it."

Nick held the baseball loosely, forgotten in his hand. I had begun to recognize he was a man of action and few words. He had been much different as a kid, always arguing, thinking. Rarely doing something. Now it was action that intrigued him. Sarah sat quietly, a little listless, her eyes narrowed. We all thought about what Jen had said.

"So, what information are we talking about?" Johnny finally asked.

"Azazel," Jen said.

"Not New Orleans and the exorcism?" I asked, glancing over at Sarah.

"No." She shook her head. "It's part of this, and it's something we have to figure out, but there's a larger picture here. Let's not get lost in the smaller one."

Sarah moved a bit then, like she wanted to say something, and then stopped. She was much thinner than Jen, though the sisters looked alike, and the motion reminded me of a slight breeze stirring the catkins of a weeping willow.

Nick did say something, though. "I know you're not saying Sarah is the smaller picture."

"We all know we're getting Sarah to the bishop and for an exorcism," Jen said. "That's the given. But let's not get lost in it."

I got it then. "You're wanting to talk about Azazel."

"You can feel the Key," Jen said. "Where is it, right now?"

I searched for it, and felt it just like I had for the past day. Southwest of us, a far enough distance away that the pull came over the horizon. Was Jen thinking the key could be in … "New Orleans?"

Jen smiled, as if two pieces of a puzzle had snapped together for her.

I had never put the two together. The revelation opened a large door of possibilities in my mind. If the Key was in New Orleans, and that happened to be exactly where we needed to bring Sarah, then that meant Azazel had always planned for her to be there. Even before I came to Grafton. Which meant there was a much longer play to his game than I had previously thought.

I straightened up, feeling my shirt slide against the Camaro. It had gotten to be a habit for me, not thinking about what the demon had planned. In the past I had never had time, I was just running from place to place. Azazel's meeting at the coffee shop took on a different light. He was driving me south. Herding *us* south. Because he wanted us there just as much as we wanted to be there.

Thanks to Jen, we all saw it now. The thought I had missed at the gas station resurfaced. This time I snagged it. Grafton had been the demon's trap from the very beginning, and I had missed it because I had been worried about Jen. Now Azazel used the same play from the same play-book. I had been worried about my friends, when I should have been wondering what waited for us in New Orleans, because it was a trap for us as well.

And I had almost fallen for it. I had fallen for it, except for Jen.

"Wow," I said.

"So he wants Sarah and the Key there," Johnny said. "Whatever for?"

Jen held up her hand, half-open, forefinger pointing up. "That's still the smaller picture," she said.

I cocked my head at Jen. What could be larger than what she had just put out there? "It is?"

"Gus, what if this all had been planned from the very beginning?" she asked me.

"But that's what we're talking about now, right?" I said. "Raphael and the factory. The drugs, Sarah's tattoo. Azazel bringing me back to Grafton."

The demon had told me as much, in the cell. *Sometimes it's about the appreciation for the thing.*

Jen shook her head now. As if we were both looking at a jigsaw puzzle that was almost complete, just one empty hole in its center, and I held a Grimm-shaped piece of the cardboard riddle. "Gus, what if Azazel has been steering you for a lot longer than that? What if *he's* the reason you found the Key in the first place?"

I froze. As big as Jen's first revelation had been, this was much bigger. Maybe too big for me to really comprehend. Azazel would have been hunting the previous Keeper. That man had been killed the same night my regiment had, when a mortar collapsed part of the buildings we all had taken shelter in. Could the demon have directed all of that?

Then there were the years of being chased. The times that I barely escaped with my life, had that just been Azazel slowing down, just enough for me to get away?

Then there were days at a time that the demon had been gone. Disappeared. I could never predict when, but had Azazel been back in Grafton during those times, playing Cole? Setting all this up?

All of it was too big for me to swallow in one bite. But it rang true. Jen had figured this out. But why would he want each of us in New Orleans? The Key. Sarah. And me. Seven of us in the beginning, my mother had said, that could do things like us. And there were seven demons trapped in a Key.

That seemed too much like an eye for an eye to just ignore.

My mother had carved a sketch in the floor of my jail cell, just a few days ago. A staff, a shield, and a feather on the floor of the jail cell. Symbols of who we had been. Who we had come from.

I still shook my head. "I can't believe it, Jen."

"Can't believe it?" Jen said. "Or won't?"

I was no angel. No superhero. I kept shaking my head. "Won't."

"Gus." Jen grabbed my arm, softly. She pulled just a little on my sleeve and pleaded, quietly, "You have to face this."

"No," I said, and pushed her hand away. "No."

"Hey," Nick said. His voice was loud in my ears for some reason. "What's the deal?"

"We have to figure this out if we're going to overcome whatever Azazel has planned. If we're going to beat him at his game." Jen's eyes met mine, trying to connect with me. "We need to know everything. About everyone."

"I believe what you are saying, Jen," I said. I ignored Nick. "Azazel wants us all in New Orleans, for some reason. The Key. Sarah. Maybe even me."

"But you won't take it a step further?" Jen asked me.

"I won't," I said. I had seen a lot of evil in this world. I had seen demons and monsters and dead babies and dead mothers. I had lived murderous ghost memory after murderous ghost memory. What force of good did that? Why would angels have that power?

The entire time I had been out in the world, running from demons, all I had seen was pain and death. I had walked battlefields and seen a soldier's head get shot off because he had stopped to try to pull along another injured buddy. I had walked through places where mothers held their babies to their chest long after the babies had passed away.

A person can only see so much of that stuff before he starts to question. The life I had lived, I had seen nothing show up and stand against what was happening. No force had protected that soldier, who had only wanted to save a brother. No force had come down and provided medicine to the little kids who had needed it.

And I had come to believe that force didn't really exist. There was good and evil, and that dichotomy didn't just exist in humans. It was everywhere. Even vampires had people like Gabrielle, who believed she could live a good life, even when I had thought her a monster when we first met.

So where was that force? The counter to the demons and creatures from hell? Where were the bright rays shooting down from the heavens, illuminating the radiant angel with a righteous sword?

I hadn't seen any. They didn't exist. And if they didn't exist, if nothing stopped all the evil I had seen, then that led me to believe nothing else existed, *up there*. All I had found was the occasional human, here and there, trying to do something to help. People like Miss Tammie. Like Greg. Like Father Benjamin.

Not me. I had run from a lot of places where bad people had done bad things to good people. Just a few days ago Greg had asked me for help, and I had turned him down. But he had helped me, when I needed it, and it had cost his life.

Jen let out a breath then, a deep sigh. Like she had held on to a hope for too long. This, *this*, was what she had been trying to find a way to say. A way to convince me of something she believed. She muttered something to herself. Maybe something like *baby steps*.

"You guys going to clue us in?" Johnny said.

Jen kept looking at me, as if she could get me to believe by the power of her gaze. Her blue eyes were open and soft and carried a little shimmer in them, like the sun had flashed over the surface of the water off a Caribbean island.

I got up and walked out of the barn. I need to get away. After I got a few steps away, Jen began speaking to the others, in a low tone. Explaining her thoughts.

Outside, the sun had set over the horizon. It had left dusk in its wake. It was light enough the stars had not yet come out. The sky was a dark purplish gray spreading from west to east. The moon hid there, behind a low-hanging cloud bank, like a spotlight under a thick cover.

I walked down the dirt road a bit. The high sides of the overgrown fields to either side herded me toward the highway. The air was cool and carried the flowery hint of pollen I always found in the south, no matter the season.

I got to the highway. A few trees stood in a field across the road. Three large maple trees, three-fingered leaves painted in oranges and yellows I could barely see in the last of the day's light. The field was overgrown. I had to break a path through, though I found a large flat area underneath the maples when I got to them. I picked one facing the barn, sat, and placed my back against the trunk. It felt sturdy behind me.

And then I thought about what Jen had said.

She had concluded a lot of things that felt right. But she also wanted me to believe I was an angel. I barked out a laugh, and the hard echo of it came back to me from the fields.

Still, it was what my mother had tried to tell me, back in the jail cell in Grafton. She just couldn't use the word, and had to resort to the sketch. If I put all the hints she had given me together correctly, then seven angels had been put under the geas thousands of years ago. My mother and I were what was left of those seven. Plus a father I had never met. All of us still under the spell, today.

What seven angels could be trapped so, back then? How had that happened, and why? Who had they been? Had they really been angels, or just seven people with incredible powers?

I tended to believe the latter. In my life, no other power had shown up and provided me a greater understanding. Truths tended to exist in actions, not words or thoughts or beliefs.

Jen wanted me to be an angel. I snorted. She saw me in a light I didn't see myself in. Just a week ago I was ready to find Jen and get her out of Grafton. Not any of my other friends. There were times I would help someone who needed it, but usually only when it didn't inconvenience me. Although, by inconvenience, I meant Azazel.

A memory from last week came back then, haunting me. Raphael and me on the hill above Grafton, Raphael giving me his deal. Then the vampire had shown me Sarah, being held in the backseat of his car.

Sarah had held back tears in the few short words she spoke to me. She had already given up on herself, and had wanted me to rescue Jen and get out of town. And that was exactly what I had been planning to do. I hadn't thought about Nick or Johnny or Sarah. Miss Tammie or Parker or anyone else. In that moment, right before the passenger window had slid up between Sarah and me, all I had wanted to do was find Jen and get her safe.

The mirrored glass had reflected a man back at me. A man who had to look away from his own reflection. A man who had found himself suddenly ashamed of what he was thinking.

I tightened my jaw, feeling my teeth on that side press hard against each other. I was still ashamed of that moment today. I was trying hard to change, to protect my friends, to put them first. Even now my subconscious screamed to me to stay on the move. To keep running. My eyes followed the highway west, until the road disappeared in the darkness.

I didn't just want to stay on the move to protect my friends. A small part of me wanted to move and *get away* from my friends. If I left them, I could put them in a part of my brain that would forget about them. Like I had done for years before Grafton. What was the saying? *Out of sight, out of mind?*

That small part of me would be thrilled to go back to a life of running day after day. It didn't want to worry about anyone else. It would be happy not knowing what happened to them. That small part of my brain told me my friends would be safer without me. It would whisper the world was more important, and the Key was more important, and I needed to go after it and keep my friends safe in the rearview mirror.

Saving Jen had changed me. I couldn't pinpoint the exact moment when, or where. But doing something small, for one person, had altered my course. A larger part of my brain had opened, a place that had been closed for a long time.

And once it had opened, other little changes had flooded through me. I hadn't wanted to help anymore, before I had rescued Jen. Greg had asked me for help, and I had told him I was too busy. At the time, I had thought I had my own worries.

After I had rescued Jen, I had freed the witches. And right after the factory in Grafton, I remembered how bad I had felt that I had let Nick down. That I hadn't found Sarah, and that I had killed the man who could have helped her with her curse. And I had promised him and Jen we would all go after her sister.

Each change in me had triggered another. Cole had killed Miss Tammie and Parker. In the past, that would have sent me running. Instead, standing in front of the burning diner, I had planned revenge. I had stood up to Raphael and taken him and his vampire army down. Over the course of one night, I had transformed from a runner to an avenger.

And I had done more good in Grafton than I had in ten years of running. Even if people, like Mrs. Cooper and Miss Tammie and Parker, had been killed because of something I was involved in. I regretted their deaths, all of them, but I also felt good that I had done something about them, and that little bit of good had taken the edge off the pain.

Maybe the good a person did didn't have to be world-saving in scope for it to be world-saving in effect. Maybe it just needed to be a small act, and that act would start another, until there was a string of acts all snow-balled together that could really, truly, change the world.

Rescuing Jen had been the first snowball for me.

I faced the barn from where I sat. Inside the open doors the soft white light of the lamp outlined the side of the Camaro. A moment later a figure blocked the light for a moment, then headed down the road, toward me.

Jen.

She strode down the road and across the highway. She stepped hesitantly across the highway and found the path I had broken in earlier. She stepped here and there across the field until she stood before me under the tree. Her hands were tucked in her pockets, and her blond hair reflected what little moonlight broke through the clouds.

A moment or two passed. The silence was filled with the chirping of crickets. The wind picked up and the tree limb shivered above me.

"Hey," she said.

"Hey." I tried to smile, but it felt broken on my face. Fake.

Another long moment.

"You remember when we first met?" she asked.

It had been in middle school. I remembered the principal introducing her to the class. *A girl, with straw-colored hair and the serious, studious face of a person searching specifically for one thing. She was tall, with a long blond braid stretching down her back.*

"Yeah," I said.

"Did I ever tell you what I thought then?"

"Was it something like 'wow, who is this dork?'" I asked.

The joke was bad. Jen still smiled, though she didn't move away from where she stood. She stayed right in front of me. I didn't look away.

"You gave this smile when I walked in," she said. "It caught me."

I didn't remember smiling at her. It wasn't something I normally did. I was surprised that I had then. The best I did in pictures was twist a corner of my lips in something like a cocky grin.

"It was shy, and it was bold," she continued. "It was all I needed to see. I knew everything about you, right in that moment."

"From a smile," I said. I sounded like I didn't believe her.

"Yeah," she said. She finally sat down next to me, and she was careful not to move too much. Our shoulders lightly touched, and the outside of our arms rested against each other. "Everything I thought proved true. Back then, you didn't care what other people thought about you. Every moment of every day, you always did what you thought was right. All the time. You looked out for us, you made sure we all were okay. Safe. You stood up to anyone and everyone. Parker, other kids at school, the sheriff …"

I remembered the sheriff. Rand and Darian, two of Raphael's cronies, had picked on Danny too much during a ball game. I had met them after the game behind the dugout, and I left them both there with a reminder to leave Danny alone. Word got back to the sheriff, and the old man had stopped by the diner a day later to lecture us.

I still had a black eye that day, and a split lip. Johnny had joked that it made me look more like my name. Miss Tammie had lectured me about it, but she had still brought a plate of food to the table.

The sheriff had walked in and pulled a chair over. He turned it backward, sat on it, and faced us. One hand kept touching the front of his hat as he lectured us about doing things in the right manner.

I had told him I hadn't started the fight, but I had made sure I finished it.

"The sheriff said," I remembered, "you don't need to finish things if those things are never started."

Jen placed a hand on mine. "And then you corrected him. You told him, 'Things wouldn't need to be finished if you would make sure those things never started.'"

We were both quiet then, remembering that day. The sheriff had hemmed and hawed and said it was always better to let grown-ups handle these things.

"I remember seeing you that day, Gus," Jen said, "with a black eye and a fat lip, staring up at this older man, the sheriff of the town, and he was the guy who backed down. As if you were going to be this man who made sure things never got started."

There was a long, peaceful moment between us, filled with a background of crickets and the rustling of leaves. Jen's hand was warm, on top of mine. We both were careful to leave it at just that slight touch.

"I'm a long way from that now, Jen." My voice was thick.

"I know you think so, Gus," Jen said.

"Would an angel have run from Danny?" I asked. "Would he have run and hid and left all you guys to fend for yourselves?"

"If Danny were here now," she argued, softly, "what would he tell you?"

Her hand squeezed the top of mine, gently. I was quiet some more. Danny's ghost had appeared over me, in Grafton. Raphael had broken my head open with a bat, and I had been dying. Danny had hugged me and had given me everything he had, all the power he had been connected to. He had allowed me to live his memories, and he had shown me how happy he had been, with me. With *us*. That happiness had blended into forgiveness, and understanding. And to some degree, acceptance.

It had been different than every other spirit I had ever pulled from. And I had become something greater, after the exchange. Danny had been a part of me that I had shut off for a long time. It had been good to get that part back.

I still missed him.

"I don't know what Danny would say," I said. Jen looked at me with her head cocked, like she sensed the half-truth. "But I can't be an angel. My past is full of bad things, Jen. I haven't always done the right thing."

"Is that what an angel is?" Jen asked. "I don't know anyone who's seen one. They haven't been around in a long time. Maybe an angel is someone who always gets back up, no matter how many punches they take, and keeps swinging."

She did know how to put words in a way I would accept them. I sighed, and the back of my head pressed against the trunk of the tree, the bark cool, smooth, and hard.

"What are you really afraid of?" Jen asked. "Why are you pushing so hard against this, Gus?"

I glanced at her, then stared deep into the night. The sky had darkened to a blue-black in the west, and a few stars had come out, one at a time, here and there. The moon still hid among the clouds in the east, a glowing masked ball of white-gray. Between the few stars in the west and the moon in the east, there was nothing but big, empty space.

It would likely always be empty. If there was a higher power, how could he have let what happened in this world continue to happen? Danny. Miss Tammie. Parker and Greg. Father Benjamin. All the witches Raphael had killed to make his drug. Azazel and everything he had done for the past few thousand years. The van with the bumper sticker, back at the rest stop, a tiny face pressed up against the window.

No one, and nothing, had shown up with enough power to match Azazel. Except for me. And if I was the best that heaven could come up with against Azazel and his demons, what did that really say about what existed above?

It made me angry, if I was the best heaven could produce against what happened down here, on earth. And it made me furious, if there was something better up there that could help, and chose not to. It was easier to not believe in any of it. No matter how Jen tried to convince me.

"Ah," Jen said.

We stayed there awhile. Neither of us spoke. After a bit I switched the positions of our hands, pulling mine out from under hers and placing it on top. Each finger of mine lay between hers, each digit fit snugly, comfortable, like pieces of a jigsaw puzzle fastened together.

CHAPTER SEVENTEEN

J en and I got up and walked back, still quiet. She was letting me process what she had said. She knew how thick my head could be.

Back in the barn Sarah was curled up in a sleeping bag, on her side, one finger scrolling down the second phone we had bought. Johnny was doing the same thing on the other phone. Nick was digging around the trunk of the car, placing one of the plastic gas cans in the back of the Camaro, holding a bunch of knives in his other hand.

These were my friends. Five of us who somehow, back in a small town in the middle of nowhere, had formed bonds strong enough to stay, even after I had abandoned them. Stronger than anything Raphael could break. Or an army of vampires.

We had been people who had once played hooky and stayed out all night at Partisan Rock, toasting marshmallows on sticks around a camp-fire. Burning a couple, occasionally, and laughing when Johnny had tried to pull a group of them off his stick and had ended up with a gooey hand of burned marshmallow and charred sticks.

Now we were all that stood between some demons and whatever Azazel had planned in New Orleans. Just five friends. Lives that could be snuffed out, quick.

If I was a real angel, I would do anything to protect them.

But if I was a real angel, would I have the power to protect them? Would that even be enough? What good was I, if I couldn't bring the full power of the heavens down on Azazel and Kimaris and the rest of the evil in the world?

It felt like too much.

I had stopped walking. Jen had taken a step or two past me before turning back. The rest of my friends had paused what they were doing and looked at us. I looked anywhere but at them.

Nick shut the trunk of the Camaro. The *thunk* broke the silence. He walked over and put his free hand on my shoulder, patting it once or twice. I didn't see the wire-frame glasses on his face anymore. Or the kid he had been. He had always followed me around in Grafton, from Parker's, from school. Always looked to me before deciding what to do. Had been someone who looked before he leaped.

He was a dangerous man now. More so with Sarah around, maybe. She herself stood behind Nick, pale in the lamplight, face sad. The two of them were a pair. Her with her curse. Nick tortured as well.

I knew he chased something he might never truly get. But he was dedicated to the effort. To the extreme. Could I be any less, for those I cared about?

I nodded at him. An acknowledgment between us.

Nick grinned. His teeth were white and straight. His face was sharp and angled, and his cheekbones stood out prominently under his eyes. He handed me a decent-size knife in a sheath.

"We all carry one now," he said.

I took the knife. It was a small thing with a white bone handle. An inscription along the handle told me it was made of silver. The sheath was thin, hard leather, and would hang horizontally on the back of my belt.

I put the sheath on. My shirt hung over it well enough. Nick went around and handed a knife to each of us. Some of them were folding knives, easy to put in a front pocket.

Jen went back to where we had started, sitting back against the Camaro. I took a seat next to her. She had a bottle of water from earlier still there, and I opened the bottle and sipped it. The water was clean, but tepid on my tongue.

"What have you guys figured out so far?" Jen asked.

Johnny waved his hand, like he was a student in class. He had pulled up Solomon's Key on the internet. He laughed and told us all the first hit he got was a video game, back in the eighties.

He had found quite a lot of information. Some of it I knew; a lot of it I didn't. The Key of Solomon was apparently a grimoire, a book of spells, speaking of how to conjure and control seventy-two demons. Which was an oddly specific number.

"Here's the thing," he said. "There's a Greater and a Lesser Grimoire. Both books apparently deal with how to perform the rituals, what to wear and say and what each demon does. The Greater is supposed to be older. The Lesser Key came around thousands of years later.

"Keep in mind, this is just me guessing," he said. "But to me – both Keys could be the same book, right?"

That piqued Jen's interest. I was curious as well. "What do you mean?"

"Well, like the Bible," Johnny said. "It's been around forever. It's been translated by different people over thousands of years. There's an argument that some books have been removed, and others put in. And whatever we read, it's a translation of a translation of a story that once began as word of mouth, right?"

There was the game where one person whispers a message into the ear of another person, and that person repeats that message to another, all the way down a line of people. The message never came out the same, when the last person spoke it aloud. The Bible in my glove box was the King James Version. I wondered what number of translations it was.

"And I'm not trying to say the Bible isn't, well, isn't *The Bible*," Johnny said. "I'm just saying it's been around for so long, translated so many times, who's to say what the original, complete work really is?"

"So," I said, "you think the Keys are one book?"

"Exactly," he said. "I mean, this is me surfing the internet. Not some Rhodes scholar. But what if they were the same book? And maybe the Lesser Key is both books together, with all the descriptions and spells and rituals about demons. That would mean the Greater Key could be something that *actually held the demons*."

"Wow." I pulled back a little at the realization. "So the Key I carried might be the Greater Key."

"Exactly," Johnny said.

It made a crazy kind of sense. The kind conspiracy theorists stay up late arguing. But it also held a note of truth. Why create a book about summoning and controlling demons, unless you had something in hand that needed such control?

"We need to find those books," Jen said.

"I'm way ahead of you." He held up his phone. "They've got an app that I can download a copy from. But I need a credit card to pay for it. Or a code for gift card. Which I also need a credit card to purchase."

Which none of us had on us. We had left Grafton with the Camaro and the shirts on our backs.

"Good work, Johnny," Jen said. "It's more than we knew."

"We can get a gift card, the next town we pull into," I said.

"I need something to write in as well," Johnny said. "It kind of sucks flipping from the internet and writing notes into this little notepad, then flipping back."

I raised my eyebrows. "A notebook? Maybe you *are* a Rhodes scholar."

There was a little laughter at that. I went back and got some more food from the car, and the other sleeping bag, laying it over Jen and us. The temperature had kept dropping outside, and the barn doors were, well, missing.

"Sarah," Jen said. "Your turn."

Sarah had researched New Orleans. Quite a number of books had been written about it, and thousands of different pages existed on the internet. Movies and television shows and books all had described the city s a haven for vampires, witches, and the undead. Voodoo was prevalent there, which Jen let me know was just a different kind of witch.

There had been a lot of death over the past couple of hundred years, especially for a major city. The amount of death was unique in application and wide in scope. The city had a history unlike any other place in the country. It seemed like the town would be a haven for Azazel.

And it also made sense that the one man who could perform the exorcism we needed would be in New Orleans. The city had a history of dead. Of evil. The sheer number of bodies that rested there was overwhelming. Thousands of people had been killed during the last hurricane there. Many of those bodies had never been found. And that short period of time may have been the least deadly in the city's history.

New Orleans had a nickname. It was called the City of the Dead. Sarah explained it to us, how that name came about.

"It started with yellow fever, back in the early eighteen hundreds." Her voice, always soft and airy, had taken on a serious tone. "Thousands of people died every year from it, for almost a hundred years."

Maybe a couple of hundred thousand dead, from yellow fever, over the centuries. Sarah described the symptoms. It was a gruesome death. People bled from their eyes and ears and mouth, from their toes, until they finally vomited blood and died.

Sarah stopped reading, and we all sat there. I wiggled my toes and wondered what I would think, what would I *do*, if I was sick enough that I was bleeding from them. How would I feel, walking around in a city where it was common for thousands of people to die that way, every year, for a hundred years?

"I think that happened to me once," Johnny joked. "After eating something Nick had made. He called it ..." Johnny put up air quotes here, and lowered his voice dramatically. "Shepherd's pie."

It was weak, but we all chuckled a little. Nick even had a slight smile. Maybe in a memory. Johnny waggled his eyebrows back and mimed sticking his finger in his throat.

The number of dead bodies in New Orleans had to be beyond what anyone could count. The number of ghosts there would be unlike anything I had seen before. Not to mention, ghosts as a whole lately had become more evil. More *wrong*. They fought me now. It wasn't going to be a City of the Dead so much as a City of Ghosts. All working against me.

I wasn't sure I was going to like this city. "Not much of a plan," I said.

"There's a purpose to the Key, I'm sure of it," Jen said. "A reason those exact demons are the ones imprisoned."

I had never thought of that before. All those years carrying the Key. It hadn't mattered to me back then what demons were imprisoned, it had only mattered that there was a demon chasing me to free them. In my mind the demons must have just been the seven worst demons at the time. And I had been worried enough about that, but if there was a reason for those seven, it spoke of a plan far larger in scope than anything we could know.

"All we're doing is guessing, though," Johnny said. "At best. Off of something on the internet."

"That's all we're going to have to go on," Nick said. He and Jen exchanged a look. The two of them had worked together, the past few years in Grafton. And he maybe understood how she worked.

"To be honest," I said, "it's the most I think I've known about anything Azazel has going on."

I gripped Jen's hand under the sleeping bag. Silently thanking her for seeing something I hadn't seen. Even if part of it was something I still was unable to conceive.

"We just keep digging," Jen said. Her grip briefly tightened over mine, then relaxed. "Keep putting it all together. Even when we guess, we're going to get some of it right. And the more right we get, the better."

She looked at me and smiled. It made me think of the smile I had first apparently given her. "It all has to start somewhere," she said.

The group of us made a little small talk for a while. Then went to sleep, one after the next. We zipped both sleeping bags together, like one giant sleeping bag, and laid it on the barn floor beside the Camaro. Then we crawled into it, like the five of us were kids, packed tightly together on some camping trip. Johnny turned off the lamp. Immediately darkness swept over us, followed by the chirping of crickets, somehow louder now that it was dark.

Over a period of time our eyes adjusted to the slow exposure of moonlight drifting down into the barn. We were all safe, together under the sleeping bags. Like back when we were kids, hiding in a poorly constructed blanket fort, tucked away from the monsters of the night. The five of us moved around, trying to find a comfortable spot, and joked and laughed as elbows connected with ribs and feet kicked each other.

Johnny started to snore. Someone poked him a few times. It was quiet for a bit. I laughed quietly after finding myself trying to race his snoring to sleep.

I didn't quite make it. It took some time to settle down. My arm lay on something sharp and edgy, and I lay there for a long time before deciding to move again. A little bit later Jen twisted a bit, and I had to carefully adjust where her knee had moved to, and let out a sigh of relief that she hadn't jerked. Then I noticed her eyes were open. She watched me with a knowing smile, and arched an eyebrow ever so delicately.

A laugh burst out of me before I had a chance to hold it back. And once I started laughing I couldn't stop. Jen joined in, and both of us had tears rolling out of our eyes. The laughing woke the others up and they joined without understanding why.

Somehow we all finally fell asleep. Together.

CHAPTER EIGHTEEN

I woke early the next day. Dusk still held on to the morning, though a yellow tinge of sunlight broke across the sky to the east. A rooster crowed somewhere, though I hadn't seen chickens or a henhouse anywhere nearby.

Nick was missing from the bag, but the others were still asleep. I was quiet enough to not wake the rest as I got up. I carefully walked around to the side of the Camaro, reaching in through the open window and pulling the Bible out of the glove box.

It was the King James Version. The Bible was light with a worn red cover. Each page was thin, and the words were dark enough that when I held one page separate the words on the back of the page blurred through the words in the front.

I didn't know what I was looking for, but I carried the book outside. I found Nick there, leaning against the side of the barn, watching the sun rise. He was dressed in his vest getup, the one holding a bunch of his knives, and his wire-frame glasses were dark, tinted with the shadow he stood in.

"I don't sleep much," he explained, to my unasked question.

"Especially packed together in a sleeping bag?"

"Yeah." He smiled a little. "Maybe especially then."

He pulled himself off the side of the barn. "Let me show you something."

He took me around the back of the barn. The sun had crested the horizon, and the shadows across the building were edged with a golden glow. There was a hard dirt path around the barn, even though the fields had grown close to the building, as if enough people and animals had walked it enough over the years they had pounded it in.

Birds twittered around us. The dirt path widened into a large round patch at the back of the barn. The doors were shut, but at one point animals had been kept here. Dark wooden posts and parts of a broken-down fence stood out around them. Brown timbers leaned from tilted posts and disappeared deep into the weeds.

In the center of the patch was a dark spot. Roughly human shaped at the edges. Like someone had lain down and traced themselves in a black ash.

"Probably burned up when the sun rose," Nick said.

A vampire.

"I think it came for Sarah," Nick said. "It was feral, like a dog."

"You found it?"

"I killed it," Nick said. He shrugged at my unasked question. "I don't sleep much."

I remembered back in the church at Grafton, Nick had been the one watching the cops come up the drive. Up in the belfry, while I had slept in the classroom below. But he had slept in the car for a bit, after we had found the help for Sarah. So he had a limit.

So a vampire had been out here, in the middle of the country. Not part of a clan or a family. It had sensed Sarah's curse and come after her, and Nick had killed it while we all slept.

"Damn," I said.

"Yeah," Nick said. "The curse is stronger."

I swore softly. I hadn't even looked for ghosts last night, a mistake I hadn't made in years. It was something I did on autopilot. The slip frightened me and I immediately searched for a spirit. Whether it was because it was daytime and the ghosts were harder to find, or there were just none around, I couldn't sense any ghost close to us.

Nick looked at my hand, where I still held the Bible. "Can I tell you something?"

"Sure."

"I used to go to church, back in Grafton," he said. "Once I found out what my powers were, I thought it was some dark thing. Something evil. I wanted to fight it."

Nick's cheeks turned a little red, and he rubbed the back of his neck. "This was a few years after you had left. I was lying in bed, at Parker's, and thinking of Sarah. And then I was just there, like I had blinked in one place and opened my eyes in another."

"Is that why you and Sarah … ?" I asked Nick. Sarah had always made sure to keep Nick as a friend. Even now. "Did she see you?"

"No." He barked a laugh. "No, she was sleeping. She and I … she's just never seen me the way I see her."

I didn't know what to say. Nick's eyes returned to the Bible I held in my hands. "So anyway, after that, I wondered what kind of person would have a power like that. It couldn't be a good thing, right? It was something born of darkness."

He swallowed. "So I went to church a bit. Talked to Father Benjamin. Read the Bible like a thousand times. Found every passage that spoke about shadows and memorized it. I wanted to find one that explained me, that told me I was okay. That I wasn't evil."

"What's the one everyone says?" I asked. "I walk in the valley of the shadow of death, but I fear no evil? Something like that."

"Something like that," he said. "That's the one everyone knows. The first one Father Benjamin told me about. And of course it was the first one I thought about. Wasn't what I was doing walking through a shadow of death? And if that wasn't evil, what was?"

Nick continued. "So over time I talked to Father Benjamin about darkness, and walking in the shadow. I never told him what I could do, because I feared it. It was something evil. I feared what he would tell me.

"Then the vampires first started taking over the town," Nick continued. "I wanted to do something. Raphael got worse and worse. Sarah started dating him. Father Benjamin and I began to argue. To me, he represented God, right? He should be doing something, protecting the thralls, killing vampires.

"He kept telling me to be patient," Nick said. His voice trembled a little, with old anger. "That he was here to protect what he could. And I thought he should be trying to protect them all."

"At one time, he was someone who had done that," I said. Thinking of the priest's spirit, on one knee back in the parking lot, an ethereal sword plunged into the ground, a golden glow around it.

"I know that now." Nick's lips twisted in a grimace. "But then I didn't understand. I thought he was wrong. He wasn't doing enough to help people, at least that's what I thought then. Here I was, watching people turn into thralls, into vampires. And the priest of the town was doing nothing.

"Then I found a passage," Nick said. His voice took on the tone all voices did when reciting something religious, a little monotone, a little inflection on the more powerful words in the scripture. *"Let him who walks in darkness and has no light trust in the name of the Lord and rely on his God."*

I grunted. That sounded like Nick, except for the trust and rely thing.

"It hit me then. I had been searching this book for something to tell me I was virtuous, that what I did wasn't evil." Nick shook his head. "But who I was was *who I was.* I was just looking for a passage somewhere, or a person somewhere, to tell me what I already knew.

"All I needed to do was trust in myself. Be the person I wanted to be. Stop looking for something to tell me who I was, and just go be that person."

"Huh," I said. My gaze drifted from the Bible to Nick. I would never have guessed anything about Nick, anything of what he had just told me. "You know, that's the most I think you've ever said to me."

Nick laughed, and it surprised me. It was a quiet thing, a murmur of a chuckle, but his eyes lit up and the smile he gave me was real. He clapped me on the shoulder. "Maybe. I don't like talking much, anymore."

He let go of my shoulder and tapped the Bible with a finger from the same hand. "But what I wanted you to know is I get it. You're going to search that thing and try to figure out what you are. Why you are that way."

"It was a thought," I admitted.

"You can find anything you want in that thing," Nick said. "It'll tell you anything you look for, if you want it hard enough." Then he paused. "So I think maybe what matters first is figure out who you want to be. Then go be it. Then, if you have to, come back to this."

I remembered how the thin pages of the Bible had blurred all the words together, under the light. What Nick had gone through was eerily similar to what I was thinking. And he had done it all alone, with no one to talk to about it.

"Let me ask you," I said. "Aren't you worried that you *have* to do the things you are doing? That all this evil in the world exists in the first place?"

I still wondered what it could mean. Azazel running free. Kimaris killing hundreds at the rest stop. Vampires and demons and wights and everything else in the world. Greg and Father Benjamin and Greg's partner dead. The young priest in Lewiston, hiding Marcus behind his robes.

Nick snorted. "You're not listening. The first thing I did was look for something like that. *Trust in the Lord*, right? Look for a greater purpose, try to find out why some righteous angel hadn't come down from heaven to smite Raphael. It's what Father Benjamin and I argued about the most.

"What I'm trying to tell you is that is in the end, none of that really mattered." Nick looked at me. "So nothing showed here. Maybe nothing's even up there. Maybe it's all a lie. Who the fuck cares? What matters is what we choose to do. What *I* choose to do."

What Jen wanted me to believe … that was too big for me. Nick was telling me that maybe the answer didn't have to be something that great. Maybe it was enough to just be what you wanted to be.

Nick was telling me he had found his purpose. And he hadn't found it in a book. He had found it in his friends. Helping them. Sticking around for Sarah, when she needed it. Even if she hadn't wanted him, like he wanted her. Doing the little things that had needed done. And that – for him – had been enough.

I didn't know if I had a purpose. Part of me felt like I did. Part of me needed the reason for my existence. For why I could see ghosts. *Use* them. A grand design, for what had happened to me, what was continuing to happen to me, and to those I cared about.

Maybe that reason would come, with time. Maybe trying to hit the home run every time I stepped up to the plate wasn't going to win me the game. Nick's way, there felt like there was something to it. The small things. Getting on base. Moving to the next. A bunch of singles could run up the score just as well as a grand slam.

Being with my friends felt good. Protecting them felt right. Making sure we were safe, we all could make it, that should be enough for me. At least for right now. Those little things could snowball into bigger things, like purpose and direction, later.

I didn't have to be some force to be reckoned with. I wasn't some avenging angel, here to save the world. I wasn't the world's answer to Azazel

"Although, now that I think about it," Nick added, looking at me out of the side of his eyes and grinning a little grin. Like he was kidding me. "It didn't take too long for you to show up, when we needed you. And Raphael did kind of get smited."

We headed back inside the barn. The rest of the group was trying to wake up. Johnny had gotten out of the bag and was standing, stretching by the car. I walked over and put the Bible back in the glove box, then stood by him.

"Man, this sleeping on a barn floor is hell on my back." Johnny had one hand on the small of his own back, and twisted back and forth. "Was that Nick laughing out there?"

"Believe it or not, it was," I said.

"I always wondered what that sounded like." Johnny grinned. Nick rolled his eyes and popped the trunk of the Camaro.

Jen didn't want to get up. So I pulled her out of the sleeping bag, laughing. She let me drag her out, so that I held her in the air against me in a big hug, her body pressed against mine. Her heart thudding softly against my chest.

I was beginning to see she was a fan of sleeping in. "You want coffee, right?"

She pretended to keep her eyes closed. Her lips pressed against my neck, and she murmured against my skin, "Your forecast right now is showing a lot of thunderstorms. Cloudy with a chance of death by witch."

I laughed and set her down. Nick had grabbed the travel stuff out of the trunk and most of us did things like eat a snack, drink some water, brush our teeth with tiny little toothbrushes that folded up. Those that needed it found a place outside to use the bathroom.

Neither Nick nor I mentioned the vampire. I think we both realized it wouldn't do anything but worry the others. I resolved to keep a closer eye on things, the next place we stopped. I couldn't believe I hadn't looked for a ghost last night.

We packed up the car and got in. I got into the driver's seat and patted the steering wheel a few times. The others buckled up, and Jen got in next to me. She had an energy drink open in one hand and sipped it with a grimace.

"They're an acquired taste," I explained.

"I imagine they're acquired by people who forsake the finer things in life," Jen said.

I smiled at her and fired up the Camaro. The engine thundered loud inside the barn, and I smiled, imagining the ground trembling a little underneath.

I backed down the driveway and got back on the road, heading west. We rolled down the windows and enjoyed the cool autumn morning. The sky was open and empty, and the sun was just high enough to get into my eyes, every time I glanced at the rearview mirror.

Johnny and Sarah took turns keeping their phones charged. They both were doing some research. Johnny would pull up a demon's sigil from the internet, one of the seventy-two of them in the Lesser Key, and pass the phone to Jen. She would let me glance at it and see if it was something I recognized from the Key I had carried.

Some I recognized; most I hadn't. Johnny kept track in his phone. "I could use a book."

"Books, coffee, gift cards," I said, looking over the hundreds of trees we passed by. "Might be a little bit in coming."

Sarah had pulled up a map of the city of New Orleans. Saint Louis Cathedral was in the French Quarter there. We would be coming in from that direction, which made it easy. Convincing the bishop to help might be more difficult.

"We're going to have to find a way to talk to the bishop," Johnny said.

"Not a worry," Nick said. "If he sleeps in the dark, I can get to him."

"We don't want to scare him," Jen said. "We want him to help us."

Nick didn't answer, just sat there, lips pressed tightly together. All business. He had done his talking for the day. Maybe for the year.

And he was right, if worse came to worst, he would be able to at least talk to the bishop. And knowing Nick, he would probably be persuasive.

We headed south through Alabama. While we avoided the interstates as much as possible, there were some sections that we couldn't avoid taking, and we had planned our route accordingly. For now, though, we were still on a two-lane road heading south.

It was a few hours until the next town. We passed some small gas stations, and filled up at one. Jen walked out with a black coffee that looked like it had been made a few weeks before. Johnny picked up a tiny spiral notebook with a pen. None of the gas stations had a gift card, though one or two did have something they called Fuel Bucks.

We kept driving, most of us quiet. The steering wheel of the Camaro hummed under my palms, and I enjoyed the feel of my weight shifting as the car swung into a curve, the tiny ball hanging from the rearview mirror swaying with each turn. Johnny took notes. Nick just stared out the window. Jen sipped her coffee, occasionally with a frown. Then Sarah found something on her phone.

"Uh-oh," she said.

"What?" Jen asked.

"They've identified us," she said. She passed her phone up. Jen looked at it and cursed softly, under her breath, then showed me the screen. It was a news report, but I just focused on the picture. There had been a camera at the welcome center on one of the light poles, focused down the exit ramp, and there was a picture of us leaving the rest stop.

Jen read the article. "While the people in the car are not known to have been the cause of what happened at the welcome center, they are wanted for questioning in an incident where a small town was burned to the ground, so the public should act as if they are *armed and dangerous*."

"That doesn't sound good," I said.

"Well, the report isn't entirely inaccurate." Johnny waggled his eyebrows, the way he did when he made a joke. "We are both."

The rest stop still hung over us a little. Everyone there had died because we had been there. No one here felt comfortable about that. Or knew what to say. It was something I had thought about for many years and didn't know how to process still. No matter how hard I tried, people died. The best way to stop all the death would be to get to Azazel.

"How did Kimaris know we were going to be there?" Jen asked.

"I don't know," I said. "In the past, Azazel had always been able to find me, when I carried the Key. Now that he has it, he shouldn't be able to."

"It's a big rest stop," Johnny said. "And we had to go that way. Maybe the demon was waiting."

We couldn't avoid the interstate all the time. There were just places where back roads didn't connect, across mountains, or large empty areas here and there. It would just take too long to get to New Orleans.

In the middle of the state, there were two interstates, like a cross on the state. The one heading west slowly worked south on a straight shot to New Orleans. We were paralleling the longer route south, thinking Azazel might be looking for us on the long straight from Birmingham to New Orleans.

"We should change cars," Nick said.

My hands tightened on the steering wheel. The hard plastic resisted the press of my fingers. I wasn't ready to give the Camaro up. It had become a part of me.

"Maybe," I said. "Let's get as far as we can."

One thing about driving the back roads, they felt liberating in a way the interstates never had. When I was running from Azazel, the interstates had been my friend. They were a fast means to travel. I could roll from place to place, and stop only when I needed to. The interstates always stretched as far ahead of me as I could see, and they opened up the country to millions of road trips a year.

But I always felt freer on the single-lane roads, with the trees flashing to the left and right, the Camaro sinking and hugging the turns, flying down the straightaways. It was funny. The interstates were large. Straight. You could see all the way down them, to the horizon. But there was a freedom to the back roads, even though the road was only visible until the next curve.

We all enjoyed the ride. It was a warmer day than yesterday, the sky was blue and held no clouds, so the sun beat down through the rear window. I let my arm hang out the window and enjoyed the feel of the cool breeze along my skin. Occasionally I held my palm up and let the wind beat against it and push my arm around in the air.

Jen had her hair in a ponytail, and we had bought Sarah a ball cap at one of the gas stations. It was red with white, and had *Roll Tide* in cursive script across the brim. She hated it.

"Okay," Johnny said, loud over the open windows. He held his notebook in one hand, and the phone in the other. The wind fluttered the papers around over his hand. "Here's what I got."

We rolled the windows up and let him talk. We knew about Buné. The guy changed the place of the dead. Johnny started on the other sigils. "The names of the five we know the sigils for are Sabnock, Vine, Malphas and Malthas, and Kimaris."

"None of them mean anything to me," I said.

Johnny looked back at his notebook. "Basically your standard demons. They command many legions of demons, are royalty down there in hell, will turn on the conjurer if given the opportunity, yada, yada, yada."

"Yada, yada, yada?" I raised an eyebrow at the rearview mirror.

He waved a *whatever* motion with his hand. "Sabnock is your basic demon, I think. He's like the king of rot—he turns wounds gangrene, spreads sickness, that kind of thing. Malphas and Malthus might be brothers. Related in some way."

Weird, to think that demons could have brothers or sisters. That they had families as well. If what I knew was true, demons were fallen angels. If they could have siblings, could they have kids? Could there be a family tree of demons, and what would that look like?

"Finally, there's Vine. He seems like a standard demon, overthrows things, can create storms," Johnny said. I glanced over at Jen..

"Here's the weird thing. All four of those demons are kind of builders," Johnny said.

"Builders?" I asked. "What's that mean?"

"It just says builders," Johnny said. "Vine can build and take down towers. Sabnock is supposed to be able to build cities and strongholds. Malthus and Malphas as well." He shrugged, and then said the word again, like that would explain it all. "Builders."

"What could Azazel plan with that?" Jen asked.

"I don't know," I said. "I don't know that I've ever known what he plans. At least, not ahead of time."

"Could he be carving out a kingdom in hell?" Sarah mused.

If Lucifer existed, how would he take a few demons striking out on their own? I couldn't imagine that going over well. And Azazel wasn't the type to make a power play.

Johnny kept reading from his notebook. "There's more," he said. "They don't just build. Sabnock furnishes his cities with weapons, Malthus is like an arms dealer, and Malphus, he's someone that 'gathers artificers.'"

"Artificers?" Sarah asked. "Like the people who make jewelry? What would a demon need to craft?"

"I'm still trying to figure out the where part," Jen said. "If they are building, then where?"

"Maybe like a Sodom and Gomorrah thing, right?" Nick said. "Building cities of sin somewhere."

"Like Vegas?" Johnny asked.

"Maybe," I said. "Maybe the places they are building, maybe those places already exist." I had been to Chicago, where ambulances ran day and night with gunshot victims. I had heard surgeons tried everything they could to get their residencies there, because of all the "practice" in the city.

"It makes sense," Jen said. "New Orleans is the City of the Dead, right? Maybe it's a city of sin as well."

Nick's face was still, like he knew I wanted him to answer the question. Being the expert of our little group. "I just don't know," he finally said. "Could it be? I mean, there's an archdiocese there, and Saint Louis Cathedral. Would those things be in a Sodom or Gomorrah?"

"What an archdiocese?" I asked.

"It's like a big religious area," Nick said. "Or maybe it's the guy running it. I'm not sure."

"I don't get any of this, then," I said. What was Azazel's plan? What could he be planning? Builders. Demons that could create armies and weaponize them. "Maybe Sarah is right, and Azazel is making a play to take over hell."

We all were quiet then. It was a big enough play for the demon. It was grand, large, and might take thousands of years to pull off. But the way Azazel had spoken of Lucifer, I hadn't ever gotten the feeling that he wanted to overthrow him. Was that how I felt, though, or how Azazel *wanted* me to feel?

Demons lived in hell. When I shot them, I was pretty sure that's where they went. Maybe to recharge, maybe to take a break. Maybe to party. It wasn't like it was a place I could visit to see what actually went on.

Hell was hell, though. Maybe conditions down there were as advertised and Azazel wasn't a fan. Maybe it was just crowded, after thousands of years. Or maybe Azazel just wanted a place with a better view.

Johnny was thinking along the same lines, but headed to a different Johnny-type destination. He waggled his eyebrows. "Maybe they're building a casino down there. Grab some cable and internet. Put in a nice place to get some drinks. Get a little fancy."

None of us really laughed, though.

"You guys aren't the best crowd today," he said. "That joke kills in all the other cars being chased by demons I've been in."

Jen burst out a laugh then. It was loud and surprised me. I think it surprised her because she covered her mouth with her hand and kept laughing. And then we all joined in, big belly laughs that died into chuckles and snickers. All of us smiled, even Sarah, who wiped her eyes.

"I wish we knew the last symbol," Johnny said. "I get the feeling it might tie things together."

"Me too," I said. The Key had little concentric circles inside the stone, and I could rotate the circles into six distinct patterns, like a demonic stone version of a Rubik's Cube. But the seventh one had always eluded me. "What about Kimaris?"

"Kimaris is basically a badass." Johnny flipped a few pages back. "Warrior. Barbarian. His name comes from Cimmeria, it seems."

"That's a real place?" Nick asked. "Conan, in demon form?"

"Guy is pretty intelligent too," Johnny said. "He's kind of a professor of demons. It describes what we've seen. He can make people into Nephilim, into warriors of his own likeness."

We had all seen that back at the rest stop. The black tendrils ripping out, each person it touched swelling into a warrior.

"A guy who can create armies," Nick added.

"There is that." Johnny scribbled something down in his notebook.

"And Buné," Jen said, her eyes slightly closed in thought. "Demons who build cities, demons who build armies, and demons who outfit those armies. Buné doesn't fit in with those, does he? Changing the place of the dead?"

"It's weird," Johnny said. "Buné and Azazel don't get along, according to what I've been finding. There's a history there."

"Kimaris thought lightly of Buné," I said. "Almost mockingly so."

"There's no connection. He's not a builder, but he's in the Key."

"I don't know," I said. Azazel had a reason for everything, though. A purpose. There would be a reason Buné didn't like him, a reason Azazel had the demon inscribed on Sarah's back. Maybe even, like the geas, something Azazel would force the demon to do, or become. "Anything would just be a guess."

"I wish we knew that last demon's name," Jen said. "Maybe that's the demon that ties all this together."

"I wish something struck me," I said. There were a couple of the drawings that had looked familiar, but nothing that I could definitively identify. Making a bad guess might be worse than not knowing. I kind of felt like knowing the last demon's name, and having that be the last detail that pulled everything together, was something people saw in the movies. Not something that happened in real life. In my life.

"Maybe those books will help," Jen said.

"Next town, then," I said. We'd have to find a real store that sold gift cards for the online store that we could download the book from. I shook my head a little. Two stores for one book. "We'll find a place."

"I looked up Azazel too," Johnny said. "Know what his name means?"

I shook my head.

"Scapegoat," Johnny chuckled. "Imagine that."

Scapegoat. That rang true, in some form, to me. A demon who had chased the Key for thousands of years. The demon who had a purpose, and no one developed that kind of purpose, with that level of dedication, without some kind of scar. That was a fact I knew intimately.

There was something in those thoughts. I wished I could figure it out. Jen had known there would be a purpose to all the demons in the Key, and I think we all felt like that task was about to be fulfilled. So we drove along, knowing more now than we had, but no closer to solving the mystery.

CHAPTER NINETEEN

The sun caught up to us and rose overhead as I drove. It wasn't too much longer before we came to the outskirts of a town. We passed a gas station here and there, then a garage. Homes appeared on the road, first one, then a couple, then dozens.

The speed limit kept counting down, from fifty-five, to forty-five, to thirty. Johnny had given us his phone so we could watch for any police alerts, but there wasn't enough traffic around for me to feel comfortable about someone actually passing a cop and logging the sighting on the same app.

I searched for spirits. It was daylight, but I still found a couple. As always, they felt under the surface, as if they hid from the sun. But I made sure to keep a running awareness of them, driving through town. The vampire outline Nick had shown me had been warning enough. I wouldn't be caught unprepared again.

A few grocery stores passed, not chain stores, but little corner mom-and-pop things. The speed limit dipped to twenty-five. I had to stop, the Camaro sitting at a stoplight, in a row of cars waiting for the light to turn green. To the right of the road were a couple of signs with blue shields, arrows telling us the way to the interstate.

All of us were quiet, stealing furtive glances down each street. Inside every building. Looking for the police. We were all hyperaware of what could happen if we were found out. I didn't want to change cars, but Nick's idea wasn't a bad one. I patted the steering wheel, a little regretfully. We'd have to figure out a way to do it without stealing one.

"There," Jen said, pointing out a pharmacy down the road, at another stoplight. A green-and-white sign let us know the drugstore was part of a large chain, with a large *W* on the sign. "There should be gift cards there."

"And something to eat," Sarah mentioned. "I'm hungry."

"Bathrooms," Nick said.

There was a gas station next to the pharmacy. And a restaurant on the other side, also part of a chain, one of the all-you-can-eat places. A ghost, tucked in an alley behind a strip mall.

The fuel gauge read a half tank, but I might as well take advantage of the stop. "Let's make it quick. Go in and get what you need. I'll fill up the car."

Sarah stared wistfully at the restaurant. "The one thing about being vegetarian," she said, "their breakfast bars suck."

"Come to the dark side," Johnny said. "Maybe try being a candy-baratarian."

She just gave him a look. Nick chuckled to himself. I drove into the parking lot and dropped them off, asking Jen to get me an energy drink. She rolled her eyes at me and grinned.

I had to wait a moment for Nick to grab a jacket out of the trunk to cover his vest of knives. He was taking the rest stop seriously as well. Then I drove over to the gas pump, taking it slow over the speed bump between the lots. The Camaro rocked gently as we went up, and the engine whined as the car eased back down.

"Don't worry," I told the car. "You're not getting rid of me yet."

The gas pump was prepay. At times like this, not having any kind of credit card did feel like a hassle. Especially when I was in a hurry. Otherwise, I liked the freedom. Not having a card, or a phone, those things people could track you with.

I wondered about the phones we carried. Could Azazel be tracing those, as Cole? Could he find us that easily? I shook my head. The demon had no idea we carried any, and had no idea what the number was.

I went in and used the bathroom real quick. Then I paid for the gas. Johnny's mention of candy bars caused me to grab a few, and a cold energy drink, just in case Jen surprised me with something different. I figured it wouldn't be a bad thing to be prepared, to have a couple of drinks, just in case.

I walked to the Camaro and started to pump the gas. While I did I took a bite of the candy bar, something with peanuts and nougat and caramel, covered in milk chocolate. It said something on the wrapper about being satisfying, so I ate the second one too. I didn't want to be undersatisfied.

I stood at the gas pump. The doors of the pharmacy opened and closed and my friends walked out. All of them carrying plastic bags of something, with the white bag in Nick's hand stretching a bit. I waved at them until they saw me.

The tank filled up. I hung up the nozzle and tightened the gas cap until it clicked. I turned to watch them cross the parking lot. Jen saw me and pulled an energy drink from the bag, waving it at me. I laughed and watched them cross the parking lot.

Then they all stopped, at the same time. They all looked behind me. Jen's eyes opened wide.

I turned around.

A police car had pulled up at the pump next to me. It must have come around from the other direction. The cop got out of the driver's side and looked at me and inclined his head, as if saying hello. His partner was already headed in to the station.

The cop by the pump looked at the Camaro.

And then he looked back at me. His eyes opened, as if in realization.

I found the ghost in the alley and started pulling. I had to fight just to reach it, and I had to fight even harder to pull. A sense of young boys, naked and afraid, came through the ethereal tap and flooded my senses. There was a scent of some kind of cherry incense, and it felt like I was in a dark room, maybe on a bed.

Great. Another pedophile. At times like this, I missed the traveling salesman from a week ago. Give me just one unfaithful husband, or wife. Just one.

I still pulled, pushing the memory away. And even as I pulled, I jumped and slid over the hood of the Camaro. With every step I moved faster and became a blur. In four steps I was by the police car.

The cop had gotten one hand on his gun. The nine-millimeter was still in the holster. His hand moved in slow motion. I moved it away from his gun, then took it and tossed it back toward the Camaro. Then I swung the cop around, grabbing his handcuffs and locking his wrists behind his back.

"Who are you?" the cop breathed out, his face white and pressed against the roof of his car. "What are you?"

A shot rang into the air. I swiveled back to the gas station. The second officer stood at the doors there, gun in the air. He aimed the gun at me and screamed for me to get on the ground. He was young and his eyes were way too open. He shouted for me to get on the ground again, his face flush, veins popping out at his temples.

The old lady at the counter of the station was already on a phone. The cop kept shouting. Behind me was the Camaro, then behind it was my friends. I was afraid another shot might hit them, especially if I tried to move and the cop missed. So I hid behind the cop I had cuffed.

"Relax, Rogers," the first cop said. He was tense, but in control. "If he was going to kill us, he would have."

"I don't kill people," I said. And then thought that really wasn't true. I killed bad ones.

The second cop kept screaming for me to get on the ground. He circled around the back of the police car and kept his gun locked on me. I turned the first cop and stayed behind him. The first cop kept telling Rogers to relax, but Rogers was having none of it.

Then Rogers was standing by the trunk and pointing his gun down the length of the police car. He had screamed so much his voice was getting hoarse. I shook my head. "This guy is too wired."

The first cop grunted in response, but his voice was concerned. "Careful, Rogers. There's a gas tank right underneath us."

I didn't want anyone else to get shot. My friends had made it to the Camaro and were hiding on one side of it. I didn't think any of them could do anything. There were no shadows here, and Jen wouldn't want to throw lightning around here. Not with the gas tanks. Behind me was a large open parking lot, but there were a few strip stores at one end. People moving to and from the stores.

I hated to do this, but it was what I had to do.

I took the energy and hardened my skin.

Slick young wet skin sliding across me—

I pushed that memory away, and at the same time shoved the first cop hard to the ground.

Rogers opened fire. His gun was a nine-millimeter, like his partner's gun. Probably a Glock. So there were eighteen shots, and I was prepared to let all eighteen strike me.

The bullets registered as little stings as they hit, like a wasp, followed by a hard press, like someone had jammed their finger into my skin. I staggered back under the first couple of shots and braced myself, one leg behind me. Each of the bullets struck me and bounced off, deformed, *tinging* off the ground around us and *ticking* off the side of the cop car.

The connection the ghost had to the ethereal plane was small. Like the spirit had been there awhile and was already fading away. Not every ghost provided the same strong connection, and I could already feel the ethereal energy start to give, like a rubber band stretched out and about to break. All I could do was cross my face, not move, just stay in one place and take each of the bullets, so they wouldn't hurt anyone else.

A couple of bullets flattened against my forearms and dropped to the ground. I searched for another spirit, feeling this one give. With all the bullets hitting me, it was hard to focus and see if there was another ghost around. Especially in daylight, when spirits usually hid.

Then the rubber band snapped, and the ethereal energy was gone. The last bullet Rogers fired hit my shoulder and spun me around. A hot pain tore through my skin and blood splattered the side of the police car, and stumbled to the ground.

"Gus!" someone screamed. I tried to push myself off the ground, but my right arm wouldn't hold my weight. My ears felt like they had cotton in them, and I shook my head a few times.

Hands picked me up and straightened me against the car. Nick. I squeezed my eyes and opened them, trying to clear my vision. My legs wouldn't lock, and I needed help to stay standing. Jen appeared, pressing a wadded-up T-shirt against my shoulder.

"That's a lot of blood," Nick said.

Was he talking about me? Johnny stood behind Rogers, who was face-down on the ground. Johnny had the gun I had thrown in one hand. Sarah had taken Rogers's cuffs and locked his arms behind his back as well.

The first cop had half rolled over. He looked at me with narrowed eyes, like he was putting a few thoughts together. Counting the number of bullets fired. "How did he miss you?"

"He didn't." Jen looked at the first cop. "Now shut the hell up." Her eyebrows were bent across her eyes. She was furious. A low thunder rumbled overhead. Or maybe I was imagining that part.

"Hey," I said, looking at Jen. I smiled at her. Or thought I did. It was hard to tell; I was something nebulous, floating in the air, like a cloud.

"He's going into shock," Jen said.

Nick shook his head, worried. "We've got to go."

"Gus," Jen said, "what do you need?"

"Hey," I said to her. Waiting for her to say it back. I tried the smile again.

Jen slapped me. Hard. Her palm stung the side of my face and a whole new pain erupted from my shoulder.

"Hey!" I shouted, angry.

"Stay awake," Jen said. "Tell me what you need."

I stared back at her. For a moment I couldn't figure out what she was asking. The shirt Jen pressed against my shoulder slowly turned red as I thought about it. Then I got it.

"Ghost," I finally said, tongue thick in my mouth. I think it came out as *Goph*.

"Okay," Jen said. "Nick, get the car ready."

Nick fished out the keys from my pocket and ran over to the Camaro. Jen and Johnny helped me across and sat me behind Nick in the Camaro. Jen had Sarah get in and hold the shirt on my shoulder, then she got in and took her place.

"Johnny, find a graveyard on your phone," Jen said. "Or a hospital, or a church."

The cotton was half in and half out of my ears. I wavered between passing out and wanting to scream from the pain. Then sirens blared, from down the road.

Jen heard them too.

"Make it quick," she said.

Nick fired up the Camaro and peeled out of the lot. Inertia pushed me back against the seat. Johnny pointed left, and Nick swung the car onto the main road. He ran the light at the corner. Tires screeched as other cars hit their brakes.

The sirens were behind us and down the road. They had an odd Doppler effect where they sounded far away, then close, then far away again. Sarah turned around in the backseat, and shook her head. "I don't see them."

Jen kept her hand tight on my shoulder.

"Graveyard," Johnny said, looking at his phone. "Maybe a mile ahead."

Nick gunned the engine and the Camaro surged down the road.

"You need to start looking, Gus," Jen told me.

Normally it wasn't a problem. My ethereal radar that I used to find ghosts usually covered a good distance. But in the middle of the day it was hard. The searing hot pain in my shoulder made it harder. And I had lost enough blood that focusing was an issue.

Still, I stretched out and looked for a spirit. I found one ghost, way down the road. Not quite a mile away. Johnny's graveyard, maybe.

I hoped the ghost wasn't like the one in Lewiston. Bile rose in the back of my throat and I didn't want to swallow it back down. Maybe this ghost would be worse, like Jo. Did I want to take on something like that again? I didn't think I could.

Jen slapped my face, hard.

"Dammit," I yelled.

"You better concentrate, Gus," she said. "Find a ghost and get fixed, or you're going to keep getting slapped."

I shook my head and bore down. There definitely was a spirit coming up. Now I just had to reach it and tap into the ethereal plane.

Nick swerved into the other lane in order to pass a couple of slow cars that were right next to each other, hogging the road. The swerve pushed the three of us in the backseat against each other. Then Nick swerved back into the other lane. I watched Sarah flip off the people driving.

"Ha," I said, and laughed when Sarah looked at me. It wasn't something I would have imagined her doing.

Jen slapped me again. This time I focused on Jen, setting my jaw. I tried frowning at her. She raised an eyebrow back at me. And waited. And watched. I was tempted to close my eyes again, just to show her I could. I was sure I would be able to open them again.

But Jen raised her hand, so I kept them open.

"Just down the street," Johnny said. An iron fence had begun to pass us on my side, running down the street ahead of us. A grassy knoll rose inside the fence, dark gray blocks of different shapes and sizes dotting the lawn in rows.

I tapped the ghost on the radar. It had been the first spirit, standing at the bottom of the hill. A young man, waiting outside the grave of an older woman. A ghostly gun in one hand. The burnt smell of gunpowder came through the connection.

I seized all the ethereal energy I could find. Jen gasped and jerked her hand off my shoulder. The balled-up T-shirt came with it. I poured energy into the wound, and the splintered bones, the tendons all began to knit together in tiny cracks and pops. Blood was made and flowed out of my shoulder and more was made, until all the veins and arteries closed up. Flesh swelled on either side of the gunshot until the two sides of the wound became one, skin tying together like the zipper of a jacket.

The hot pain in my shoulder chilled into the searing, freezing pain of healing. My head immediately cleared. My mind no longer floated on a cloud, drifting in a haze, but was in the backseat of my car, the sirens of cop cars behind us.

Jen poked my shoulder once, then twice. Her head tilted to one side. The pokes felt like they would any other time. I let go of the ghost before any other memories came across and took a deep breath, letting it out in a big exhale.

"Whew," I said. A little ethereal energy still ran through me, and like always all my senses felt sharper. The scent of warm copper blood flooded my nose, and I heard the police sirens, crystal-clear in my ears. Every muscle in my body thrummed in anticipation of movement, like I had drunk a thousand expressos.

Johnny looked back with a worried grin. "Here I thought you were invincible."

"It was close," I said. That was the story of my life. It always seemed to be close.

Heading toward the graveyard had brought us closer into town. More buildings passed by, taller and wider. Traffic thickened around us, enough that Nick had trouble getting around the cars ahead of him and had to slow down. Sarah still looked out the back of the car, but the sirens maintained their distance for now.

Jen still faced me in the backseat, her back to the front. Her eyes shimmered a bit. The front of her shirt and her arms were covered in my blood.

I smiled at her. "Hey."

She shook her head and looked at my shoulder again, her lips pressed tightly together.

I glanced at it as well. There was a lot of blood. How could I be an angel, if a bullet could almost kill me? How could I be something strong enough to stand up to Azazel, or Kimaris, or all of the other evils in the world? No matter what had happened back at the factory. No matter what my mother had left scrawled on the floor of my jail cell. No matter what I had felt when Danny's ghost had poured into me.

"Still think I'm an angel?" I asked Jen, half-jokingly, my voice low.

She punched me in the chest, hard. Then spun around and faced the front seat. Johnny caught something on her face and turned back to face the road.

"That's not funny," Jen said, angry. Then in a whisper, "I just got you back."

The sirens kept blaring. They would get louder and softer. Sarah stared through the rear window. "I still can't see them."

I still had enough of the ghost left that my senses were augmented. My ears picked up the *whump-whump-whump* of a helicopter's blades chopping the air. I swore. "They called in support. There's a helicopter coming this way. Once it finds us, the cars will just box us in."

"I can make it," Nick said. "We just got to get to open road."

"That's going to be impossible, man," Johnny said. "We're coming up to the main part of the town."

The city was much larger than I had thought when we first found the pharmacy. The roads had gone from two-lane to four-. Tall apartment buildings and offices broke over the horizon, swelling larger as we drove, until they stood on top of us.

It would be impossible to outrun the police. But running was something I was used to. And hiding. "Look for an industrial district," I said.

Nick swung down a side street and kept driving, taking whatever turn was handy. Johnny punched something up on the phone and began pointing out where to go. The sky was blue overhead, cloudless, and the helicopter appeared as a tiny dot to the east. A black insect against the blue background. "We have a minute or two, maybe, before that thing gets on top of us."

Johnny kept directing. Nick drove into more side streets. We got to a run of streets of older buildings, and a few homeless people appeared. One guy stood at a corner with a torn-up sleeping bag wrapped around him, a long gray beard hanging down from his chin. Trash littered the streets, and then we passed a few boarded-up places. Closed stores and shops.

"Start looking for something closed with a garage," I said. And as soon as I said it, we pulled into a block full of shops. Electricians, plumbers, air-conditioning repair men, with trucks and vans with signs painted on the side like "The Knife Guys" and "Cranford Mechanical." Middle-class Americans and small businesses. Even a few of the mobile phone vans I had seen up North. Most of the shops were open, but a few were closed.

"There," Nick said. He pulled in front of a store. There was sign in the front letting anyone know that the area was up for lease. The front window was broken, with a board half covering it. The inside was dark, unlit.

"Now we just got to get in," Johnny said.

A couple of trucks and sedans were parked at meters on the street. A blue coupe just down from the closed shop. Managers and assistants, directing technicians in the field to trouble calls and installs.

Nick pulled around the corner, into the shadow of the building.

"Drive this thing back around," he told Johnny, throwing the Camaro into park and letting the car idle. Nick got out quickly, popping the trunk and crawling into it with a crackling of water bottles and plastic grocery bags. He shut the trunk from the inside with a thump, and was gone.

"Hmmm," Sarah said, still looking out the back. Like she had never seen Nick work before.

Johnny slid over to the driver's seat. He shut the door and backed the Camaro back out onto the street. By the time he had turned the nose of the car toward the building, the garage door was rolling up. Nick stood off to the side, pulling a thick chain hand over hand.

Johnny drove in as soon as there was clearance, and then Nick shut the roll-up door behind him. The whole thing might have taken thirty seconds.

The sirens swelled from down the street. Nick creeped over to the half-boarded window and peered out from a corner. Johnny played with the keys and then switched the Camaro off. The engine chugged quietly to a stop. The rest of us stayed in the car.

The sirens got louder. And we all heard the helicopter overhead. It was low enough and loud enough the sounds of the blades thumping in the air echoed in my skull, like someone hitting me in the head, over and over.

The wave of sound built, crested, and then washed away down the street in a flash of cars, blue and red strobe lights circling. None of the cars stopped. The helicopter never paused in flight.

We all let out a collective breath. Little by little we all exited the car. I got some water out of the trunk and drank it. I was really thirsty. Sometimes I wondered if my body made new blood and bone and skin from all the ethereal energy.

Sometimes, after a long fight, I would feel like I used to after days of driving on energy drinks and coffee. Exhausted to a degree that I couldn't move. Maybe I used the ghosts to push past my body's natural limits, and I just needed to give it sustenance. Or maybe right now I was just really thirsty.

"Safe for now," I said after my last gulp of water.

"We can't stay here forever," Nick replied, looking at Sarah.

Jen looked at me, her eyebrows lowered and her jaw tight. She had watched me drink the entire bottle.

"We'll have to stay here until tonight," I said. When the cops lost us they would start circling back. They could even search block by block. We'd have to play it by ear.

"That puts us behind," Nick said.

"I got it," I said. It had been just bad luck, but I hated that I was the person who hadn't noticed the cop car pull up. And then I had gotten shot. All of that had led us to this. "We all know. We still have some time, though."

"I don't like people getting hurt because of me," Sarah said, out loud.

"Don't worry about it." I understood where she was coming from, having had people hurt just for being near me. And it wasn't like I wasn't perfectly able to get hurt, all by myself. "It's something I'm used to."

"Tomorrow's the day," Nick said again.

"Nick," I said, "*I got it.*"

"I still don't like it," Sarah said, again.

I nabbed another bottle of water and went to the side of the shop. It was a large garage with enough room for a couple of cars and an open area to the side of the garage.

The open area ran along the side of the bays and ended at the boarded window we had viewed at the outside, and there was a tiny door in the concrete wall behind a table that might have held a cash register at one point. Enough light broke through around the front window to let you see through the gloom in the shop.

I walked to a far corner of the area, passing a large metal workbench topped with a few old rags. The towels were black with grime and age. Scattered around the rags were mismatched nuts and bolts, and the thick oily smell of grease was strong.

I sat beside the bench and put my back up against the wall of the shop. It was cold concrete, and part of me felt like I was back in the jail cell in Grafton. I drank some more water, still not looking at my friends. Not looking at Jen, who was apparently mad at me.

She knew I didn't believe what she thought. And so what if I cracked a joke about it? It was what I did. When things got dark, I needed to make them light. So I didn't bear the full weight of what I carried around with me.

Or what I *had* carried. The Key still pulled south, a little more to the west of us now, and south. That's the way we would travel. If we could use the interstate, we would get there in no time. Just a few hours, maybe.

But we couldn't use the interstate in the Camaro. And if they found the Camaro, they would know we were in a different vehicle. It seemed like a lose/lose proposition.

I finished off the water. I was coming down off the high I got after using ethereal energy. Or maybe I was just realizing how close to death I had gotten. My heart beat way too fast in my chest. If Jen hadn't kept me focused, I wouldn't have been able to tap into the ethereal plane. I had lost too much blood, too fast.

My hands shook some. I crossed my arms and hugged myself tight, like I was cold. I took deep, even breaths until my heart slowed down, and closed my eyes.

My friends talked a little among themselves. I tried not to pick out any one voice. I focused on my breathing and exhaustion and recovering. Like before, these close calls were getting too regular. It said something about me, that I was used to doing this. Used to going from almost being killed to quickly running.

After a bit, footsteps wandered over. Light steps, but with a purpose. Someone stood in front of me for a long moment.

I opened my eyes. Jen. She had changed out of her blood-covered shirt, and wore a blue T-shirt with a soda logo on the front, red and white. Her eyebrows were still lowered, as if she was still a little mad. Or maybe still thinking about things. She held an energy drink in one hand.

"Hey," she finally said.

I took a deep breath and tried a smile.

She plucked at her new thrift shirt. "I'm thinking I didn't get enough of these."

My smile turned into a grin, and I bobbed my head in acknowledgment, tired.

Jen smiled a little smile in return and sat next to me. In one hand she held an energy drink, and tilted that a little toward me. "Peace?"

Our eyes met, and as always there was an underlying connection between us. It hit me almost like a jolt, a feeling of being together that thrilled me and scared me. Apparently her too.

"There was never a war, Jen," I said, softly.

"I know," she said. She opened the drink with a metallic crack that echoed in the tiny garage, and then sipped it. And grimaced at the taste. "I just didn't know what I'd do if you had died."

I understood her. I had felt the same, back in Grafton, when my mother ran Jen through with her sword: a momentary burst of terror, followed by a slow-growing realization that the person you loved was dying.

Back at Raphael's mansion, I had watched my mother run a sword through Jen. I had watched her drop to the ground. And I had sat in the jail cell, not knowing if she still lived and fearing the worst. Alone, wondering why I still lived, when Jen was dead. Having nothing left to live for except hate.

"I understand," I said, trying her drink. It was cool and bubbly and tasted like grape. "I guess I'm just used to getting shot at."

"And you joke about it," Jen added, "at the worst moments."

"There is that," I said. And smiled again. "I can't promise anything, but I'll see what I can do."

"I'd rather you see what you can do about getting shot in the first place," Jen said, smiling a little as well.

"We might just have to keep buying shirts," I said. "And maybe laugh at a bad joke or two."

"Maybe." Jen bumped her hip against mine. "Your jokes are really bad, though."

"Yeah," I said. I was really tired, so maybe what I said next came from a more honest place than normal, a place I was usually kept locked. "I worry you have this hope with me, that I'm some avenging angel that can save everyone. Protect everyone. And that I'll fail."

Jen paused a long moment. There was a laugh that interrupted us. Johnny stood next to Sarah and they both were laughing at Nick. All of them held wrappers of something, something they had bought back at the pharmacy with a large V on the front beside a picture of some kind of green vegetable.

Sarah looked like she was in more pain today than yesterday. Maybe that was my imagination. A wince briefly appeared at the corner of her eyes, but she still smiled and ate one of her veggie bars.

Nick had a couple of packages in his hands, and his mouth was stuffed. His jaw worked up and down, over and over. Johnny held a bottle of water between his thumb and forefinger, dangling it in front of Nick. Sarah laughed again. Nick shook his head and tried another bite from the package, a bunch of crumbs falling to the floor when he did.

"He's good at that," I said.

"Johnny?"

I nodded. "He's got better jokes than me, I think."

"Is that a real debate?" Jen asked, arching her eyebrow. She placed an arm on mine. Her fingers wrapped snugly around my wrist, and her thumb rubbed the outside of my hand.

She waited for me to speak. It took a while. I knew we were going to talk, but I wasn't ready for it. There was a lot in my past I held back, and I didn't want to go through it all.

But Jen deserved to know. She believed so much in me, she needed to know why I didn't do the same. So finally I gave in.

"I ran for a long time, Jen," I started out. My voice was a little rough, but I had opened the door, and I was going to let it all out. "Because of Danny. When he really needed it, I failed him."

"Gus," Jen breathed out, almost a whisper. She held my arm tight and squeezed.

"I've failed others, since then," I said. A tear slipped down my cheek. More followed, silent and slow, each following the last. "After what happened, after his ghost appeared and he hugged me, I thought I understood what he wanted me to do."

Somehow my head had ended up in my hands. "I thought Danny wanted me to forgive myself. I thought he wanted me to be okay with what happened. And I tried, Jen. I thought I had at least accepted it."

It had been easier when I was on the run. Easy to convince myself I was doing some vague good for nebulous group of people I called the world. I protected them all, I told myself, keeping the Key from Azazel.

It was much harder, even with Danny's lesson, to protect those around me. Harder to be a part of their lives, knowing I might lose them. It almost hurt, smiling and laughing and crying with my friends, when at any moment they could be gone.

Jen knew what had happened with Danny. He had opened himself up and forced me to accept the ethereal energy he was connected to. Danny's ghost had felt so different than others. Happier, pure. When he had hugged me, and I had lived his memories, I had seen how he had viewed us all. How he had loved us all. And how, in the end, he was proud of standing up for me when I needed it. Even though that act had killed him.

Danny had lived life with joy. He had lived it without reservation. And he had lived it for us. Not for the world, just for us.

"I thought I was strong enough. I thought I had learned the lesson." I lifted my head, shook it slightly. Still wondering how I could have thought I was a different person. A *better* person. "But then Kimaris happened. It reminded me, any of us could die at any moment. We're all targets now. Not just me."

My free hand clenched tight into a fist. "And if I can't protect us, then what am I good for?"

Another moment of silence between us. It was something we were good at, quiet moments next to each other. Our thoughts ran along the same lines, but still found different destinations.

"I didn't mean to place a larger burden on you, Gus," Jen said, finally.

She knew, like I did, that she was talking about what she believed me to be. What my mother hinted at. Some kind of bastard half angel.

"I know, Jen," I said. The thing I knew was, what Jen wanted me to be might be the only thing that could keep my friends safe. And I laughed inside, a bitter laugh, wondering if I could ever be something good enough, strong enough, to protect those I cared about. "I know."

Another moment. Jen took another sip of the drink, letting me gather myself together. I finally wiped both of my cheeks, and inhaled deeply through my nose, sucking up the wetness in my nostrils. Like a kid, after bawling.

"Can I tell you something?" Jen asked. Carefully. Seeing if I was ready.

"Always," I said.

"We may not all make this," Jen said. Her eyes open, deep, and serious. Earnest. "Azazel may kill us all. Whatever he's planning may succeed. Any and all of those things *could* happen."

Her hand kept that same grip on my arm. Fingers, tight to my skin. Anchoring me to the moment.

I finally answered, "That's a strange kind of pep talk, Jen."

This was a strange conversation. It stopped and started. As if both of us were afraid to keep it going. Still, Jen was strong. Stronger than me.

"If you had just died," she continued, "I would have been devastated. I would have been angry and furious and depressed and sad. I would have been torn apart and I may even have blamed myself some. I would have cried for a long time. But I would have kept going. I'd have made it mean something."

The anger retribution brought could fuel a person, maybe even long after despair had faded away. "I get what you are saying," I said.

"You get it, but you don't *get* it," Jen said. "You've been shot, broken up, cut, thrown, and who knows what else, just in the past few days. I've *watched* all that happen. Don't you think part of me fears that I won't be enough, the one time you need me?"

I was quiet. I had never thought about what I did, and how it affected others. Only about what I couldn't do, and how it affected me.

"Danny wasn't trying to just get you to forgive yourself," Jen said. "He was *proud* of what he did. *He* made his choice. You didn't make it for him. And I think, at the end, he wanted you to remember how happy you had made him, how we all had made him. And maybe *you* meant enough to him that what happened in the alley was worth it.

I shouldn't have wiped my cheeks before. More tears ran down them now. I remembered what had happened; I would always remember that day. Raphael about to kill me. Danny, stepping in the middle. He had been the one to make a stand. Danny had thrown a baseball and broken Raphael's nose. Danny had stood up for me, in that moment. And Danny, ultimately, had paid the price.

I had always blamed myself. I had never looked at it from Danny's side. From Jen's side. Maybe I just didn't think I was worth it. How could I, looking at my past? Everywhere I went, people got hurt. With nothing I could do about it.

"Think about it, Gus," Jen said. "He didn't give up his life for you just back in the alley. He also gave himself up as a ghost. He gave himself twice for you. He felt like you were worth that. He wanted you to know that."

I resisted what she was telling me. Her message wouldn't work for me. And Jen felt it. I could tell, and still she tried to persuade me, her voice low, but passionate. Urgent.

"You have to *get* it, Gus. You have to understand we're all here with you. That we all understand what can happen to any of us. That *we've* made that choice. All of us need to keep fighting, whatever happens. We need to get Sarah to New Orleans, whoever of us lives or dies. Because *someone* has to."

She was right, I got it, but I still also didn't get it. Not inside, where it mattered. I didn't want to live in a world where my friends died and I lived.

"And all of us are worth that," she added, at the end.

Failing to protect them was something I didn't want to think about. The thought itself existed outside of the circle of something I could accept. It existed only in vague terms, and even as I tried to pull that acceptance inside myself, some inner core of mine refused it entry.

I wanted to be the first out, every time, having given everything I had. I wouldn't let my friends die. Not on my watch. If that happened, I would have no one left to blame but myself. It would always be my fault. That I didn't know enough. That I couldn't *do* enough.

"You're right, Jen," I admitted, finally. "I may not ever get it."

I thought she would be upset at me, but Jen surprised me. She smiled instead. Happy. It was the smile that made me feel stronger. Bigger. Better.

"That's why I believe in you, Gus," she said. "You're the guy that is always going to stop these things from starting. You can't accept anything less. You'll never let it go. You always protect those you care about, and yet you always fear you are not enough."

Her eyes saw me in a different light than I saw myself. I shook my head, which seemed to be the thing I always did when we had these conversations. Taking in what she told me. Internalizing it, even though I wasn't sure I believed it. Even though Jen did.

"We all count on you." Jen's hand slid down into mine. Her palm was warm and a little moist, her skin soft and pliable against mine. "And it's hard, that kind of responsibility. But you have to be the one that stays strong. Even if one of us dies, it's not going to be your fault. It's going to be *our* fault. It's all of us, or nothing."

She took a breath then, and really looked at me. *Through* me. "You've got to promise me you'll keep swinging, Gus."

I couldn't do that. When I had first gotten to Grafton, my only thought had been to rescue Jen and run. But I had changed since then. I was going to keep the fight going. Keep my friends safe. I was going to be that guy who took every bullet for the people he cared about, so they didn't have to.

"I don't know if I can make that promise, Jen," I said.

She squeezed my hand hard, both of her hands around mine, and stared at me. I avoided her eyes for a long moment. Jen waited.

I finally looked.

"I mean it, Gus," she said. Each word firm. "You promise me."

The corner of my lip turned up in a sad grin. If she only knew how many times I had failed, before a few days ago. I was just coming to terms with a person I was becoming. The knowledge was fragile, and the slightest of breezes could blow it all down.

"Jen," I said in protest.

"Gus," she said, simply. "You know, better than any of us, how dangerous all this is. So you have to be the person who stays strong, if any of us die. *Any* of us. Even me."

The last two words hit me like a bomb. I didn't know if I could handle losing any of my friends. Not again. Not after my past. But Jen, if I lost Jen …

That would be the end of me. The end of my world. And certainly the end of this person I was trying to become. She didn't seem to understand how much I needed her. Fear ran through me. My hand now tightened in hers.

Jen's eyes were open and earnest. She saw something with a clarity I could not. But I denied what she hinted at. My head made little motions to the left and right, as if saying no, no, *no* of its own volition.

"Not you," I said, finally. My voice hoarse.

"Gus, it's a heavy burden for you if any of us die," she said. "I understand. Maybe more so if it's me. But you have to promise me. Look at them. They are going to need you."

Nick and Sarah and Johnny were still talking. The group was a little obvious about leaving the two of us alone. Apparently whatever vegetarian bar Sarah had bought required a lot of chewing. And a lot of moisture.

"Jen," I started. Then stopped. Not sure what I wanted to say. What I could say.

"Just promise me," she said. "For me. For my peace of mind."

I could maybe do it, for her. For her to be able to relax, so Jen could focus on helping her sister. I could do that. "Sure," I said. "Sure."

Jen wasn't quite buying it. She knew me too well. "Your word, Gus," she demanded.

If that was what she wanted, I'd give it to her. I blew out a deep breath. "Fine," I said. "You have it."

She leaned closer and said her next words softly, accenting each one, her lips pressed next to my ear and her breath hot on my cheek. "If you don't, Gus, I'll haunt you. As a ghost."

Then she pulled back from me, an impish grin on her face. Her eyes were lit with some inner humor. Waggling her eyebrows like Johnny did when he was making a joke. Her voice a little *too* dramatic for the moment. "Forever."

Fear ran down my spine. Goose bumps rippled down my arm. For a moment I only saw Jen as an ethereal blue, a spirit. In that vision she looked past me, eyes open, unseeing and unknowing what had happened to her. Just a ghost, wandering the world.

If that happened, I would never be able to touch her again. I would never hear her laugh. Feel her smile. The press of her lips, on my jaw. I would never have someone who could hold me up. Keep me standing. Against all comers.

"That's not funny, Jen," I said.

"There." Jen grinned, like she had been leading me to this realization the whole time. She waggled both eyebrows at me. "That's what I've been trying to tell you. Those kinds of jokes never are."

I snorted. Women. They always throw the things you say back at you, when you least expect it.

CHAPTER TWENTY

There was a washroom behind the only door in the place, and the water still worked. I went in there and took off my shirt, trying to wash the blood off me as best I could. The water was bitter cold and I braced myself each time I splashed water on my skin.

I rinsed my hair under the spigot, washed my face. The water ran red down the drain, then turned pink, and finally clear. After I was done I looked for a cloth or paper towels, but the dispenser was empty and likely had been so for a while.

I went to get one of the last T-shirts out of the car. The cotton stuck to my skin in places where it was still damp. Nick handed me one of the veggie bars and I tried it. It was spicy and hard and dry and I quickly washed it down with some water. When I did Nick grinned a little, and I tried to grin at him back.

Everyone was quiet. There was a feeling of the calm before the storm. The air was humid and just warm enough in the shop to remind me of some of the hot rains I had been in in the South. They always felt like standing underneath a lukewarm mist of a shower. Just warm enough to not be refreshing, just cool enough to not be relaxing, and the drizzle not hard enough to make a person feel clean.

Johnny was on a phone, a gift card on his lap. Sarah had another card in her hand, the phone in the other. Jen sat next to her sister, and they both were looking at something on her phone. Like in the barn, we all took seats like we were sitting around a campfire.

"Did anyone buy some real food?" I asked. "Maybe a candy bar?"

Sarah looked up and stuck her tongue out at me. Jen smiled.

Johnny had a bag by him, and he dug out a box of the toaster pastries and tossed them over. "Best of both worlds, brother."

They weren't his flavor, s'mores, but beggars couldn't be choosers. I took a bite and sighed when chocolate and marshmallow washed the spicy vegetable thing out of my mouth. What some people put into their bodies, I would never understand.

"What's going on?" I asked.

"We bought some gift cards back at the store," Jen said. Little scratch-off cards with digital codes people used for money. "We're downloading an app right now."

"A police blotter," Sarah said, a little proudly. It made me think it had been her suggestion.

I raised my eyebrows and grinned. "Great idea."

"Right now not a lot about us," Johnny said. "No pictures and videos. A few posts on the internet from some news sites talking about a shoot-out at the gas station."

"Maybe we'll get lucky," I said. No pictures or video would be good. Though they still had the video of the Camaro heading away from the welcome center, they didn't have any clear pictures of us.

Both phones sounded off then, blaring a klaxonlike alert. I didn't know how such a small device could put out such an annoying sound. Both Johnny and Sarah rolled their eyes at the same time.

"You had to jinx it," Johnny said to me.

"What?"

He tossed the phone to me. The screen was locked, but there was a message bubble in the center, with AMBER ALERT at the top of it. Below those words were a description of the Camaro, and where we had last been seen, and what direction we were headed in. Like yesterday, we were called Armed and Dangerous.

"Dammit," I said. "We'll have to make sure no one saw us come in."

It was the middle of the day. A lot of the stores and shops along this road had looked either out of business or out to lunch. But all it took was one person looking out a window at the right time, and we would be caught.

Nick silently got up and went to the window. He hid off to the side and looked out, facing us. His eyes narrowed as he watched the street.

I had an idea, but I didn't think the group would like it. I didn't know if I liked it. And after our last conversation, I *knew* Jen wouldn't like it. My plan flew in the face of the change in myself I was trying to make, and like I was reverting to the old me. The runner I used to be, not the fighter my friends needed me to be. But the alert had heightened the feel in the room. We all wondered how we were going to make it out of this town now.

I brought my idea up.

"We should split up," I said.

Everyone stopped what they were doing. Jen looked at me, tilting her head like she did when she was puzzling something out. Johnny frowned.

Nick, though, agreed. He caught my eyes, like he understood. And it was likely he did. Of the whole group, he had been somewhat of a loner, like me.

I was trying to be careful not to fall back into my old pattern. I still fought the urge to run, all the time. I worried this idea I had came from that part of my life, and that there was a small part of my brain trying to convince me to *get away*.

I still fought that voice, and I worried it colored this decision. But Nick and I thought a lot alike. We would do whatever it took to protect those we cared about. But he had stayed in Grafton. He had fought to protect those he cared about. So I felt like in a way he was letting me know he felt like my idea was solid.

I let out a low breath I didn't know I had been holding. I was doing the right thing.

"We need to get another car today," I said. "You guys will take that one and straight-shot it to New Orleans."

Jen shook her head then. She knew where I was going.

I pressed on anyway. "I'm going to take the Camaro and run. Try to draw all the police away."

"Gus," Jen said.

"It makes sense, Jen," I said. "I'm the one here that can survive a shoot-out, if that happens. This is what I'm good at."

Running and drawing the danger away. I had thought I had been doing the right thing, all those years, running from Grafton after Danny had been killed. And I had thought I had been doing the right thing, running with the Key, keeping the world safe from the demons Azazel would release, if he ever got it.

This time, though, I would be doing the right thing, because all of them would be safer on their own than with me. The Camaro would draw a lot of eyes, especially if I wanted to be visible, like I was making a break for it. I'd be able to get far enough away that my friends could make it to New Orleans.

"You're not going alone," Jen said. Her jaw was set, like earlier in the car.

"It's best," I argued. "I can keep myself safe long enough to get out."

Jen got up and marched over to the bench. She grabbed my bloody, hole-filled shirt at the shoulders and shook it out. Like it was some kind of flag for Camp Jen.

"It's a risk," I said. I understood her anger, but I also had taken care of myself a long time on my own. She needed to realize that. "But I can't stop a stray shot from taking someone out while I'm driving. I can keep myself safe."

Quiet spread through the garage, with the tension between Jen and me. The rest of the group watched us. Jen was worried, but irrationally so. I had made it a long time on my own without dying. The years behind me were littered with times when I had taken a beating and kept moving. The close calls were too numerous to count, and I always got back up.

Hell, I even might have actually died back in Grafton, after my mother had put her sword through my heart. Sometimes I could still feel the hilt of the blade, snugged up against my chest. The action had been so fast, the force so violent, and the metal so sharp that the sword had barely even vibrated.

Everyone looked at each other, like they were letting all the information settle. Jen balled up the shirt and threw it angrily, but the shirt opened back up and flopped to the floor almost immediately after the throw.

She stood there and looked at the shirt, just a few feet away. I wanted to smile, but held it back. Jen looked at the shirt, we all looked at the shirt, and then she shook her head and snorted.

Nick broke the silence. "It makes sense. We're getting short on time."

Sarah winced but didn't say anything. She had just said she didn't like people getting hurt because of her. And now we were going to take more chances to get her to where she might be able to be helped.

I remembered her back in the car on the hill above Grafton, telling me to find Jen and leave. Maybe she was still that person from back then, maybe she had given up on herself and didn't believe she was worth all this trouble. Or maybe she just didn't allow herself to hope. Maybe she had fallen into despair so deep she couldn't see a way out, and was just enjoying her last moments around her friends while she could.

"Look at it this way," I said. "We're making ourselves an easy target for Azazel. If we split up, we give him more things to worry about. We may even surprise him."

Jen stared at me. Her eyes flashed. She was likely thinking all of this through in a million different ways. But she didn't say anything against it.

"If we do this," she asked, "what's the plan?"

"We take today and figure it out," I said. "Maybe pick a spot where we'll meet up."

"We're still cutting all this close," Johnny said. "Even if we make it to New Orleans sometime tonight, we've got to figure out a way to get to the bishop. With all these reports coming in, it's not like he's going to have a welcome mat set out for us."

"I think I can do something there," Nick said. "A way to get there earlier."

"How?" Sarah asked. There was a note of hope in her voice, and it felt good to hear.

"Traveling the shadows," Nick said, "I can cover a lot of ground, faster than a car. Probably faster than a plane. What I can see, I can move to."

He had done that back in Lewiston. Popping in and out all over town looking for the witches. Traveling from power pole to power pole, stepping out of the shadow, seeing the next spot, and walking there. He was just going to do the same thing, on a much larger scale.

It would be fast. Nick would blur across the state, traveling from spot to spot almost at the speed of light. The trip would take an immense amount of focus and will.

"How long can you hold up?" I wondered aloud.

Nick shrugged. "Long enough."

He stood by the window, a silent shape, thin and wiry and angled and ready for motion in a moment's notice. It was almost as if he had made his body a tool, to use as needed. I tried not to look over at Sarah, but still saw her look away from Nick. I couldn't read her face, but Jen noticed the same motion.

I swallowed hard, knowing how I felt about Jen, and what he felt for Sarah. Nick would do it as long as he needed to. He would be a man on a mission.

Nick had noticed Sarah looking away, but the motion never registered on his face. He took it all in and then sank back into the corner of the window, returning his gaze outside.

Johnny broke the silence. "So Nick gets there and finds the bishop. Then somehow convinces him that we aren't mass murderers, and we need his help."

"What if he doesn't want to help?" Sarah asked. As if, in her mind, that had always been the probability.

"I'll convince him," Nick said, simply. "I'm sure he sleeps in the dark."

Nick is a dark fucker. Johnny's words, but there were times when they really rang true. I liked him, though, more and more as I got to know him again. Parts of both of us had changed from when we were kids, yet some parts had stayed the same, and helping our friends no matter what was something we both agree on.

I was one hundred percent with Nick on what he was saying. What he was ready to do, and why. I recognized his reasons, and I would have done the same, for Jen.

"I like it," Johnny said. "How do we stay in touch? We only have two phones."

"We're definitely not going to be able to get another," Nick said. "Not today."

"You guys need one, and Nick needs one," I said. I held up a finger, knowing Jen was going to protest. "You all need to communicate and set this thing up. I'll memorize the numbers and get a phone and get in touch with you."

"We'll need a backup plan, then," Jen said. "In case a phone gets lost."

I nodded. "Let's pick out a spot in New Orleans. And maybe a time. If something happens, that's where we'll meet."

"Like one of those spy-thriller movies," Johnny said. He started thumbing through his phone, and read something from whatever he had searched. "Secret Spots and Hidden Places in New Orleans."

"Let's not overthink it," I said. "Easy and simple is best."

"Not as much fun, though." Johnny did his eyebrow thing.

"How about the cathedral?" Nick said. "That's where we're going to need to be anyway, right?"

Johnny was still thumbing through his phone. "There's a park right across from it," he said. "Jackson Square. Looks like a big grass oval crossed with a couple walkways."

"Good enough for me," I said.

"So, if I'm getting this right, this is the plan," Jen said. "We find another car sometime today. Gus takes the Camaro and leads the police on a wild-goose chase. Nick gets to New Orleans and secures the bishop's help. And then the rest of us get there in the second car."

"Simple is best," I said.

"There's a lot that could go wrong," Jen said. Looking at her sister. Looking at me.

"That's why simple is best," I said. "I can't think too long-term, too far down the road. In the Rangers I learned how to identify, isolate, and overcome. That works best for me. No plan survives the first shot."

"Easy to say," Jen said.

"Easy to do," I argued. "We all walk by putting one step in front of the other."

Jen didn't reply. Inside I grinned. She wasn't thrilled, but we had a plan and it was one I was comfortable with. One I believed we could execute. We still needed to know more about what Azazel had planned, but getting Sarah an exorcism was our first priority. After that, we could worry about the demon.

We all just had to get there.

Nick stood by the window. His eyes never left the street. He looked alert and awake now. Maybe he really didn't need a lot of sleep, but Nick would need it after tonight, if he was going to shadow-walk all the way to New Orleans.

Sarah jerked like she just remembered something, and touched a few places on her phone. A tinny voice read an article aloud, the voice echoing in the small garage. Sarah turned the volume up a bit, but the phone's speaker was small. The sound was clipped and static broke through every time the reader stopped talking, like someone clicked off the speak button on a walkie-talkie.

I wondered if that static walkie-talkie sound was manufactured. It didn't make sense for us to hear it on an app. The voice kept speaking. There was an overview of what had happened at the gas station, a fairly good description of me, and brief descriptions of the rest of us. Everything the voice said about us was manufactured. I decided the sound was fake too.

The voice repeated a hotline number for people to call, and then repeated the message from the beginning. Sarah turned it back down some. This station was going to play our hits all day.

Jen walked over and took a seat next to me. Her face still carried a serious expression, like we were back in school and I hadn't done my homework. She shook her head at me.

"I know," I said.

"I do too," she said. Both of our voices were low, knees pulled up to our chests, and both of our backs were against the car. Jen turned to look at me, her head angled up a bit, as if she was looking up at the ceiling for an answer.

"It'll work, Jen," I said.

"It's a good plan," she agreed, even though her jaw was still tense, tight. "Maybe I just have to get used to the fact that you like to be in the worst possible danger."

I tried a grin. It felt a little sad. "I don't know that it's something I like. But if the choice is between you all and me, I'm going to choose me."

She sighed. "It's so hard to get used to now, for some reason. Just a few days ago I was scared for you, when we all went after Sarah at Raphael's. But I wasn't afraid like this."

"Watching someone get shot alters how you feel about things a bit," I said. I had watched it happen in the army, and each time I witnessed how people got by, after real bullets took chunks out of living flesh and left behind cold corpses.

It had been my life for a long time. I had seen similar things, running from Azazel over the years. There was a time I had taken a subway in

New York, hoping to hide in the tunnels and make a break out of the city. Azazel had derailed the train and killed dozens and injured others, just because I was around. I had left that accident and watched those that survived sob and cry and pound the dead bodies of loved ones who had left.

And then there were the ghosts like Jo. What did living their memories do to me, over time? Each time that I used ethereal energy, did I become more like them? Did I care about human life just a little bit less? Was any power worth that cost?

There was a lot of death in my life. I lived on the edge of it, all the time. So I was more used to it than Jen, but I hoped I hadn't become cynical about it. Because I would pull from all the ghosts in the world to keep her alive, I'd live a thousand of Jo's memories, to keep my friends safe.

"You might be right," she said. "I'll manage it."

"I don't want you to manage it, Jen," I said. Her eyes opened a little in surprise.

"Getting angry at me shows you care," I explained. "You have no idea how alone I felt, running from Azazel, wondering if what I was doing meant anything to anyone. Whether what I was doing was worth it. Sometimes I felt so alone I wanted to scream for someone to reach out and shake my hand, pat me on the shoulder, or even just say hello."

That desire was why I had been caught by Azazel, that night at the motel. Because the burger had been delicious, but I had also wanted to feel human again. I had enjoyed having a beer, eating the burger, and talking to the bartender about a football game. Those moments helped to remind me I was still human.

And it was what Azazel had said, in that motel room. It was that feeling that was always going to trap me. No matter how hard I tried to make myself, I still needed someone to care.

I smiled again, and this time it felt a little more real. "Having you be mad at me makes all of this worth it."

Jen snorted and bumped her hip against mine. Our legs pressed up against each other, feet drawn up so that our shoes lined up. My arms hugged my knees to my chest, and Jen laid a hand on top of mine. "It's always been us, hasn't it?"

"It has," I said. Our eyes locked. Those two words were the most important I had ever said to Jen. The moment became real, between us. We had always been meant to be together, forever and always.

I wondered for the millionth time why I ever left. It had been the quick decision of a frightened boy after a horrifying act, and I wished now I had been wise enough to see and choose differently then. Ten years I wasted, when I could have been with Jen.

I flipped my hand around on my knee so that her fingers could mesh with mine, and we sat like that for a bit. Listening to the same report being read over the scanner app, and the occasional crackle of other voices, from fire departments and police cars.

"Good," Jen said. "Because I'll probably get angry again."

I grinned. "Think of it this way, you wanted me to figure out a few things about myself. This is just part of it."

Even though I meant it in jest, it struck me that what I had just said was the truth. Whatever I'd done in life, and wherever I'd been, I had always tried to protect others. I don't know that I had ever done something just for myself. Or at least not consciously. I had always made my decisions based on how I could help others. As a young kid in Grafton. In the army. Running from Azazel. Now.

Maybe not the best decisions, looking back. But ones I felt were right at the time.

I followed the thought. It gathered traction like a train slowly chugging up a steep hill. When I had run from Grafton, I had done it to keep my friends safe from Raphael's retribution. When I had run with the Key, it was to keep the world safe from the demons held in it. When I had kept myself alone, running from Azazel, it had been to keep others safe from the demon.

It all took a cost from me. But I had always been willing to pay it.

"I've run a long time, Jen," I said. "And maybe I'm going too much the other way now, but it doesn't feel that way to me. It just feels like I'm going to do everything possible to keep you all safe."

I paused a moment, trying to come up with the right words. Jen was quiet, though her fingers tightened around mine, and let me puzzle out what I wanted to say.

"I don't think I'm who you think I am," I finally said. "But that doesn't mean I'm not going to give it my best shot."

Jen smiled then, and it was one of her smiles that made my heart beat a little harder, that made it difficult for me to breathe.

"How can I argue with that?" she asked me, and squeezed my hand one more time. Each of our fingers locked tight, and our thumbs had wrapped around the sides of each other's palms, and every knuckle on both of our hands was white.

CHAPTER TWENTY-ONE

We rested as best we could throughout the day. At times each of us used the washroom, tried to clean up. We found some paper towels in the garage, and I tried to clean out the backseat of my car. I divided some of the stuff in the trunk so that we could put it in the new car.

Of and on, traffic passed by the shop. There was a slight scare later in the afternoon, after a police cruiser stopped on the block for a bit, behind an orange sedan that had been parked there all day. But the cops never got out, and after a bit they drove on.

Johnny pulled out his notebook, and started writing some stuff in it for Nick to give to the bishop. Notes about what Tabitha had told him, some of what the witches had found about all symbols and scripts on Sarah. At one point Jen took Sarah into the washroom and took a few pictures.

There was a little discussion about all the information we had found about the demons in the Key. Johnny still thought they were building something in hell. Not a casino anymore, but some kind of fortress. Maybe gathering together and prepping an army. There was a logic to it, I guessed. Like a forward operating base. But I still felt like we were missing something obvious.

"They couldn't be building something on earth, right?" I asked, looking at Nick. He was as close to a priest as we could get.

He shook his head. "I don't know. I wouldn't think so."

"I think they have to be summoned first," Sarah said. "It's one of the things I heard the witches talk about. They have to be summoned in a certain symbol, composed of certain things. I can't remember what."

She told us what she had overheard in the house. Like I was with Nick, I was surprised to hear Sarah speak so many words at the same time. She had been so different as a kid, always laughing and teasing me, when I was over at Jen's.

"Gertrud seemed to know the most," Sarah said. The witch who reminded me of a Valkyrie. "Once a demon is summoned, it can travel back and forth between hell and the place it was summoned from. They can get free only if they kill the person who summoned them."

"So that's a no, then," I said.

Johnny's thought made a lot of sense, building fortresses, creating an army, and building weapons for it. But Azazel was more subtle than that. Whatever he planned, it wasn't going to be leading a demonic army from hell to raze the earth.

It was too simple, too straightforward, for Azazel. Unless he was counting on its simplicity to fool me, and he was ready to have an army at hand while I was occupied with all the different schemes Azazel could be thinking.

I shook my head. I had just said simple plans were the best. Could that be what Azazel was planning? An attack on earth while I looked for ghosts? Those thoughts circled over and over as the sky darkened outside.

After a bit it was dark enough that we had to pull the lantern out of the trunk. We circled together and ate a last meal of sorts. Toaster pastries, protein and veggie bars, and energy drinks. Nick grabbed his bag from the pharmacy and brought out a large bag of peanut butter cups, and we ate a bunch of those as dessert.

Jen and I shared one in a kiss. Sarah *yecched* but still smiled. Even Johnny grabbed a few cups.

"And thus the great debate ends," Nick said. Like he had been waiting for that moment.

Johnny grabbed another. "No shame here. They aren't candy bars, but they *are* effing delicious."

We all laughed. My mouth still tasted peanut butter and chocolate, and I still felt Jen's lips press up against mine, wide and curved in a large smile. We were all a little nervous, but as ready as we were going to be.

Tomorrow night, this would be over, one way or the other.

"I know this feels like farewell," I said to everyone, but glancing at Jen. "But we'll all be together tomorrow night. Remember, simple is easy. Get to New Orleans. Get to the bishop. And get that exorcism."

"And then get the bastard that started all this," Nick said.

"Hear, hear!" Johnny said, tipping a bottle of water to Nick.

"Hear, hear," I said, tipping my energy drink.

Then our phones started beeping again, like the AMBER Alert from earlier. A high-pitched beeping, over and over, until we grabbed the phones and acknowledged it.

We all looked at Johnny. "Us again?" I asked.

He had his phone up, and his eyes opened wide as he read it. He shook his head. "Nope. But things have definitely gotten worse."

"How could they have gotten *worse*?" I said.

"Kimaris," Johnny said. He read the message. "Effective immediately, all civilians are required to stay inside their homes and avoid contact with others, *as a precaution*. There may be a contagion or virus spreading. Signs of the virus *may be* a swelling and discoloration of skin. Some skin may crack with weeping sores. Repeat, *as a precaution* all civilians should remain inside until further notice."

Kimaris was looking for us, and in doing so, he was spreading through the population like a virus. Maybe learning where we were, by surfing through their memories. There was no way to really know what the demon was capable of, but Kimaris would know where to start his search, with what had happened on the news.

From there, he would just have to start taking over people, gathering more and more under his command. Building his little armies of clones. He wouldn't care if they were cops or civilians, and maybe he could just keep gathering people until he learned where we were at. Or gathered one of us.

I shivered at that thought.

The phone kept up its piercing alarm, with the same warning, until Johnny figured out a way to turn it off. The messages listed locations the contagion had been reported in, and Johnny said that the locations got closer and closer to where we were hiding now.

"Maybe no time like the present, huh?" I asked.

We all looked outside. A slow dusk had rolled over the street, and shadows were plentiful.

"Might take a bit," Nick finally said. "Be ready with the door."

He walked to a corner of the room. To my eyes it looked like he kept walking, and a line of shadow just waved over him, like a cloud passed. Each part of the shadow that touched Nick obscured him, like a fuzzy place existed between the light and the dark.

And then Nick was fully in the shadow. And then gone.

I walked to the window. Sarah came up next to me. We saw motion in the orange sedan, Nick looking around for keys. He flipped down the visor, looked in the glove box, the center console. It all took just a few seconds, and then he waved at the garage.

And then he disappeared again, appearing in a truck farther down the street, so that I just saw the motion inside the cab. It was far enough away I couldn't be sure. Then the motion was gone. Nick would do the same thing down the line of cars, street after street, mile after mile, until he found one with the keys in it.

It seemed like something he had done before.

"I want to tell you something," Sarah said. Her voice, always light, was almost ethereal now, and cracked when she spoke. She looked a lot like her sister, blond hair, full lips, just thin where Jen was curved, angled where Jen was strong. Her eyes glistened and she wiped a tear from one cheek.

"What is it?" I asked.

"I've been wanting to tell you, and maybe now is the last time I can," she said. "Just in case, you know, you don't make it."

Sarah was like her sister there too. I opened my mouth to reassure her, but before I said a word she laid a hand on my arm and shook her head, stopping me from speaking.

"Or I might not make it tomorrow night," she said, and swallowed, maybe wavering on whether or not she could tell me what she wanted to say. What she needed to say.

"It's okay," I said. Jen looked over from the Camaro, head tilted a little, and I waved her away.

Sarah's eyes kept flicking to my face, then looking away. Over and over. She took a deep breath and let it out, like an explosive decompression.

"Just say it," I told her.

"You won't think bad of me?" she asked, in a tiny-girl voice that pulled something out of my heart. I had spent the least amount of time around Sarah since coming back, but back in the day she had been like a little sister to me, and now I regretted not taking the chance to talk to her.

"Come on, Sarah," I said. "You know me better than that."

But maybe she didn't. Maybe she was still trying to figure me out. I had been gone a long time, and I had been much different when I first came back. That man had stared at his reflection in a car window, as it had rolled up between Sarah and him, and found himself wanting. Could I blame her for thinking me anything but that person? I held myself back from making a fist.

"Okay," she finally said. "Danny came and saw me the day he died."

"Okay," I echoed, trying to keep her going.

"He was just being Danny, you know?" Sarah said. Her voice trembled a lot. Her fingers played with her necklace, and the tiny clasp at the end of it. "He wanted to know if I liked Nick. Because, you know, Nick liked me."

We had all known back then about Nick and Sarah. And we all still knew it now, apparently. But to hear Danny had been concerned about it, it made me think of back in the diner in Grafton. When Nick had been furious with me, and demanded to know what had happened to Danny.

Danny in some ways for me existed in this existential realm. Danny was laughter, he was how we all felt good together, he was a part of our group existing outside of time and space. Where the sun always shone and the skies were always blue and the crack of the bat sent baseballs far into the fields.

I had never pictured him being concerned about more mundane things, like Nick and Sarah. I had never pictured him worried about getting a homework assignment. Whether or not it might rain that day. Or if Danny had been a sounding board for Nick, listening to Nick worry about Sarah, listening to Nick wonder if he could ever get her attention, if she liked him the way he liked her.

I wondered if Danny had asked Nick about Sarah first. Or if he had listened to Nick and then, in his Danny way, decided to help. Danny's way would have been simple, he would have just gone over to Sarah's and asked her how she felt. Maybe told her how Nick felt. And, in doing so, would have made Sarah feel guilty, for possibly using Nick.

If it had been the same day, Danny would have been heading back from Sarah's when Raphael and his friends had found him. The day they had killed Danny. The day I had run away.

"I yelled at Danny," Sarah said. "I told him it was no business of his who I liked. And he better butt out of it. And he walked away with such a sad expression on his face I almost stopped him and apologized. Because he was Danny."

"I know," I said as tears surfaced in my own eyes.

"But I didn't," Sarah said. She began to hiccup. "I let him walk away. And then he ... and then he ... and then he—"

"Hey," I said, and wrapped my arms around her in a hug. Sarah cried then, loud sobs into my shoulder. Tears ran down my face as well. Jen looked at me and I waved her back again, and patted Sarah on the back with gentle pats, telling her it was okay.

We all had our secrets. We all had things that shaped us. I was just beginning to know mine, but Sarah had her secret, with Danny. Her life had changed after Danny was killed. Sarah carried a dark loathing about herself, what she did, and I was one person who understood the need to punish yourself, when you believed you had committed something really, horribly wrong.

Sarah was like me. She had punished herself the rest of her life for what she had said to Danny, for what a young teenage girl had said quickly, without thinking. She had pushed away everyone, even her sister. She had run to Raphael. And she had committed herself to a dark life as penance.

Even after her rescue, she felt like someone who had given up, and I now understood why. But I didn't ask her about it. I just held her and let her sob. I let her get it all out. Her whole body shook with it. After a while the sobbing became a crying, and then the crying became a sniffle, here and there.

"You and I have some of the same demons," I said then.

Sarah nodded into my shoulder.

"But I was lucky enough to see him again," I said, my voice low. "And you weren't."

A sniff, and another nod.

"All I can tell you is that when I saw him again, he was happy," I said, softly in her ear. "Every memory of his was about all of us. Playing together. Laughing together. I can remember each one clearly. He loved you, he loved all of us, without reservation."

Her voice trembled. "I just wish I could tell him how sorry I was."

"I would say he knows. I would tell you it wasn't a memory he had kept," I said, and swallowed myself. "You know, I think about him a lot."

"You do?" Her voice was tiny again.

"Not just a lot," I said. "Always. Your sister and I talk about it. I think about it. I even dream about it sometimes."

"Are they bad dreams?" she asked, in her tiny voice.

"They used to be," I said. "But not anymore. And maybe that's because of what I'm trying to do. Maybe because when I saw him, I knew what I needed to do, and then I tried to do it."

She waited then, and I waited a bit as well. Feeling a fragile, young body, in a fragile, young mind, and wondering if the words I spoke would help her make it. I hoped they would. I promised myself I would see that they did.

"I'm trying to live my life in a way that Danny would be proud of me," I finally said. "And you should too."

She sniffed again, face pressed into my shoulder, the shirt there damp and warm. "Is that enough?"

Sarah had punished herself for years. Much the same way I had myself. And she thought she deserved it. She needed a way to make herself feel better. Hopefully, what I had told her would open that door a little. But it would take more convincing, and more time, for Sarah to heal from this wound.

It was amazing to me, the little moments in life that shape us. Maybe sometimes it was missing a phone call from a loved one, right before they passed away. Or maybe not stopping by just to say hello, when we had the chance. Or a final moment of anger, before never seeing them again.

"It will be," I said. The words were strong and reverberated from my chest. I hugged Sarah tight so she could feel them. "And you already know it. It's why you wanted to talk to me about it right now. It's what Danny would have wanted you to do. And you felt it, and you did it."

There was a long pause there. The sniffling slowed to a stop. When Sarah spoke again, her voice was stronger. "I did."

"You did," I agreed.

There was a longer pause. "Thank you," Sarah said.

"Oh, Sarah," I sighed, and realized something then. "We shouldn't have to thank each other for being the friends we are. It should just be something we do."

Headlights from a car lit up the window then, outlining Sarah and me in a bright white light. We both looked and saw a four-door black sedan sat in front of the shop, Nick at the wheel. Something large with a lot of room.

I waved at Johnny. He walked over and worked the chain to roll up the garage door. Nick pulled the car in next to the Camaro. The machine hummed a bit like it was something heavy and comfortable with speed. Sarah hugged me one last time and patted my chest before letting me go. "I'm glad you're back. I missed teasing you and my sister."

I winked at her. "I maybe didn't miss that as much as you." She snorted.

Nick got out of the car, looking at me curiously through his wire-rim glasses. The lenses reflected all the light and shadows in the room, but his eyebrows lowered in anger, as if I had done something to hurt Sarah. Jen pulled Nick away and talked to him in a low voice. Nick looked like he wanted to argue.

Sarah wiped down her face. I wiped mine as well. There would never be a time I would think about Danny without tears. Though there were smiles as well. Some lives were too happy, too innocent, to ever be forgotten.

We all gathered and started moving stuff around between the cars. Packing a bunch of things into the slick car Nick had found. He even had a key fob, and used it to pop the trunk.

We finished packing. It didn't take long. Nick went to the passenger side and grabbed a screwdriver and another license plate. "I took a few minutes to find another car that looked like this one."

"Won't they know their plate is missing?"

"Hopefully not for a few days," he said. "I switched their plates."

Smart. I still felt like Nick was angry at me for some reason. The two of us stood behind the new car. He knelt and screwed the plate in, not saying anything more. He stood after he was done and the two of us just stood there for a moment.

As much as I told Jen I would be fine, I didn't know it for certain. Things could happen at any moment. And Sarah's lesson was fresh in my mind, as well as my reply. Living life like Danny would have wanted me to. So I hugged Nick, a little awkwardly, since it wasn't something either of us was used to.

Nick had initially pulled back, then stood there awkwardly as well. I pulled him closer. There were a lot of hard edges under his jacket where knife handles poked out from his homemade vest. A moment or two later one of Nick's hands oddly patted me on the back, as if Nick hadn't been hugged in a while either.

"You take care of them," I whispered into his ear, and then let go. Jen might have had the largest amount of raw power in our group, but I was starting to believe Nick was the most dangerous.

"Of course, man," he said. His face was almost expressionless, except for his eyes, which were still open and a little surprised.

"And take care of yourself," I said. Nick was going to have a rough night. I knew a little bit about giving everything I had for a cause, for a person. To do something impossible on the slim chance I could save a life. It was draining, at the best of times. And it could be much worse, in a time like this. Especially when there was no other choice.

Even if it was worth it.

"Of course," he repeated, still a little stunned.

I let him go then. When I did, Sarah was standing next to us, and enveloped Nick in just as big a hug. If he had been stunned before, he was beyond stunned now. For a long time he didn't know what to do, but Sarah waited until Nick hugged her back, and when he did she gripped him hard for a long moment, and then let go.

The hard edge I had always seen in Nick left him when Sarah let go of him. Like a knife blade suddenly sheathed. Anger still existed underneath his surface, some kind of sharp edge rested there, but it had been put away for the moment.

He looked at me and grinned a small, silly grin. He was just Nick now, the kid who had lived with me at Parker's. Like a younger kid brother. He had always followed me, and mimicked me somewhat. I hadn't realized it then, but he had been someone who had looked up to me.

I took a breath. Then I looked at the group. "We all ready?"

They were all quiet. It was a somber moment that could have gone on a while. I didn't think anyone wanted to break it. So it was up to me.

"Tomorrow, then, five o'clock?"

Johnny waggled his eyebrows. "It's a date."

I wondered if it would be the last time I saw him do that. Then I shook my head. I would make it back. They all would make it there. Then the bishop. Then Azazel. Simple as pie.

I snorted.

I hugged Jen, hard. Part of me didn't want to let her go. She didn't tell me to be careful, and maybe she felt like the words would have been wasted. But she hugged me just as hard in return.

Then I was at the driver's side of the Camaro. Just me and my car again. It had never let me down, and I started feeling better about my chances. I opened the door, then stopped, one hand on the roof of the car, one hand on the windowsill.

"Which way to the contagion?" I asked, grinning. It was my cocky grin, and it felt good to wear it.

"Make a left out of here," Johnny said, waving a hand that way. "A mile or two."

"All righty," I said. "As soon as you guys feel it's safe, start rolling."

"We will," Nick said.

I got in the Camaro, looking back to watch Johnny roll up the door. He paused for a moment, a big smile still on his face. The passenger door opened next to me and closed with a light *thunk*, bringing in a scent of honeysuckles and rain.

Jen was already buckling up. I frowned. "What do you think you're doing?"

"I'm coming with you," she said. "The rest of them all already know it."

I shook my head a little with a smile. I had been outplayed. Jen had waited until the last second before letting me know. There would be no way to get her out of the car.

Johnny rolled up the door behind us. I glanced back. He stood to the side of the entrance, against the wall, taking quick looks up and down the street. The clock was ticking.

"I'm not going to be able to talk you out of this, am I?" I asked.

"Nope," Jen said. She waggled her eyebrows at me, mimicking the Johnny motion. "You and me, right?"

I cursed, but it was a curse without anger, and shifted the car into reverse. The Camaro was ready and pulled out with a thundering rumble, and it curved backward onto the street. "Of course you're right."

"Was there a question about that?" Jen asked, both of us looking down the street in front of us. The corner of her mouth curled up in a smile.

"You don't have to look so pleased about it, though," I told her.

"Don't I?"

I rolled my eyes. We pointed east now, down the street. I put the car into drive and floored the gas. The Camaro leaped forward, the rear wheels screamed across the blacktop, and then the two of us took off like the car was powered on jet fuel.

CHAPTER TWENTY-TWO

It was dark enough it could be night now. Bright streetlights lit our way, and the Camaro didn't hum so much as rumble, like a lion warning other predators away.

We headed east. The city became more, well, more city-ish as we drove. Blocks grew taller, buildings grew more packed, four-way stop signs became streetlights, red lights glaring ominously in the distance.

But the city was empty as well. Block after block flashed by. Very few people were out. I was surprised to think that people actually were listening to the warning about the contagion. Maybe there was more about it on a network, and people were at home watching it.

Some people were still out, occasionally one wore a mask, but we encountered very little cars. I had clear lanes and used them. I made sure to be aware of ghosts, in the background of my mind, as the spirits came into and left my radar. It was a large enough town that plenty of them were around.

"It's weird that this feels so empty," Jen said.

"Yeah," I said. I wasn't used to people taking warnings like a virus this seriously.

I punched the gas and got around one of the few cars on the street in front of me. We came up on a red light, and I took a peek at both sides before shooting through it.

Jen looked over.

"Have to get the cops attention somehow," I said.

Jen didn't say anything, but one of her hands crept forward and placed itself on the dashboard, so that she was bracing herself. We flew through a couple more red lights, brakes squealing at one as we passed.

I hammered the gas pedal down. The Camaro responded with a rumbling roar. Ahead of us flashing blue and red lights appeared. Police cars parked, blocking off the street ahead. As we neared, the cops started to turn back and look at us. A few ran to their cars.

I hit the brakes and the Camaro skidded to a stop. The nose of the car waved back and forth as the front tires dug into the street. I sat there for a long moment, as if we were a group of people not expecting to find the police ahead of us, and unsure of where to go next.

One of the cops was ready. She spoke into the two-way radio on her shoulder. Her other hand already had flipped the leather strap over her gun, and was pulling it out. Other cops were running toward us from down the street.

I threw the Camaro into reverse and gunned it. The cop stopped talking into the radio and pulled her gun. But we were already heading north, down a side street. After we went a block I slowed down long enough to see the first police car turn into the street after us, and then I hammered the gas pedal down.

Whether Nick had done something back in Lewiston, or Tabitha, the Camaro felt more alive now than it ever had before. More responsive. More ready. It launched down the street, handling turns with grace, wheels spinning around sharp corners, leaping forward each time I punched the gas. The baseball hanging from the rearview mirror jumped each time I did, as if urging us on.

More police appeared behind us. I kept them in the rearview, slowing only if they lost sight of the car.

The one police car became two, then three, then nine. The plan was working. There would be enough attention on me and the Nephilim of Kimaris that Johnny and Sarah would be able to get away without a second look from anyone.

I tapped a ghost, just enough to augment what I could hear and see and to speed up my response time. A quick wash of stomach pain shot through me, something the ghost had eaten or drunk, and I forced away whatever memory the spirit had pushed on me.

My sight grew clearer. My hands were quick on the wheel. I saw farther, even in the dark of night. And my hearing took in *more*. Back behind us was the *whump-whump-whump* of the helicopter.

I grinned. "We got the chopper too," I said. Which gave free rein to Johnny and Sarah.

"Get to da chopper," Jen said, grinning back. A line from a movie we had watched together as kids.

The helicopter closed the distance quickly. Soon it was above us, and a spotlight circled the street around the Camaro. I weaved a little, here and there, making the person handling the spotlight zig and zag the beam across the car. It was unnecessary, maybe, but I enjoyed making him work for it.

Sirens sounded ahead and to my left. My mind did a quick calculation and I floored the gas pedal. We reached an intersection seconds ahead another wave of police cars and flashed by them. There was a huge screech of tires and popping sounds as some of the newer cars slid into the cars that were following us. A couple of the cars spun in circles and slammed against parked cars on the street. The spotlight left us for a moment and circled around the pileup in my rearview.

"Wow," Jen said.

I slowed down just a bit, not enough for anyone to notice, but enough to get a few cars back on our tail. The spotlight returned. I pressed the gas pedal down. The Camaro surged down the street.

The dance continued in that fashion, until we made it to the outskirts of the city and into the country. Another helicopter came in from the east, adding another spotlight to the road. It brought a bunch more police cars, darker in color. State police.

There was oddly more traffic on the road out here, cruising past suburbs and out into the country. Like people had yet to hear about us, or the virus. I had to swerve around cars, into oncoming lanes, dodging headlights heading toward us. At one point even stop at a stop sign to wait for a couple of big rigs to cross right to left in front of me.

The eighteen-wheelers took long, arcing turns toward us that seemed to take forever. The first truck's headlights flashed across our windshield, and I held a hand up against the glare. Between all the headlights and the spotlights, the entire intersection was lit as bright as day, and could see large fields on the other side of the rigs. I glanced up at the helicopters, hanging above our heads, and listened to the sirens gaining volume behind us, and my hands drummed the steering wheel.

"You like this, don't you?" Jen asked. Grinning a bit.

I smiled in return. I did like this. Jen had been right earlier, I did like danger. But not for danger's sake itself. I liked putting myself before my friends. I liked risking my life to save theirs. To protect those I cared about. It meant something to me; it was a higher purpose of my own that I served.

I loved the thrill of the fight, when everything I gave was to protect my friends. If I checked out, it would always be because I had given everything I had. Because I had nothing left. Jen had seen that in me as a kid. She knew me better than I knew myself. It was funny, and I wouldn't admit it out loud, but she was usually more right about things than I accepted.

Something dark flashed ahead of me, a black tendril framed by the spotlights, snapping through the air in a quick moment. It had moved so fast I almost missed it, even with my augmented senses. The eighteen-wheeler directly in front of me stopped in the middle of the intersection. A face pressed against the driver's window and screamed. I watched the skin darken to a bronze color, just slightly, against the glass.

Kimaris. The demon had found us.

That was both good and bad news. Good for the others. Not great for Jen and me.

I punched the gas. The rear end of the Camaro fishtailed on the road. Jen rocked to the side and caught herself.

"Kimaris," I said.

"Shit," she said.

I swung the Camaro off the side of the road and around the big rig. Dirt and gravel kicked up behind us, and we bounced up and down on the grass. The car slid a bit when I goosed the pedal, and then the tires grabbed purchase as I found the road on the other side of the rig. We shot off into the night.

Both spotlights found us for a moment, and then wobbled off the road. As if the operators of the lights had suddenly released them. Both helicopters hung in the air behind us for a long moment, hovering uncertainly over the land, and then in a synchronized motion turned in our direction.

We were going to run out of time faster than I had hoped. But I was more prepared as well. I had kept a running awareness of ghosts, and there was a large field of them a few miles ahead. Another cemetery. If we were going to have to fight it out, I planned on bringing plenty of ammo to the party.

The rig behind us backed up. Police cars swarmed around it, like locusts. Other cars were involved now too, trucks and minivans and even a bright yellow Volkswagen beetle. To my left a tractor slowly rumbled its way toward us, across a large field of hay.

"This feel a little déjà vu to you?" Jen asked me.

I grunted. Back in Grafton we had led vampires to the water tower, baiting them with balloons filled with a drug they were addicted to. The vampires had jumped in front of the car, jumped out of houses, and chased the Camaro as a horde of creatures ready to kill.

It did feel the same. Eerily so.

"No water tower this time," I said, focusing on the road. All of a sudden it was everything I could do to stay ahead of the fleet of vehicles behind me and the helicopters overhead. And all of a sudden I was worried about Jen.

"We're going to have to fight it out," I said.

She looked a little sad. "You see the minivan?"

I had. We had raced by it. It was one of those that had the family on the back of it, a bunch of white stick figures, all holding hands. And a baby-on-board sticker.

"How many kids are back there, you think?"

"Whatever's back there isn't a kid anymore," I said. "Or a wife or a husband. Or a policeman."

"It still feels wrong," Jen said, a little arc of electricity racing down her arm.

She was facing a decision I had wrestled with for many years. In the past, people always died if I didn't run. Fewer people died when I did.

I had still been caught on occasion. I had tried my best, but people had still died. I didn't know what to do about it. It felt like there should be more meaning to it all. All I could do was add it to the tally that Azazel owed me.

And, if I was being honest, if it was between all the minivans and cops and tractor-riding farmers out there and Jen, I was always going to pick Jen and live with the consequences.

"You know I'm worried," I said to her. Just one bullet, aimed or stray. One overwhelming horde of demons tearing her apart.

"Me too." she looked over at me, one eyebrow arched. "One of us has already been shot today."

I rolled my eyes and laughed a grim laugh. "That's a fair point."

We raced down the road. The country opened up around us, large fields stretching far and wide, round bales of hay spread sporadically through them. Then the cemetery, nothing fancy, just a chain-link fence surrounding dark square edges in the night. A little churchyard. Ghosts littered the lawn, and I pulled a good amount from one, feeling the jolt of power course through me.

The helicopters closed in quickly overhead. They flew low enough it seemed like they might try to dive into the car. Jen looked at me, and this time I did see little flashes of blue and white roll around in her hand.

"Are they the demon?" she asked.

"Probably," I answered. It seemed likely, but I couldn't see them and didn't know for sure. Jen clenched her fist and looked backward, trying to get a glance. Neither one of us wanted to fire the first shot, and yet we were stuck in this world where we were afraid the first shot fired at us would kill us.

Thunder rolled down from the fields in front of us. It felt like a wave washing over the car. My augmented senses felt tiny vibrations in the steering wheel as the rumbling sound traveled through the frame of the Camaro.

Beyond the cemetery lay a church. Likely the whole thing was a churchyard. The building was old and wooden, with a brick base and white wooden walls. A tall steeple held a small bell at its top.

I spun the Camaro into the parking lot.

The helicopters veered off at the last second, rising high overhead.

I drove the Camaro over the blacktop and slid it to a stop beside the church. Jen and I got out. I already had my shotgun in my hand, and I had the knife Nick had given me still in the sheath on the back of my belt. I hoped Jen had hers. The two of us raced to the front doors.

They were locked. I banged on the door with a hand.

The spotlights found us again. Headlights brightened up the walls of the church around us as cars found the parking lot. They had been freshly painted, and a tiny metal cross hung on either side of the door, just a little above us. As far as I could tell, there were no windows.

I pounded on the door some more. Maybe the father here was slow, or old. Or maybe a priest didn't live in this one, though I had thought that was the rule.

The rumble of cars entering the lot got louder. At any point one of the Nephilim with a gun could open fire. I was worried, especially about Jen, when a bullet could take her quickly from me, at any moment. I pumped the shotgun and fired a shell at an angle where the handle of the door met the frame.

The buckshot splintered the wood and the door creaked open. I herded Jen inside just as doors started slamming shut from the parking lot.

It was dark inside. There was a creamy kind of melted-wax smell in the air. There were a couple of wooden pews up front, but the rest of the rows were folding chairs.

I tried to place the chairs so they would brace the door, but they kept sliding out across the wooden floor. Nothing really worked. The doorjamb splintered inward pretty spectacularly around the hole. I even bent the chairs and used a little ethereal energy to try to slap something together that would hold the door closed, but whatever I tried was a no-go.

"Dammit," I said.

"You shouldn't curse in the house of the Lord," a voice echoed from the front of the church. It was an older man's voice, and a little-high pitched, but firm.

The lights flicked on. I grabbed the shotgun, quickly seeing the altar. A large cross hung on the wall behind it, one of those crosses with a statue of Christ hanging from it. To the right of the building was a tiny table with unlit votive candles beside the Virgin Mary.

Between the altar and the table stood an older man, a dark brown robe wrapped around him, one hand on a light switch on the wall. The robe was fuzzy, and the man wore big white fluffy slippers with rabbit heads at the toe of the slippers. Each of the heads had big rabbit ears, and one of the ears flopped down a bit. The priest, if that was who he was, blinked like he was still a little sleepy.

"Father?" Jen said, or asked, or likely something between the two.

"What do you all bring here?" The priest's gaze remained on my shotgun.

"I'm not sure you'd believe us," I said.

He tilted his head. "I've heard a lot of crazy things in my time."

"I'm sure you have," I said. "But this is on a whole other level."

A voice called out my name from the parking lot then, loud and strong. A battle cry, from warrior to warrior.

Kimaris.

I turned and edged the door open. The parking lot had filled with cars. The tractor, even the tractor-trailers lay by the side of the road. Somewhere between fifty and a hundred people stood in a semicircle in the parking lot, and some of them held guns. A few cop cars in the lot, some with pistols in their hands, some with shotguns and at least one assault rifle.

The demon stood before of them, still in the semicircle, though, like there was a barrier he wasn't yet willing to cross. Or couldn't cross. His skin shone bronze, even at night, and he was just as big and powerful as at the rest stop. He wore the same getup. The black trench coat over a red shirt, and his sword once again poked out over one shoulder. The helicopters circled overhead, and the spotlights flashed across the lot between us.

"You need something, Kimaris?" I called out.

"Make this easy," the demon called. "Send your friends out, and I'll let you live."

Friends. So he hadn't seen or noticed it was just Jen and I. Point for our team.

"Why not come and get them?" I asked.

"It would be interesting." The demon's whole body grew a tiny bit larger, as if he flexed. "I have not had the opportunity to test myself in that fashion in a long time."

"Why my friends?" I asked, curious. "Why not me?"

The demon grunted, and frowned. "Azazel has made it a condition of my release."

Oh. Azazel hadn't just opened the Key, he had used it to summon his brother demon from the Key, and had laid a condition on his acceptance. Interesting.

"Why not kill him?" I asked. "You don't seem like a guy who would take orders from someone else."

"Perceptive," Kimaris replied.

I sat and waited. I wondered if Kimaris had been the first demon summoned by Azazel, or the first demon summoned that had accepted the condition Azazel had given. It spoke to a greater plan to all this, the one Jen had started us looking for, and that plan was right on the edge of my understanding, if my brain would just grow large enough to encompass it.

"All warriors have a code," Kimaris finally said. "I will honor mine. And once the honoring is done, I will extract my vengeance on my brother."

Strange, then, that Kimaris had a code, when many demons did not. The rest of the crowd stood patiently behind him. Like statues. I wondered what the demon meant. He had been imprisoned long before churches were a real thing. Maybe the place just had to be a place of faith? Of worship? Was the belief of the members of this church the only thing protecting this church? I remembered the minivan with the Believe bumper sticker back at the welcome center, the tiny face pressed up against the van's window.

I didn't know.

I would need to make a decision, though. I wondered if Kimaris, even now, was bringing more warriors to us. How far could the demon reach?

I held a finger out to Kimaris. "One moment, please."

"Of course." The demon bowed his head, just a little. "There is time yet for you to make the right decision."

And he waited. Which was awfully decent, for a demon.

I turned back. Jen stood next to the priest, as if she had been explaining things to him. "Can a demon get into a church?"

"Surely you're pulling my leg." The man frowned. He had woken up some. "Do you mean a real demon?"

"Yes," Jen and I both said, at the same time.

The priest pulled back his head, like he wasn't ready to believe something like that, but he pursed his lips, as if thinking.

"A demon could not just enter a church," he said. "He couldn't just walk in."

"Just speculate for me," I said. "Could a demon *theoretically* get into a church?"

"I don't know what you're asking," the priest said. Worried. Not understanding.

"Let's say we're in a church," I said. "And a demon is outside a church. How could that demon get in?"

He paused. I felt the rush of everything happening outside. Kimaris. All the clones. The upcoming battle. I wondered if we could hide in here, and be safe. I didn't think so. Even if Kimaris couldn't come in, he could just shoot the place up. Or burn it down.

The priest looked at me. I think he was torn between telling me demons weren't real and knowing if he said that, he would be revealing himself as not really a believer of his own faith. So he stood there and said nothing.

"There's got to be something," I said. "Just hypothetically."

"Hypothetically?" The priest jumped on the word, as if it were a lifeboat in the middle of an ocean. "Hypothetically, the church would have to be desecrated somehow."

"How's that happen?" Jen asked.

"What's out there?" the priest asked. "Maybe you all should leave."

"Not right yet, Father," I said. "Will you answer the lady's question?"

I think he humored us in the end, hoping that would get us to go away. "There's a few ways. The easiest is to not have Mass in it for a few years."

"Anything else?" I asked. Kimaris wasn't likely to wait that long.

His gaze wandered from the door to the shotgun in my hand. "Fire. Burn a church down, something that caused serious damage to the integrity of the church. Remove the symbol of the faith."

That could definitely happen here. The protection the church offered against demons wouldn't provide the same shield against bullets. Maybe that's why so many churches were brick or stone.

The priest tilted his head, like a thought had struck him. "Since you said the word *demon*, there's some old tales. Human blood spilled in a church can desecrate it. Or if filth is brought inside its walls."

I didn't know if me getting shot would desecrate this church, and let Kimaris easily come in. The second word didn't make sense. "Filth?" I asked.

The way he said filth made me think, not of dead animals or horse shit or anything like that, but something or someone with bad intentions.

"Filth," he said. "Something or someone with no faith. Pure evil. A person or being that couldn't just walk into a church, but if he was snuck in somehow, that would desecrate it. He would have to be brought in, without knowing he was brought in."

That didn't make sense. If Kimaris and I fought outside, and somehow we wrestled and ended up inside the church walls, was I accidently bringing filth in? Would that be enough? How could you sneak a demon into a church, without the person doing the bringing knowing about it?

I shook my head. The line of thought robbed my attention from the problem at hand. It would just be a matter of time before Kimaris had the people outside start shooting. And someone surely had a lighter out there.

Whatever time I bought, it wasn't going to be enough. We were going to have to fight. Right. Now.

"How do you want to do this?" I asked Jen.

She smiled and held up her hand. Tiny blue streaks arced across her fingers.

The priest stared at them, and stammered.

"Relax, Father," I said. "We're not the kind of filth you should be worried about.

"If I go after the demon, can you keep the rest of them occupied?" I said to Jen.

A sharp cracked of thunder answered from outside the church, followed by a long, low rumble. Jen's response.

Kimaris would go after Jen. I wanted to use that. I hoped if his focus was diverted enough I could hit him with the shotgun. Or get close enough to use Nick's knife. Either way, if that happened, we knew the rest of his warrior-clones would fall down dead, and that would give us enough time to get away.

"Make sure you beat his ass," Jen said. I knew, as I did in these moments between us, that she was thinking of the tiny red shoe back in the welcome center.

"Absolutely," I said, then looked at the priest. "Father, you got a place to hide?"

He really stammered then.

"Seriously," I said

"We have a tiny cellar." He motioned to the front of the church, to a small door beside the small table of votive candles.

"Go get in," I said. "Lock the door behind you. We'll give you a minute or two. Don't come out, no matter what you hear or feel, until the morning."

"I don't know what is going on," the priest said.

"You shouldn't be any different than the rest of us," I said with a grin.

The priest looked at the two of us. Jen raised her eyebrows and cocked her head to the door. He seemed to listen to her better than me, and finally made his way to the cellar. I waited until he walked through the door and closed it, and I waited some more until there was a faint thump of another door closing behind that one.

"I don't want you worried about me," Jen told me.

I remembered my mother's sword at the battle at Raphael's, punching forward out of Jen's stomach.

"I don't know that I can promise that," I said.

"I'm serious," she said. "I can take care of myself. You can too. If we're going to make it out of here, we have to trust each other."

"I've always trusted you, Jen," I said, frowning.

"Not like that," she said. "We have to trust that we're both strong enough to survive this. I have to trust that you can keep yourself alive, so I can focus on what I need to take care of. I want you to trust that I can keep myself alive, so you can get that bastard."

I took a moment, then I took another. Jen would always see things clearer than me. And I finally nodded.

She smiled.

I opened the door and we both walked out. I held the shotgun loosely in one hand. Kimaris grinned, and licked his lips. A chill wind blew across the parking lot and Kimaris's coat fluttered behind him. Clouds gathered above and hid the moon. The air brought the wet scent of rain. The cloud thickened enough that the helicopters dropped down from their great height above us.

Jen and I stepped down the couple of stairs and stood side by side in front of the crowd. I became aware of all the ghosts in the churchyard beside us, then picked one at random and tapped it. I was prepared for the spirit's resistance and readily overcame it. A faint memory of blood filled the back of my throat, and I quickly swallowed it, and the memory, down.

Kimaris frowned, waiting.

"Where are the rest?" he asked.

"We're all you got tonight," I said, ratcheting back the pump of the shotgun. "You always bring a sword to a gunfight?"

Kimaris got it then, that we were here for a battle.

"As it should be." The demon grinned, and then went for his sword.

A large bolt of lightning forked down from the skies and hit around Jen, hard enough that the wave of force pushed me to the side. I had to brace one leg against it, just to stay standing. Kimaris too, and the demon threw a forearm up to protect his face.

Blue light flickered over me, from Jen. She had a perfect circle of lightning rolling around her, like a shield. Jen caught me looking and winked. She had learned a new trick. I didn't have to worry so much about protecting her. So I snagged as much energy as I could from the ghost and began shooting at Kimaris, shell after shell.

Lightning thundered across the air, the strikes pounding over the heavy whine of helicopters in distress. Another strike followed, beating the ground along the front of the crowd, tossing bodies into the air. The bright flashes were almost strobelike in their brightness, and the bodies tumbled like stop-motion animation, pausing in the air as every strike hit.

Kimaris had drawn his sword, slicing in front of the air, somehow deflecting all the buckshot with it. I tried several different angles to hit him, and each time he moved the sword to block the shot, almost as fast as I fired. Scattered pebbles flew through the air and hit a Nephilim, who screamed at the touch and started firing back.

Two seconds had passed, and the battle was fully engaged.

Jen circled away from me and faced the crowd. Bullets hit her shield and evaporated, disintegrating with a sound like a thick bug hitting a bug zapper. The sound at first was a couple of pops, and then became a heavy rain of zaps as more and more of the crowd fired at us.

Bullets pinged off me, deforming against my skin and ricocheting away. I made sure my connection to the ghost was strong, and kept pulling and reinforcing my skin and strengthening my muscles.

At the same time, more lightning struck the ground around us, a strike here and there blowing Nephilim into the air. In one hand Jen held the knife Nick had given her, and if a warrior came close she would flick the knife out and the Nephil would burst into a cloud of thick ash.

The wind picked up, and fat drops of rain started spattering the lot. Heavy clouds thickened the night skies, and below them the choppers spun and crashed to the ground. First one, and then the other. Red and yellow flames bloomed up from each impact.

Kimaris closed in while my vision was elsewhere. I got another shot off as the demon struck out with his sword. I jumped to the side and a metallic ting rang in the air as the shotgun was wrenched from my hand.

Kimaris grinned and pivoted quickly away. He raised his sword to strike at Jen's back. She was just pulling her knife hand back from a puff of ash.

I leaped and grabbed the demon's sword arm, landing in front of Kimaris and twisting my hips. I powered up with energy and threw the demon over Jen's head. He flew deep into the parking lot, tumbling through the air like a doll before disappearing into the crowd.

Even though Jen's back was to us, a lightning bolt crackled through the crowd, thundering into the ground right around where the demon had landed.

I grinned. We made a good team.

More bullets struck me. I felt them as I always did, tiny stings and fingerlike punches. I used more ghost to harden my skin and body. Sick memories ran through me, like a movie reel spinning faster and faster. A man with binoculars who watched a young girl undress across from his house. A younger kid stealing money from homeless people who slept on the street. A middle-aged lady who had poisoned all the pets in her neighborhood except for her own cat.

I pulled from them all. I looked at my arms and waited. For me it was a millisecond, but I had hoped to see the armor grow out of my skin again. There was a small part of my mind analyzing everything, trying to figure out how I had triggered it, back in the factory at Grafton. It would certainly be useful now. I had hoped I could create it again with a large amount of ethereal energy, like all the cops then.

So I waited some more. But the armor was a no-show. I was going to have to do without it.

I yanked Nick's knife from the back of my belt and went to work, cutting through the crowd on my way to Kimaris. Each cut left a puff of black ash behind me. Bullets and knives and arms struck me and bounced off.

Bodies thickened around me and slowed me down with a sheer press of numbers. Hands grabbed at the arm holding the knife. One Nephilim grabbed me in a headlock. I broke his arm and he fell off. I screamed and swung madly until I stood in a thick black fog.

A black fog through which a sharp black sword descended.

I saw the blade at the last second and deflected the cut with Nick's knife. A sharp ring echoed through the air. Kimaris followed the blade into the large cloud of ash, a long black scorch down one side of his body, part of his trench coat on fire. He cut again. I wildly parried it.

The demon's eyes were focused and he stepped much lighter than he should have been able to, dancing across the ground. I ducked and rolled and dodged well-timed swings. My hand stung each time I had to use the knife to parry. Each time, I barely was able to hold on to the blade.

Dammit. I had brought a knife to a sword fight.

We fell into a pattern. Then Kimaris quickly reversed a cut. Something freezing slipped along my hand, and the knife glittered as it twirled away from me. Kimaris smiled.

The ground shook around us as thunder echoed across the crowd. Multiple forks of lightning struck around the demon and me. Bodies and bits of bodies, hands and legs and heads, all tumbled through the air, like they all were in a glass jar that was being shaken.

Jen still stood in the same spot she had been in earlier, looking our way. She tossed strikes of lighting over and over all around us. Ozone became the only scent I took in.

I wasn't holding up my side so well, but she had hers locked down.

Kimaris frowned at Jen. He looked at the scorch on his side. The edge of the cut down his coat still twinkled with burning embers. He set his jaw and threw his sword, like a missile.

The sword struck Jen. There was a loud bursting clap. Jen flew back through the air and bounced off the front wall of the church, then fell to the ground. The lightning shield flickered out and I watched her try to get back up. She shook her head once, then again.

A lot of the crowd around me were picking themselves up. A lot of them moved toward Jen. Tiny flashes of blue light streaked out from her hand and picked a Nephilim off, here and there. But there were enough left that they began to surround her, and moved closer, like a press of zombies.

I screamed and went after Kimaris. We stood and traded punches. Each time I connected I put all the energy I could into it, but the demon was a big bastard and shrugged every blow off. It felt like my fists were punching concrete and that I wasn't doing any real damage to the demon.

I kept pulling and kept swinging. I ducked and dodged, and when the demon hit me hard enough to break something, I tapped more ethereal energy and repaired it. Maybe with a scream. Kimaris packed a punch.

Then I rinsed and repeated.

I kept one eye on Jen, though. She had pulled herself up and lay against the wall, one hand up. A few of the crowd still had guns, and when they fired a flash of light would burst from her hand. Other little streaks of lightning still forked out occasionally, but not large enough or fast enough to keep all the Nephilim away.

It wasn't going to be long before she was outnumbered and surrounded, and then Jen would get torn apart.

I turned and ran toward her. Kimaris grabbed my arm and swung me overhead through the air. I seized more ghost right before I hit the parking lot with a loud crack. The pavement shattered and gave around me.

My head rang like someone had hit a gong. I shook it and tried to get up. It felt like the ground was moving underneath my legs. Kimaris stood before me and I dove at his stomach, picking the demon up and pile-driving him into the ground.

We rolled around together. We traded head butts. I ended up on top of the demon and tried kneeing him in the groin. He laughed and grabbed me in a huge bear hug, squeezing me against his chest, my arms trapped inside his. Each squeeze popped a few ribs, and I had to keep pulling ghost to repair them.

Kimaris rolled, trapping me underneath his body. His arms tightened like a vise. I tried to find Jen, even lying upside down, but no longer could see her through the crowd around the church.

More and more of the demon warriors picked themselves up and headed toward her. The tiny flickers of lightning coming down became guttering arcs, and then those died out. We were both going to die. I flailed and pushed against the demon's chest with both my hands, but I didn't have the leverage or the strength to break his hold.

"I'm going to watch you watch her die," Kimaris said. His breath was hot against my cheek, and smelled like greasy meat.

I screamed and pushed, hard, but the arms wrapped around me were like iron. I swelled inside with the amount of ghost I had taken in. Unless something happened soon, Jen would die, and I would quickly follow her.

The memories played on by. I was the young woman, shopping for antifreeze, putting it in feeders. I was the man who pushed his wife down the stairs, and when she still moved I walked down and stepped on her neck. I was the guy who shot his friend during a hunting trip, and later slept with that man's wife.

Kimaris chuckled, lips wet against my ear. I screamed and pulled and pulled and pulled and punched my fist against the demon's chest. If I only had Nick's knife –

Kimaris's chuckle ended in a bubbling gurgle. The demon's arms relaxed around me, going limp. His eyes opened wide, and he tried to say something, but instead cold black blood ran out of his mouth over us both.

My hand balled up against his chest. Something ethereal shimmered around my fist, and a matching shimmer came out of the demon's back. I rolled Kimaris off and pulled my hand away from his chest.

The ethereal sword came out of the demon's chest. It was long and crystal-like, almost transparent except for the sharp edges, which glimmered like starlight. Wisps of blue drifted from me and swirled in light circles around the sword. My fist was wrapped on the hilt, a simple cross of crystalline metal, pointed at each end in little diamonds.

The blade hung in the air for a moment. The dark night wavered a little behind the sword, like heat rose off the transparent blade.

And then it disappeared into thin air.

All the Nephilim dropped to the ground around us. Like someone had unplugged them.

Kimaris lay on his side, blood still pouring out of his open mouth. He tried to push himself up but couldn't make it.

I got to one knee. Kimaris rolled over on his back. His eyes found mine and discovered something that made the demon smile, almost ruefully.

"Fucking Azazel," he said with a sigh.

And then he died.

CHAPTER TWENTY-THREE

I didn't know demons could die. Not for lack of effort, on my part. But that's definitely what I watched happen with Kimaris.

Usually in my fights with Azazel, I would get a shot in, and he would disappear, leaving a charred outline of his shape on the ground. I thought I had killed him the first time that happened, and realized when he returned a few days later that that was just Azazel fleeing.

This death was different. Kimaris melted before me. His skin turned into putty, and then ran loose like a thick liquid, leaving black bones to rest in a gooey bronze puddle, dark with blood. Then the bones caught fire, a quick flare-up from head to toe, and the body was gone.

It left a horrible stench, and I gagged and stumbled away. Jen still lay against the front of the church, and waved when she saw me. I let out a deep breath and worked on putting one step in front of the other, making it her way.

"Hey," she said, smiling, when I got near. One hand held her side tight, though I didn't see any blood.

"Hey," I said.

"We kind of made a mess," she said.

I snorted. The front of the church had hundreds of bullet holes in it. Bodies lay around us, both whole and in a variety of pieces. Two shoes, feet still inside, stood in front of Jen, as if someone had been blasted into bits right in front of her.

Both of us were covered in gore. I sat down next to her with a groan.

Jen raised an eyebrow, which might have been as much energy as she had. "Is Kimaris dead?"

I was tired myself. I couldn't raise either eyebrow. "I'm pretty sure," I said.

"Did I see you holding a sword?" Jen asked.

"Yeah." I shook my head, wondering at the blade. "It just appeared."

"Like the armor?" Jen asked.

"Yeah."

"You need to figure that out," Jen said. "We could have led with it."

I laughed, and then groaned again. Then I tapped into a ghost and healed the bruises pooling in my body.

Jen tilted her head. "What did you just do?"

"Used a little of the ethereal energy to heal myself," I said.

"Think you can do me?"

"Now?" I asked, smiling a little lecherously. "Shouldn't we clean up first?"

She laughed then, a big laugh, which caused her to wince and hold her side tighter. "No, silly. My ribs."

"I don't know," I said.

"You did back at the motel," she said.

"I did," I said. "But maybe that was Danny."

"What's it hurt to try?" she asked.

She was right. And healing broken ribs had become a specialty of mine. I placed my hand over hers. Like every time, my fingers slipped through her fingers, like a puzzle fitting together. Jen smiled at me, and I felt like I always felt, like we were two pieces of the same person. She was just the better half. And then I found a ghost and pulled.

It was the lady with the cat. Her spirit was still around. Her gaze was angry and red, and she shook her bottle of antifreeze at me and spat. I took from her spirit anyway, letting the energy flow from my fingers and into Jen's, and then watched it swim up Jen's hand to her arm, and spill out over her stomach.

At the same time, a single memory chased me.

Fucking dogs chasing her cat ... Every fucking time. She keeps talking to the neighbors and they keep laughing. They think it's funny, her Sophia caught in a tree ...

So she poured antifreeze into bowls, into hamster water-bottles, into empty bottles of beer she had found at the front of the neighborhood. All the time she poured she talked to herself. Muttering about the people who lived around her.

The neighbors keep laughing and tell her just not to let the cat out. Her fucking kids never shut the door in time. But cats and kids should all be safe. Dogs shouldn't run free. If a dog chases her cat, they can chase her kids.

That morning the old man laughed and told me to get a life. What a considerate fucking neighbor to have.

She would get a life. She would get many lives. And she would start with that guy's dog.

She placed all the bowls out. Put the water bottles on trees. Put the beer bottles back at the front of the neighborhood.

The next day she woke up and went for a walk. A dead dog lay right in front of her house. Birds lay across the lawn, here and there. Squirrels too. All kinds of animals, everything. Dead.

Not her cat though.

A cop car sat in front of her neighbor's house. The old man, face red, pointed over at her. He was screaming at her, and all she could think of was the life she had gotten. She looked back and laughed and went over and kicked his dead dog...

The tap into the ethereal plane shrank, the ethereal energy dried up, and the ghost disappeared. I shook myself out of the memory with a gasp. Jen gasped at the same time, and then took a deep breath. Then another. Like she was testing something.

"Wow," she said. Moving her arm around.

"Yeah," I said. I was still trying to forget the memory. I was a big fan of dogs. But part of me was surprised, and happy. I could heal my friends. I wasn't exactly quite sure how, but I could.

Unlike the sword. That thing had appeared, but I wasn't sure how, or why. Or even *what*.

"I caught glimpses of something," Jen said. "A lady, did she poison something or someone?"

"Dogs," I said. "That's from the ghost. What I have to live through, every time I use one."

"Like back at the motel?" Jen asked. She shuddered. "That's how you have to do it?"

"It kind of stays with you, doesn't it?"

"It feels oily, and sick, somehow," she said. "I don't like it."

"Yeah," I echoed. "Me neither."

We lay there for a bit, not moving. Both of us were exhausted. It wasn't long before flies began to buzz around, though, and the scent of blood and feces thickened around us.

"We should get moving," Jen said. "Find a phone and call Sarah."

"Yeah," I said. Even with the last bit of ethereal energy I had pulled, I still was exhausted inside.

Jen looked at the parking lot. "What do you think they're going to say about all this?"

"Another terrorist attack," I replied. It was the way the world worked. It would explain anything away it couldn't understand, it couldn't prove.

"Seems far-fetched."

"Maybe," I said. "But I'm going to let the world worry about their own stuff. Right now I'm just concentrating on me, you, and our friends."

We finally got up. We took a minute and walked around. I found my shotgun, but neither of us found the knives we had lost. And neither of us wanted to search through all the bodies and pieces of bodies to find them.

We went inside the church. I knocked on the door the priest had locked himself behind, to let him know everything was okay and that he could come out. He had taken our warning to heart, though, and didn't come out, and wouldn't come out until morning.

I'm sure it sounded like a war had been going on outside, so I couldn't blame him.

Both of us were mostly silent after that. The inside of the church seemed to mask all sound. Even our footsteps on the wooden floor barely echoed as we walked across. The adrenaline rush had left the both of us, and for a while we just concentrated on cleaning up and getting ready to roll down the highway again.

The back of the church led to a little place where the priest had stayed. We found some clothes that didn't really fit, washed ourselves in a cold shower real quick, and tried them on. The best Jen could find was a blue sweatshirt that stretched a bit over her chest, and I found a white T-shirt that was too tight to wear. The shirt tore as I tried to pull it on. I gave up and grabbed the last shirt out of the Camaro.

We picked the best slacks we could out of the closet. The priest had been really skinny. The pants were a little loose on her and a little tight on me.

"Your ankles show." Jen pointed out, and laughed.

I rolled my eyes. But she was right, they did show.

There was a phone there, an old landline. Jen tried it, but there was no dial tone. Which didn't surprise me. I bagged up our old clothes and put the bag in a trash can out behind the church. And I left some money on the counter for the priest.

Then we walked back outside, where the Camaro waited. It stood off to the side of the church and had made it through the battle unscathed. It shone wetly under the dark night.

I popped the trunk. We had more pastries left. And protein bars. Jen grabbed the last of our energy drinks and surprisingly kept one for herself. Then we got into the car, popped our drinks, ate a quick calorie-heavy meal, and headed out.

CHAPTER TWENTY-FOUR

The car thrummed under our seats, full of power and ready to roll. We took back roads for a bit. Just a few miles from the church we passed a couple of cop cars. One had nose-dived into a ditch on the side of the road. Another had flipped. Like the cars had been flying down the road and then the people driving them had, well, immediately stopped driving them.

Jen was so exhausted she was pale. I told her to get some sleep, but she wanted to stay up and keep me company, so she cracked her window in response. Cold air whipped in and flooded the car, bringing with it the wet smell of fields and forests around us. Clouds still hung overhead, interspersed a bit. They dotted the night sky and gathered together to the east of us, as if they still marched to the battle there, and were just a little late.

"Where do they go?" Jen asked.

"Where do who go?" I asked. For a minute I thought she meant the clouds.

"The ghosts," she said. "The lady's spirit, it just disappeared. Where did she go?"

That was something I thought about a lot, and I hadn't yet found an answer I liked. "I don't know."

"Do they ever come back?"

"No." Not that I had ever seen.

"That would be scary," Jen said. "If that was all that was left of you, and then you were gone."

She shivered then, and I didn't know if it was from her thoughts or the chill wind.

"I thought I was killing them in the beginning," I said. "So I always tried not to take too much."

Lately, though, I didn't know how much I cared about ghosts like the lady with the cat, or Jo, or spirits like the trucker at the rest stop. Maybe they all deserved to be erased from the earth. But a part of me feared, when Danny had hugged me and given me all his memories, that there was nothing left of him. That he was truly gone.

It made living my life in a way he would have wanted more important to me now. I glanced at Jen. She caught my eyes and stared back, lying back against the seat, wind stirring her hair, tossing it back and forth. Maybe she was too tired to pull it back.

"But that's been a little hard to not do, lately," I said.

"It makes you wonder," Jen said. "Why they are here in the first place. Where they go when they leave. Where the other people go, if they die and don't become ghosts."

We were thinking the same thoughts. I kept quiet, though, because for me the thoughts were too real. Too personal.

Jen thought I was an angel. If I was, what did that make ghosts? Were they an echo of a person's soul? Was a spirit just what was left, after life had fled a person? Was there a place, when Danny died, where he still lived on?

I wanted to believe so. But if I did, that led to a larger belief. One I wasn't ready for. Might never be ready for.

Jen waited, giving me time to process. Inside I shook my head. She knew me better than I knew myself. The road rolled underneath us. I guided the Camaro into a steeply banked turn and the two of us sank a bit into the seats with the inertia.

"You're awful quiet," Jen finally said.

"I am," I agreed.

Jen smiled a sleepy smile. She knew where my thoughts had been going. She always did. Her eyes closed for a long moment.

"There's something about you they recognize," she finally said.

"The ghosts?" They all did fight me now. Like they were waiting for me. Maybe there was a spirt grapevine, and word had gotten around. Maybe fighting me was the last hope the spirits had to stay in this world, in some form. Maybe they just disappeared, and no one liked to be forgotten.

"Yeah," she said.

"What do you mean?"

"I felt it for a moment, when you healed me," Jen said. "Right after she started kicking that poor dog. I felt her rage, and her pain, but some of it was part of the memory, and some of it, I felt, was toward you. I just felt it. That she knew who you were. And she knew what was happening to her."

I was quiet some more. I couldn't argue that I had felt the same lately. Even before I tapped into them. Jo was a ghost who had recognized me, even before I had pulled at him. Recognized me and maybe lined up the worst of his memories, so that I would be horrified by what I had lived through.

"But I can't be sure." Jen's eyes closed again, and her voice was almost a whisper. "I think maybe I want something so much I imagined it all."

"Either way," I said, "we don't have to figure that out now."

"Mmmm-hmmm," Jen murmured.

Funny she doubted what she had felt. Jen had hit on something. The ghosts did recognize me. Maybe not me as a person, but something I represented. A natural order, long missing from their world. Some force I was a part of and didn't understand, which had always been there, waiting, like judgment.

A stop sign came up, in the middle of nowhere. I slowed to a stop and looked over at Jen. Her chest rose and fell evenly, her eyes were closed, and her hair lay wildly across her face. I leaned over quietly and rolled up her window. I carefully brushed her hair back with my fingers, and then I placed a gentle kiss on her forehead. Her skin was warm and soft under my lips. Like always, the scent of honeysuckles hung around her like butterflies around a flowering bush.

God, I loved this woman.

I froze then, startled by the realization. It was raw and passionate, filled with everything I was afraid of and everything I wanted. And I had always felt that way about Jen, but the force of the thought now, how it had just come out, caused my heart to beat harder in my chest.

I took a breath and let it out. Then I put the Camaro in drive and kept driving. I had always loved Jen. What would have happened, had the sword Kimaris had thrown killed her? Or the warriors afterward? Would she have been a ghost, like Danny? Or would she just be gone, forever?

Fear ran through me. Goose bumps tingled up and down my arms. Either way, my life would be over. It wasn't something I ever wanted to think about. I promised myself, I would do everything in my power, and if that wasn't enough, I would make sure to be the first to go.

I drove for a while after that. I was taking back roads, following signs to try to navigate a way parallel to the interstate. I would get on it later, but I wanted to put more distance behind me first. We needed to find a store and a phone and get in touch with our friends. We had a lot more work to do in the following evening. Thoughts of ghosts and who they were, or where they went, could wait until later.

I shook my head and pressed the gas pedal down. It was definitely too late at night, or too early in the morning, for these kinds of thoughts. I followed the road signs west, staying parallel to the interstate for a few hours. I didn't have a map, and a few times I took a wrong turn and had to double back. Strange how fast I had gotten used to the phone's app directing me.

But a few hours later I started taking the turns toward the interstate, following the green signs with the blue shields on it. The fields and the trees became homes, each with a half acre of lawn, the lights out in the house and cars parked silently in the driveways. Those inside were asleep, not knowing who or what traveled through the night.

The Camaro powered along the road, content, the engine humming. I fondly patted the steering wheel, and smiled. The car fit me.

The sky cleared of clouds, leaving little twinkles of starlight in the west. The white face of the moon looked down upon us. It was still almost full, and so bright I was sure I could turn off the headlights and drive the car by moonlight.

We got lucky as we neared the ramp. A large megamarket was there, one of the stores that sold food and clothes, electronics, auto parts, and garden supplies. A gas station lay in front of it.

I slowed down and pulled into the gas station. Jen woke then and smiled. The attendant didn't even look up when I prepaid. I pumped the gas and then drove over to the megamarket. There were multiple entrances, but one of the doorways was dark and locked. I parked nearer the lit one.

"Going in?" Jen asked, curling into her seat some more.

"Grabbing a phone," I said, and smiled. "Maybe a new shirt."

"See if they have coffee?"

"Sure."

I walked in, taking a blue basket by the door at the front. Then I stocked up on bars and energy drinks. I also picked up some jeans and a few shirts. They were the cheap ones with a superhero logo on the chest, and each of them had funny sayings like *I'm just saying you haven't seen JetMan and me in the same room together,* and there was one I actually smiled at, *I have no superpowers, so I'm guessing I'm the villain.*

I purchased a phone as well, adding what Johnny had gotten the other day. Chargers, earbuds, all that stuff. A few prepaid cards. The shop didn't have any hot coffee, so I walked the cold aisle and tossed a few cans of flavored lattes into the now-heavy basket.

I passed the fruit and vegetables at the front. There was a stand of flowers, and at an impulse I picked up a few. A group of yellow sunflowers with blue lilies.

I brought everything to the car, leaning in and putting the bags in the backseat. I pulled out the phone package and handed Jen a drink, but she looked at my other hand. The one holding the flowers.

"Are those for me?"

"They are," I said. A flush warmed my cheeks. I hadn't ever given anyone flowers before. Then I rolled my eyes at myself and handed them over.

She smiled and took them, putting her face into them and taking a deep breath.

Then she sneezed.

I laughed, and she smiled. Her hand grabbed mine for a moment and squeezed it, then laid the flowers in the backseat. We both changed clothes in the car, and she ended up with the shirt that said she might be a villain. I grinned again.

I started tearing the phone stuff out of the packages. Jen cracked the canned latte, took one sip, and grimaced. "I think I'd rather have your energy drink."

"Too sweet?"

Her nose wrinkled. "Just tastes fake. It's not real coffee."

We got the phone working. Jen called Sarah first, putting them on speaker. They were still on the road, but close to New Orleans. It took longer; the interstate had a lot of construction, and of course there had been an accident.

"You guys good?" Johnny asked, his voice far away, as if Sarah was holding the phone.

"We are," Jen said. "I think we don't have to worry about Kimaris anymore."

I could hear Johnny's whistle.

"That must have taken some doing," he said.

"It did," Jen said. "But we're good."

"You sure?" Sarah asked.

"We are," I said.

Jen talked with Sarah for a few more minutes. She let us know that Nick had made it. He had called them, and also had been texting a bit. It was going to take longer to get into the city than we thought. Nick had the news.

"I'll let him tell you," Sarah said. Jen took it off speaker and talked for a few minutes.

We called Nick next. His voice was stronger over the speaker, and excited. Like he hadn't just traveled hundreds of miles on foot. The first words out of his mouth were that he had talked with the bishop.

"And get this," he added, "he knew Father Benjamin."

Both Jen and I grinned.

"Man, that's a good bit of luck," I said.

"He's ready as soon as Sarah gets here," Nick said. His voice thrummed with energy.

I pumped my fist, and Jen smiled, her eyes a little wet. It was a huge break for us. We were going to be able to save her sister. We were going to keep our band together.

"It's not all good news," Nick said to us then. "There's a curfew in town."

"In New Orleans?" I asked.

"Yeah," Nick said. "Same thing as in the town yesterday. A virus. It's been really bad for the past two days here."

Jen and I looked at each other, the same thought in our minds.

"That's not all," he added, "sometime last night all the people infected died."

I cursed silently. Not just Azazel, but Kimaris had been waiting for us in New Orleans, and apparently had been building an army there, which had collapsed when I killed him.

"How many people?" I asked.

"Literally thousands," Nick said. "They're still finding bodies. Could be tens of thousands. They've got the streets locked down. Everyone is being told to stay inside."

"Going to make meeting at the park rough," I said.

"I'm working on that," Nick said. "The bishop is going to try to help. But he may not be able to do anything. It's the government shutting everything down."

"Dammit," I said.

"Planes and trains are still running, but the police and National Guard are everywhere. It's martial law here," Nick said. "They're even blocking the entrances into the city with checkpoints for taking temperatures, monitoring for signs of infection, those things. From what I can tell, they are turning most people away."

I swore again.

"I'll figure something out," Nick said.

Maybe. The city on lockdown due to a plague, and my face on the news. It was a bad combination.

"I'm guessing you guys took care of things," Nick said. "With what's happening here."

He meant the dead bodies. More people killed that Azazel was responsible for. I smiled at the thought of the ethereal blade. Maybe I finally had something for him.

Jen gave Nick the rundown. He was quiet when she told him I had killed Kimaris.

"So, dead, dead?" he asked.

"Dead, dead," I said.

There was a smile in his voice. Nick was the happiest I had heard him, since we were kids. "Maybe we got something for your other friend, then."

"We're on the same page," I agreed. Though conjuring the sword brought a lot of questions, at least for me. What was the blade, really? Was it something I always had, or had conjured from somewhere? Why me?

There wasn't enough time to worry about all that right now. I just had to figure out how I had made it appear, and do it again, one more time.

Maybe I knew how.

"Get some sleep, Nick," I said. "Going to be a long day."

"Will do, bro," he said. Like we were kids again, back at Parker's. "If I can."

We all said our good-byes. I promised we'd call again when we got closer. He promised he'd let us know what was going on. Then Jen hung up and looked over.

"Switch seats with me."

"What?"

"You heard me," she said. "You let me sleep. It's your turn."

I didn't know if I could. I had fed off Nick's excitement, and I was worried about figuring out how to get into New Orleans. But we changed places anyway. Jen adjusted her seat and mirrors, fired up the car, and we took off. Heading for the ramp to the interstate.

Nervous energy still ran through me. I kept moving in the seat, and even tried laying it back a little more. Jen placed a hand on my arm, like always, and the warm contact felt good, soothing. Like always.

It was still dark out, and the hum of the Camaro's engine quickly lulled me into a good sleep. Some things just fit me.

CHAPTER TWENTY-FIVE

I woke as the car slowed down. The sun had crested the hills in the east and glaring sunlight reflected onto my face from the side mirror. I raised my hand to block it, and pulled the seat back up.

Jen had the radio on, something low and pop-sounding. I yawned a little, and even though I still was a little tired, I had recovered some as well.

Jen grinned. "Good morning, sleepyhead."

"Pop music," I groaned. I had always been a rock guy.

We were coasting up an exit ramp. There were signs of gas stations and restaurants and hotels at the top of the ramp. A strip mall sat off to the right, with a few small stores in it. I made sure to look for ghosts, and found a few.

Tall power or phone lines crossed the road in front of us, measured every few hundred feet. A truck sat off to the right, directly in front of one. The road was blocked off around the truck, and it had a long metal arm raised high up to where the lines hung off the pole, and a guy stood in the bucket with a yellow hat and orange vest.

We sat at the ramp. Plenty of shops lay on both sides of the road, to our right. Jen headed to the building I figured she would. One of the popular chain coffee places that seemed to be by every exit. She clicked the blinker and turned right.

She did love her lattes.

"How far are we?" I asked.

"Just a few hours," Jen said. "Thought we'd get some coffee and make a plan."

"Good idea," I said. I checked the phone. Johnny and Sarah had texted a bit ago. They were sitting on the interstate at one of the road-blocks. I called them.

"It's a bit weird, man," Johnny said to us. "They're turning cars around and sending them across the median ahead of us."

"Are you guys getting through?" I asked.

"I think so," he said. "Nick called us an hour ago. The bishop pulled some strings. Religion has gotten big here in the past few days."

"Still," he added, "I'm nervous."

"I understand," I said.

"Sarah keeps checking the internet," Johnny said. "There's no real mention of us in the local news. And our descriptions weren't great to begin with."

"Let me know," I said. "If they make you get out of the car, send me a text before you do. I don't care what it says. If they nab you, I want to know I need to come get you."

Johnny laughed. "I hear you, man. Will do."

I wanted to call Nick, but just sent him a message instead. If he was still getting sleep, he needed it. I left something saying to call me when he woke, then set the phone in the console.

Jen pulled into the parking lot by the coffee place, parking a little around the side. It was a square building with lots of big windows, and a green sign, almost a clone of the one in Lewiston. She tucked the Camaro between a large black sport utility vehicle and an even larger red truck, hiding it from the road. "Want to go in?"

"Sure," I said, remembering the coffee cake from the other store.

I'm sure we looked like people on a long road trip. Our shirts were already wrinkled, and our hair was matted funny from sleeping in the car. We both stretched as we got out. Jen yawned and covered it with her hand.

She still looked tired. A little pale. Like Nick, I had no idea how much the power she used took from her. It had to be a lot. I remembered how hard lightning had struck around me the night before, and how many bolts had crashed to the ground.

I could always pull more energy, if another ghost was around. My only limit was self-imposed. As long as enough spirits existed near me, it was always just a matter of how long I could keep fighting. Jen's power seemed more internal, and always took something from her. She needed rest, to recover. It was something I needed to learn about, if we ever had a day off.

She grabbed my hand and we walked inside. I took a deep breath of dark roasted coffee. The place was busy and we stood in a short line. Jen wanted a large vanilla latte with some whip, and something to eat. I checked and saw they had coffee cake, and I swallowed down some extra saliva that had suddenly appeared in my mouth.

It got to be our turn, and I ordered us two of what Jen wanted. It sounded good. I then ordered some of the coffee cake with extra cake, and the girl at the register smiled.

"I'm serious," I said, smiling. "Let me get three or four pieces."

The case didn't just have coffee cake there. There were thick muffins topped with big blueberries and a sugary crust. And they looked good, so I added, "And a couple of those muffins."

The cashier put it all in a bag. She took our names for the coffees. I went to pay, and as I did a shadow crossed across the shop, as if a heavy cloud passed overhead. Then there was a long, low rumble of thunder.

I left the change and turned around. Jen stood a few feet from me, facing the area with tables. Her body was taut with tension.

Azazel sat at the center table, just like in Lewiston. Wearing the same white pin-striped suit. He leaned back comfortably in his chair, legs out and crossed, and sipped from a tall cup. Just seeing the demon had me reach out and tap one of the spirits I had found.

"I remember him," Jen said to me, her voice low. Surprised. "He was sitting next to me, at the motel in Grafton. After the fight."

"That's Azazel," I said, and firmed up my connection to the ghost.

The rumble grew louder. The man across the street in the bucket looked up at the sky, hand on his helmet. The guy in the truck was on the phone. The advertisement on the truck was for that same mobile company, the one I had seen on the front of the paper back in Lewiston.

The company was building out the largest wireless internet for the fastest service.

Funny that the largest wireless internet still depended on lines being run through the ground, from city to city, all across the country.

"Careful," I said to Jen, my voice low as well. People stood in front and back of us. Others were seated at tables, enjoying a morning coffee with no idea what could erupt in their midst.

Much like earlier, the demon waited. He held his arms out to his sides, as if asking us if we were coming over or not.

Jen and I each carefully took a seat, like we were gunslingers sitting down at a high-stakes poker table.

Azazel set his cup down and winked at me. "I missed you, Grimm."

"So you keep saying," I said. "You looking for another friend, now that you're one short?"

"So he *is* dead," Azazel said. "Good for your side."

He grinned his demon grin, the one full of teeth. I got the feeling he wasn't surprised, and maybe even a little happy about it. Had I taken care of a problem for him? Was everything I did part of some plan?

Jen sat next to me, her back straight, hands underneath the table. She carefully observed our interaction. Maybe filing it away for later.

"So, what are you doing?" I asked. "Sending more cops our way?"

"You know," he said, shaking his head, "things are never as much fun when you expect them, Grimm."

"So, what's the plan?"

"Maybe there is no plan," Azazel said. "Maybe I'm making this up as I go along."

I snorted, and shook my head.

"Just say it," Jen said. Her voice controlled.

The demon looked at her, curious.

"Say what you came to say," Jen told him again. "And then go wait for us to come around and kill you."

"Wow," Azazel said. "Grimm, haven't you told her about me? Didn't you explain my need for the appreciation of a thing?"

"I did," I said. "You'll find she's a little more direct."

"I don't like wasting time either," Jen said. "So say whatever it is you feel you have to say, whatever thing you have to appreciate, and head back to New Orleans. Unless you want to go right now."

Every minute I was with Jen, I found something I liked more and more about her. We were all quiet for a minute. The barista called my name, and I went to get our coffees. She handed over a bag as well; I had forgotten to grab our breakfast.

While I did, Azazel and Jen sat and stared at each other. Maybe getting each other's measure. I brought our coffees back and set everything on the table in front of us.

"I like this," I said to the demon. "It's rare that I find you speechless."

"You will never find me in a state other than what I want to show you," Azazel said.

"I disagree," I said. The demon seemed a little rattled, and I wanted to press him a little more. "We know all about your plan, Az."

What I said didn't have the effect I had intended.

Azazel just laughed, loud enough that the other customers looked at us. "You do?" He wiped his face, as if there were actual tears on his cheeks. "What I have planned has been happening for thousands of years. How could you possibly know that? In a couple of days?"

"We know about the demons in the Key," I said. "And we know what you plan to do with them."

"Shit, Grimm," he said. "You've got it all figured out, then."

"We're close," I said. "You know it. And the closer we get, the better chance we can stop you."

"I could show you what I'm doing, I could put it right in front of you," Azazel said. "And you still wouldn't get it."

"Try me," I said.

The demon looked around, then pointed at the guy working on the phone line. "How many people you think pick up a phone call and know everything that goes into it? All the different metals in the wire, the switches, the components? How the signal crosses an entire country, from one house to another? How a signal moves from tower to tower, crossing oceans?

"All those people would tell you, I know all about how a phone works. And ninety-nine point nine percent of them would be wrong." Azazel bent forward a little, toward me. "Are you that point one percent, Grimm?"

"I'm starting to think I am," I said. "And the next time I stop you, I won't be sending you home either. You'll be wherever Kimaris is now."

His eyes narrowed. "What do you know about my home? Where I'm forced to live?"

I was quiet. I had touched a nerve. It seemed important.

"You done yet?" Jen asked.

"No, I'm not *finished* yet," Azazel said. He grabbed his coffee and sipped it. "What I'm doing now, really, is sitting here at the end, appreciating a thing."

The words *at the end* bothered me. It spoke of a finality in New Orleans. And try as he might, Azazel could not hide the excitement underlying his words.

"I told you, back in that cell," he said, "all games come to an end."

"Don't bet on anything you don't want me collecting on," I said.

"My bet has been placed a long time," he said. "New Orleans is it for me and you, Grimm."

Goose bumps ran up and down my arm. I remembered the conversation clearly in Grafton, between Azazel and me. The new game he wanted to play.

The world's safety ... or Jen's?

Jen looked over at me. I took a deep breath, and let it out. Suddenly shaky. Her words, back in the garage, came unbidden to me.

We may not all make this.

Promise me you'll keep swinging, Gus.

I'll haunt you as a ghost forever ...

I tore through the ethereal energy of the ghost. I had no idea if it fought me or not. I barely registered its memories.

Azazel's eyes had just begun to open a bit wider when I threw the table aside and jumped him. The two of us tumbled back over his chair and rolled across the floor, wrestling I grabbed both of his wrists and head-butted him. He made a sound, so I did it again. And just because he was hard-headed, I did it one more time.

The demon was laughing. That was the sound I had heard. I stood. Azazel still chuckled on the floor, even with blood pouring from his nose. So I yanked him off the floor and pushed him against the wall with one hand.

"Maybe we don't get to New Orleans, Az," I said to the demon.

He wiped a tear from his eyes, grinning his stupid perfect-teeth grin. I balled up some of the ethereal energy in my other hand, and wished for something like Nick's knife to appear there. Exactly in the same way I had done with Kimaris.

My hand was empty. And then it wasn't. The sword flickered into existence, more solid than it had the night before. It was almost a midnight blue, though still translucent, and the sharp edges of the blade shimmered in crisp, sharp lines.

I grinned, and turned from the sword to face Azazel.

At the same time the hand holding the demon to the wall fell against the wall. As if the demon had slipped my grip. He was gone.

I screamed. Angry. Furious.

The whole thing had taken just seconds. Some people were standing in the coffee shop, frozen in place. One or two had their phones up. Quite a lot of others were screaming too, beginning to run out of the place.

Our table had flipped upside down. Our coffees had landed on a few other customers, who had jumped out of their seats and were wiping themselves off. Jen had just finished standing up, and one of her hands flickered with electricity. Thunder boomed outside, and a hard rain started to fall.

I looked at my hand, and let the sword go.

It disappeared.

Then the ghost memories hit me. Bad ones. A man had lived next to the interstate, close by, and had selected and killed people as they stopped here. People who looked like they wouldn't be missed.

And then he had eaten them.

In a single moment I lived a thousand of his memories. I tasted human flesh, charred from a wood fire, the smell of burned meat thick in my nostrils. I licked my thumb and smacked my lips. I popped cubes of half-raw meat into my mouth and chewed. The skin stretched around my teeth and a piece got stuck between my teeth, and I – as the ghost – reached up with a nicely trimmed fingernail to clean it out.

I knelt and threw up in the shop. Inside, I was a mess. My stomach rejected everything I had eaten, and my mind fought horrific memories. Toward the end the man had carved pieces from his victims while they were still alive. He had eaten them as they watched.

And I lived all that. There was a tiny boy once, his mouth duct-taped, still screaming as the man had cut off his toes and popped them into his mouth like popcorn.

A hand laid itself on my shoulder. I fought it off, ready to fight something. But it was only Jen behind me, her eyes open and worried.

Others in the shop, those close to me, stepped back like I was contagious.

My eyes wouldn't look at Jen. I had almost hit her. The memories were getting worse, and part of me felt like they were taking me with them. A bad apple always ruined the bunch, and I had eaten a lot of bad apples. I closed my eyes and shook my head at myself and worked to swallow the bile down.

I fought a dry heave, retching up nothing. Jen stepped closer, and patted me lightly on the back, rubbing her hand up and down my spine. I swallowed again and tried to keep whatever was in my stomach down.

She handed me a bottle of water, the label of some glacier up North. It was half-drunk and I polished it off. I wiped my mouth with the back of my hand. I stayed on one knee. Rain still rattled the windows outside, but almost all of the customers were now out in it. Just the cashier girl and a barista remained, frozen behind the counter.

"A bad one?" Jen asked. Meaning the ghost.

I nodded. In some ways, worse than Jo.

"We probably need to go," she said, worried about me.

"Yeah," I said. I needed a moment or two more. Adrenaline raced through me from the fight, mixed with horrific disgust. The killing was one thing, but the relish and excitement at the eating was not something I had encountered yet. It was sickening, and the memories were inside me now, and I didn't know how to let them go.

I rubbed my face with my hand.

"You okay?"

"I will be," I said. Taking large, deep breaths. Keeping the memories inside me at bay.

"Go wash up," she told me.

I went into the bathroom. My hands shook underneath the faucet. I splashed my face with water, and gargled some of the vomit taste out of my mouth.

Azazel had directly threatened Jen. That dominated my thoughts. But I also had summoned the demon-killing sword and the demon had fled. He was afraid of me. And whether or not Azazel thought New Orleans was the end for us, I was going to make sure it was the end for him.

I took a few more deep breaths. I dried my face with some paper towels. Then I headed back outside.

The store was almost empty. Jen stood by the register, talking to the girl there. Jen had rescued our bag of coffee cakes and muffins, and had two new coffees on the counter beside her. Apparently she had talked the barista into making them.

The girl looked at me warily, but Jen kindly thanked her and left a nice tip on the counter. I picked up the coffees and we left. The rain had slowed to a drizzle, and completely stopped before Jen took the first step out the door.

The pavement was dark with water, and we stepped around a puddle of water as we both headed to the driver's side of the car. She arched an eyebrow, as if asking me if I was okay to drive. I let her know I was fine. Driving the Camaro relaxed me. She handed over the keys and we both got in, each of us taking a moment to adjust our seats.

I started the car. Jen handed over a muffin. I ate in one hand and drove with the other, the coffee sitting between my legs. We merged back on the interstate for our last leg to New Orleans.

The engine sounded smooth on the road. The rpm's settled under two thousand and held steady. The steering wheel vibrated slightly under my hand. There was a lot of traffic and I weaved in and out of it in a natural rhythm, pushing myself faster.

"You're really worried, aren't you?" Jen finally said.

"Yeah," I said. I wanted to get there and kill Azazel.

"You know that's what he wants, right?" she said.

"I don't get it."

She sighed. "Gus, we talked about this. He keeps throwing your friends in your face. He threw me in your face. As soon as he does, you let go of everything else."

I left off the pedal for a moment. The car slowed down and I got into the right lane before holding our current speed. She was right.

"Still," I said, "I'm going to kill him."

"Sign me up," Jen said. "But we should be throwing him off. Not allowing him to throw us off."

Oh. That's what Jen was trying to do. Threaten Azazel and have him more concerned about what we could do. And I had screwed that up.

"Dammit, Jen," I said. My fingers tightened on the wheel.

"It's okay, Gus." She smiled at me, and laid a hand on my lap. Offering comfort. "I guess it's nice to know some things never change."

"What could he be up to?" I asked.

"We got to figure that out," she said. "Soon."

"Yeah," I sighed. Time was running out, and we were no closer today to knowing what Azazel had planned than a few days ago. Just names of the other demons in the Key. Except for one. And I had the feeling that one mattered.

She looked around her seat for a minute, then opened the glove box. Then checked the center console. "Where'd you put it?"

"What?"

"The phone."

"Console," I said.

Jen looked again. "It's not there."

The phone wasn't where I remembered putting it. Jen looked around the seat some more, and unbuckled her seat belt to climb into the back of the Camaro and look for it there.

"It's not anywhere in here," she finally said.

"Did I bring it into the coffee place?" I asked her, trying to remember if I did or not. If I had brought it in, maybe I lost it in the fight.

"I don't know."

"Yeah," I said. Thinking I had put it on the console, but maybe I had brought it in and lost it in the brief fight. "I left it here. I thought."

"We can't go back and get it now," she said.

"No," I agreed. Part of me was surprised I had lost it. It had been the only time I had carried a cell phone, been responsible for it, and I had lost that thing in minutes.

It would have been great to have for the research. We were running out of time to figure out Azazel's plan. And we needed to get a hold of our friends as well. "You remember their numbers?"

"Yeah," Jen said. "It would be nice to have, though."

"We'll just have to do it the old-fashioned way," I said.

"Wild-ass guessing?"

"No." I remembered how my hand had felt holding the ethereal blade, knuckles white, fingers wrapped around the hilt. The way the hilt felt a little like leather. "Just make it simple. We get to New Orleans, find Azazel, and kill him."

"Not much of a plan," she said.

"Doesn't have to be," I said. "Hard for things to go wrong with a simple plan."

"I've heard you say that before," she said.

"It's gotten me this far," I said, wryly.

I thought about the plan, and liked it more and more. It was odd, Azazel's plans were convoluted, and ran over the centuries. Grafton was an example. The demon had plans backing up plans. He had strung events and people together, giving a small push to a person here, building up to a large event there. The two of us were almost opposites. Simple, easy, direct was where I functioned best.

CHAPTER TWENTY-SIX

I hated it, but we had to ditch the Camaro. The interstate became too congested, and it was taking too long to get to New Orleans.

As we got closer to the city the traffic thickened like a school of fish, vehicles slowly drifting westward, stopping and starting in a slow rhythm. A lot of cars were already turning around, zooming up the shoulder of the interstate and taking the next exit to circle back the way they had come.

To our north an occasional train rolled by. And big jumbo jets still flew east and west above us. It was still early morning. The sun had risen red in the east, coloring the clouds there in hues of crimson and orange. The planes appeared as dark dots behind us and grew larger as they moved west, big silver fishes high overhead, unaware of the little schools below.

We hadn't seen any police cars, although emergency vehicles were everywhere. The trucks were parked off to the sides and flashed signs on their backs, the arrows directing traffic. Large electronic boards crossed the interstate, posting messages in scrolling digital letters, warning of a contagion in the city and asking all people without critical business in New Orleans to turn back.

I felt like our business was pretty critical.

I finished off the coffee cakes while we were stopped, surprised to eat more than Jen. She told me they were just too sugary. I raised my eyebrows. The pastries she normally ate seemed worse to me. We nursed our coffees as long as we could. Mine was a nice blend of thick cream and dark roast, and cut the cakes perfectly.

We finally took an exit, maybe fifty or sixty miles out from the city proper. Just far enough that the city was a dark smudge in the west. An hour out, maybe.

Jen looked at me, an eyebrow arched. Wondering. At the top of the ramp I crossed some train tracks, then headed north down the road until I found what I was looking for, a rental storage place. It was a bunch of long white square buildings with roll-up doors at each unit.

I hid in the car and had Jen go outside to rent one. She came back out with a combination lock and a four-digit code to get past the gate at the front.

"They ask for a license?" I asked.

"I had enough cash to take care of it," she said.

Good. We had plenty of cash, and we only wanted the unit for a bit. I hoped to come back and get the car, once we were done here. I didn't have a plan for the Camaro, long term, but I've never thought that way anyway. I figured why start now? It was a car I liked to drive.

We pulled the Camaro through the gate and navigated the buildings until we got around the back. The roll-up door opened easily and we parked the Camaro in the unit. I left the keys in the car, tucked in the side seat.

Then we popped the trunk. I emptied the duffel bag and started packing it with things we might need. A little food, but mostly the shotgun, my .38, and ammo. A few things I had kept from Grafton. The picture Danny had taken of Jen and me. The bag of cash. Some of Nick's knives he had left. And a flashlight.

I would have loved to pack more, but ammo was heavy. The bag was made of a thick canvas, but I'd have to carry it awhile. At the last second I went up front and pulled the tiny baseball from the rearview mirror, and tied it around the edge of the duffel bag. Then I threw the bag on my back and the two of us locked up the door.

"Nine-five-one-one," she told me, getting up from setting the combination.

My look was blank.

"The day we met, dummy." Jen playfully kicked my shin.

I grinned. "I knew that."

"Sure." She rolled her eyes. "Sure."

We walked out the front, through the gate again. I wondered if the person inside had noticed the Camaro, and if they had, if they had recognized it. Or Jen. Or if there was some camera somewhere recording all of this, with someone watching, recognizing, even understanding what was about to happen. Who really knew?

I guessed it didn't matter, really. In my mind either we were coming back here, opening the roll-up door with the combination from the day we had met, or we weren't. Not much mattered more than that.

Jen mentioned being hungry. She had recently burned a lot of calories, and I had eaten all of the cake. We got some more to eat, at a fast-food place with chicken on a sign above it. It was the South, so we ordered some fried chicken breakfast biscuits and a pair of sweet teas. The biscuits were thick and moist with butter.

No one really paid any attention to us. The place was packed, the exit was packed, and all everyone could talk about was the contagion in New Orleans. Questions abounded around us, people talking about whether it was real, or wondering how many times a country was going to let a virus "escape" their labs before we all took action. I took it to mean war.

"What's the plan?" Jen asked.

I had a mouthful of biscuit and chicken, and had to sip a large amount of sweet tea to get it all down. "Nick said the trains were still operating."

"Is there a station here?" Jen said. Her eyes looked up, like she was trying to remember the exit. "And will they stop?"

"It won't matter," I said. I had spent a lot of time on the run. We'd get on.

Jen looked at me mysteriously, and I winked at her.

We finished our breakfast and walked toward where I had crossed over the tracks. There was a gas station on the east side of the road, and on the wall of the station was a pay phone. Jen saw it first and pointed it out to me.

"I keep being surprised to see those still around," I said.

She went inside and got a prepaid card, and came back out. We dialed her sister first, and the phone rang for a bit without being picking up. Jen tried again with the same result. We looked at each other.

She tried Nick next. He picked up on the first ring. Jen held the phone between both of our ears.

"Nick?" Jen asked.

"Jen?" His voice came out tinny, like something was up with the wires. "Grimm with you?"

"Here," I said.

"Good," Nick sighed. "We got problems."

"Is Sarah okay?" Jen immediately asked.

"I don't know," he answered. "They're missing."

Jen's face went white. I took the phone from her hand. "Tell us more, Nick."

"I don't know any more," he said. "I fell asleep." His voice was angry, as if he was mad his body had required rest. "We had just finished talking and they were coming up on one of the checkpoints. They thought it would be thirty minutes. I told them I was going to close my eyes, and call me when they were through.

"Next thing I know, the bishop had come in to check on me," Nick said. "They never called."

"Okay," I said, putting my hand on Jen's arm. "Have you checked the news? The police stations?"

"Yeah," he said. "Nothing on the news. And the bishop has had a few people check the stations around the east side. We can't find them."

"That doesn't make sense," I said. If they were at a checkpoint and the police nabbed them, then they would be in one of the local cells. And surely there would be some news coverage, if the police had recognized them. "They didn't text you or anything?"

"Not a thing," Nick said.

I cursed. I hated it that I had lost my phone. I had asked them to text me no matter what. And maybe they had, but I had lost it fighting with Azazel.

A cold fear ran over me.

I *had* left the phone in the car. I knew it now.

Azazel hadn't been there to talk to me. He never had. Everything he did had a purpose. He might not have even known we were using phones, he might have just done a quick search and found something that suited his needs.

He was a master of planning, but he had always proven himself to be a quick thinker as well. Great at adapting to situations. Plans don't last for thousands of years unless a person can do that.

So Azazel had taken our phone, and he had used it to call Johnny and Sarah. Maybe they had texted us that they were at the checkpoint, and the demon saw the text.

From there it would have been simple. Maybe he had told them he had us. Or maybe he even had pretended to be me, or Jen. But any way about it, he had used the phone to get Sarah. Because he had a purpose for her. A purpose that had begun millennia ago.

This time Jen took the phone from my hand, and she searched my face, her eyes worried.

The Key pulled at me right then. Hard enough that I stumbled against the wall of the gas station, and caught myself with one hand on the plaster. Then the Key ripped open again, somewhere in New Orleans, but where before it had felt like a zipper, this time it felt like someone tearing a thick blanket in two.

My legs trembled, and felt like they couldn't hold me. I leaned against the wall. The Key screamed at me, long and bloodcurdling, although I was the only person who heard it. Waves pulsed over me, like subsonic pushes of a supernatural creature in a hard labor.

The Key's scream dwindled, as if it had run out of air. Something dark and malignant entered this world. And another. And another, until the Key had birthed four evil creatures.

Jen grabbed me, shook me. "Grimm?"

"Key," I managed to get out. The Key felt like it had been cut wide-open, and the pain echoed along the bond I had with it.

"Shit," she said. "Nick, where are you?"

She waited a moment, listening, then told him, "Stay right there. We'll be there as soon as we can."

"Jen," I said.

"Nick," she said again, more serious. "I'm telling you to stay there."

He must have said something again, and Jen finally agreed. Then she grabbed me and held me against the wall, almost holding me up. I relaxed in her arms and took deep breaths.

I expected to see fire raining down from the sky over New Orleans, but everything around me looked normal. The city was a dark smudge, distant on the horizon. Maybe a building or two poked out from the skyline into the hazy blue sky.

I shook my head. Behind us came the swelling sound of the train's horn, long and loud, carrying through the air and over the earth. And yet it was muted, when compared to the scream of the Key.

"You okay?" Jen asked.

She had just been asking me that, just an hour ago after I had lived the memories of the cannibal ghost. And here she was, asking it again.

I would have to be.

"Yeah," I answered. "I think things are coming to a head."

"Then let's get on that train," Jen said. "There's a demon we have to kill."

I smiled. There was the sword. One demon, two, or four, it wouldn't matter to me. I would kill them all.

And I would kill Azazel with them.

Simple plans really were the best.

CHAPTER TWENTY-SEVEN

Getting on a moving train was easy enough, for someone with my particular skill set.

I had never done it with someone else, though.

Jen and I got to the tracks in plenty of time. The train was headed in from the east, a big silver engine, sleek like a bullet, an orange-and-white-and-blue ribbon horizontal along its side. Car after car stretched in the distance behind the engine.

The two of us walked down a bit, along the tracks but away from the road. Long bits of grass waved us on by. We found a spot where a tiny rise in the ground blocked the interstate from our sight, and then we waited.

The train came on. It brought the clickety-clack of its wheels on the tracks, followed by the low rumble of something massive rolling along the rails. We were close to the tracks, and the weight and power of the machine shook the ground under our feet.

I faced Jen. "I've never done this with someone. It might be tricky."

"Just tell me what to do."

I tightened the bag over my shoulders and had Jen hug me, like we were teenagers in a gym, dancing to a slow song. "Hold on tight."

She snaked her arms around me, and underneath the bag, then squeezed me.

"Tighter," I said.

She held on tighter. I wrapped my arms around her and hugged her back. My nose was by her ear, and the scent of honeysuckle from the nape of her neck calmed me a bit. The Key opening again had really rattled me, but I found it amazing that just a few minutes with Jen made everything right.

"How do you always smell like that?" I asked her.

"Like what?" Her lips nuzzled against my throat, and her mouth smiled against my neck.

"Honeysuckle," I said. "And a fresh rain."

"Witch's secret," she replied.

The train rumbled by us. I faced the east, and couldn't tell if the engineer had seen us, but there was no blaring horn, and the brakes never engaged. The clickety-clack of the wheels was all around us, the rumble of the engine swelled into a roar, and then silver car after silver car cruised by us.

"Put your legs around me," I told Jen.

She hopped a little and crossed her legs around my hips in a quick motion, distracting me a bit with a memory of our shower.

I steeled myself and reached for a ghost, taking just a little energy. I watched car after car pass us. Most of the cars were full, but toward the end they emptied a bit. I'm not sure why the back of a train is never as full as the front; everyone gets off at the same time. Maybe it's something residual in the past, or some subconscious effort to always be first.

"Ready?" I asked.

"Ready," she said.

A few cars from the end, I leaped into the air.

I funneled the energy into my legs so the leap would take us over the train. I overestimated a bit and shot a bit farther up than I intended, and for a moment both Jen and I were looking at cars sitting in traffic. A little girl in pigtails looked back at us from the backseat of a blue coupe, eyes wide-open.

We fell and landed on the top of one of the cars. My balance was off and we hit the roof a little heavier than I wanted to. I slipped and fell, but still kept an arm around Jen. We rolled a bit across the roof of the car, my free hand slapping for a handle, or a light. Something on the top of the train.

There was nothing, so I used a little more ghost and pinched the roof. The metal crinkled underneath my fingers, and the two of us jerked to a stop.

We lay there, side by side, the breeze fluttering through Jen's hair. She pulled her head back from my neck and looked at me.

"Soo ... tricky?" she teased, her lips curved, her eyes alive.

I grinned back. "We're here, aren't we?"

"Don't we get to ride inside the train?" she asked, raising her voice.

I got to my knees. On the roof, the train seemed like it was moving much faster than when we had stood beside it. The wind buffeted us as we crawled down to the far end, where the cars joined.

I pulled a little more ghost before we got too far away, and let Jen down right in front of the door, on the platform there. Then I hung down from the roof and dropped.

Jen tried the handle of the door, and funny enough it was unlocked. Sometimes I had to break it open. It was likely the conductor had already made his way through, us being so close to the city. No one expects someone to sneak onto a moving train.

We walked in and found seats in the back. I slung our bag in front of us. The few people inside the car turned to look at us, with at best quizzical expressions. I gave them a little wave, but they turned back with the same bored looks they had turned our way. Maybe everyone here was more worried about what waited for them in New Orleans.

I knew I was.

"Nick is going to meet us when we get in," Jen said. "He said the bishop is going to get us past the checkpoint."

"Okay," I said. That had been what they were arguing about, at the end of the phone call.

I hadn't worried about the checkpoint. If they wouldn't let me past, I would make my own way through. I hadn't planned on sneaking around when I got to New Orleans. I was going to get off the train, find some spirits, and go demon hunting.

"He told me to tell whoever met us at the train that our names were Jen and Gus de Sedella," Jen said.

I frowned. "Do either of us look like a de Sedella?"

Jen shrugged. "He said it's a code."

The parking lot on the interstate rolled by us. Car after car locked into a pattern that would never change, a puzzle that could never be completed, just shifted into something different, as cars occasionally changed.

Jen held my hand the whole time. She had to be worried about her sister. I was too. But I was also strangely confident. I had a way to kill demons now. And I had a way to find them. The Key would pull me to it, and I would follow that line all the way back to Azazel, and whatever friends he had with him. I tangled her fingers in mine and clasped her hand in return, making sure Jen felt my grip as something strong and absolute.

CHAPTER TWENTY-EIGHT

I t took maybe an hour for us to stop at the platform. The train went through several stages of slowing down, and blared its horn as it did. Warning everyone ahead, all the roads we crossed, the people driving around, announcing our presence.

Here they are, the train seemed to shout out, repeatedly, followed by a long *Here they aaarrrrrrrreeeeeeee.*

The final few miles were over a blend of swampland, older tracts of land on which sat shacks of homes, and lots of water. One of the lakes rested around New Orleans, but I wasn't sure which one. But the water was dark and muddy and little waves rolled across the surface of as if a breeze blew across it.

The train pointed to the skyline of New Orleans, tall office buildings and apartment complexes. We entered the city proper, passing run-down streets, the occasional store or gas station. Trash lay at each corner we passed, walls of buildings were covered in graffiti, though the blocks were suspiciously empty of homeless people. I wondered if they had been Kimaris's first victims.

The station was pretty empty, except for soldiers in National Guard uniforms lined up by every car. Every person on the platform had a mask on, one of the blue cloth masks with strings that looped back behind the ears. I watched one of the men arrange the mask to keep his nose covered as we crawled beside the station.

The doors slid open as soon as the train rocked to a stop. One last horn blew through the air. A young man walked in. He wore a uniform much like one I had worn in the army: a camouflage shirt, pants, and ball cap. A name tag over his right pocket, a patch signifying his rank on his shoulder, and a blue mask over his face.

He held a card in front of him and read from it. It was a little hard to understand him. The mask muffled his words, and his voice cracked a few times as he read. "Please do not exit the carriage until you are told you can. Please be aware that New Orleans is under martial law due to a severe contagion. This contagion is life-threatening, and only those who live in New Orleans will be allowed off."

Another guardsman came up behind him. She had her hair cut short underneath her cap, and wore the same blue mask. The patch on her shoulder had a cross on it, surrounded by the wings of an eagle. In one hand she held a laser thermometer. The young woman moved around the young man and started reading the temperatures of each one, then asking questions. When she was done, she moved to the next row, and the young man then followed up with more questions for the first group.

I took that moment to pull my bag and tuck it underneath our seats. It barely fit. Then we waited until the medic got to us. The thermometer was a little like a gun, point and shoot, and she read a spot in the middle of Jen's forehead, then mine.

She frowned and read mine again.

"How contagious is this thing?" I asked.

"We're not allowed to speculate," she answered in a clipped tone. Her voice was easy to hear, behind her mask. "Have either of you experienced feverlike symptoms?"

"No."

"How about rashes? Skin discolorations? Coughs?"

"No to all three, ma'am," Jen said.

"Okay," she said. "Wait here please."

She went back to the front of the car. The young man was next. "Do you all live or have business in New Orleans?"

"Business," Jen said. "Jen and Gus de Sedella."

The young man remained expressionless. "You don't look like pastors."

"Who said we're pastors?" Jen said.

"I just assumed …" The soldier looked at us both, and waited for us to fill in the blank. When we didn't, he walked back and talked to the medic for a moment. She said something in return. Then the soldier turned and waved us forward. "Follow me please."

I let Jen follow him. I got up and slung my bag over my shoulder, conscious of the metallic sounds clinking inside it. But the young man didn't notice or didn't care.

He led us off the train and onto the platform. It was warmer than it should be, this late in the season, and the air was muggy. We had been the only people who left that car. The soldier led us up to another man by a white plastic table. The table held hand sanitizer and masks.

"Grab a mask," the man said.

We both grabbed one. The paper cloth had folds that opened up and stretched over my mouth as I hooked both strings of the mask around my ears. Jen did the same with hers, and I flashed my eyebrows at her.

"Follow me," the man repeated, when we were done.

We followed him through the train station. Rows of brown plastic chairs with plastic arms sat on a tan squares of tile. A group of guardsman had set up more of the plastic picnic tables at one end. Two men and a woman, all dressed the same as the solider we walked behind, all wearing masks.

There was a young man with them who wore a brown shirt that wasn't quite a robe, tucked into blue jeans. He had long brown hair tied behind his head with a simple white band. A cross hung on the front of his shirt, and he had on a white cloth mask.

"These people say they are the de Sedellas," the solder said as we came up.

"Did you get their identification?" one of the soldiers asked at the table.

Another soldier looked at the young man with a cross and shook his head. His was the first voice I had heard that sounded Cajun, where each word got drawn out and blended with the next. "We won't need that."

"Shouldn't we check?" the first soldier asked.

Jen just stood there. I was somewhat thankful the mask hid our faces.

"Come on, Miller," the older soldier said. "What criminal wants to come to New Orleans *now*? Especially with everything else going on now." He looked at the young man with the cross and long hair. "Is this them?"

"Thank you, sir," the young man said, his voice was firm and serious.

"There you go." The older soldier waved us on.

We followed the young man, who moved with sharp, economical motions. He held the door outside for us, opening the door not all the way, but just enough for us to walk through.

Outside, it was warm and muggy. A Humvee stood off to the side of the station, a dark sedan idling in front of it. The sedan had heavily tilted windows.

The sun was a glow of orange descending in the west. It was bright and warm outside, and too muggy for the season. A breeze would have made the day nice, but the air was still around us.

The young man turned to look at the two of us, taking off his mask. His cheeks and chin were sharp, and freshly shaved. Though he looked like he was eighteen or nineteen, his face was serious and composed. "Fergus Grimm and Jennifer Cooper?"

He shook our hands. Every motion of his was precise. "Good to have you here."

"Who are you?" I asked.

"Bartholomew," he said. "I'm what you might call the understudy of His Holiness, the bishop."

"Isn't that one of the names of the apostles?" Jen said.

"That's correct." His lip twitched. "You can take off your masks. Let's do away with that fiction."

Easy enough. I slipped mine off my ears. "What did the soldier mean when he talked about everything else going on?"

Bartholomew looked at us both a moment. "Four cities have had what are being called terrorist attacks."

"Four," I repeated. Four cities. Four demons. Johnny had talked about them, the four demons who built towers and cities. Vine. Sabnock. Malphas and Malthus. But why? And which cities?

The young man answered the question before I asked it. "Paris. Mexico City. Hong Kong. And Cairo."

"Like Kimaris?" Jen asked. "Are they calling it a plague?"

Bartholomew shook his head. "Details are scarce," he said.

Within hours of the Key being opened, and four demons being released, four major cities had been placed under attack. If this was all part of Azazel's plan, I didn't get it. Jen looked a question my way.

"None of that makes sense," I said. And it didn't, in the world that existed between Azazel and me, in our fight. This was part of his greater plan.

"We can talk on the way." Bartholomew urged us to the sedan, motioning to the backseat as we neared. He got into the passenger seat in the front.

Jen and I got in. I put my bag on the seat between us. The car was running. The air inside was cool and dry and a stark contrast to the feel outside. Nick sat in the driver's seat, and turned to the backseat as we got in. He had black circles under his eyes, and his hair was a mess, but he still was Nick. Edged, sharp, and ready.

"You guys good?" he asked.

"Good enough," I said.

"I'm glad you guys made it," Nick said. I guess he had been worried that we wouldn't.

"Us too," I said. "It's nice to have someone here helping us."

"Understood," the young man said. He could give Nick a run for his money on brevity.

"The Key's been opened again?" Nick asked. He must have heard Jen and me talking over the phone.

"I think four of the demons were let out this time," I said.

"And you heard about the four cities?" Nick asked.

"Just now," I said.

"Be nice to know which demons are where," Nick said.

"Any weird reports of activity?" I asked.

Bartholomew shook his head, a brief back-and-forth.

"It would make sense that the four demons are the ones we think are related," Jen said. "How about cities being built somewhere? Or armies showing up?"

"Demons can only build in hell," Bartholomew said.

"What about dead changing places?" There was what we had learned about Buné, so I asked the question. "See any corpses coming out of the earth and walking around?"

"I believe that would qualify as unusual activity," Bartholomew said, as if he had already answered my question.

I didn't know if it was because he was just being brief, but his answer felt rude. I tried not to take it personally. Jen might have noticed the same thing, though, and put her hand on my thigh.

"You're right," I finally said.

The young man nodded, as if agreeing with my agreement. "We understand you killed a demon?"

I nodded back. If he could be economical, so could I.

"It's been a long time since the church has recorded the death of a major demon," he said.

"There will be a few more before this day is done," I said. I searched for the Key, and it surprised me by pulling from the north and east. It had been south and west for so long, the different direction had me turned around.

Bartholomew frowned. "You plan on going after the demon now?"

"No time like the present." I unzipped the duffel bag and ruffled through it.

"His Holiness would like to speak to you," Bartholomew said, as if that took precedence over anything we wanted.

"His Holiness can wait an hour or so," I said. "Azazel has my friends, and where that guy is concerned, every moment counts."

Bartholomew looked at Nick, briefly. Apparently the two of them had had a similar conversation. Nick's hand tightened on the steering wheel. "I told you."

Bartholomew's lips thinned, which made me think the young man didn't like repeating himself, but was gracious enough to do so. "You plan on tracking the demon through your connection to the Key."

"Got it in one," I agreed. I found the .38 and spun the cylinder, checking the load. Then I tucked it in my jeans, behind me. The handle dug into my back a bit.

"Can I ask you one question, before you go after this demon?" Bartholomew said.

Jen's eyes were lowered a little in thought. In times like these, I had become aware she liked to watch the interplay between me and whoever I was talking to. She would file away information and bring up her thoughts to me later. It was a level of introspection and thoughtfulness I didn't think I would ever have.

Nick's hand stayed tight to the wheel. Bartholomew had talked him into a course of action Nick was hoping I would change. Nick and I were a lot alike in these moments. Both of us shared the same sense of failure and the same requirement of duty to our friends. We would argue against any course of action except the ones we felt would satisfy one or the other.

Still, I listened while I got ready. I was a multitasker. "Sure."

"Has the demon ever had the Key, since he's taken it from you?"

I paused with my hands in the bag. Azazel had never appeared around me with the Key. He had been careful about that. "You think I won't find him."

Bartholomew corrected me. "We think there are too many variables."

"My friends aren't variables," I said.

He lifted a shoulder, a brief motion. "Apologies. But you still know what I mean."

And I did. Dammit. He was right. Wherever the Key was, there was a good chance Azazel wasn't with it. And that meant my friends might not be there as well.

"And you know this demon well," Bartholomew continued. "What are the chances the Key is where it is because it's a trap?"

I took my hands from the bag. I looked away from Bartholomew. Again, he was dead-on.

Still, this was Johnny and Sarah. They deserved everything I had. Azazel knew that, and probably had planned accordingly. But I didn't really have an off switch, and fought Bartholomew. "Whether it's a trap now, or a trap later, it's always going to be a trap."

"Fair point," he said. "But *right now* the reward is unknown. Will your friends be there? Or just the Key?"

Our eyes locked for a long moment. Bartholomew was much older than he appeared. I ended up looking away, knowing I had let him talk me into it. "Fine," I said.

Nick shook his head, but he must have agreed with me, or he would have argued more. He had hoped I would have a different answer, and I hadn't.

"Your friends will be okay," Bartholomew said. "Demonic rituals are best performed at night. That is the time, and the place, where both the Key and your friends will be."

"And it will still be a trap," I said quietly. Jen squeezed my leg. I turned to the side window. Like back in Grafton, outside a car holding Sarah prisoner, I saw a reflection of myself in a passenger window of a car. This time, though, I was on the inside of the car, and the reflection I stared through was faded, transparent. Missing something.

"But a trap for which the price will be known," Bartholomew pointed out.

I barely make out my face in the window. Just an outline of a nose, cheekbones, stubbled skin. Shadows, where my eyes were. My lips moved as I made a quiet promise to myself. Whatever this trap was, all my friends were coming out of it. Alive.

There was a long moment of silence in the car.

Then the car shifted into drive with a quiet *thunk*, and the vehicle pulled smoothly out from the curve. Nick drove us along empty streets, with Bartholomew pointing out turns in tiny, economical motions. We passed a gas station on the corner, no cars at any of the pumps. Nick's eyes met mine in the rearview mirror.

"You all had the same talk?" I asked.

Nick grinned a grin without any humor. "I do my best work at night anyway."

As tired as he looked, he was ready to shadow-walk the city to find Sarah, as soon as night fell. I understood that.

Nick drove on. Very few people walked the streets. Most of them were soldiers, some were police. All of those wore masks, some a blue cotton, some colored in camouflage. Occasionally there was even someone wearing a full-face mask, like they wore in those movies where a virus wipes out the world. We passed a police car on one corner, the cops sitting inside, the car's lights flashing.

"You never said the demon's name," Jen said to Bartholomew.

"Correct," he said.

"Why?" she asked.

"If you name something," he said, "it holds power over you."

I wondered what he was. I flicked on my ethereal vision. He showed no differently than other humans did in my sight, with the white spark inside his chest like Jen or Nick. Otherwise his body was dark to me, like a shadow.

Jen's spark always flickered with an electric blue. Nick's spark was somewhat dim, as if it merged with the darkness around. If Bartholomew had a supernatural power, he hid it well. Nothing revealed itself in my sight. He appeared to be a regular person, with a strong white flame flickered in his chest.

Looking around with my sight reminded me to check for ghosts. I was worried I might not see any during the day, even though we were in the City of the Dead. I didn't need to be.

"Wow," I said aloud.

"The city has its beauty," Bartholomew said, mistaking me.

I put my hand on top of Jen's and held it, tightly. I had never been anywhere like this. Not New York City, not Chicago. Not over in Afghanistan. There weren't a hundred thousand spirits. Or five hundred thousand, but millions. So many, even in daylight. They were so thick over my ethereal radar they appeared as large blobs everywhere, clumps of ghosts so stuck together that the ethereal blueness I assigned to them darkened in hue to midnight.

Part of me felt like they were pressing on the border between our worlds, rising to break away from the ethereal plane they existed in and enter the land of the living. The car cruised along, and we passed one of the thickest concentrations of them, to the north. They were all enclosed in a white brick wall, and over the top of the wall were pointed tops of mausoleums. Even maybe the top of a miniature pyramid. The marble edges of each crypt glowed with an echo of an older world, letting me know I still looked on with my ethereal sight, and I blinked it away.

"Saint Louis Cemetery Number One," Bartholomew said.

"Are there so many cemeteries that they all have to be numbered?" I asked.

"Yes," he said, simply. I was beginning to feel brevity was his trademark.

New Orleans really was the City of the Dead. So many spirits filled that cemetery I had trouble picking just one out from the rest. They were all dressed from different ages and stations: aristocrats in lace dress, people in modern suits, powdered wigs and sharp fades, timepieces mixed among Rolexes. Anyone and everyone could have been there.

Saint Louis Cathedral appeared before us, a white castle of a building, with a clock in the center. The clock told me it was almost three in the afternoon. Three large steeples pointed from the top of the cathedral, one large steeple in the center that rose above everything, and a smaller steeple to each side. Stone crosses perched on the top of each, on the front of each, between each of the steeples, and across the white brick of the roof.

A lot of the streets were one-way in this area, leading us to take a specific route, even though no other cars were on the street. Bartholomew directed Nick to circle around the front of the cathedral. We had to go all the way around and to the back, where there was a beautiful Antebellum-style mansion. Big and white with a double-decker porch, tall circular columns holding up each floor, magnificent windows with black shutters, and a green lawn with a black iron gate around it.

We drove up to a keypad by the gate. Nick typed in the number Bartholomew told him. They rolled apart, pulling in to either side. Nick parked the car in the half-circle roundabout in front of the mansion, and we all got out. Again, I found myself slinging my bag over a shoulder, listening to the *clink-clinks* inside it.

A man opened the big front door. He was dressed simply in white robes with a little gold trim. He wore no hat, oddly enough. In every picture of every bishop I had ever seen, the priests had worn a pointed white hat with a gold cross on the front. Instead, a tiny ring of dark hair circled his balding head.

Without seeming to rush, Bartholomew got to the man first and kissed a ring on the man's hand, bowing briefly. The man waved Bartholomew away, smiling a little in embarrassment. Up close the robes couldn't hide his large belly, even on his thin frame. He faced us with a bulbous nose, red with broken veins, like a heavy drinker might have.

"Archdiocese?" Jen asked.

"Bishop, if you please." He smiled. His voice was maybe the most priestly thing about him. It was deep and resonant and even though he spoke in a low, friendly tone, the words traveled high around us. "The archdiocese is what I administer."

We all introduced ourselves.

"Have they told you of the terrorist attacks?" he asked. When we told him what we had heard, he continued. "I believe your demon is enacting the last stage of his plan."

Your demon. Azazel would love that. I tried not to roll my eyes. "Do you know what his plan could be?"

"Not from the information we have right now," the bishop said. "But maybe now that we are together, we can learn more."

He welcomed us into his home. The doors opened to a large room with wraparound staircases leading to a balcony above. The floors were all tiled in white with gold edges. The steps were marble, and flecked with golden veins. Everything was tasteful, and expensive.

Paintings lined the walls, like I would expect in a church. Halos around heads, robed men bowing before a woman, a tiny infant in a crib. There was one that struck me, a golden painting of a hillside with maybe a large coffer on top of it, a pair of wings on the top of either side of the box. Rays radiated outward from where the coffer sat on the hill.

We entered a library, or a study. Hundreds or thousands of books circled us from three of the walls, organized in tall oaken bookcases. A large polished desk rested directly in front of us, with tall windows behind it holding tasteful white drapes. A few comfortable-looking chairs were placed directly before the desk, and a reading chair sat off to the side of the room, the dark red leather worn and the padding of the seat sunken in.

The bishop took the chair behind the desk, sitting in a practiced motion. He leaned back a little, with a sigh. A moment later he opened a drawer and pulled out a tiny silver flask and took a sip. He swallowed, took another, and patted his considerable stomach.

The three of us sat in the chairs before the desk. I took the center one, with Jen and Nick on either side. Bartholomew stood off to the side, between windows, with his arms behind his back. The sunlight glowed behind the drapes and lit the entire room.

"So," the bishop began. His voice was just as resonant as earlier, even more so since the sound was contained in just this room. "We have a little time, and a lot to do."

CHAPTER TWENTY-NINE

It was quiet, in the house. As if no one else existed, like it was just us in the entire world. The room was comfortable, dry and cool. It was also brightly lit, not only by the windows, but by a large chandelier above us. The chair I sat in had plenty of cushion, enough so that I barely felt the .38 tucked in the back of my jeans. Jen looked at me, her lips curving just a little, a smile of comfort. Nick's glance was more serious, his jaw closed tight, his cheekbones sharp.

A sweet scent was in the air, like someone had burned incense. I wondered if it was frankincense, or myrrh. It was sharp and woody, and the scent smelled the way figs tasted, plumlike and sugary.

I wondered what he meant by *a lot.* I had a couple of goals tonight, and they weren't mutually exclusive. Rescue Sarah and Johnny. Get Sarah her exorcism. Get the Key. Kill Azazel.

That was the order of things as I saw them, and I said so.

"That's your plan." The bishop smiled.

"Simple is easiest," I said. It was going to be my mantra tonight.

"You don't mention any of the other cities," he said.

"I'm not worried about them right now," I said. "I just want to get Sarah and Johnny safe."

"Any idea of how to do that?" he asked.

I didn't feel like I had a plan. I would follow the pull of the Key to where it led. Seemed simple enough. "I kind of work best on the fly. I figured I'd get to where the Key is and work the list from there."

"Hmmm." The bishop frowned. He bent forward, his stomach pressing against the top of the desk, and he picked up a pen and a tiny pad of paper. The pad had a golden cross on the top right corner of each white sheet. "I find writing things out helps me work a problem. Let's write your list down in reverse order. If you know what you have to do at the end, how you start sometimes is easier to figure out."

"By end, you mean killing Azazel," I said, looking at Bartholomew. The young man wouldn't say the demon's name, but apparently didn't care if I did.

"Exactly," the bishop said. "How about telling me about it? How are you able to kill demons?"

"You mean, other than I've learned how to do it?" I didn't need to know more about it, other than that the blade could kill demons. The look on Kimaris's face came to mind, a little surprise, a little regret, and maybe realization of a deceit. "Not much."

"Humor us," the bishop said, exchanging a quick glance with Bartholomew.

So I talked about the fight with Kimaris. How I had used Nick's knife to kill the Nephilim, and then wishing for a knife when Kimaris had held me down. How the blade had just appeared, already inside the demon's chest. I finished with summoning the sword in the coffee shop, and that Azazel had fled when I had.

The bishop wrote a few things down while I spoke.

"And the Key," he asked, "what do you know about it?"

I told him what I had learned while I carried it. It wasn't a tremendous amount. Solomon had created the Key as a prison for seven demons, and that Key had been passed on from Keeper to Keeper during that time. Azazel had chased us all, but the only way he could get the Key was if someone handed it to him. None of the Keepers had, and Azazel had told me he would occasionally kill a Keeper, if one bored him, just to try a new Keeper out.

"From what we've learned, though," Jen added, "Solomon once commanded dozens of demons. At the least. I'm not sure why the Key was made, or why those seven demons are imprisoned in it."

Johnny had finally downloaded the books, the Greater and Lesser

Keys of Solomon, but we never had a chance to really look at them. We had simply run out of time.

"This next part is me, of course," the bishop said. "We'll have to bring your sister Sarah to the cathedral for the exorcism."

"No matter where we find her?" Jen asked. "What she's not even in New Orleans?"

"We still need to get her to the cathedral," the bishop said. "It is the holiest place in the city. The curse is strong, but I believe I can break it there. At least from the pictures I've seen."

The three of us looked at each other. In our minds there was never a question of him not being able to do the exorcism. It appeared as if the bishop worried a bit about it.

He held up a finger to forestall any questions, though, and wrote more down. "The important thing is to get her to the cathedral before midnight. It has to be done before then."

"Once we find them," I said. Still worried that they might not be at the same place the Key was. "That doesn't give us a lot of time."

"It does not," he agreed. "Time will be in short supply tonight, to accomplish a great many things."

The bishop looked at what he had written, holding the paper out some and squinting a bit. I didn't think we had any more information than we would have if we had just talked about it, but he seemed to come to some kind of conclusion internally.

"What do you know about Azazel?" he asked.

I snorted. "Not enough. Delights in making things complicated. More about the appreciation of a thing than the doing of it."

"We found out his name meant scapegoat," Jen added. "But there's not much more known about him than that."

"There's not a lot known about any of that time." The bishop waved a hand at the books circling his room. "Demons and angels, all of that happened way before we started writing. Everything was passed down generation to generation, orally. Those types of stories change as they are told, and exaggeration becomes indistinguishable from the truth."

His voice resonated through the room and entranced us. It was easy to see, even with his belly and his drinker's nose, how he could capture a congregation with a speech. How he could lead a sermon.

The bishop flicked his pen across the paper, crossing something off his pad. "Azazel does mean scapegoat, though. Sometimes I wonder if he was *the* scapegoat. Lucifer always was blamed for the fallen angels, but I wonder if he, in turn, blamed someone else."

Something in that struck me. And I wasn't sure what about it did so. But it was a piece of the puzzle. Azazel had been among those who had fallen from heaven. Did he now want to leave hell? Where else could he go?

Could that be why these cities were under attack? Could Azazel be trying to build his own empire? Something felt right about that idea to me. But it couldn't be, if Bartholomew was correct and demons could only build in hell.

The older man shook his head. "But I digress. Following the fall there was a war on earth between the angels and fallen angels. They were yet to be called demons. But the war lasted thousands of years, and took its toll, as both demon and angel fell.

"We all hear the questions so many times today," the bishop continued. "Why doesn't God appear? Why doesn't he send an angel anymore? Why does he allow evil to exist in this world?"

That reasoning was the core of my argument with Jen. It was why I believed I couldn't be an angel. If heaven existed, there should be someone better than me patrolling its corridors.

"We haven't seen an angel in a while," the older man went on. His eyes drilled into me. "Maybe that means there are no more."

His eyes drilled into me. Bartholomew shifted his glance slightly, between the bishop and me. I shifted in my seat, uncomfortable. Jen laid her hand over mine.

I wanted to ask if any of this mattered, but I had a feeling it did. He was leading us somewhere. Or maybe he was leading me somewhere.

"Toward the end of the war, the scales were tipped. A trap was laid, and seven angels disappeared from heaven. Seven who had been among the leaders of their side. After that, the rest of the angels disappeared."

I started, thinking of the jail cell in Grafton. My mother, her hands twitching the handle of her sword, leaving behind a message without words, a scrawl of her blade on the concrete of a feather, a shield, and a staff.

My mind played back her words. *"How many through the years?"* My *mother shrugged. Her hands still worked her blade. "But in the beginning, there were seven."*

Jen's hand squeezed mine.

"So you know about the geas," I said.

The bishop nodded. "The Templars are of Solomon as well. What I am telling you comes from their lore. The geas was the first attempt at binding and controlling others. Until then, binding creatures to a purpose, none of those things had *become* yet."

"What are you saying?" I asked. "That the geas didn't exist before then? Summoning didn't exist?"

"What's the lesson of the Garden?" the bishop asked.

I had never been religious. Nick was the guy who came up with an answer. "Free will."

The bishop smiled. "Exactly. Choice. We all exist here, with only, truly, one absolute. Free Will. The ability to decide for ourselves who to believe, and who to follow. To believe in God in heaven, or to listen to Lucifer's lies. There was no geas, no summonings, no bindings or control in the beginning. Earth is a battlefield, and the ammo is, or was, choice."

Another memory came back to me. I had asked my mother how long we had been under the geas.

"Millennia," she had replied. *"Longer than I know of. My mother had it, her mother before her, and so on...."*

And now I knew the answer. We had been the first. We had been entrapped since the beginning.

The bishop continued. "After the geas, the rest of the angels mostly disappeared. The fallen angels had won. Sin, vice, evil appeared in abundance. Sodom and Gomorrah were destroyed. The name *demon* appeared then and then grew in the stories.

"Then a wise man took it upon himself to strike back. He learned how to call and bind the demons. He figured out their weaknesses, bound them, and used them for good."

Here the bishop paused. "You've carried this Key for a long time. Have you ever wondered how Solomon first learned how to call and bind demons? How to build a circle and safely control one?"

It had never occurred to me. I lived in a world of the supernatural. Magic and monsters existed. The Key had just been a different variation of the same evils, and I had never questioned how it had been built, only why.

Kimaris, outside the old church, had told me Azazel had made killing my friends a condition of the demon's release. A condition such as a summoner might have for a creature who had been bound. Who would have taught Solomon how to bind other demons? It wouldn't have happened on a whim, it would have been according to a plan. One that had lasted thousands of years.

"Azazel," I said aloud. "He's responsible for it all, isn't he? The geas. The summonings. Teaching Solomon."

Bartholomew's eyebrows rose, briefly. He might have been surprised I had made the connection. Jen's hand clenched mine, as if she was having the realization herself. She had thought Azazel had a part in my life, long before I had. It just had turned out that it was thousands of years before.

"It's what I believe," the bishop agreed. "He is responsible for introducing humans to *hidden knowledge*. We just have never known, for certain, what that knowledge might be."

Why would Azazel teach Solomon how to summon and bind his brothers and sisters of hell? Was that the hidden knowledge? I didn't know, but I couldn't rule it out. Azazel was capable of anything, and would do anything, to carry his plan to its end. He would have lied to Lucifer, if he thought at the time it would get him what he wanted.

"That's why you think he's really to blame," I said. "Why he's the scapegoat."

"Yes," he answered. "Maybe for a great many things. Maybe for the fall. And maybe for corrupting the one agreement between Lucifer and God, by removing choice and free will from the creatures on earth."

None of this was founded in any kind of fact. Just stories and maybe rumors, passed down by word of mouth for generations until one day being written on paper. But it made sense, and it fit Azazel. The demon wouldn't want to just extract vengeance, he would want to do it in the worst possible way.

"I think Solomon must have known something, though. He worked against the demon, while learning as much as he could," the bishop said. "In the end, before he passed, he created an order who would later become the Templars. And he also created the Key. In that Key Solomon put the seven demons he most believed were critical to Azazel's plans."

"Why not just put Azazel in the Key?" Jen asked.

"I don't know," the bishop answered. "My guess? Solomon had never learned how to properly summon Azazel.

"But Solomon was able to make it so the demon would always have to chase the Key, and create almost impossible conditions for Azazel to be able to get it."

Those conditions had been one of the few things I had learned from the previous Keeper. All the demon needed was for a human to hand him the Key. A great test of a person's will was Solomon's Key. Run until the demon kills you. Or hand it over and give him enough evil to control the earth.

Nick was still in his chair. He had given the Key to Azazel for Sarah, because he thought I was dead, and because he didn't know what the Key was. There was a part that still blamed himself for giving it to the demon, would always blame himself.

Nick's eyes met mine, holding a dark anger. His jaw tightened. Even though I would have done the same, in Nick's place, I understood what he was feeling. That kind of self-recrimination.

Azazel had figured out a way around Solomon's conditions. Even if it had taken thousands of years. Though, in all honesty, that seemed a bit long to me. I'd have thought he'd be able to do it faster. Maybe the Keepers had been a match for the demon.

"So the seven demons in the Key are the demons Solomon believed were the most crucial to Azazel's plan," Jen said. "What plan?"

"Who knows?" The bishop said. "World domination. Overthrowing heaven. Overthrowing hell. All the great evils. The rumors are many, and each as viable as the last, and nothing definitive about any."

"It'd be nice if we had that part," I said.

"If we assume Azazel had a purpose for those demons," Nick said, slowly, as if he was figuring out something along the way, "then we should believe he had a purpose for the geas as well."

The whole room was silent. The bishop shook his head, as if something new had been revealed to him. The man wrote something down. Even Bartholomew raised his eyebrows.

Then everyone looked at me. I wondered what, if anything, Father Benjamin had communicated to the bishop. I was suddenly scared, and I didn't know why. There was just an overwhelming fear of the unknown.

Azazel wouldn't have created the geas as a test, or as a stepping stone to figuring out how to bind and control a supernatural being. He would have done it as part of a purpose, as a plan. Everything would have been a plan. Even Solomon.

"What do you know about me?" I asked.

"Enough," the bishop said. "The geas of each of the Seven had been passed to seven different vampire clans. It was how the vampires first learned how to control, an ability they used and grew.

"Those clans passed the control of the geas from master to master, through the years. The vampire clans warred among themselves, and took part in other wars. The Seven became the Six, which then became the Four. Then the vampires realized they could breed their captives, and pass the geas from parent to child. It took a long time, but the Four eventually became the Two."

My parents. Something occurred to me. "Were they bred with other humans?"

"That's our guess," the bishop agreed. "So if the angel was killed, the geas would fully pass from them to their child."

My mother had told me my father was under the geas as well. So he was the other surviving angel. But that didn't make sense to me. Why would two different clans have my father and my mother produce an offspring that would contain both parts of the geas?

The bishop looked at me. "We had no idea there was a Third, until Father Benjamin contacted me, and mentioned he had met someone not a Templar, but who could see the things we did. You see, the powers of the Templars work through belief. Only those with faith can do what we can, can see what we do. Unless, perhaps, that person is a part of what we have faith in."

And that had been what my mother was trying to tell me, with her sketch of a feather, a staff, and a shield.

I was, at least partly, what Jen thought I was.

I took a deep breath and let it out. The realization was too big for me to grasp. I had told Jen I wasn't what she thought I was, and I believed that. How good could a side be, when I was their best representative? Maybe their only representative?

Thousands of years was a long time for the good side to be losing, I had said to my mother.

"It is." She had nodded. "But maybe it's time for it to win again."

I got out of the chair and walked away from the group. The library was big, and I got away from everyone. I wanted to leave the room, the house, everything and everyone. I faced the corner, though, put my hand on one of the shelves there, and took deep, controlled breaths.

"If what you are saying is true," I said, "then at best, I'm only part angel. Not the real thing."

"Maybe," the bishop said. "Or maybe, being part of something is enough."

The whole room was quiet. I sensed them all looking at me. I even knew Jen wanted to come stand next to me, to support me, but I also knew this was something I needed to work out on my own. Because that truth, if I came to the conclusion on my own, would be greater.

I breathed in and out. The wooden shelf was cool under my hand, strong. Like oak. The surface had been polished many times, and I slid my hand along it, looking at the books. Different sizes and shapes, some well worn with broken spines, others brand-new.

My mother had let me know my father was also under the geas. So the two of them were what was left of the original seven angels, after thousands and thousands of years of wars and breeding. And for some reason, they had conceived me.

Not for some reason. For one reason. I balled my fist.

Maybe it's time for it to win again.

My parents had planned me for a reason. My mother had known things she couldn't tell me, because of the geas. Maybe things about Azazel. Maybe what she and my father had planned. But it was clear whatever Azazel had planned, whatever he was doing, whatever he had done, I had been put on this earth to stop him.

I tapped my fist on the shelf, feeling the soft strike of flesh against wood. In front of my book was a copy of *Paradise Lost*, by John Milton. It was one of the worn copies. A corner was peeling back from the edge. Milton had searched for the one truth, out of the millions of fragments that existed. I had some pieces as well, and was looking for them to fit together, to give me something greater.

Bartholomew hadn't moved, but both Jen and Nick had turned in their chairs. Facing me. Nick's glance was thoughtful, but Jen had a corner of her lip curled up, ever so slightly. Thinking.

I didn't think it mattered now. Whatever my parents had planned, it was far away from here and now. Azazel had first created the geas. He had a reason for binding angels to his purpose. If I was an angel, or a part angel, he would have a purpose for me as well. I just had to figure out his scheme before tonight. Maybe it was good the bishop had wanted to write all of this out.

"So, Azazel wants three things in the same place at the same time," I said. "Sarah. The Key. And me."

"That is what I believe," the bishop said. I wondered if that was the real reason Bartholomew had convinced us to come back here first. To make sure I heard all of this, from the bishop himself.

"You believe Azazel is going to make sure I'm there," I added. If that was true, then I wouldn't have to follow the Key to wherever Azazel was tonight. We wouldn't have to worry if Sarah was going to be there either. The demon would find a way to get me there.

And that fit the demon's pattern, up until now. Azazel had led me here, with the pull of the Key. He had forced me here, with his threats to my friends. He had checked up on me along the way. The demon had done everything possible, other than buying me a plane ticket to New Orleans.

The bishop let me come to the final conclusion on my own. The real reason Bartholomew brought me here. One I didn't like.

"So you want me to stay away," I said.

"All we have to do, to win tonight, is keep you away," the bishop said.

"It's not about winning," I said. "It's about saving."

He shook his head, his voice somber and full of remorse. "This demon has planned this for more years than we have history. Whatever his plan, it will fundamentally change our world as it exists. We simply cannot take that chance."

"It's not going to be up to you," I told him. I remained in the corner, and folded my arms over my chest.

"I'm asking you to really think about it," the bishop said. "The fate of the world might depend on this."

"I don't need to think about it," I said. I had run forever, all in the name of *saving the world*. My friends had suffered during that time. Vampires had overrun the town I had been raised in. Even now, with rescuing Sarah, we were still trying to fix the damage we had walked away from Grafton with.

Was the world any better today than a few years ago? While I had been running around, keeping it safe from the demons in the Key? It might arguably be called worse.

Running had been so easy. Escape always was, when we could convince ourselves we were doing it for the greater good. For years I had lain awake at night, sometimes in the backseat of my car, telling myself I was keeping billions of people safe throughout the world by running away. I lied to myself, and told myself not to fight, because I was keeping the Key away from Azazel, and that was more important than a life here or there.

We convinced ourselves we were doing the good thing, the right thing, but there was no stick to measure that effort by. How many people had I helped, hiding in that car? Running from the fight? Keeping the Key away from Azazel? Three? A billion? Was the number even something I could measure?

I realized suddenly I could. The answer was always going to be just one. I had only helped myself, by running, because I hadn't been willing to tackle the really tough things. I had run from every confrontation. I hadn't helped those I might have been able to otherwise. I had let Grafton become Grafton, and allowed all my friends to suffer there. Because I had run away. Because running only kept one person safe. The person on the run.

I was still circling around what the meaning of good really was. I didn't know what the large concept of it was, the overhanging principle, in this world. How I could measure myself against it. But it had to start with putting those I loved above myself.

Putting myself first had a cost associated with it, a price. One I could see in the mirror, every time I failed. If I could even look in it.

Which I never had, on my own. Glances at myself had come in reflections, and in those moments I had seen who I had become. And I had never liked that person. I couldn't face him, when I had failed Danny. I couldn't face that reflection, for years, while I was running.

I think, if the bishop could understand what I had done, what I had learned, maybe he would be able to see his actions in a different light. Maybe he would understand, *see* how he had changed, inside, with his compromise. I squeezed Jen's shoulder, cautioning her about what I was going to say. Her heart thumped under my palm. Our hands found each other.

"So you want me to sit out," I said. "What's your plan?"

"I will do everything I can to rescue your friends," the bishop said.

"What kind of chance will you have, if you leave the one guy behind who can kill demons?" I asked.

"It's a small enough chance either way," he said. "The world should come first, don't you think?"

And there it was. The bishop didn't understand. Maybe *couldn't* understand. So easy to do something for a nebulous goal, like the world. Something where you can't really face the consequences of your decision, and not look the person in the face whom you failed.

Easy to talk that talk.

Much harder to walk my walk. To put everything on a line for a friend. For someone I cared about. To put the needs of my friends above my own.

I shook my head. "I'm going."

"Even though the demon wants you there?"

"Even though," I said. "I'm going because my friends are there. Azazel is just a perk."

The bishop sighed. "I was hoping I could convince you."

He motioned a hand at Bartholomew. The young man didn't move. I went to move and found out that I couldn't. It was as if I weighed a million pounds.

I fought against the weight, but I didn't budge. I breathed in and out okay, and my heart beat fine, but I couldn't move a muscle. I tried pulling a ghost until ethereal energy burned through all my body, but my legs couldn't move an inch. No matter how hard I pulled.

Jen sensed something and stood up beside me. Nick as well. Thunder rolled across the front of the mansion.

"Wait." The bishop held out a hand. "Listen, please."

The skies darkened outside. Nick had a knife in his hand.

The door to the library opened, and several men and a woman stepped in, assault rifles in the air and pointed in our direction. Four in total, all of them kitted out in vests and helmets. Each of them had the same feel I had gotten from Greg, back in Grafton. Dangerous people, who had once served.

Templars.

Everyone froze. Except for me, since I was already frozen.

The bishop took a breath and stood. As he did his round belly rubbed against the desk, pinching his robe there for a moment. He tugged it down absentmindedly, as if it was a motion long practiced.

I used my sight. The Templars looked much like Greg had, covered with golden sigils. Bartholomew looked the same as in the car, no golden glow, no trace of power. Nothing but a white spark in the middle of his chest.

In the ethereal world the bishop appeared as a real knight. His stomach was flat, his head encased in a sharp plumed helmet. He was tall and well built and outfitted in golden-plate armor, a red cross painted over his chest. Some of the plates looked tarnished to me, dull. But maybe that was a trick of the light.

I shook my head and blinked back to my normal vision.

"We are prepared to help, as much as we can," the bishop said. "If you two give me your word, you both can go. But if we have it out now, we ruin any chance we have of stopping the demon, saving your friends, or performing the exorcism."

Nick shook his head and set his jaw. He still had his knife out. "You betrayed me."

Nick was furious. He and I both got it, at the same time. There was a reason this room was so brightly lit, why we all stood underneath a chandelier. No shadows to travel.

I would not want him that angry at me.

"No one has betrayed anyone," the bishop said. "I'm doing the best I can."

"By holding one of us hostage?" I snorted. "So much for the lesson of the Garden."

"Was it me that brought the Key into the world? Who gave it to the demon?" The archbishop's eyebrows lowered. "Or is it up to me to try to fix what has been laid at my doorstep?"

"And you think you're doing that by leaving me on the sidelines?" I asked.

His eyes met mine. "It's not an easy choice. But I am responsible for hundreds of millions of lives."

We were on opposite sides of that coin. I had been on his side. I had already learned that lesson. I wondered if he was about to learn it too.

"I'm responsible for four," I said. "And you're putting them all in jeopardy."

The Templars had spread out in the room, angling their guns in toward us. Bartholomew stood there, not moving, not appearing to have a concern in the world. Whatever he was doing to me didn't seem to strain him.

The bishop went silent. I think we both knew we weren't going to talk each other into what we believed. To me doing something for *the greater good* ended up sounding a lot like *the end justifies the means*.

Jen looked worried, and she turned to me, her hands balled into fists. "I don't know what to do."

"That's easy, Jen," I said. "You go save your sister."

While she did that, I was going to figure out a way out of this. And get there to help. But Jen and Nick had to carry on without me, and they needed to be focused.

She looked at me for a long moment, and as she did the thunder died off outside, in a slow, echoing roll.

Nick stood there, knife in hand. His thumb rubbed the hilt, as if he still debated what he was going to do. The Templars still pointed their rifles at him.

Just a week ago Nick and I were at odds. The first thing he had done when I saw him in Grafton was punch me, blaming me for Danny's death. And probably a lot more things.

He trusted me now, though. And he not only trusted me, he was willing to take on everything in this room with just a knife. It meant a lot to me.

I had some great friends.

"Nick," I said, "nothing we can do about me right now. But I'm trusting you to get everyone back safe."

Nick made no motion that he heard me. He kept up his stare at Bartholomew, and the bishop. He had thought they had wanted to help us, and Nick had brought us here, only to have everything change at the last second.

Nick's jaw flexed once. He flicked a glance at me, in agreement. Then he quickly tucked the knife back underneath his jacket. When he did, the Templars relaxed a bit.

"I have your word, then" the bishop said.

"As long as my sister is your priority," Jen said. "And not just stopping whatever Azazel has planned."

"You can trust me to do what I need to do to keep my friends safe," Nick added.

"Is that your word?" the bishop asked.

"It's what you get," Nick said. He was the forgiving type. "If you're not good with that, lock me down with Grimm."

I'm sure the bishop thought there were only two ways this was going to go down. Either they rescued Sarah and stopped the demon or they didn't. He was gambling that we'd be thrilled with the first case, and in the second case, well, there would be nothing left to settle.

"Hopefully that is enough," the bishop said.

And, either by coincidence or through divine providence, that happened to be the moment when Nick's phone started to ring.

CHAPTER THIRTY

The light had darkened outside from a bright yellow to a dark orange-red. Embers of a once bright flame, now burning their last. Dusk would come soon. I wasn't the only person to check. One of the Templars pulled the drapes aside a bit, and stared to the west.

The room was quiet except for a repeating jingle, like wind chimes being struck in the same way, over and over. Nick fished the phone out of his front pocket and showed me the face. My name was on the top of it.

"Wait," the bishop said.

The phone kept jingling.

"You can't let him know you won't be there." He looked at me. "He might change his plans."

"So you want me to lie, then?"

"To a demon," he pointed out.

I raised my eyebrows. "Going to be hard for me to talk to him like this."

The bishop looked at Bartholomew. The young man didn't move, but I suddenly found I could move my arms and the top of my body. My legs, though, still felt like they were part of the floor, and my hips were locked down.

I wondered how Bartholomew's power worked. It seemed like he could make any part of me immobile, just by increasing its weight. Like I had become concrete. Or something much heavier than concrete.

Nick handed me the phone. It was still ringing and vibrated in my hand. I winked at Nick, and pressed the red X on the phone to end the call. Then I tossed it back to him.

My arms froze before Nick had caught the phone, each arm swinging back to my side like pendulums, as if they weighed thousands of pounds.

The bishop looked at me, flustered. His eyebrows lowered. "Why?"

"You're asking me to lie to a demon," I said. "That's something he's pretty good at. He'd see through it in a heartbeat. But hanging up on him, that's something I would do. Azazel knows that."

"What if he kills your friends?" the bishop asked.

I didn't think Azazel would. He would want every reason for me to show up. I worried some about Johnny, but I didn't think the demon would kill him if I wasn't around to *appreciate* it.

So I wasn't expecting what happened next.

The Key opened again, nearby. So close I could point it out on a map. Like every other time, it felt more like a birthing than a door opening. Its scream was close and loud in my ears, so loud I had to shut my eyes. I struggled to breathe.

Jen was next to me. Her warm hands held the sides of my face. "You have to release him," she said.

They didn't.

"The Key?" she asked me.

I tried to tell her yes. The pull from the Key felt like it was tearing something inside me. Pain blossomed in my chest and in my gut. But Bartholomew never released me and I started to choke where I stood.

Jen put her forehead against mine and talked me through the pain. I got to a point where I took short, quick breaths. She eased me through it, waiting until the Key closed again. Then she held the side of my head and kept talking, as the pain receded, and the scream faded.

One demon out. One left.

And no idea what was waiting tonight.

I finally opened my eyes. I had pinched them so tight my jaw hurt. The Key's pain had been tremendous, and tears ran down my face. Jen wiped my cheeks for me, and kissed me briefly on the lips. "You okay?"

I nodded, not trusting myself to speak.

"We'll settle with them for this," she said to me, her hand still on my cheek.

"Your sister first," I said, low, my voice hoarse.

"I know," she said. "But you are item number two on my list."

Jen wanted me to know she was there for me. Which was nice. I hadn't had that until she had come along. I let out a deep exhale.

The bishop watched all of this.

I explained what had just happened. "Azazel has let another demon out."

That made five demons who could be waiting for my friends. And Azazel. It seemed like overkill. We were missing something.

"Was it because you didn't take his call?" He was still upset that I had hung up on Azazel.

I shook my head. "Whatever he's planned, it's been for thousands of years. It's not like he can call an audible at the last second."

"We still need to talk to him," thebBishop said. "We need to know where he is."

"Where he wants me, you mean," I said.

"That is what I mean," the bishop said. "If you will."

"I could feel the Key. It's nearby," I said. "If you have a map, I think I can show you."

"You wouldn't mislead me?" he asked.

I just looked at him in response. I didn't feel like the question was worth answering. Misleading him about the Key wouldn't help my friends.

"Fine," he said. "We'll get a map."

Two of the Templars left the room. The woman stayed by the door, right next to the light switch. The other Templar stood in the corner by Bartholomew, holding his rifle so the barrel rested lightly on the glass, staring out the window. It was getting darker by the minute now.

My friends were about to face more demons in one place than had been gathered in thousands of years. And they were going to go without me. I struggled to move, and fought, but this wasn't like the geas. It was as if my whole body had become rock.

"Any chance you could let me sit?" I asked.

Bartholomew's lip twitched. It was worth a shot. We all stood there for a moment, as if everyone was unsure of what they were going to do. Or what was next.

Jen and Nick both stood near me. Nick rubbed his face a few times. The bishop had turned to Bartholomew and talked quietly, the young man occasionally responding in one-word answers.

"I'm worried," Jen said to me.

"How can you not be?" I said, and tried to give her a reassuring smile. If Jen was worried, I was panicked. I wouldn't show it to them. I just promised myself I would find a way out. There had to be a way to beat this.

I didn't like not being there for my friends. I didn't like being held from the one thing I believed I could do.

At what point did I begin believing in myself, and that I was strong enough to protect my friends? Just yesterday I had sat in a garage and told Jen I didn't know if I was enough. A day later, I wondered if they could do this without me.

I snorted. Maybe all it took was someone telling me I couldn't do it. My smile grew wider at the thought. That was a truth that resonated with me.

I wouldn't believe a truth, even if everyone in the world swore it was so. But one person tells me I can't do something, and I'm all about proving him wrong.

"It's not funny," Jen said.

"No, it definitely is not," I said. But I let my grin grow wider anyway. There was something there, about proving people wrong, that gave me hope I was not out of this fight.

"If we can get the lights out, I can get you free," Nick said to us both, his voice quiet.

If Bartholomew had let me, I would have shaken my head. "Sarah and Johnny first."

"Whatever they have planned," Nick said, "it's all going to go south when Azazel doesn't see you there."

"That's what I figure too," I said. Nick had been the guy studying theology at one point. "What can you tell me about Bartholomew?"

The young man heard me, and his eyes focused on me over the shoulder of the bishop.

"Other than he's got the name of an apostle?" he asked. "Nothing. But the apostles were teachers, I think. They went around healing the sick."

"He doesn't show any kind of power," I said. "Not like anything else I can see."

"What did the bishop say?" Jen said. "Their power is about belief?"

I flicked back to my ethereal vision for a brief moment. The Templars, the bishop, they all still showed golden. I tried to look past the symbols, though, and the armor. Underneath. It was like peering through gold-tinted sunglasses, but the spark in all of them looked white. Not like Jen or Nick; their sparks held a color, or a shade.

Nick started, as if he had just remembered something. "The apostles weren't just sent out to heal, they also were tasked to drive out demons."

Bartholomew could be valuable in the upcoming fight. But it appeared he was going to stay here and hold me. The bishop worried that much about what Azazel had planned.

"I wish we knew more," I said. I wondered how Bartholomew could drive out demons. All it appeared he could do was make statues out of people. "But in the meantime, you guys find Sarah and Johnny and get them back."

"We can do that," Nick said, looking back at Bartholomew and the bishop.

"Don't be heroes," I stressed. "Get in, get them, and get out. Be careful. Be safe."

The words sounded silly to me, but I had to say them. Both Nick and Jen would do whatever it took to save Sarah and Johnny. Whatever the cost.

Nick arched an eyebrow. "You mean, like you?"

I took a deep breath. I wouldn't be there to take the heavy hits, to protect my friends. And it was something I was good at. And if I wasn't there to take Azazel's best shot, then that shot could fall on one of them.

Jen put her hand on my arm. She knew what I was thinking. "We'll be fine."

"I just don't like not being there," I said.

"Tell you what." The corner of Nick's lip curved slightly, like he was sharing something he thought hilarious. "It'll be weird, when all this is over, to not have to listen to Jen yell at you again for getting hurt."

Jen snorted, and I laughed. What Nick had said was close enough to the truth that we all could get a chuckle out of it. Who knew Nick had a sense of humor?

The bishop frowned at us. Maybe he thought we weren't taking this seriously. Then he came over, navigating his belly around the corner of the desk.

"I hope after this, we can talk," he said.

"I doubt it," I said. "But we'll see."

"I don't think you understand the weight I carry," he said.

"I might be the one guy who *could* understand that," I said. I had, after all, thought the same thing once.

"Millions of lives. Hundreds of millions. Maybe billions," he said. "I have to protect them all."

"Then you're doing it wrong," I said. "You should have the same amount of compassion for the one person as you have for the many."

"But I'm doing that," he argued. "We *are* going after your friends."

"So you say, but you don't really believe that," I said. "I don't care that you are lying to me. But you should make sure you aren't lying to yourself. You're hedging your bet, leaving me here. You're *hoping* you've figured out Azazel's plan. You're *hoping* you can beat him without me."

I wanted to lean closer and whisper what I said next. The moment deserved that kind of gravitas. I wanted to talk into the man's ear, my face next to his, and have him understand how close I was to a piece of the truth he didn't understand, with all his oral histories and his responsibility for millions.

But I couldn't move, so I just said it out loud, for everyone to hear. "If there's one thing I've learned about Azazel, it's if you aren't completely committed to beating him, you aren't going to win. The demon always has a cost. And if you aren't ready to pay it, he's going to know it, and make you pay something much greater."

That struck a nerve, because the bishop set his jaw. He did speak in a low tone, and if it wasn't menacing, it was certainly angry. "What could you possibly know about paying a cost?"

"You're the one telling me I'm one of the few remaining angels left," I answered. "Why don't you tell me?"

My words echoed in the room and descended into a quiet of anticipation, like the stillness before a fight. Bartholomew actually tilted his head, as if in thought.

I locked my gaze with the bishop's. "I can see you, you know, in the spirit world."

He frowned. Maybe it was something he hadn't thought about.

"There was a Templar in Grafton," I said. "And I thought he had died foolishly, in a gas station, trying to help me. He had called his choice a fulcrum. I didn't know what he meant then, but I think I do now. A town full of vampires, a drug that controlled them, all these evils that had affected many."

Instead, Greg had died trying to help me save Jen. "Instead, he paid a cost he believed would tip the world in a better direction. I thought he had chosen poorly, that he could have done a greater good, for more people, instead of dying to save one."

I would never know why Greg had made the choice he had. If he and Father Benjamin had known about me even then. It seemed, when Father Benjamin had given his life and commanded me to look at him in the spirit world, that the two of them had guessed at something. And both had paid the price.

"So I see you in the spirit world, standing there in your golden armor," I said to the bishop. "And I have to believe you once knew what I'm talking about. Maybe it's a founding principle in your order. And maybe you forgot, or the weight of millions became too much."

I set my jaw now, and made sure he saw how angry I was. "So I'm trying not to judge you. But right now I see a man who's afraid to fully commit to destroying evil. A man afraid to pay the cost."

I stopped talking then. And not because I wanted to, but because I had become a statue from top to bottom.

Bartholomew opened both hands to me, and raised an eyebrow, as if he was asking me if I wanted to continue. The rest of the room was quiet. Jen's hand was on my arm. Nick wore a tiny smile. The two Templars had their guns down. The woman by the light switch broke the silence.

"Was that Greg?" she asked. Her voice was quiet, but sharp, with an undertone of concern.

I couldn't answer. I couldn't move.

"Let him answer, Bartholomew," the bishop said.

"It was," I said. "He was a good man."

The Templar remained by the door, her bottom lip tucked under her front teeth.

Nick's phone rang again. He held it out to us. My name on the screen, one more time. He looked at me with a question on his face.

I motioned up and down with my head, and Nick hung it up.

"Things are going to get real, soon," I said.

"What do you hope to gain by this?" the bishop said.

"Provoke him into doing something he might not want to," I said. "Seeing as I'm sidelined for the fight."

The two Templars who had left came back in. Both of them had on backpacks, and they looked heavy. One had a rocket launcher strapped to his back. They were loaded for bear, and it gave me some hope. If they armed like I armed, if there was silver in the payload of the launcher, then all they had to do was get one close enough to a demon.

Just sending one back to hell, even for a little bit, would be a win tonight.

One of them held a map, unfolded. He handed it to the bishop, and then motioned to the man and the woman who had remained on guard. Then the Templars all changed places, the two without backpacks leaving, the two with backpacks taking their places. One by the window, one by the light switch.

They were taking no chances with Nick.

The bishop flapped open the map and held it in front of me. It was a tourist's map, showing all the famous places in New Orleans. The French Quarter, the Voodoo Temple, the Garden District. The blue Mississippi River winded its way from left to right.

During the drive here the pull of the Key had flipped again. It was now southwest again. So we had passed the place where Azazel held it. And that place was just a few blocks away. Maybe not even a mile.

"There," I said. "The Lafayette Cemetery."

I didn't add the number.

Bartholomew nodded to himself, as if he had made a bet. The bishop flipped the map over. The cemetery had a larger picture on the back, from the top down. It was one of many pictures of many different cemeteries. But the Lafayette Cemetery from the top down looked like a big cross.

Azazel was nothing if not a showman.

"It is not far," the bishop said. "From there to the cathedral."

He spoke in his sermon voice. The reassuring one. As if he wanted to tell us we were all in this for Sarah. But he was only trying to convince himself.

"You going to take rocket launchers in there?" Jen asked.

"I can guess what you think of me," he said to us. "But I will do whatever it takes to beat this demon. *And* to help your friends."

Part of me felt bad then. I had introduced a chink in the bishop's armor. Or maybe it had always been there, and he had been unaware of it. Either way, he was about to face something no Templar had faced since Solomon.

"You can still beat him," I said. "Just let me go. Then you have me and your apostle."

The bishop shook his head. "Then doubt wins. I will be enough."

He looked around at the group. "We will be enough."

"There's movement outside." The Templar by the window moved his rifle up to his shoulder, sighting down through the glass.

Nick took a few steps to an open window. The bishop moved to one as well, although a little less nimbly. Bartholomew stayed where he was.

"I don't know what I'm seeing," the Templar said.

"Nick?" Jen asked, her hand still on my arm.

"Not good," was all he replied.

Maybe a ghost could see what was going on. I search my ethereal senses and tapped the closest one, in the cemetery nearby.

There was the memory first. It was an older ghost, of a time hundreds of years ago, and there was a taste of bread in its mouth, and a hunger in its belly.

And it was moving. Which threw me off. Ghosts normally were tied to a spot. I had never seen one stir away from where I first saw it. But this one's arms moved, like it was crawling. And then I realized the ghost wasn't moving as much as it was directing the motions of a corpse. It was locked inside a body, controlling it like a puppet.

Like the wights in Grafton. Those had been bodies animated with the spirits of animals. These were corpses animated with actual spirits.

I zoomed out on my ethereal radar. The blue clumps were all shifting there, like a mob. Shuffling through the streets en mass. Like zombies. Picking one at random, I took a little from it. A ghost of a man tied into a woman's body.

All the spirits seemed to have been placed in whatever corpse had been closest. I checked out the Saint Louis Cemetery. The first cemetery, and the closest. There were hundreds of corpses breaking through the rotting wood of their coffins and digging their way out of the earth. Each one clawed through the cold, moist ground like an animal burrowing out of its den. And each one was headed to the spot I made on the map.

"Lafayette Cemetery," the bishop said, as if he had been staring at the corpses walking the street and thinking the same thoughts.

"Give me the phone," I said.

Nick held it out. We both waited, since I still couldn't move.

"So you can lie to the demon now?" the bishop asked, pursing his lips.

"I can't lie any better than before," I said. However, I didn't think what I planned on saying would be a lie. "But I can give him something to think about. Maybe distract him."

The bishop waited a moment, then motioned his head at Bartholomew.

I seized the phone from Nick and hit callback on the most recent number. Then I put it on speaker.

It went to voice mail. It was my voice, though I had never recorded a message. *You've reached the number of Fergus Grimm. I can't come to the phone right now, likely because I'm dead, but if you leave your name and number I'll happily not call you back.*

I rolled my eyes. Fucking Azazel and his jokes. I dialed again and let it ring.

The demon picked up on the first ring. "Grimm! You *do* answer your phone."

"Hey, Az," I said. "You having a party?"

"Just a few *old* friends," Azazel said, and waited. And waited.

"Hilarious," I finally said.

His voice was cheerful, excited. "You're welcome to join."

"I'll be headed that way shortly," I said. "Want me to bring anything? Chips? Beer? A sword that will rid the earth of you forever?"

"We're good here," he said. "You can bring your friends, though. Plenty of fun to go around."

"They'll be there," I said. "Save some fun for me, though."

"I admire your optimism, Grimm," Azazel said. "It's been the best part of the past few years. I'm going to hate seeing you after tonight."

"With any luck you won't have to," I said.

It went quiet over the phone. It struck me, all of this had started when Jen called me, after I had fought Azazel at an old motel. And it was going to end tonight, after this call.

"You know where I'm at, right?" he said. His tone serious. Ready.

"Lafayette Cemetery," I said.

"See you here." The line went dead.

"See?" the bishop said. "I told you he wants you there."

"Of course he wants me there," I said. "That was never the question."

He just didn't think I could beat Azazel at his own game. And maybe the bishop was right. Maybe I couldn't. But it wouldn't be for a lack of effort.

I handed Nick his phone. The other Templars came back, tactical packs strapped to their backs. I didn't know what they had in there, but I hoped each one of them had an extra army in there.

The woman walked up to the man who had brought in the map. Both of them stood by the window, facing outward. I assumed watching undead corpses walk the streets. Both of them talked in low voices.

Nick's phone blared then, the loud earsplitting tone that meant AMBER Alert. Nick rolled his eyes and turned it off.

"I'm beginning to hate that thing," I said.

The bishop turned to the room. "It is time, then."

I could move both arms, so I hugged Jen, hard. She felt solid in my grasp, real. Her body pressed against mine and we felt right together. Her hair in my face, her cheek warm against mine. I worried so much about losing her, about losing any of my friends, but especially Jen.

"You guys hold on," I whispered. "I'll be there."

"I know," she whispered back. Suddenly confident.

I tried to lean back a little. Her eyes were shiny and serious. "How?"

She smiled at me, an innocent yet mischievous grin. It thrilled me.

"I just thought, tonight we need a miracle," she finally said. "And who better to bring us a miracle, than an angel?"

CHAPTER THIRTY-ONE

The group left quickly after that. I clapped Nick on the shoulder. He did the same to me, as if we both understood each other. The Templars waited until he left the room first.

Nick is a dark fucker. Johnny's words, once upon a time. I had learned more since Johnny had first spoken them, though. Nick was committed to a cause. To a friendship that for him had always existed, going back decades. To a love that he might never get in return, with Sarah. He was as determined as I was, in all the ways that matter. He was as good a friend as I could have wished for, and as dangerous an enemy as anyone could fear.

The Templars followed him out. Jen held my hand a long time, until it was clear the bishop wasn't going to leave until she did.

We had said all the words that mattered. But I still wanted to find more. There was a moment neither of us wanted to let go. It was full of fear and hope. My heart raced. I had trouble breathing through the emotions racing through me. Once Jen walked out that door, I didn't know for certain I would see her ever again.

"Last chance," I told the bishop.

"We all do what we think is right," he said, his eyes clear.

Jen squeezed my hand and walked out.

Then it was us three.

"You think me uncommitted," the bishop said. "I can see why. But I promise you I will do everything I can to save your friends. And to protect them."

"If you fail," I said, "it won't matter."

"I understand," he said.

My jaw flexed. We looked at each other for a long moment. I couldn't think of anything to convince him, and he couldn't say anything to salvage his conscience.

Azazel was going to eat him alive.

"Maybe I am hedging my bet," the bishop finally said. "If I die, I won't live to see what comes next. You will. So if anything happens, I'll count on you to fix what I couldn't."

"You should just take me now," I said. There was an old adage, an adage heard in every book, said in every movie, even the speech of a president. *The only thing necessary for the triumph of evil is for good men to do nothing.*

There was more to it than that. Evil existed in many forms. The bishop couldn't choose which to fight, when to fight it, and with what. He had to fight the same evil that existed in a boy who stole a pack of gum from a store with the same level of investment as taking on Azazel. He had to trust himself fully, and know without reservation that if he failed, he would inspire others to keep the fight going.

Leaving someone in reserve wasn't an option. Leaving people behind might make the bishop a martyr, but it would never inspire others. It would only leave a wondering sense of what might have been.

I had those kinds of friends. That kind of commitment.

The bishop looked at Bartholomew, and some message passed between them. Then he walked out as well. The door shut behind him.

Then it was just the two of us.

It was fully dark outside. The doors of the sedan outside opened and closed. Its engine fired up and purred. A second engine, a larger chugging one, appeared. It was a sound that reminded me of my time in the army. The powerful thrumming motor of a Humvee.

The Templars had come prepared. I wondered if they had a regiment here, or if they had gathered from other places. They had worked well as a team.

"How many would be left?" I asked. Four seemed like a lot to me. *Recruitment levels were low,* Greg had told me, before he died.

Bartholomew's lip twitched. I was beginning to think it was his go-to move. "Not enough."

It was easy to see why the numbers were down. Things were simple to believe when there was a defined good and a defined evil. Banding together against an evil was obvious, when it seized a plane and flew it into a building, or when corpses walked the streets. It was much harder to deal with something rotting from the inside, biding its time like a cancer. In those cases, evil always waited until it was too late to do anything about it.

That rot had been happening a long time in this world. Even I succumbed to parts of it. I was supposed to be an angel, and unlike Bartholomew, I had no faith in anything greater.

"You're supposed to drive out demons, right?" I said. "You know you would be helpful in this fight. Why are you following his plan?"

"I never plan anything," he said. "I lean on my faith, in times like these, to follow the right path."

Bartholomew was feeling loquacious. "What if the bishop dies?" I asked.

"I cannot pretend to know the mind of God," he answered, as if he said it many times. "I can just trust my faith to show me the right way. Even if it results in the bishop's death. Or mine."

Hard to argue with a zealot. And I needed to not only argue, but win that argument. My friends were minutes away from a battle they might not walk away from.

So a moment I had dreaded felt that much worse, when it came.

The Key opened, one final time.

I recognized its scream for what it was now. Because the scream echoed inside me. When the Key tore open, something inside me tore open as well. When it birthed the final evil it held into this world, every stone in the Key, every fiber of my being protested against it.

Bartholomew had left my arms free, but both legs were still frozen. I started pulling on ghosts, fighting the pain of the Key. And the Key recognized me. It screamed in pain as it reached out to me. There was an energy to the power of the Key I recognized as the Key ripped open.

An ethereal power.

I pulled at more and more ghosts. Bartholomew tilted his head, understanding I was doing something, but unaware of what it was.

I tried to push that energy into the Key, along the invisible line that tied us together. I fed it more and more energy, trying to hold it shut. The Key accepted the energy, and the lips of the horrible womb fought the demon pushing its way out.

The demon gathered itself, and labored hard against the Key.

I screamed.

The Key screamed.

The demon screamed and hurled itself against its prison.

The womb burst. In that moment I saw a woman, kneeling in the middle of a cemetery. Dark hair over her shoulders. Trembling. Exhausted. *Freed.*

Underneath her shimmering red lines ran along the pavement. The lines crossed and headed north, south, east, and west. They were bulbous things and flared bright crimson. Yellow sparks popped out along them. It was as if two comets had cut underneath each other and headed out across the earth, and in the distance the lines rose and began looping, as if going from pole to pole.

Then the demon sensed me. Her eyes locked with mine, from miles away. She smiled. All her teeth were pointed.

The vision ended.

I trembled where I stood. At least my body did; my legs still couldn't move. I shook and tried to breathe and wiped my face.

Bartholomew stood there, his back against the wall, facing me. Other than the angle of his head, he hadn't moved. But he understood the Key had opened.

"What do you know about demons?" I asked, my voice hoarse.

"As much as anyone can," he said.

"The last demon is a woman," I said. "We know the names of the six demons, but we could never find the last one's name."

"I couldn't tell you the name of a demon, based on its sex," the young man answered. "There simply is no way to know for sure. Things like genders get lost as names get passed down through the years."

"There has to be something," I said.

I had caught Bartholomew's interest, asking about demons. His jaw worked, as if he was chewing something. "How did you discover the names of the other six?"

I told him about the Key, how it had concentric circles, like a puzzle. That by turning each circle, patterns would emerge, sigils would form. And six of those symbols were the six demons we could name.

"But I never could find a seventh symbol," I said. "No matter what I tried, no matter how many times I would work the Key, the sigils never made sense. Nothing ever lined up."

"Could you not make any symbols with the Key?" he asked. "Or was it that you could make too many?"

It could have been either. "Yes to both."

Bartholomew paled. "You speak of Oriax."

"Tell me about her," I said. If he was worried, then I was more so.

"If Azazel is a schemer, Oriax was the glue behind his schemes," he said. "She is a great masker. What is the truth is presented as a lie. What is a lie is presented as the truth."

That didn't seem so bad. Oriax wasn't a warrior, like Kimaris. She didn't create armies, or fortify them. She didn't cause the dead to rise from the grave. Hell, Azazel was a great liar himself. The world wouldn't be that much worse off with another. "There could be worse things," I said.

"You don't understand," Bartholomew said. "Nothing will be as it seems. Friend could be foe. Foe could be friend. She can mask and transform anyone into anything else."

The young man thought aloud. "The bishop will have no idea what is true, and what is fake."

"You mean my friends are walking into a trap," I said. I got what Azazel had planned all along. Whatever he was going to do, Oriax would hide it for him. Until the moment Azazel needed it.

What if Sarah wasn't really Sarah?

"We've got to warn them," I said.

Bartholomew just shook his head.

"This changes everything," I said.

"It doesn't," he said. "In truth, the bishop expects to die tonight."

But my friends didn't. And I wasn't about to let them. I flung myself at whatever weird power Bartholomew had over me. I tapped into ghosts and screamed. I flung my arms around and tried to grab anything to pull myself away from where I stood. My legs, though, simply ceased to move. As if they were too heavy to respond.

Finally, I froze entirely. Like a statue. Even my head. I was getting tired of this.

Over our heads, high in the night, a rumble of thunder rolled across the night. Flashes of lightning danced across the windowpanes. In the distance came a constant thumping, the firing of a heavy .50 caliber machine gun.

The battle had begun.

I almost burst with ethereal energy, and had no place to use it. And my friends were walking into a trap.

Bartholomew waited until I calmed down. His eyes were sad as he revealed a truth. Maybe *the* truth, for them. "The bishop's real victory, if he lives or dies, is keeping you away."

I got it then. The bishop expected to die. He was going to do what he could for my friends, but he expected them to die as well. Azazel needed three things tonight for his plan to succeed. The Key. Sarah. And me.

The bishop was going to do whatever it took to keep me out of the equation.

At the cost of his life. At the cost of my friends' lives. He was going to leave me here and hope that in the future, I'd face the demon again. He was going to lose this battle, in hopes of winning the war. He had even told me, *I'll count on you to fix what I couldn't.*

And there was nothing I could do about it.

Or maybe there was.

Bartholomew took things on faith. The Templars' power worked on belief. Jen believed I was an angel. Nick did too, all my friends, I thought. It was only me who couldn't believe, who didn't have that kind of faith.

With what I had seen, with what I had endured, it was hard for me to believe in something greater. No matter what others believed about me, I was just beginning to understand things about myself. I had just learned that caring for and protecting my friends felt more right to me than anything I had done before Grafton.

I didn't doubt that feeling, but I still doubted my ability. I had walked away from Grafton thinking I had gotten a vital piece of myself, a small piece of the truth about who I was. But there were more pieces to gather. There was more to understand.

A deeper truth to comprehend.

In order to do the greatest good for my friends, I had to figure out a way to trust myself. I needed to know I could handle whatever was thrown at us. I had to believe in something greater *in myself*.

Another piece of truth fell into the jigsaw puzzle of who I was.

My arm twitched. The ethereal energy I held expanded inside me. It was like it had been poured from a bucket into a wide, cavernous pool.

It wasn't belief in myself; that wasn't it, on its own. I could be afraid, but I couldn't fear failure. I needed to have faith that I was strong enough. I had told the bishop he was hedging his bets, but I had been doing the same, this whole time. I needed to trust myself *without a doubt*. That I could and would be enough.

I would never believe in something greater, unless I believed great things about myself first.

The pool of ethereal energy swelled into an ocean. Armor grew out of my arms then, my legs, my chest. Black-blue plates, edged in gold, slid over my skin like a glove. Like it had done back at the factory in Grafton, only this time the armor covered my entire body. Blue-white light crackled across it all and disappeared into the floor below.

And just like back at the factory, something tugged on my back. At the time I had thought the tug a hood, or a cape, but I had been wrong. The tug had been wings. They spread to either side of me, a ghostly, ethereal white. The room grew brighter around me.

All the weight disappeared from me. I was free to move. If Bartholomew's power rested in his faith, he would be powerless to stop someone in whom he had placed his trust. Like an angel.

Jen had her miracle.

Now I just needed to get there.

CHAPTER THIRTY-TWO

The library was silent inside. Outside, the lightning bolts grew more urgent. Miles away electric blue strikes repeatedly stabbed into the ground. The echoing thunder waited long seconds before rumbling against the windows. The small delay felt like hours to me.

I had to hurry.

Bartholomew stood, expressionless. It was as if he worked through the acceptance of a knowledge greater than he had originally believed.

I had just done the same thing, so I recognized the look.

At first I tried to fly. Turns out that was harder than it looked. My wings wouldn't flap, and I wasn't sure how to get them working. Or if they worked at all. Maybe they were just for looks, being transparent, and I didn't have the time to figure it out.

"Is there a car?" I asked.

Bartholomew blinked.

"Car," I said.

He shook his head. "They took it."

That left running. I tapped into the reserve of ethereal energy inside me, the large ocean that had opened up. Power thrummed through me.

"See you there, then," I said.

Bartholomew held out an imploring hand, even as I jumped out one of the windows. The glass shattered outward over the lawn. I landed and started to run, as fast as I had ever done. This ocean of energy was different from how I normally felt when I worked with ghosts, tapping them for their connection to the ethereal plane. This energy existed all around me. I could breathe it with every breath. The deeper a breath I took, the more energy I inhaled. It pumped through my lungs, into my blood, and raced around my body like a shot.

I took off in large leaps and bounds. I headed toward Lafayette Cemetery, straight like an arrow, as the crow flies. When a building got in the way, I leaped over it, sailing through the air.

I passed thousands of corpses, all heading in the same direction. They shuffled and shambled, slow enough they seemed like they stood still. Here and there a piece of dead body had fallen to the ground, little corpse crumbs leading any who followed to the cemetery.

Dark shapes fluttered past them, and after a couple of blocks I realized they were vampires. They were fast, but I was faster, and as I raced by I watched their twisted, enraged faces. Trapped by the call of the curse. Their eyes open, in fear. The creatures felt Sarah's curse and were being drawn toward it. Against their will.

She wouldn't have too much time left now.

None of my friends would, if I didn't get there.

I viewed the world differently than before. It was as if I was looking through the world with both my ethereal and normal vision. The ethereal blues and whites existed all around me, just less strong than I was used too. Buildings, streets, trees, they all existed in edged blue outlines and sapphire shimmers.

I crossed under a telephone pole. The red lines under Oriax ran above me, heading east. On my next jump I looked farther into the distance, watching the lines leave the cemetery and loop into the distance, at the four points of the compass. Telephone poles carrying a deadly message.

In the coffee shop in Lewiston, Azazel had flapped open a paper in front of me. He had wanted me to look at it. I recalled the front page had an article about Grafton, but there was a smaller article underneath. A much more important article now. One about a new phone company, using different technology, building a new infrastructure across the world.

"I could show you what I'm doing. I could put it right in front of you," Azazel had said. "And you still wouldn't get it."

I leaped hundreds of feet into the air. The jump seemed effortless. I traced the phone lines as they looped their way outside New Orleans. There they appeared to circle and double back in a pattern I couldn't discern.

I had seen the vans everywhere. Azazel had even pointed out one to us, at the last coffee shop. A couple of guys repairing a line, or maybe even installing one.

I landed the next street over and jumped again. I took a deep inhalation of energy and rocketed straight into the air, as high as I could possibly go. The city spread out and lay underneath me in a grid of buildings and streets, the square blocks glowing in my sight.

I pushed my awareness even higher, until I saw the entire city from a bird's-eye view.

The red lines were arranged as a large pentagram. Large enough to encircle all of New Orleans and some of the surrounding area. The lines traveled through the Mississippi River, up into part of Louisiana, and out into the Gulf of New Mexico. The red glow subdued under the ocean.

At each point in the pentagram large red trunks glowed. Five of them. Each of the trunks broke off and headed different directions, and I guessed where they were headed. Paris. Mexico City. Cairo. Hong Kong. Each of those cites would have a pentagram around them as well. And likely a demon as their newest inhabitant.

How many people you think pick up a phone call, and know everything that goes into it? All the different metals in the wire, the switches, the components? How the signal crosses an entire country, from one house to another? How a signal moves from tower to tower, crossing oceans?

I hung at the apex of my jump for a long moment. Under the clouds the air was cool and clear, with a faint smell of ozone. Above me and around me lightning flashed, illuminating a great understanding.

What do you know about my home? Where I'm forced to live? Azazel had asked.

Azazel was a fallen angel. If the demon didn't want to live in hell, and he couldn't return to heaven, where else could he go?

I had my answer.

I knew what Azazel planned now. Maybe what he had planned from the beginning, thousands of years ago. Maybe he had always wanted earth for himself. And he was close to having it. All those other cities, all had long histories, and large numbers of dead and undead.

Buné was raising all those corpses even now, all across the world, if what was happening here was any indication. All of those demons in their cities would have hundreds of thousands, if not millions, of creatures willing to welcome them into their new homes.

And New Orleans would truly earn its name as the City of the Dead.

It all made sense, and yet it was so monstrous in scope it was impossible for me to take it in. That pentagram around New Orleans was so large, and glowed so vibrantly, such an angry red, I believed I would be able to see it from space.

I wondered, briefly, about the fifth trunk on the pentagram. It led northeast. There was another place, another pentagram somewhere, that we didn't know. And didn't have time to figure out. We would just have to stop them now.

I descended back to earth. The heavy wet air whipped past me, battering along my skin. Azazel had pulled me here, with a purpose. The demon wanted me to choose between protecting my friends and allowing Azazel to create a literal hell on earth. Or hells, in this case.

My mother had revealed there was greater evil in this world than I knew. True evil. Not the little evils I had seen, vampires, child molesters, but a malignant force. She had said it was driven to overwhelm everything or destroy. *There is no middle ground for it,* she had told me.

I thought Azazel was that force.

And the demon wanted, needed me there.

If New Orleans had an evil force acting upon it, then I would be equal to its opposition. There would be no middle ground for me either. There was no middle ground in me. I had always been all in or all out. And when I fought, it was with every fiber of my being.

Azazel believed he had directed me here. But someone else had a hand as well. My mother had led me to believe that, that there was a reason she and my father had conspired to have me.

Maybe it's time for good to win again.

I had a purpose. Maybe they had me as a way to fight the geas. Or maybe the creator of the geas. To take on evil at its root.

The blacktop cracked underneath me when I landed. Corpses bounced into the air. Then I took off again. In my hand, unbidden, was the ethereal blade.

If it came down to a choice between Azazel's plan and my friends, I knew which one I would make.

But I hoped it wouldn't be necessary.

CHAPTER THIRTY-THREE

I stayed on the ground as I neared the cemetery. Lightning still flashed ahead of me, constantly, the strikes powerful enough they reverberated through my feet. The .50 caliber machine gun had gone silent, though small arms fire popped in the air, and assault rifles kept up a steady chatter.

The mass of corpses thickened around me, and I flicked my blade out. It cut through dead bodies effortlessly, and each one dropped to the ground after the sword passed through. After each cut there was a tiniest wisp of a thought from the ghost, a promise of hate, a feel of envy, a quick memory. All of that washed away in the pool of energy inside me.

I came upon the cemetery. The street I headed down ended at a pair of black iron gates, a large concrete wall spreading out from each side of the entrance, which was barely large enough for a truck to pass through. I cut through corpses on my way to the gates, and saw a sign on the road beyond the entrance, as if it had hung over the gates but had been torn down as something had driven through. *Lafayette Cemetery No. 1.*

New Orleans really did number its cemeteries.

I stepped across the sign. The red line ran past me along the path and out past the gates. The inside of the cemetery was laid out like a giant cross, a concrete pathway heading north to south. Ahead of me, in the distance, another path crossed it, east to west.

Mausoleums lined up side by side. They ran the length of each side of the roadway. Most were single-story large buildings, built in white plaster, concrete, or marble. Occasionally a cross or an angel perched on the point of a roof. Bricked-up doors faced the path, some of those broken open, as if something had burst out.

Bullet holes tattooed the mausoleums, and dead bodies littered the walk. Some of them still moved, even though they were missing an arm, or legs, or their head. My friends had fought their way down this path.

The sedan lay halfway down the path, flipped over onto its top, parts of the undead scattered underneath it. The car was empty. The Humvee was a little farther in, crashed into one of the crypts, the .50 caliber machine gun torn off its top. One of the Templar men lay close to the vehicle, not moving. The rocket launcher next to him, empty.

Ahead the flashes of lightning grew brighter, louder. The firing of the machine guns grew urgent. Jen stood where the paths crossed, in her shield of lightning, directing strikes at the corpses pressing in from the tombs. Occasionally she reached out and a bolt thundered down among the crypts, throwing up a blast of rubble. Nick flicked in and out of the shadows around Jen, hacking at the corpses with a pair of giant knives.

The bishop stood a few feet away. He looked as he had in my ethereal vision earlier, as a knight. Golden armor fit his built frame, and he swung a great sword, chopping his way through the zombies. A pair of Templars stood by his side, the leader and the woman, firing their assault rifles into the crowd.

Nick's knives didn't have the same effect they did on other supernatural creatures, like vampires or demons. Neither did the bullets. The rounds burst through dead skin, tore off chunks of bodies, arms, legs, or heads, but nothing killed the corpses. All Nick and the Templars could do was reduce the zombies to bits and pieces, and leave the carcasses twitching on the ground.

Along the side of the path was Johnny and the last Templar. They had Sarah between them, and were headed toward the Humvee. Her eyes were shut, and she hung as if lifeless. Johnny's eyes opened when he saw me run by, sword outstretched and leaving lifeless corpses as I passed.

I jumped and landed beside Jen, swinging my sword in an arc before us. Each time the blade tugged through a corpse, a little memory pressed itself upon me, washed away in the pool of power I had inside. I used that power and pushed outward from my body. A shock wave rolled out from me then, like a boulder had been dropped into a pool, and as the wave passed over the corpses they fell to the ground by the hundreds.

Almost like the explosion at Grafton, at the factory.

I took a breath, looking over everyone. For a moment, we were all together, and safe.

"Grimm?" a voice called out from the crypts. Azazel. "You finally show?"

"I didn't think you'd start the party without me," I answered.

Thunder rolled overhead, but the lightning had stopped for a moment, as well as the rifles. It left the cemetery eerily muted and quiet.

I winked at Jen. "Hey."

"Hey." She grinned. "Nice wings."

The bishop walked up. He had removed his helmet, and his was forehead beaded in sweat. His nose, oddly enough, was sharp and no longer colored with bursting red veins. He didn't look happy to see me. He had been ready to die, as long as he could keep me away.

But here I was. With wings and armor and a sword. An angel fully empowered to defeat an evil.

Then he grinned. Maybe in hope.

Hope. It was what commitment revealed. Hoping good would triumph, instead of fearing evil would. Hope inspired, when the righteous faced the monstrous. When a group of friends banded together in the face of an insurmountable evil.

The bishop was maybe thinking the same thoughts. "It seems we are committed, then."

Behind him dark shapes fluttered among the tombstones and crypts. Vampires, running by all of us, and toward where Azazel had spoken. Running right past where Johnny and the Templar were carrying Sarah.

Oriax. The reason I had come.

"Wait!" I called back. Johnny stopped and looked back. The Templar took another step before he realized I was shouting at them.

I didn't see anything different about Sarah. So I left it up to the sword. I placed the edge of the blade against her skin. Johnny freaked out and tried to grab my hand.

The blade cut through the illusion. Both Johnny and the Templar jumped back, seeing they were carrying one of the corpses. A withered young girl from a crypt hundreds of years old, in some kind of lacy, rotting dress.

I checked Johnny next. He was still Johnny, though, and my guess was that Azazel had set up a way for Johnny to escape with Sarah. Hiding some of the lie with a little bit of the truth.

"You okay, man?" I asked, after testing him.

"What?" he asked. He looked at the sword, at me, and at the corpse on the ground. His eyes opened wide. "What?"

"You okay?"

He shook his head. He looked exhausted but otherwise unharmed. The others had closed in. Jen's shield had dissipated, and she gave me a tired smile.

I quickly told them about Oriax, and the red lines. About the pentagrams, and what I believed Azazel's real plan was.

"So he still has Sarah," Nick said, grimly. His jacket hung in tatters around him.

"It's been what he wanted all along," I said.

"That explains it," Nick said.

"Explains what?" I asked.

He motioned where thousands of pieces of corpses littered the paths. "This was too easy."

One of the Templars snorted.

"They pressed us just enough to keep us busy but still give us time to get away," Nick explained. "To bring the corpse to the cathedral."

There was a moment of quiet then, when everyone realized how close that had been.

"For the pentagrams to work, they would have to be powered by a sacrifice," the bishop said. "They need power *invested* in them to work. Power comes in the form of sacrifice. The greater the sacrifice, the greater the power."

The size of the one around New Orleans seemed almost as large as Louisiana. The power required to invest in it was hard for me to imagine. "These things are just so big."

"If we had taken that corpse into the cathedral, into a place full of hundreds of years and millions of prayers of worship, the resulting desecration," the bishop said, "would have been powerful."

"Enough?" I asked.

The bishop held his hands open, palms up. "It's not like we've seen anything like this before. I would guess, though, that Azazel knows exactly what he needs."

"Then we need to make sure he doesn't get it," I said.

"Work the list?" Jen said.

"Simple is easy," I said. "Nick, follow the vampires to Sarah."

He disappeared into the shadows before I finished. I went to talk to the bishop, but before I did Nick was already back, growing out of the shadows he had just stood in. His knife was in one hand, and dripped black blood.

"Found her," he said.

"Tell us," I said.

"There's a large mausoleum in the center," he said. "Sarah's inside that. There's some stairs that go down, and a large open area. She's there, in some kind of circle.

"Your best friend is there," Nick said, twisting his lips. He meant Azazel. "And two other demons. A man and a woman."

Oriax. And I guessed Buné.

"Sarah's on some kind of altar," he said. "And there's some kind of circle there keeping the vampires out."

"Bishop, can you and your Templars take her to the cathedral and get the exorcism done in time?" I asked.

The lead Templar gave a thumbs-up.

"Yes," the bishop said.

The zombies were returning, in little clumps and gatherings. I had bought us some time, but thousands more pressed in from outside the cemetery, coming from all over New Orleans. It had earned its moniker.

"Then here's the plan," I said. "Crypt. Sarah. Run."

I pointed at Johnny and the Templar with him. "You two guys grab Sarah. Nick, Jen, and I will be the distraction. Bishop, you cover the stairs and the getaway."

No one had any questions. One of the Templars handed Johnny a gun, a Beretta nine-millimeter, and a couple of magazines. Nick slid one of his hundred knives out of his vest and gave Johnny that as well. And we were as prepared as we were going to be.

"I'm killing Azazel," I said to Nick and Jen. "You guys get to divide up the other two."

Jen smiled. "This whole distraction plan sounds familiar."

"Yeah." I grinned back. We had much the same plan when we had tried to rescue Sarah up at Grafton. "I guess I only know the one."

The zombies behind us had passed the Humvee. Others were streaming down the other three paths, all coming to a head here at the center. For a moment it felt like a horror film, with all the groans and shuffling of steps.

"If you guys are ready," I said, "no time like the present."

We followed Nick. As soon as we stepped off the path we encountered vampires, all pressing around a single mausoleum, circling it. The crypt itself was as wide as any three tombs in the cemetery.

There were well-dressed vamps and undead dressed in ragged clothes. Each one of them strained wildly against what called them. Zombies pulled down the vampires at the edges, killing them one at a time. The vampires didn't even resist, they were so taken with the call of the curse.

Nick didn't even stare, just waded through the center of the crowd, cutting his way through if he needed to. None of the vampires fought back, so it only took a few moments to get to the front of the crypt. There a pair of concrete doors beckoned us, slightly open.

We went through the door. Marble stairs led down from a little landing. At the very bottom, a tiny glow of yellow light barely reached the bottom step.

The last Templar in, the woman, shut the door and held it against anyone else who might try to come in. Another Templar cracked a couple of glow sticks and tossed them. The green lights were just strong enough to reveal the edges of the steps.

I slapped Nick on his shoulder. The two of us went first, stepping quickly and carefully down the stairs. No vampires or zombies were present. We got to the bottom of the steps, and found ourselves in a square cavern the size of a large basement.

Sarah lay on a tomb in the middle. She appeared to be sleeping, although her tattoos writhed along her arms, face, and neck. She did lie on something like an altar, and a small reddish light radiated from underneath her. Azazel stood in front, leaning back against the bier. A man stood far off to the left, with old stringy hair and a thin, emaciated face. My guess was Buné.

On Azazel's right was the woman I had seen leave the Key. She smiled with pointed teeth, like a shark. "This is him?" she asked, her voice echoing sharply in the room.

Buné nodded. All three of the demons were covered in armor, much like mine, just a different color. Black, with glowing red edges, like coals and embers. Buné had the Key on a chain around his neck, as if he had been the demon who had opened it last.

"He does not seem like much," she said. "Not like the Uriel of old."

The two groups stood there, facing each other. A righteous good versus a merciless evil.

"You the guy that has all the corpses walking around?" I asked the stringy-hair demon.

He bowed his head.

"It's a shame you two were the last demons out," I said. "You're not going to get a lot of walking-around time."

Oriax snorted. "You were right," she said. "He does think he is funny."

Azazel was quiet, though. He seemed content to sit and watch me. It was unlike the demon.

"Nothing to say?" I asked him, circling the tip of my sword in the air.

He smiled at me. One shoulder lifted, then dropped. His voice sounded hoarse. "Nothing that is needed."

"Then put on the music," I told him. "And let's dance."

I took a breath of ethereal energy and leaped at Azazel. At the same time something slammed into me. Buné. For a creature who looked frail and old, he packed a hell of a punch. The two of us bounced off the side of the crypt wall, leaving a crack in the foundation.

We rolled across the floor. Buné was a match for my strength, even as old as he looked. The demon had his arm around my sword arm, keeping the blade away. His voice was hot and wet against my ear. "The end comes."

I folded my legs up and kicked him off me. At the same time, a lightning bolt arced through the room and knocked Buné into the corner opposite me. Azazel still waited at the bier.

Jen arched an eyebrow at me, but had a little smile on her face. I grinned back at her. We understood each other. I had said I was going to kill Azazel, so she had taken Buné out of the equation, and had pointed out to me that Azazel still was breathing.

In my defense, Buné had attacked me first. Azazel would get his.

Nick flickered through the shadows around Oriax, trying to get close so Nick could use his knife. In turn, the demon dodged and swung and connected enough that blood started to show up through his vest.

I got up and tried for Azazel again. A lightning bolt sizzled across the room and twirled Oriax around. Nick was able to make a real cut, and Oriax screamed and scrambled away with supernatural ability.

Azazel had pulled out a sword, in a stance that said he had used one before. It was black, but different than the blade Kimaris had carried. It was elegant and dual-edged, the edge glowing red.

I swung, worrying at the last second about the transparent nature of my sword, but the two blades connected hard enough that the impact jarred my shoulder. Then Azazel pressed forward, timing his swings in a perfect rhythm. My worry grew. The demon had had thousands of years to master an art form I only played at. I had to give ground, holding my sword at crazy angles to block each incoming strike.

Azazel's face was focused. Determined. I fell back, opening up the area behind the demon. Johnny and a Templar ran forward and threw Sarah's arms around their shoulders. She was asleep, and her feet dragged across the floor as the two rushed her back to the stairs. The bishop waited, his sword at the ready, protecting the exit.

I blocked one of Azazel's swings and kicked the demon away. A loud boom echoed through the room. The Templar carrying Sarah staggered and dropped to the ground, part of his head missing.

Johnny lurched a step or two under Sarah's full weight. Then he stood there, trying to hold her up.

Buné trained a large six-shooter at Johnny from the corner of the room. The gun was big and black, with a long, smoking barrel. Like in the westerns. I parried a blow from Azazel and got ready to try to jump in front of Johnny.

The room exploded with a roar of a thousand cannons. Blue-white lightning flashed through the room. The force of the blast threw all of us into the edges of the room.

I picked myself up, trying to see. I had to blink several times. Everything appeared in my vision like overexposed film, white and gray figures on a black background. I staggered against the wall and waited until my vision cleared.

The night sky was above us. Jen had blown the entire top off the mausoleum. All that was left was a giant pit and the staircase leading out behind us.

Johnny and Sarah were already up the stairs, the bishop following. The Templar leader next to him. Jen stood in front of the bottom step, her lightning shield back and arcing around her. Daring any of the demons to chase.

Buné picked himself up out of the rubble. Parts of his armor smoked, in faint white wisps. His hands dug around in the earth, as if he looked for something.

Oriax leaned against the far wall. Nick appeared in the middle of the room, pulling the Templar's gun from his holster, and then Nick flickered around Oriax. She had slowed some, and he pressed his attack, sweeping with the knife and following it up with a shot from the nine-millimeter. Oriax shook her head and leaped out of the pit. Nick's blurring shadow followed her.

More by luck than anything else, I had my blade up when Azazel swung again. He had pulled himself from the side of the cavern and attacked, focused. It was unlike him to be so quiet. Maybe that was the way we all got when we were in sight of a goal we had reached for our entire lives.

We didn't trade blows. I more deflected his. Dust rose around us from the explosion, a white plasterlike fog. Zombie corpses appeared at the top of the pit and began falling in by the dozens, with hundreds more behind them.

Buné had found his gun, and Jen seemed to have her hands full with it. The gun kept firing, more than the six rounds it appeared to have. Each bullet hit the orb of lightning surrounding Jen and threw sparks in a large arc behind her. She had both hands up, as if reinforcing her shield.

Minutes passed and felt like hours. We needed to keep going long enough for the bishop to get Sarah to the cathedral and start the exorcism. I didn't know we were going to get that time. I had no idea where Nick and Oriax were. Buné seemed to be keeping Jen occupied. And Azazel was like a man possessed, his sword everywhere and nowhere. I struggled with my parries, guessing more than seeing, and I started to block a swing that never came.

My brain screamed a warning. I dropped to the ground as Azazel's sword split the air over me. It had been a near thing, but also a break. The demon had overcommitted in the swing. I took advantage and jumped into the demon, leading with my shoulder, and the force launched both of us out of the pit.

We hit the wall of another crypt, breaking it in. I got up quickly, but Azazel lay on the ground, dazed. He shook his head as if to clear it. I reversed my sword in my grip and went to stab the demon in the chest.

A shot boomed out. A hot searing pain ripped along my shoulder. The bullet spun me around and I tumbled to the ground.

Azazel was still gathering his wits. Buné fired another shot. I scrambled back behind one of the crypts. My blade had disappeared, and I put a hand on my shoulder. I tried to heal myself, pushing ethereal energy into the wound like I always did, but it was as if a hot black spot existed where the muscle of my shoulder was.

The hole wouldn't heal.

Buné climbed out of the pit then, the Key jingling as he stood. He smiled at me and spun his six-shooter around on his thumb. "You humans, with your fancy blessed silver bullets. You ever wonder why we didn't have something similar?"

Malphus and Malthus. The Armorer and the Artificer. The demons had bullets that might be able to kill angels, or at least return them to where they came from. Azazel's plan covered a lot of angles. He was building something on earth, and he meant to hold it.

Buné fired again. A piece of concrete exploded behind me. I held my shoulder and ran, ducking behind tombs, dodging until I got back to the front of the big mausoleum.

The vampires were gone. I hoped they had followed Sarah.

Jen stepped out of the doorway as I neared. She looked exhausted, was as white as I had ever seen her. But she walked with a determination.

"Have we given them enough time?" she asked.

"I don't know," I said. "The more, the better."

"Have you seen Nick?"

I hadn't. "I haven't seen Oriax either," I said.

"What's wrong with your shoulder?" Jen pressed her palm where the bullet had entered. I winced, and her hand came away red. "Can't you heal it?"

I shook my head. I wondered if I looked as tired as she did.

"Hold on a minute," she said. She pulled a small knife out of her pocket. "This is going to hurt."

And it did. Jen dug around the wound and pried a tiny black ball out of the muscle. I bit back a scream. The ball popped out of the hole, and I caught it in one hand, then quickly dropped it.

The bullet had burned my hand.

We looked at each other. I took a deep breath of ethereal energy, and the wound closed up as we both watched. I tried summoning the sword, and it flickered back into my hand.

Corpses shuffled our way. Hundreds upon hundreds, tight together like sardines. They pressed inward until the mass of undead circled us, stopping just a few feet away.

"Grimm?" Azazel called out from the tombs. "I didn't think you'd turn tail, here at the end."

I wouldn't know why he wouldn't think that. I had spent a good part of my life running from him. I just hadn't planned on it tonight.

"Just taking a time-out," I answered.

Jen still had her hand on my shoulder.

I tugged her hand down. Our fingers locked together, as if we were holding hands back in grade school. I tried pushing a little energy into her, like I had healed her before. This time I was just trying to heal her exhaustion instead.

She shivered, and took a breath. Then squeezed my hand, tight. A tiny bond sprang between us. It thrummed and crackled, alive with power.

Jen was powerful. And I was an angel. But that gun of Buné's was dangerous, and Azazel knew his blade. It was an even match, at best.

"Have you ever taken lessons with that thing?" Jen asked me, waving at the sword.

I snorted. "No."

"So why are you trying to learn now?"

It was a good question. Why was I trying to fight a master swordsman with a blade? I grinned at Jen. "You're right. I should be playing to my strengths."

She winked, and I felt a little better about our odds.

"It's probably time we finished this," I said.

Thunder rumbled in the clouds, as if in answer. The air stirred around us, with the wet feel of a heavy rain. Even here, surrounded by rotting zombies in a cemetery, I caught a hint of honeysuckle.

The two of us stood together, backs against the crypt door, shoulder to shoulder, hip to hip. We took a breath, and then another. Getting ourselves ready.

Our hands found each other, and clasped tightly together, for another moment. Then we both let go. The air had all the feeling of the showdown at the O.K. Corral, and I wouldn't want to go into it with anyone else. Just Jen and me, together against the world.

CHAPTER THIRTY-FOUR

W e each circled around a side of the crypt. Jen went left, I went right. Metaphorical guns blazing.

Lightning ringed the edge of the pit and blew corpses away. My sword took care of those on my side. We each carved our own path to where Azazel and Buné both waited.

Azazel slumped. The arm not holding his blade hung low, as if something had broken in the limb. Buné held his gun in one hand, and seemed the more energetic of the two demons. Even now he grinned.

Jen and I stopped in front of the demons. The four of us faced each other. Azazel stood closest to me. He raised his sword in a mock salute.

"You seem to be down a demon," I said.

Azazel shrugged. It was odd that the demon had nothing to say, at the end, but I was also glad. He had always had too much to say, before.

"You're friend isn't here either," Azazel said.

"Isn't he?" I suddenly glanced behind the demon. He fell for it, and I jumped him.

Jen was right. I wasn't a swordsman, but I was a hell of a brawler. And I needed to bring my kind of fight to this party.

Azazel turned back at the last second, raising his sword. I slapped it aside and stepped in close. Then I breathed in more energy and head-butted the demon. He staggered back.

I swung my sword then, hoping to end it, but Azazel got his blade up in time to block it. So I stepped in again and let my sword disappear, picking the demon up and swinging him into an outer wall of a crypt. The wall shattered.

I stepped inside. It was just Azazel and me in there. The demon was struggled to get up, holding on to the stone coffin inside. I picked him up and slammed him repeatedly into the coffin, until the coffin broke into slabs. Then I pounded him into the floor.

All the years of being chased. Of the demon threatening my friends. All of the pain and anguish that had followed me, I put all of that into the beating.

It felt great.

"Nothing funny to say now, right?" I said, standing over Azazel. "Nothing to say about Jen? No threats about my friends? About your plan? Nothing left to *appreciate?*"

The demon crawled away from me. I flipped him onto his back. Black blood spotted his face, and his armor had cracked in a hundred places. Outside the crypt I heard Jen and Buné, still going at it.

Then I summoned my sword.

"Appreciate this, motherfucker," I told Azazel.

And stabbed that bastard in the heart.

CHAPTER THIRTY-FIVE

As soon as the blade pierced his chest, I knew I had everything wrong. But the motion was too violet, too fast to stop. The blade slid through the demon until the hilt slammed into his chest.

Azazel disappeared.

A wispy red stream of mist flowed out from the body. It was like the blue ethereal wisps of energy I pulled from spirits. The wisps were crimson colored, like drops of blood, and flowed so quickly east I might have imagined it.

I didn't imagine what was left, though. Not Azazel, but a stringy-haired older demon with an emaciated face and empty eyes.

Buné.

Oriax had switched them on us.

Outside, far in the distance, a scream began. Long and full of burning pain. Back the way we had come in. *The church?*

I didn't feel right all of a sudden. Dizzy. Weak. My sword disappeared. My armor too. I staggered up and stepped outside the crypt, feeling weaker. The pool of energy I had been drawing from shrank inside me, like it was evaporating.

Azazel stood across the pit, holding the six-shooter on Jen. Who no longer had a shield of lightning to protect her.

The scream in the distance became a thousand screams. Millions. The voices of prayers that would forever go unanswered.

Saint Louis Cathedral, desecrated. A massive sacrifice. To power a monstrous curse. I had killed Buné, and when I did his essence had left his body and gone to the only place it could go. The only vessel that could hold it. A place *built* to hold him.

Sarah. Buné's symbol, carved onto her back. Something alive, and not the container of energy I thought it might be. But definitely a container.

The bishop thought he was just exorcising a curse from Sarah. Not a real demon. He wouldn't be ready; he wouldn't know.

Azazel had found a way to bring filth into a church, without anyone knowing.

The red lines blew up around us all, so bright everything burned crimson, like the three of us stood under a giant heat lamp. A scarlet wave washed over us all, turning the ground the color of blood and bringing along a thick smell of sulfur.

I realized *changing the place of the dead* meant something entirely different than what we had thought. It wasn't about moving a dead person from one place to another. Or not only that. It could also mean moving the place where the dead lived to an entirely new place. Like each of the pentagrams, spread across the earth.

Azazel had his cities now.

"I told you, Grimm," he said. "I'd make it a choice."

The demon fired his gun.

The bullet took Jen in the chest, and she tumbled to the ground.

I screamed and ran toward Azazel. He grabbed me and swung me around into a tomb. There was an explosion of pain. Something in me might have broke. I healed what I could, but the ethereal energy was leaving me, fast.

I got back up and punched the demon.

He took the punch and laughed. Then he tossed me aside again. This time I hit a crypt and rolled across the ground and got up, much, much, slower.

Azazel walked toward me. He had a big grin on his face. "Just like we can't return to heaven, angels can't survive in hell."

I shook my head. Either the crimson color had covered everything or I was bleeding more than I thought. I got to my knees.

Azazel bent over. "I hope now you can appreciate the scope of the thing, Grimm."

I spat on the demon. He grabbed my shirt with one hand. I snatched at his shirt, and ending up ripping the Key off his neck.

"Look at that," he said. "You did end up choosing the Key."

He laughed at the reference. Then he tossed me in the other direction. I bounced a couple of times and landed on my back, next to Jen. My back cracked over something and all of a sudden I had a hard time moving my legs. But Jen was still there. I pulled her over onto me, the two of us facing each other.

Blood welled out of a hole in her chest. It was thick and red and spilled between us both. "Gus," she whispered, once.

"Jen," I said, and my voice faded into a low cry. "No, no, no, no, nooooooooo."

Her hands trembled, finding mine. The Key rested between us, her body on top of mine, her mouth next to my cheek, her breath coming out in shorter and shorter gasps.

I screamed. What I had left in my ethereal bank I pushed into her, trying to get the wound to close. But the wound refused, just like my shoulder had.

And then my reserve was gone.

I searched around for ghosts. There were plenty here, all around. But I couldn't tap into any of them. They all resisted me, as if they had new strength inside the pentagram. As if the ethereal plane wasn't a part of this world. As if they had found the place they belonged.

"Jen," I begged.

She smiled.

Then she shuddered.

And then she lay still.

Any energy I had left went with her. I lay there, too broken to cry or scream or rage. Empty. No desire to move, to live. Nothing left, even for revenge.

A dark shadow drifted across my face. Azazel. The demon squatted next to me, and held his gun so that the barrel rested on his shoulder, as if he was taking a break.

"What's funny is how this all happened," he mused. "I was going to use Raphael, you know. I was going to have him order your mother to kill Buné, when I needed him to die, right in the middle of the exorcism."

I didn't want to hear any of this. I couldn't have cared less. But I couldn't move either. Azazel seemed to know it, and the demon loved an audience. The appreciation of a thing. He squatted down and grinned.

"And then your mother fled with Dominic," he said, "and you killed Raphael. So I had to change things up, at the last second. But I always have a backup plan. And I was glad I did, because this ended up being much more fun."

I had nothing to say. I just held Jen close to me. Her hair lifeless against my cheek. Not feeling her heart beat against mine. Not feeling her chest rise and fall, with her breath.

"And now, Grimm, I kind of want to let you live," Azazel said to me. "I don't know that I've ever broken someone as completely as I have you."

He had lowered the gun so that it pointed between my eyes. I kept them open. I was happy to go.

"But all games come to an end," the demon said. And pulled the trigger.

There was a click. Then another click. And another, as Azazel pulled the trigger over and over. The demon swore, then looked past me. His jaw flexed.

"You," he said.

A white nimbus drifted across my vision, as if someone carried a large lamp lit through this new, scarlet world. The bubble of light pushed against the night, and the grass inside turned back to a normal, green color.

As the nimbus came over me, it brought with it a trickle of ethereal energy inside it. As if the old rules still applied inside the bubble. I gathered what I could and tried to pour it into Jen.

The white circle enveloped me. As it did, it pushed Azazel. The demon stepped back once. Twice.

"You may save him now," he said to the bearer of the nimbus. "But sooner or later, I'll get him. He knows it. I know it."

"So be it," a voice answered. "Begone."

"You have no power over me here," Azazel shouted.

"And you have none over me, anywhere," the voice said. "Do you want me to force the issue?"

The demon disappeared.

I frantically found little bits of energy and pushed it into Jen. Every drop I could feel or find, I seized. I wrapped her in my arms and cried and screamed as I drained myself dry.

Then she was gone.

The nimbus was directly over me.

A hand placed itself on my shoulder. Bartholomew knelt at my shoulder. I think he asked me if I could get up, but I didn't know if I could, and I didn't want to try. I just lay there and cried, for what seemed like forever, wanting to hold on to Jen one last time.

CHAPTER THIRTY-SIX

B its and pieces were told to me, through the next few days. Some things I remembered. Some things I wanted to forget.

Bartholomew finally got me up, and half carried me out of the cemetery. My hand gripped the Key still, tightly. Even though its purpose was over.

"We need to get Jen," I said to him.

"Shhh," the young man said. One of my arms draped around his shoulders. The white nimbus moved with us. Everything inside it looked normal. Everything outside the bubble was a night-colored crimson, a dark scarlet hue.

A few steps later. "Where's Jen? We need to get her."

"Just another step," Bartholomew said.

And so we made our way to the cathedral. It was twisted and black and charred, inside and out. The towers hung over a bit, as if sick. All the crosses had been blasted off, leaving pits in the stone and on the roof. The front doors of the church were gone, and all that was left was a gaping mouth.

My friends were there, Sarah and Johnny and Nick. The last Templar, the woman, sat on the ground with her back to the Humvee, but the bishop wasn't around.

Nick looked at me, then to Bartholomew. The young man shook his head. Sarah buried her face in her hands.

Nick and Johnny took me from Bartholomew.

"Nick," I said, "we've got to go get Jen."

His face turned away then.

"Hey, man," Johnny said, "let's get you in the car."

I didn't want to get in the vehicle. Something about the action told me it was final. That if I left, Jen was gone for good. So I struggled and threw punches. My friends took it all, working me over to the open door of the Humvee. In the end, they waited until I tired, and then they packed me in.

From there, if I functioned at all, it was on autopilot.

The Templar drove us out. The nimbus around Bartholomew seemed to protect us from this new world that had been created. Creatures began to appear on the road, deformed versions of humans. Vampires and were-wolves. Sometimes the monsters fought each other, sometimes they stepped in front of the Humvee. The only real danger came from a few bullets that struck the side of the car.

The drive took a few hours. As we came close to the border we encountered other humans heading out, some of the people running, others walking in large groups, trudging along side by side. Toward the end we encountered traffic jams, but the Templar deftly drove off the road and kept going.

Then we were out. The night sky returned to a deep, dark blue. Stars winked into existence. The moon burned a bright white. And in the east a faint tinge of orange appeared on the horizon.

Somewhere east of the city we found a hotel. They put me in a bed. The room faced west, and during the night the red glow of New Orleans burned against the drapes. During the day the glow was still bright enough to tinge the day crimson.

I had spent this entire time using my ethereal sight, from when Bartholomew had grabbed me until now. I blinked and let it go. The red glow disappeared with it. Everything looked normal, to the west. And yet everything had changed.

We stayed there for a few days.

I slept for the most part. I woke every now and then. I ate nothing. Someone had found a chain for the Key and hung it around my chest.

When I did wake, Johnny, or Sarah, or Nick would be in a chair next to me. Each time I woke I would ask about Jen. Whoever was there would shake their head and hold me down as I cried and screamed.

I finally stopped asking. Then each time, when I woke, it was quiet. Just the light breathing of the person in the room with me.

Johnny started talking, one time. He filled in bits and pieces of what had happened in the cathedral. The exorcism had worked, but it also hadn't.

Sarah had been laid on an altar. The bishop had started, and somewhere in the middle Sarah's skin began to stretch. She woke and began screaming. Buné began climbing out of his sigil. First a hand clawed out of her skin, then another, and then the demon's face appeared, as if he was building himself out of Sarah.

The bishop had stopped the demon there. Johnny and Nick had held Sarah down, and Johnny had watched as the bishop completed the ritual. Buné screamed and sank back into Sarah's back, and then his symbol disappeared.

At the same time, the church exploded in black magic, desecrated. The bishop had just looked at Nick, and nodded, and then he was blown apart in the backlash. Johnny still remembered the wall behind the bishop, holding a large cross, spattered with his blood and bones.

I cared about none of it.

Sarah never talked when she sat with me. I had overheard her tell Nick she feared I would blame her for Jen. I didn't have the strength to tell her I blamed no one but myself.

Nick badgered me when I woke and he was there. He would bring in food, water, drinks, but nothing that I touched. He cursed me and told me I was better than this. He got angry and yelled at me to get back up, telling me I always got back up.

Maybe I had done so, once. But not anymore. For a brief period of time I had learned what it was like to be with someone who understood me intimately. Who had my back, no matter what. Who believed something out of me I had never believed in myself. And then I had failed her, just like I had failed Danny.

"Dammit, Grimm," Nick shouted. "Fight, you son of a bitch. You going to let that demon get the best of you? You going to let him get what he wants?"

It wasn't worth an answer to me. He had gotten what he wanted. And he had taken everything I had wanted as well.

One evening, Johnny started talking about the news. New Orleans had become a real City of the Dead. Some of the people there had fled after Azazel burned his own hell upon the earth, some had stayed there, and most had died.

Azazel had set up his own kingdom, composed of most of the state of Louisiana, and some of the Gulf of Mexico. Everything inside the pentagram. The United States had moved the army in, and had locked down access into the state. There were even naval warships in the Gulf, and talk of a meeting in the future between the demon and the president.

The other cities were the same way. Mexico City, Paris, Hong Kong. Each had declared itself its own nation. Supernatural creatures had moved to the cities, who offered sanctuary for all. The same for real humans, the liars and thieves and murderers. All of them found a new place to live. Nations without persecution, or laws. Where anyone could do anything they wished.

The world was in shock. The United Nations were still meeting and trying to figure out not only what to do. But what had actually happened.

The city we hadn't known about turned out to be Rome. Which made sense. Azazel would want to take out his competition. Very few people had made it out there. Bartholomew had talked to me, once, and let me know he was going to head back there and meet up with what was left of the Templars, and see if they could make it to the Vatican.

There was some hope that it still survived.

None of that mattered to me.

"Johnny," I said once, my voice hoarse.

I rarely talked, so he immediately perked up.

"Why didn't we get Jen?"

"We keep telling you," he said. "You're not making sense."

"She's still there," I said.

He shook his head. "No. Bartholomew only saw you there."

That didn't make sense to me. And I didn't make sense to them. The days passed. Finally, I grew too weak to get out of bed.

Sarah got Nick. His face was angry, the same way it had been when I first saw him in Grafton. When he punched me and ran off. He and Sarah held each other for a bit and talked. The motion reminded me of her sister, and I closed my eyes until she left.

Then it was just Nick and me.

"Look," he said. He held a bottle of water and a protein bar. "I need you to eat something. You're going to die soon if you don't."

I didn't respond. I didn't feel the need to eat, or drink. I just wasn't hungry. Or thirsty.

"I know you are hurting," he said. "But we all still need you. The *world* needs you now, more than ever."

I did move then, but I glanced away. I was tired of the world. I was tired of believing I was doing good, when the people I cared about most suffered for it.

There was quiet for a long time. The bottle of water and the protein bar were dropped on the bed, beside my hand. Nick sat in the chair, heavily.

"I wish I could get to you," he said. "For a long time I had held on to the slimmest of hopes, against the most impossible of odds. It was all I had, until you came back."

Outside, it was dark. Overcast. I couldn't see the lights of New Orleans anymore.

"So I know a little something about where you are at," Nick said. "About being so deep in a pit you can't see a way out."

I closed my eyes. Maybe this time I would never open them again.

"You keep asking about Jen," Nick said.

He did have my interest then. But I didn't show it.

"She wasn't there," Nick said. "And you think she's dead."

I didn't think. I had watched her die. I had felt her die.

"I want you to think about who you are," he said. "About *what* you are. About what you've *done*. And I want you to think about all the stories in our past, thousands of years ago, of people being brought back to life."

I kept my eyes closed. Even so, my heart picked up a beat or two. I knew some of the stories he talked about. Everyone did. Lazarus was one of the larger ones, but other stories existed, in our past. In a book, in one place, really.

"I've never seen someone love someone else like you." Nick's voice broke. "You don't have to give her up. If anyone can find a way, it would be you. If anyone can do the impossible, *it would be you*."

My mother had brought me back to life, after she had stabbed me through the heart. Though I wasn't sure if I had been really dead for that long. And if she could, who was to say I couldn't do the same?

Nick got up and went to the door. He paused there. I think he knew this would be the last time we talked, unless he could change my mind.

"You can't let him win now." His voice was low, but it carried. "It's not what she would want, and you know that."

The door opened and closed, and then Nick was gone.

And I idly thought, my mother had brought me back from the dead once.

I let out a shuddering breath. I would keep going. I had promised Jen. I would have to find a piece of myself and tuck it away, where nothing could get to it. I would need to believe that part of me is greater than the evil around me. It's what my mother did to survive in her world. I would have to do the same to live in mine.

That piece would always, for me, be the memory of Jen.

I sat there in the dark for a long time. Outside, there was a sound of car doors opening and shutting. The murmur of voices. Someone drunk shouting about the end of days.

After a while I took a sip of water. My throat was so dry and raw it hurt to swallow. But I did. And then I sipped some more. Then I opened the wrapper and tried to eat a little of the bar, but I choked on it. I had to mix it with the water to get it down.

I lay there until I finished the bar, and the water. It woke a ravenous hunger in me, but I didn't want to ask anyone to get me anything. I wasn't ready for the celebration they would feel my eating would be. I just wanted to get myself to a place where I could go on.

Nick was right. Jen would want me to continue. She had *told* me to, back in the garage. To stay strong, for the others. As if she had known something like this might happen.

But I wouldn't go on like I had been.

The hunger inside me warped and became something else. An unrelenting anger. A malevolent force that would drive me onward. Azazel, I promised myself, would pay. And he would pay in the most painful way I could imagine.

Inside that pain and anger I kept a small part of myself. A memory of who I had been. Of who I wanted to be. A memory of Jen, of who she had been, and of who she wanted me to be. I believed in that vision of her, of us, as much as I had ever believed in anything in my life.

Then I wrapped that kernel in all the anger and rage I had. I buried it deep. But I kept it there. It was so cool, inside the maelstrom of burning pain that was me now. I lay there and let the rage burn and tried to feel the coolness, deep inside, until I finally fell back asleep.

Sometime later, I woke. I almost cried again when I caught the fragrance of honeysuckle and rain. Then I opened my eyes.

Jen floated above me, face-to-face, of the ethereal world, a ghost. Her face looked upon mine, her eyebrows arched with worry.

Something small and round lay on my chest, warm on my skin. The Key. The scent came from there.

She smiled, and mouthed a single word to me. *Hey.*

Enjoy *Ghost Town* and looking for more of the Grimm Saga?

Why wait? *An Ethereal End* is available at your favorite bookseller right now…

Also - take a moment and visit chrisjcranford.com, be a part of the Grimm Universe. Discover all the other worlds I'm building. Or just reach out and say hello.

And next, keep on reading about Grimm and his friends with this sneak peak at the next book in the saga …

AN ETHEREAL END

I stood among clumps of grass, the uncut stalks waving slightly under a small breeze, the patches of turf spreading out into a large field and becoming brush. The brush was mostly green in Louisiana, even this late in the fall. The pasture spread before me, growing and alive, the field heading west. At least, it was all alive until it hit an invisible line.

Everything after that line was dead. Brown. Lifeless. Patches of tan clay dotted the landscape there, the fields mottled, as if the earth carried a disease. Tall weeds poked out with brittle stems, some of which had already snapped under light gusts of wind. The soil was hard, a nip seemed to be in the air, it was going to be a cold November. Especially for this far south.

A pale blue sky curved above me. Thin wisps of braided clouds trailed each other, stretching out over the western horizon, strung like torn bits of cotton. The sun, a faded yellow, radiated no warmth to those standing underneath.

I pulled my jacket tighter around me. Not my army jacket; that had been thrown away weeks ago. Something Nick got me, a black jean jacket with some kind of fur lining. It felt too warm around me, but I was weak enough as it was, and my body seemed like it couldn't make up the heat it lost. I hadn't eaten or drunk anything in a while, and just this morning got out of bed. The first time in a week.

Tiny pops echoed from over the southern horizon. Like the constant rattling of firecrackers. Gunfire. Occasionally there was a large rumbling boom of larger guns, or the whistling of missiles tracking targets. The president had sent the army into New Orleans two days ago. They were struggling to pull out survivors now.

They were calling the area the Dead Zone.

A few feet from where I stood marked the division. Right beyond the line. The fields appeared little different by my feet than beyond, except for the hard line of death. When I looked with my ethereal sight, the vision I used to see the spiritual energies around us, I saw everything more clearly.

A hard red line appeared in front of me, north to south. A crimson boundary. Everything inside the line took on a smoking shade of scarlet, as if glowing embers burned underneath the ground and colored everything above. Grass, soil, trees, all had a crimson hue, as if they rested underneath a heat lamp.

The line was part of a pentagram that had been built around New Orleans, spanning thousands of acres. It had been carefully constructed using phone lines across most of Louisiana. Azazel had wanted his own kingdom, away from both heaven and hell. The demon had wanted his own piece of earth. And he had finally gotten his foothold.

I didn't know what Azazel's next steps would be. Creating his cities had been a plan thousands of years in the making. Five such pentagrams had been created, all around major cities. New Orleans. Mexico City. Paris. Hong Kong. Rome. All powered when Azazel had sacrificed another demon, Buné, during the desecration of Saint Louis Cathedral.

And he had killed Jen.

My jaw flexed.

"You sure you want to do this?" Johnny asked. He and Nick stood by, wearing dark flak vests under dark blue jean jackets.

"Yeah," I said. I was into one-word answers today. I didn't have the energy for much more.

Today was a day about finding a purpose, for me. To see if I could go on.

On the road next to us was a hastily constructed checkpoint. The army had erected barricades once they saw they couldn't take the city. To keep people out, or keep whatever was in the pentagram, in. Sawhorses held orange-and-white-striped two-by-fours across the road. A big stop sign mounted in the middle of each long strip of wood. A couple of military army jeeps, painted dark green, parked behind each.

Soldiers lay against the Jeep, tied up with black cable ties. Four of them.

They hadn't wanted to let me by. And I had asked politely.

Sarah sat in one of the jeeps. She looked much like her sister, just a thinner version of Jen. Blond hair, fragile where Jen had been strong, narrow where her sister had been curved. She was dressed just like the rest of us. A flak vest, a nine-millimeter in one hand. None of us were taking any chances anymore.

"No one comes out, man," one of the soldiers said. A man needing a shave. Young for a sergeant. His name tag read Lutz.

"We did," I said. Multiple large booms thundered from the south, resounding across the horizon. The attack had stepped up. Dark clouds bloomed up, one after another, explosions tracing their way west. Toward New Orleans.

And I was just going in for the day. There was something I needed to see.

"We need to get going, if we're going," Johnny said.

He was right. I was just making sure I could make it. "I can still go on my own."

"We've had that conversation," Johnny said. And we had. My friends weren't going to let me into the Dead Zone alone. They hadn't wanted to before, and they definitely weren't going to now.

We had gotten here. The soldiers weren't going to let us by. I had tapped a ghost and subdued them in an angry rage. And then I had collapsed.

Which was why we were standing around now. My friends were waiting for me. Ethereal energy wasn't a replacement for food or water. I was too thin. Emaciated starving myself. From wanting to die, after Azazel had killed Jen.

I had gotten up this morning with thick black circles under my eyes and too-prominent cheekbones. I had rinsed my hair under the bathroom sink, and the dark curls had hung limp from my head, like a plant that had been without water for far too long.

I looked for Jen, using a kind of spiritual radar. Usually ghosts would pop up on it, like dots on a map. I hadn't found her, though spirits were hard to find in the daytime. And it had made me doubt I had seen her at all.

Until last night I had thought my life was over. I had failed Jen like I had failed Danny. I had lost the one person I would have given anything for.

Nick had been the one to convince me to keep going. I had been ready to die, just lacked the energy to pull the trigger. I just lay in the motel bed they had brought me to, not eating or drinking anything they brought.

It was a slow death, but I *was* dying. My friends had known it. They had all tried to convince me to keep going, to get back up. They had held water to my mouth and it had just dribbled down my cheeks. I hadn't responded to anything they did, until last night.

Nick had come in last night for a final attempt. He had told me he had known what it was like, living with the slimmest of hopes, something so thin the idea was barely worth thinking about. And he wanted to give me that same hope. Something to live for, even if the thought was ludicrous.

He thought I could bring Jen back to life.

"Grimm?" Johnny asked.

I held a hand up. I was weak, but I needed to move. If I stopped moving, if I lay down, I might never get back up. But I also knew what it felt like in the Dead Zone. I knew I wouldn't be able to access the ethereal plane, to use its energy to keep me going. And I wanted to keep going.

I needed to see if Jen's body still lay where she had fallen.

I found a ghost nearby and tapped it. There were plenty around. The memory of the spirit forced its way through my mind, making me live it. A woman, screaming at a man, stabbing him over and over in the chest before slitting her own wrists.

It was one of a thousand evil memories I had lived, and had pushed down inside me, I was hoping that they disappeared then, but I feared I just put them all into some kind of vault, cramming more and more inside, feeling the pressure of all the evil acts, waiting for the day the door would burst back open and let all the memories live me instead.

The ghost fought me, like they all did now. But I subdued it and pulled the energy in. And I crammed the memories alongside a thousand others, deep inside me. Another price I might have to pay later. Another bill that would come due.

Ethereal energy flowed into me, and I fed it into my body. It didn't replace nutrition, but I hoped it would hold me for a bit. For long enough to get me in and get me out.

A light thrumming ran through my nerves, and I took a deep breath and let it out, standing a bit taller.

Nick arched an eyebrow at me. His wire-rim glasses had a piece of tape across the nose. Cuts and gashes crossed his face, from his fight with Oriax. He had held her off so that Jen and I could take on Buné and Azazel.

I nodded. I was as ready as I could be.

Nick walked over to Sarah, talking to her for a bit. I tried not to focus on his hand on her arm, or the way she looked at him, worried.

"You shouldn't go in," Lutz said again. One of the many times he had said it, like he had been handed it on a card, and he read it, over and over.

"Shut up," Nick told him. And the soldier did. Nick had an air about him that scared people. He was thin, wiry, and looked like a nerd. Until you looked at him twice. That was the moment you understood he was dangerous.

I had good friends. Nick maybe the best of them. His idea had been crazy, but it also had gotten me thinking. If not quite believing.

I had woken up later that night, after he had left. And I had found Jen floating above me, as a ghost. Watching me sleep.

This morning, part of me hadn't believed it. I thought it had been a dream. But maybe what Nick thought was possible. The first step was going back to the beginning. I would find Jen's body, or I wouldn't, and I would go from there.

I needed a purpose. Right now it was going to be bringing Jen back. It was what I had, and I would do it, or I would die trying.

ABOUT THE AUTHOR

When Chris isn't trying to figure out how to write a bio, he spends time contemplating the fate of the universe. Probably while walking into a door jamb. He's accepted that the two go hand-in-hand.

He currently resides in Florida, though he has some Magellan in him, and loves to wander.

It is his dream to write stories that – through their telling – influence others to live a little better. Stand a little taller. Smile a little wider. Hold someone a little longer. Fiction should be the dream real life aspires to be.

Dogs are his buddies. Football is his hobby. Books are his passion.

Find out more about Chris here:

www.chrisjcranford.com

facebook.com/chrisjcranford
x.com/chrisjcranford
instagram.com/chrisjcranford

www.ingramcontent.com/pod-product-compliance
Lightning Source LLC
Chambersburg PA
CBHW060227030726
47499CB00004B/1214